COMMON PLEAS

(A Tale of Whoa!)

By

J. Randolph Cresenzo, JD

Common Pleas (A Tale of Whoa!)

By J. Randolph Cresenzo, JD

© 2016 J. Randolph Cresenzo. All rights reserved. Copyright 2014-1-144-1555761

No part of this book may be reproduced, stored, or transmitted in any written, electronic, recording, or photocopying without written permission of the publisher and author. The exception would be in the case of brief quotations embodied in the critical articles or reviews and pages where permission is specifically granted by the publisher and author.

Although every precaution has been taken to verify the accuracy of the information contained herein, the author and publisher assume no responsibility for any errors or omissions. No liability is assumed for damages that may result from the use of information contained within.

This book is a work of fiction. Although the places are of historical and physical fact, names, characters, and incidents either are products of the author's imagination or are used fictitiously. Any resemblance to actual persons, living or dead, events, or locales is entirely coincidental.

If you can't find it in your favorite bookstore, this book may be purchased by contacting the publisher at Lulu's bookstore at www.lulu.com/shop, at www.barnesandnoble.com, at Apple's www.ibookstore.com, at www.amazon.com, and/or through the author at: J. Randolph Cresenzo, Attorney at Law, 612-A Business Park Drive, Eden, North Carolina 27288

Many thanks to Jamee Grossman, Greensboro, North Carolina for her wonderful ideas on cover design.

Publisher: LuLu Publishing Services
ISBN: 978-1-329-65953-7
1. Law 2. Trial 3. American Southern Culture 4. Humor 5. North Carolina 6. Rockingham County 7. Legal 8. Death Penalty 9. Thriller 10. Courtroom 11. Drama
First Printing: January, 2016

Printed in the United State of America

The Beginning

The summer afternoon seemed typical. Hot. Humid. Almost windless. The water at the bottom of the field was still.

Even birds were scarce. It sweltered. Crickets and grasshoppers perched on weeds with strands of wheat orchestrating their cacophony. All awaited the coolness of dark.

The farmer had invited his younger brother to take a walk in the field. Most probably the younger brother had looked forward to seeing the growing rows, to hear how the crop was coming, to listen as the efforts that went into the field were detailed and explained.

The two worked their way toward the middle of the field. Observations were made about the soil, the different rates of growth in different parts of the field, when the harvest would take place. The older brother held a hoe, using the handle to point, as a staff and as a walking stick.

The field seemed fertile, full of promise.

The brothers reached a slight rise in the field, a promontory from which the slight waves caused by an imperceptible breeze could be noticed.

Something toward the right caught the younger brother's eye. He thought he may have seen shafts of wheat quiver as a rabbit slipped away from the brothers' presence. He concentrated on the movement, raised his arm to indicate, and prepared to mouth what he had detected to his older brother.

Before words could leave his lips, the point of the slate hoe began to crease through the hairline of the younger brother. Having been swung at a speed in excess of 80 miles per hour, the hoe dug deeper, passing through the cranium and entering the younger brother's brain cavity in mid-thought. Arteries continued their function of delivering flow despite the diversion caused by sliced pathways. Sympathetic reflexes took over, causing the younger brother's right arm to rise in defense.

The older brother had closed his eyes as he began his swing. Not to avoid the result, but in an effort to put all of his might and strength into the swing. He had succeeded.

Even before his knees buckled, before his collapse, before his lifeblood had flowed, the younger brother was dead.

And so Cain had killed his brother Abel.

The creature created in God's own image—Man---had become the only living animal to kill its own for reasons other than self-defense, food, territory, or preservation of its species.

And Cain, the first-born of all mankind, had committed humanity's first murder. This first-born of all mankind became the original defendant accused of murder.

His Judge?

God Almighty.

The Judge's first question? "Where is your brother Abel?"

And then humanity's first perjury: "I know not."

The verdict? Guilty of murder.

The sentence? Banishment. No more crops. A cursed life.

Despite the lesson taught as one of the Bible and Quran's first stories, every culture of mankind—without exception--has persistently produced murderers motivated sometimes by reason and sometimes by no reason at all.

And, for reasons of simple self defense, these cultures have devised mechanisms to confront and deal with murderers. Some better than others.

This story is about one of the others.

Chapter 1

"The law is a jealous mistress and requires a long and constant courtship. It is not to be won by trifling favors, but by lavish homage."

U.S. Supreme Court Justice Robert Story

(1779-1845)

Twenty miles from the North Carolina/Virginia state line stood the Rockingham County Courthouse which, as directed by the county justices of Rockingham County in 1787, was located in the geographic center of the county.

The present courthouse—the third in that location--was rebuilt in 1907 after a fire destroyed the old courthouse at a cost of $25,000.00. It sat in a decidedly rural area skirted by eight or nine oak-shaded Victorian houses that had survived development of the county into four towns no closer than 8 miles from the courthouse. Tobacco fields dotted the roads between the courthouse and the towns.

The building was composed almost entirely of bricks made from sand mined from the banks of the nearby Dan River and fronted by two massive brick pillars. Its center-heart was what many envision as a typical Southern American courtroom: Judge's bench at the front, witness chair to the left of the judge, jury box to the witness's left, and two counsel tables sitting in front of two chairs. Heart-of-pine floors that had been oiled echoed squeaks as jurors, witnesses, and onlookers took and left their seats among the rows of pews divided by a waist-high gated partition behind the counsel tables. Spittoons for those prone to chewing tobacco or simply wanting to spit had been removed from the courtroom in the 1960s, but ashtrays were provided so judges, counsel, witnesses, and courtroom attendees could still enjoy the locally grown tobacco products during court proceedings.

To the right of the jury box a door led to the jury room, which was often appropriated by attorneys during non-jury sessions as a meeting room to discuss cases, swap stories, smoke, and socialize. Another door in the jury room opened to a hallway that contained a water fountain and an entrance that led to the small lobby of the Superior Court Judges' chambers.

The Judge's lobby was monitored by a secretary who sat behind a desk placed equidistant between the doors to the chambers of the resident Superior Court Judge and the chambers of the visiting Superior Court Judge. It was the practice in North Carolina to have judges regularly come from outside the immediate area to assure the appearance that the important decisions vested within the jurisdiction of the Superior Court were made without local bias or prejudice. Therefore, judges from other areas of North Carolina often "visited" the Rockingham County courthouse to hold six-month sessions of court.

On this day visiting Superior Court Judge Amos Burgwyn stood in his chambers behind a tall roll back desk. The desk was designed to be used from a standing position so no chair was provided for its use. Thick tomes in cherry bookcases surrounded the rollback desk along with four oaken chairs. A push-button phone with five additional buttons that would light up if someone was on hold sat perched on an end-table. A coat tree where robes were hung sat next to a second door which opened directly into the area behind the judge's bench in the courtroom. The room's only window looked down into one of the three parking lots that surrounded the courthouse.

Flecks of gray peppered the Judge's hair and a pair of reading glasses hung on the end of his yellow notepad. His unzipped robe revealed a white button-down collared shirt, a maroon tie, black pants, and a middle-aged bulge. He had driven from his home in Jackson County, North Carolina to hold court in Rockingham County, a trip of more than 200 miles.

Judge Burgwyn was not at the courthouse that week to preside over any jury trials. No jury had been called for the February 11th, 1985 Non-Jury Session of the Superior Court of Rockingham County because it was an administrative "plea week," a week in which defendants pled guilty under the terms of plea bargains hammered out between prosecutors and defense attorneys. Hundreds of felony cases would be disposed of in that single week, and Judge Burgwyn would render sentences in each of them.

Plea bargains weren't just an accepted practice of the court system--the sheer number of felony cases demanded that deals be cut, reducing charges by the very system that had initiated the charges. On occasion Superior Court Judges would refuse in their discretion to accept a plea bargain and enter judgment because their consciences dictated that the plea bargain was either too harsh or too lenient. Judges served as a stopgap to prevent unconscionable plea arrangements from sliding through the system. Under such circumstances a denied plea bargain could be re-negotiated and was, as a practical matter, usually continued for re-grouping by the opposing sides or re-presented before another judge.

The judges' secretary had left a message with Judge Burgwyn that the assistant district attorney and a defense attorney wished to meet with him to discuss the circumstances of a particular felony plea in chambers. Both sought the Judge's assurance that the plea would not be embarrassingly rejected in open court and that their agreement would be honored by the Judge.

Judge Burgwyn had just re-arranged some papers on the rollback when his phone buzzed. The attorneys had arrived.

Chapter 2

"You can't help getting older,

but you don't have to get old."

George Burns

Assistant District Attorney Gerry Wiles and Defense Attorney Bob Lee Pender stood in the lobby, both holding briefcases and files.

Judge Burgwyn welcomed them with a handshake. "Come on in, gentlemen. And how are you doing today, Gerry? Nice to see both of you fellas. Have a seat. Have a seat."

Gerry Wiles dropped his briefcase next to the chair. "Just fine, Judge. Hope you're doing fine, too."

Charles Gerard Wiles lived the life of a statistic. He wore conservative gray suits purchased at Belk's Department Store, earned just above the American median income, loved his average-looking wife, and was raising three children who maintained just above-average grades in school, one of whom had just left for Guilford College. He had recently voted for Ronald Reagan a second time and was happy that re-financing of the mortgage on his brick rancher had reduced the interest rate to 12.75% per annum. When it was warm, he'd rent a room at the motor court on Saturdays so the kids could go swimming. His laugh was almost nervous and invariably brought a finger to the side of his nose. He kept a canoe propped up against the rear of his garage, drove a Ford Fairmont to work, and drank alcohol in moderation.

As an assistant district attorney Wiles had immersed himself in his work and paid attention to the small details that win and lose trials. He was more often than not self-righteous and condescending of defendants who succumbed to the very human frailty of breaking rules, or in his case, laws.

Truth be told, Gerry Wiles loved the inner workings and mechanics of the legal system. He found it fascinating and stimulating.

Burgwyn responded to Wiles' pleasantries. "Yeah, my boy and his Cindy brought my new grandson over this weekend. So I'm doing real fine, Gerry..."

The Judge and Bob Lee Pender had known each other in law school. Bob Lee had passed the stage where he found trials as exciting, competitive, and pressure-laden as he had in his younger years. His role in the legal profession had evolved into simply and methodically carrying out his self-imposed responsibility of using the law and his years of experience to prevent smaller men from being run over by bigger men. If society had to suffer a guilty man's verdict of not guilty to do that, then the overall cost was worthwhile.

"Bob Lee, nice to see you again. You still have your farm here in Rockingham County? Still raising a few cows?"

Outside of the courthouse premises Bob Lee would have called the judge by his first name. They might get together at social gatherings, drink too much, swap lies and stories, check out women's asses, and make sure the other one got home safe. But protocol demanded that within the confines of the walls of the courthouse —particularly in chambers— that in addressing the Judge, proper respect be displayed for the office held by Amos Burgwyn, even in informal conversation.

"Yeah, Judge, I've still got my cows. They keep me busy. I sold the house in town and built another one up on the farm just outside of Mayodan, toward the Virginia border. I've kind of moved in with them, so to speak."

Bob Lee scuffed at his shoe.

"Can you believe it's been over 30 years since we were at Wake Forest Law School, Judge? 30 years… The place just isn't the same. Wake's gone more national with fewer native Tar Heels from small towns to send back home to practice law and medicine. What changes we're seeing… Dr. Lee, Dr. Divine, Sizemore---all gone. Dr. Rose is still there inspiring the young ones. But we're getting to be dinosaurs ourselves, Judge."

Robert Lee Pender was a direct descendant of the great William Dorsey Pender, a West Point graduate and Confederate general who had died of wounds suffered at Gettysburg. He had been named in honor of General Pender's commander.

"You grew up in Mayodan, didn't you, Bob Lee?"

Bob Lee answered honestly. "No, Your Honor. Never did. I thought about it, but it never did make sense to me to grow up. Nope, never did."

The three chuckled.

Amos Burgwyn smiled at Wiles and pointed at Bob Lee. "He's telling the truth, Mr. Wiles. This guy has never, ever grown up. I've known him over 30 years, and he hasn't changed a bit."

Bob Lee looked around the judge's chambers. Thirty years was plenty of time for a practicing trial lawyer to develop a self-image of having learned the law, harvest life experiences, and impart accumulated wisdom upon juries and those seeking advice. Bob Lee knew more than he was willing to admit, even to himself. In the past few years more middle-aged people had started calling him "Sir" in his office and cafes, and younger attorneys more often deferred to his opinions, but it still caught him off guard. Reality kicked in his bathroom mirror after a shower--it seemed as if an unrecognizable bald, overweight man had broken in and was staring back at him. Hell, he thought, his belly button had gotten so deep, he could probably dispense a roll of lifesavers from it.

The seriousness of most situations confronted in a courthouse eluded Bob Lee. Not all of the situations, because some situations were sobering. Rape. Robbery. An innocent falsely accused. But most of the situations were not momentous in the scheme of things by Bob Lee's measurement. The courtrooms brimmed with cascades of emotion in which both sides of a dispute perceived the justness and importance of their cause to be of gargantuan importance, whether the cause involved a petty theft, traffic charge, divorce, dispute of apartment rent, or murder. And in the midst of this tumult Bob Lee found humor--and sadness. Arteries were clogged by stress, lying and misleading under oath were commonplace, and manipulation of the truth to win a momentary point was typical. It never occurred to lawyers and parties that their performances in the courthouse spoke more of what they were than their Sunday confessions. Bob Lee saw it, and the children looking up from below saw it, but it made no difference. It was the accepted situation, the given human condition.

It just seemed so natural to him not to take it so seriously. Almost protective. He and the Judge were about the same age. Gerry was about ten years younger, but both the Judge and Gerry seemed old and tired. My God, he thought. They act as if they really believe that their efforts in this courthouse had a lasting effect in the scheme of things.

If the truth was told, court houses were little more than the big steam valves of society. When folks were angry and determined to act, a decision was made to either reach for a gun or to go running to a magistrate to have a warrant issued. Most went to the courthouse. The good news was that by the time the steam blew off--and a number of months and continuances of their cases had passed--everyone was generally dissatisfied but still alive. Justice or not, violence had been averted and the pressure dissipated.

Gerry Wiles and the Judge will probably both drop over before me, he was thinking. They'll probably get light-headed, faint, and be dead without a whimper before they hit the floor. Or die in a quiet hospital room surrounded by loved ones. To each his own. Not me, he was thinking.

Bob Lee intended to go out louder. He had no expectation of arriving after his journey to the grave in a perfectly preserved body. He smoked. He drank. He chain-sawed from stepladders, rode an old Harley, still tried to ski the black runs, bush hogged on his farm tractor through hilly thickets, and even went skydiving every other year or so. He projected his journey would end with him skidding in broadside, screaming, scabs and all, totally worn out. With a thud.

Judge Burgwyn interrupted Bob Lee's reminiscence. "So, Gentlemen, I'm supposed to have lunch with Sheriff Bailey. Let's get down to what we're here about. What's your business?"

Chapter 3

I had been a lawyer for less than three years when Judge Denny assigned me to represent the four Graves brothers for breaking into an abandoned farm house. We first met in a cramped conference room behind the old courtroom, with only a small table separating me from the small chairs on which the brothers sat.

It became immediately apparent that I was superior to the Graves brothers in every way. I was educated, white, earned a decent living, and was buying a house. The Graves brothers were blacker than black--African black-- with nappy hair, and they muttered and meekly stared down when they spoke, bore the appearance of recently freed slaves shown in Civil War tintypes, and wore tattered clothes and worn shoes. They smelled.

I tried to explain the charges to the four drooped heads when I noticed that one of the brothers, who appeared to be the youngest, had leaned back against the corner of the room and was apparently doodling on a legal pad he had found in the room. "Hey, pay attention, will you? This is important." I went back to the charges, but the doodling brother kept at it and became a bigger distraction. "Hey, what's your brother doing? Can you get him to stop that and listen to me? This is serious." A brother leaned over the pad and said "He drawin.'" "Drawing? Drawing what?""Look like a hairy dog upside down to me, it do. Yep, a hairy dog."I finally spoke directly and firmly to the doodler. "Look at me. Look at me! What is it you're drawing? Show it to me."

The doodler, still peering down and apparently unable to return my look, flipped the pad around so I could see the source of his efforts. I was astonished. A wolf. In sheep's clothing. The doodler had drawn a wolf in sheep's clothing to absolute perfection. Not a simple drawing. Vivid in detail. Strong and direct lines. Photographic in its appearance. Incredible. Stunning.

"Dear God", I thought, "A wolf in sheep's clothing. Please grant me wisdom and understanding. Please forgive me."

    Sheriff Efron Bailey conveyed the distinguished air of a rock-solid common man. Stocky, with a steady gaze from azure eyes, he seemed never to forget a face or name. He had been elected 14 years earlier and was serving the second year of his third 4-year term.

    There was no more beloved man in the county. A uniform and badge were unnecessary for him to warrant respect. His usual attire consisted of a gray or blue suit, an appropriate but undistinguished tie, and a wide-brimmed hat which, when indoors, was held in one hand or the other while he warmly shook hands and zeroed in on eyes.

Sheriff Bailey seemed to be at every public function and funeral, and he addressed everyone he met as "Sir" and "Ma'am" with Southern gentility. His countenance was best described as "courtly."

The High Sheriff was a masterful politician who was respected and quietly feared for the authority he wielded. As was his legal right, he chose his deputies for their physical size, family name, and the precinct of their residence. Since there was no civil service or job protection for employees of a sheriff's department in North Carolina, deputies were hired and fired at the whim of an elected sheriff. If an incumbent sheriff lost his job by failing to win re-nomination in the Spring Democratic primary, which was tantamount to re-election, so did each of his deputies. Each deputy was expected to reach out to family and friends and to carry out any other duties assigned to assure that his home precinct voted correctly.

One of the deputies' assigned duties involved the very serious business of selling tickets to the annual Sheriff's Fish Fry. Held each May at the county fairground, thousands of tickets sold for a "minimum" of $5.00 each. It was a social event attended by multitudes of locals and politicians from across the state. For accounting reasons, it was presumed that most citizens were not very concerned and gave the minimum of $5.00. But "concerned" citizens were encouraged to contribute more or purchase tickets that they promised would be "given away" to raise money for an unspoken and unmentioned fund. Concerned citizens included civic-minded elderly folks possessed of an abounding faith in their good Sheriff who received a

Sheriff's star for the back windows of their vehicles and expected an understanding ear in the event of a traffic stop.

Other concerned citizens included operators of gambling houses, moonshiners, and a myriad group of miscreants who simply wanted to be left alone if the need arose. "Fish Fry Money" with its several connotations in reality had a number of uses: the re-election of Sheriff Bailey, bribes for whatever favor or action may be needed, funds for those with a true short term need in return for an expected favor owed the Sheriff in the future, and a secret "retirement" account that had accumulated in an amount known only to the sheriff and the Caribbean banker he would visit during his annual vacation cruise with his devoted and portly wife.

Another source of funds for the Good Sheriff's needs involved a truck stop/motel known as The Train Stop. Overseen from a protective distance by a high school graduate by the name of Ricky Dean, The Train Stop was a single link in a chain of seventeen counties that snaked from Alleghany County, Virginia down the Shenandoah Valley and across the Blue Ridge Mountains into North Carolina and then westward across the Smoky Mountains to Hawkins County, Tennessee. Prostitutes would move in and out of various locations for two or three weeks at a time and, along with them, would come marijuana and cocaine from Tennessee, cocaine from Virginia, and white liquor, or moonshine, from North Carolina. The overhead for Dean included a manager or two at each location and monthly cash contributions from each location to each local sheriff.

Sheriff Bailey had no interest whatsoever in being involved in the management of Ricky Dean's affairs. That would be up to Dean. As a matter of fact, both Dean and the Sheriff had intentionally never met or even spoken. The Sheriff had purposely attained no idea of Dean's appearance or the sound of Dean's voice. Distance between the two partners was necessary, understood, and protective.

Chapter 4

"A company is known by the people it keeps."

Anonymous

Ricky Dean was not formally educated beyond high school but he was brilliant in his effectiveness. His stated residence was in an 1800 square-foot ranch house near the Virginia/North Carolina border in Axton, Virginia, but the bulk of his assets lay in accounts located in Switzerland and the Caribbean. He chose his managers on the basis of fealty, paid them a reasonable amount, but--to guarantee that wealth would not be flashed among the locals--bathed them with at least two lavish vacations each year with seemingly unlimited expenses and beautiful women.

None of the managers Dean hired were worldly, but each had an earthy sense of his locality. More importantly, Dean instilled an abiding faith in his own business-related loyalty and in his ruthlessness. Each local manager, with canine-like obedience and reverence for Dean, supervised the girls without complaint, distributed drugs and alcohol to trusted underlings who remained unnamed to Dean, kept aware of and reported threatening competition, and quietly and tactfully forwarded the monthly contributions to the Sheriff. Most importantly, job security demanded a low profile in the midst of all of this activity.

Six years earlier Dean had chosen Harley Ames to manage The Train Stop. Ames was an illegitimate 34-year-old raised six miles from Reidsville in the Williamsburg area of Rockingham County. He had worked at fruit stands and cut wood while living in his mother's trailer before he began bussing tables at The Train Stop, where he had met Dean over a bowl of pinto beans, onions, cornbread, and Texas Pete hot sauce. Within a short time he was overseeing the cafe when Jimbo Curtis, Dean's manager of The Train Stop, was away. With this on-hand experience and simply by keeping a sharp ear, he became aware of the inner workings of The Train Stop.

Harley was not a friendly drinker. His teenage years had brought two convictions for a couple of Ernest T. Bass crimes--felonious assaults while drunk that involved everything but throwing rocks through windows—and then a third charge for another drunken assault and a charge of cocaine possession, both of which led to his being charged as a Habitual Felon. This was shortly after his 21st birthday. A person convicted for being a violent habitual felon in North Carolina could be sentenced up to life imprisonment without parole. Dean had heard of Harley's plight and sent word to Sheriff Bailey that his faithful underling could use some consideration, and shortly thereafter the detective's notes and written records in the evidence room inexplicably disappeared. The necessary evidentiary chain of custody needed to be established before the cocaine could be introduced into evidence at trial was no longer available to the State to be used against poor innocent Harley, who was apparently the victim of some nefarious vendetta. The charges were quietly dismissed, and upon his release word was conveyed to Harley that Dean had gone to bat for him.

Within a few months Ricky Dean stopped by The Train Stop for another lunch. Harley approached his table, but before Harley could thank him, Dean asked him to come to his Ford F100 pickup truck after he left the cafe. Dean left and within minutes the two sat in the truck. Harley began thanking Dean and gushed that if there was ever anything he could do in return just to let him know. To Harley's surprise Dean chirped up and said, yes, Harley, as a matter of fact, there was something he could do. Dean handed Harley a small package and asked him to deliver it right away to the occupant of a green Chevrolet Nova waiting two exits down the highway.

Harley took the pouch and hopped into his Chevrolet Apache pickup truck. He had driven less than a mile when the blue lights of a sheriff's patrol car caused him to pull over. Two deputies promptly searched the vehicle and found the package containing heroin behind the seat. Harley was placed in the back seat of the patrol car where the deputies advised Harley of the penalties, promised him that he wouldn't slip past the Habitual Offenders charge this time, and demanded to know the source of the heroin. When Harley wouldn't speak up, he was driven to a spot near Troublesome Creek, handcuffed to a poplar sapling, and beaten to the brink of death. The deputies then took their key, removed the handcuffs, stood back as Harley seeped to the ground, and left him, broken and thrashed, near the creek bank with the heroin.

Harley had remained silent, except to insist that the heroin was his.

When he came to, Harley crawled to his knees and feet and stumbled his way back to his truck. Before the sun rose, he had called The Train Stop asking for Mr. Dean. When Dean returned his call, Harley explained what had happened, apologized, and told Mr. Dean he still had his package.

He had passed the test.

Harley's mother died of throat cancer the next month. He never received a funeral bill.

Within six months Jimbo Curtis dropped dead in his shower. Harley was sent word that a guest from Tennessee--a friend of his friend Mr. Ricky Dean---would be meeting with him at the boat ramp on Belews Creek Lake marina. It was there that an offer was made that Harley couldn't refuse. One condition of the offer was that Harley would partake in no drinking and no drugs. Rules were laid out. Protocol and expectations revealed. Harley became the efficient and loyal manager of The Train Stop.

Affable in his demeanor, Harley discovered a hidden talent in his management of The Train Stop. He loved to walk the edge and was good at it. As long as he smiled, stuck to the rules, and did what he was told, life would be good. Very good. He was suddenly exposed to more money than he had ever known and an ever-changing menu of girls.

And, for the first time in his life, he had a Protector, a father.

Chapter 5

"158 years ago, and two and a half centuries after the death of Machiavelli in 1572, at the urging of a Dottore Ferroni of Florence, Italy, the Duke of Lombardy caused to be erected a marble memorial to Machiavelli in the Church of Santa Croce, in Florence, Italy. These words are inscribed upon the base of the memorial:

TANTO NOMINI NULLUM PAR ELOGIUM

Five years ago, and 153 years after that event, I met Hamlet. Hamlet became not only a source of joy and lively conversation, but a loyal friend who will always remain a part of my being. I therefore feel particularly qualified to honor him with these words today:

HAMLET

TANTO NOMINI NULLUM PAR ELOGIUM

which, in translation, say

HAMLET

TO SUCH A NAME NO PRAISE NEED BE ADDED

Lourinda Stokes, from the Memorial Service for Hamlet

Gerry Wiles spoke up. "Well, Judge Burgwyn, we've got a manslaughter case here. My friend Bob Lee represents a 50-year-old woman by the name of Lourinda Stokes from Casville, just east of here. Lourinda has no prior record, Your Honor. None whatsoever. She's worked over at the American Tobacco Factory for over 20 years and is active in her church."

Wiles paused to arrange his thoughts so the situation could be understood. Judge Burgwyn had picked up his yellow legal pad and started jotting a few notes.

"I don't want to speak too much for Bob Lee, but Mrs. Stokes was married to a man by the name of Glenn Stokes. And, to be honest with you, Judge, I knew Glenn Stokes. I've prosecuted him several times for beating Lourinda up. He'd beat her real bad, your Honor. What caught my attention is that each time I prosecuted him, there were no alcohol or money problems involved at all. There was no evidence of either of them drinking or money spent so there'd be some kind of excuse for what he did to her. He just enjoyed her beatings. Did it for the fun of it. I'd look at photos of Lourinda all punched up like Conan the Barbarian had gotten ahold of her and then there'd be Glenn, clean as a whistle. He was a mean bastard, Judge, if you'll pardon my language."

Judge Burgwyn showed the trace of an understanding grin. "I hear you, Gerry. So what are you leading up to?"

Bob Lee had yet to say a word.

Gerry continued. "Well, Your Honor, the evidence for the State would indicate that Lourinda met a guy at the truck stop over in Ruffin. One of those guys who would listen to Lourinda and understood--you know how women are..."

"Yes, I do, Gerry. And...?"

"Well, Lourinda told Glenn she was going to a Mary Kay meeting down at the beach near Wilmington, and one way or another Glenn got wind of the fact that she was with the guy from the truck stop. Oh, I forgot to mention something..."

"What's that, Gerry?"

"Lourinda had a pet. One of those midget pigs."

Burgwyn sat up. He laid his note pad on the roll top desk. Murder. Mary Kay. A pig. Sometimes he couldn't help but love his job.

Bob Lee finally chimed in. "They call them potbellied pigs, Gerry. Not midget pigs. It's not politically correct to call them midget pigs anymore."

Gerry continued. "Bob Lee's right, Judge. It was a potbellied pig, not a midget pig."

Having been corrected, Gerry went on.

"Lourinda's pig was almost five years old. She never had kids herself and named her little pig Hamlet, and boy, did she baby that little fella. Hamlet had his own bed next to Lourinda's with one of those fake birth certificates you can get down at South of the Border hanging over it, sat on the couch and watched TV with Lourinda, and, I swear this is true, Judge, she'd march along with Hamlet in the 4th of July parade in downtown Yanceyville each year she had him. Put a pink ribbon, a little green Swiss Alps hat, and a leash on Hamlet, and everyone loved seeing him. I heard he was house trained, too."

The Judge had zoned in on Gerry and was engrossed in the facts. "So what's a pig got to do with all of this, Gerry?"

"Well, when Lourinda got back from Wilmington, Judge, she drove up to find Glenn in the back yard drinking beer with several carloads of Mexicans and having a barbecue. When Lourinda asked what he was doing, Glenn said he had renamed Hamlet. Said his new name was 'Lunch'."

Wiles waited a short moment for effect.

"Glenn had made Hamlet into a barbecue, Judge. Right there on the spot. Just to be mean and get back at Lourinda. He killed and ate Hamlet. All she had for his remains was part of a shoulder... a pork shoulder and three little feet. She had those remains cremated and put in an urn and interred in one of those pet cemeteries down in Greensboro."

"This is starting to take shape, Gerry."

"Yessir, you can probably see where I'm headed, Judge. Lourinda just couldn't live with what Glenn had done.

Less than two weeks later Lourinda cut Glenn's throat from ear to ear in his own bed. Caught him while he was asleep. He's probably in hell, now, but we all know that's at least second-degree murder, Your Honor. But I can't just dismiss a case because someone murdered a devil. And that's what we wanted to talk to you about, Sir."

"Go ahead."

"Well, I've gotten the go-ahead from my boss on this, and you know we run a pretty tough office here, Your Honor. We're eighth in the state in death row convictions, which isn't too bad for a county our size. And Bob Lee and I have known each other for years. We've seen a lot together and bumped heads more often than we'd like. But when I talked this over with other members of the DA's staff, we just couldn't see Lourinda being convicted of 2nd degree murder for killing that pet-pig-eatin', wife-beatin' SOB. So we've agreed to manslaughter, Your Honor.

"And?"

"Now we realize she'd face a maximum sentence of ten years, your Honor, but my boss and I have agreed with Bob Lee on a flat sentence of five years. We realize it'd be up to the parole board if they wanted to let her out early for good behavior or other credits. And, if you just can't see yourself sentencing her to five years under these circumstances, we'd understand fully and simply ask that the case can be continued until another judge comes in."

"Is that about it, Gerry?"

"Yes, it is, Your Honor."

"Do you have anything to add, Mr. Pender?"

"No, Sir, Judge, I believe Gerry summed it up pretty well."

"Then let's go into the courtroom and close this case."

Chapter 6

"Of all of the animals, man is the only one that is cruel. He is the only one who inflicts pain for the pleasure of doing it."

Mark Twain

Johnny Wayne ("J.W.") Fulcher could best be described as a human being who had yet to fully evolve. With an IQ of less than 70, he was driven by animalistic instincts. He wanted what he wanted. He wanted it now. Food. Sex. Money. It didn't matter what he had to do to get it. If he had to bully, shove, or kill, then so be it. He loved sex with women or animals, marijuana, white liquor, and his motorcycle.

He had been raised by his grandmother. His mother was 16 years old when he was born. His precise biological father was unknown at the time of his birth, but as years passed and the boy developed definite physical features, it became apparent that his immediate lineage could be traced to an angular man of Lumbee Indian heritage who had worked as a laborer in a local lumber mill and become a father again at the age of 50. His mother had left Johnny Wayne with his grandmother, floated down to Kitty Hawk with one of her boyfriends to work as a waitress, dabbled in drugs, had several cars repossessed, and, after living with a string of different men, eventually weighing less than 70 pounds died at the age of 44 of lung cancer.

During all of these events the grandmother misappropriated government support checks sent for Johnny Wayne's benefit to buy cigarettes and beer and looked at Johnny Wayne as more of a Golden Goose than a ward. Johnny Wayne's few meals were generally frozen dinners served on a newspaper supplement covered kitchen table. The grandmother never considered having him participate in any activities after school that involved any effort or participation on her part. Johnny Wayne grew isolated, resentful, mean, and larger every year.

His first encounter with the legal system in Rockingham County occurred in the seventh grade when he beat a classmate. An offhand remark on a Fall afternoon led to more than a mere schoolyard fight. Johnny Wayne inflicted a beating that intensified into such ferocity that onlooking students were horrified into believing his victim would be killed. The young victim lost eyesight in one eye. The event was addressed by the school administration, the juvenile court system, and even the local department of mental health. Instead of a suspension for days or even weeks, Johnny Wayne was expelled from school for the year. The juvenile system's efforts produced no more than a mound of assessments, lame recommendations, a curfew, and no meaningful long term solutions. At the end of the day, Johnny Wayne was left home with his grandmother for the remainder of the school year to be neglected and free to roam, smoke, drink, and steal.

The next years were, for the most part, predictable. In and out of court. Drugs. Alcohol. No regular employment.

Johnny Wayne learned that one means of livelihood lay in earning a feared reputation. Anyone conducting business with Johnny Wayne Fulcher, whether it was over drugs, gambling, or otherwise, knew that their end of the bargain had better be kept. Johnny Wayne was known to have beaten many people who simply suggested coming up short on their end of a deal.

One of Johnny Wayne's big "hits" came when he heard of the savings of an elderly widower. The man distrusted the Federal Reserve and held no faith in banks. He believed his money was safer in his home where he could personally protect it. Money was stashed in the walls, in the basement, under his bed. A life savings worth of money. When word of the old man's stash reached Johnny Wayne, he went to the old man's front door, knocked, and talked his way into the house. Once inside, he tied and taped the old man to a kitchen chair. After two hours he was moments away from keeping his promise to cut the man's throat when he was finally told where each and every cent of the life savings had been stashed. Before untying him, Johnny Wayne convinced the old man beyond all uncertainty that his grandchildren would be slowly and painfully murdered if he ever whispered or spoke a word of the event to anyone. The old man believed him. And for good reason. Johnny Wayne Fulcher meant it. In his mind, he had not threatened the old man. He had made a promise. Johnny Wayne Fulcher left the homestead with over $160,000.00 in cold cash and silver and gold coins. Oddly enough, word of the robbery became a whispered topic in the community, but law enforcement never investigated the unreported incident. Fulcher's status had been enhanced.

Johnny Wayne's reputation for being involved in violent acts for which he seemed to pay no price, coupled with a massive size and a bulbous mullet wrapped in a red bandana, contributed to his bearing the distinction of being recognized as the most dangerous man in Rockingham County.

Oddly enough, what made Johnny Wayne predictably unpredictable stemmed from his lack of awareness that he could so easily and quickly get into trouble with the law. It was almost a talent, one that had become well-developed by his late-30's. One minute his demeanor would be normal and engaging, and the next minute all hell would bust loose with blue lights.

When Johnny Wayne was first told that the Good Sheriff Efron Bailey had asked that word be sent directly from him to Johnny Wayne that he was terribly upset and losing sleep over the fact that a child molester had escaped conviction by a jury, no further translation was necessary. Johnny Wayne had no reservations about killing the bastard, throwing his dead carcass down the shaft of an abandoned well on the farm he had inherited from his Grandpa, and sending word to the Good Sheriff that there was no reason for him to remain upset. No reason whatsoever.

An understanding had been reached between Sheriff Bailey and Johnny Wayne.

Johnny Wayne had his Get-Out-of-Jail pass. He needed one. Time and time again. Whenever his temper got the best of him, he always managed to sleep in his own bed at the end of the day. Deputies would appear, calm him down or send people off, drive him home instead of to the jail, and when the morning sun rose, he somehow found himself at his own kitchen table. The same kitchen table Johnny Wayne sat behind as he looked out the window at the well house on the edge of his yard.

And, whenever anything or anyone particularly upset the Good Sheriff, the Good Sheriff knew who understood and who would do what was necessary to help him sleep without remaining upset. Like Johnny Wayne, he enjoyed good sleep in his own bed.

This understanding was unspoken between the Pit Bull and his Master.

Chapter 7

"He's too lazy to have his own babies."

Unknown

Carlton Purvis was 46 years of age and another constituent of Sheriff Bailey. He had done pretty well until his wife Iola died. Until then, he and Iola made payments on their Clayton mobile home with Iola's paycheck from Wal-Mart but could never quite afford to gravel from the road to the house. Living just three miles outside of the community of Lawsonville had its advantages. It was close enough to get into Reidsville and far enough away to be able to keep a chicken or two without being bothered by local police.

Later on Carlton's obituary would read that he was a "self-employed handyman." He could never quite get up and go to work on a regular schedule when he was sober, much less so when he was drinking. And even if Carlton wasn't drinking, he looked as if he had been. His red face was perpetually four days short of a shave and his regular uniform consisted of an STP ball hat, dirty clothes, and well-worn shoes.

Carlton had a history with his right hand. He had only worked three days at a plant that molded hot plastic into garbage cans when his index and middle fingers were amputated by a machine called The Chopper. The Chopper's function was to turn large cakes of plastic into smaller ones for quick melting. A swift thinking co-worker scooped the digits up and carefully placed them into a Hardee's cup of ice. The local emergency doctor directed that the ambulance streak Carlton and his detached fingers to the teaching hospital over at Wake Forest University's medical school, and for a time, everything seemed to have started pointing Carlton's way. With his fingers sewn back on, Carlton looked forward to undertaking as his main duty simple endorsements of fat Workman's Compensation checks.

But the checks didn't start coming soon enough. Carlton's Workman's Compensation claim was taking a while to process. Carlton's wait had become intolerable only three days after his return from the hospital, so he unwisely rifled Iola's pocketbook and helped himself to some hard earned cash which was, to make matters worse, Iola's Thursday beauty parlor money. Iola discovered the theft at the laundromat and came home to find Carlton drunk from his thievery. One thing led to another, and before long a serious lapse of judgment on Carlton's part caused him to take a clumsy but missing swing at Iola. Bad mistake. Iola gripped Carlton's newly-attached digits like a vise, gave them a lawnmower yank, and off the fingers came. Both of them. Carlton, writhing on the floor, watched helplessly as Iola ran down the hallway, slid open the door to the porch, and slung her two-fingered fastball into the yard where an old blue tick hound from next door sauntered up, leaned forward with a wet nose to take a good sniff, and ran off with his find into the woods.

Carlton's bad luck didn't stop there. His Workman's Compensation claim was denied when other workers verified that Carlton had been drinking on the job the morning of the de-fingering. So, with eight fingers and a lifelong psychosomatic revulsion to honest and meaningful labor, Carlton once again resumed his daily work routine among the malingering unemployed.

His business associates among the rarely-working and persistently idle would meet at the He'sNotHere Bar or The Train Stop and sip a mixed beverage of tomato juice and beer called RedEye during work hours while spouses labored or disability checks were being processed. Outside of the two establishments this collection of riff-raff smoked marijuana and snorted cocaine in parked cars or side alleys. Law enforcement turned a benevolent eye with the rationalization that breaking up the illegal activity which was concentrated in such a small vicinity would only serve to disburse it around the county. And anyone who has ever wondered "How is it that winos sleeping on park benches can still afford wine?" would wonder the same about Carlton. He always seemed to have money for cigarettes and beer. The answer was Iola.

Carlton's den didn't change much after Iola died in her sleep. There were still ashtrays full of butts, old Parade

Magazine inserts on the table, and Formica peeling up on the counters. A kerosene space heater kept the room warm when it got cold. But his access to her earnings did change.

Remarkably enough, the Board of Directors and Shareholders of The Great American Guaranty Corporation of Chicago, Illinois and Carlton Purvis shared a common interest in Iola. Both relied on Iola Purvis to sign a check, lick a stamp, and mail the $329.00 a month house payment.

When the payments got behind and the foreclosure letter arrived, Carlton started asking around for someone to loan him money. One of the places he asked was while sipping a Pabst beer at the counter of He'sNotHere at 10:30 one morning as George Michael pranced in his Wham sweatshirt on the video screen behind the bar. One of his fellow unemployed business associates suggested that he might want to talk to Harley over at The Train Stop.

Before lunch Carlton had stopped by The Train Stop and found one of Ricky Dean's most recent associates, the manager Harley Ames. He asked, in the most earnest and heart-rending way, if he could borrow money to save his house. Carlton pleaded that wouldn't have any place to go and that his wife had risen to Heaven. He was all alone. It was just pitiful. Harley Ames insisted he was truly, truly sorry but just didn't see how Carlton could ever pay him back with his errant employment history.

So Harley had an idea. In spite of all, Harley knew the social circles Carlton ran in and believed he saw the makings of a decent street vendor of illegal wares. Another block in the Ricky Dean pyramid. If Carlton would be careful, and Carlton would be smart, Harley just might be able to put him in touch with someone who would entrust him with some unnamed items to sell on a strictly commission basis. When these unnamed products were sold, Carlton was to pay all the money he received to the same person, and this person would then pay him his commission on the spot. These would be strictly cash transactions. He could easily earn $500.00 within the next week. All under the table with no taxes taken out. But if he double-crossed this person, Harley warned, it would be hell to pay. Hell. Literally. Understand? Harley wasn't about to say what was to be sold. It wasn't necessary.

Harley Ames hired Carlton Purvis on the spot. And a new and improved Carlton Purvis was born. Entrepreneur Extraordinaire.

Chapter 8

"You're not drunk if you can lay on the floor without holding on."

Unknown

Johnny Wayne Fulcher was pissed off. It started as a typical sunny Sunday afternoon get-together at the farm. Almost 40 people had come to drink, smoke dope, swim and fish in the pond, and party. Bellies and teats hung, bras and shirts were scarce, and voices graveled from cigarette smoke laughed and coughed in unison. Undefined country rock music blared from a cheap radio on the porch and charcoal smoke burned eyes as hamburgers were flipped. Sobriety was lost. It was another normal Sunday at the Fulcher farm.

But then, by happenstance, Johnny Wayne Fulcher thought he had seen Grady eyeing his Queen Bee.

Queen Bee was Johnny Wayne's woman. Although they had never gone through a marriage ceremony in North Carolina, most people considered them a couple. The

Queen Bee called Johnny Wayne her Baby, spoke of anniversaries, occasionally wore a ring on her wedding band finger, and mentioned how many years they had been together. Johnny Wayne had beaten her time and time again, and yet, for some reason, she couldn't leave him.

They were a good fit. The Bee kept a pocket pistol either in her bra or her purse and turned a blind eye if Johnny Wayne had a poke with one of the drifting teenagers who ended up at the farm every now and then. One of the first things noticed about her was the white-bleached hair stacked atop her head in a beehive hairdo which favored, from a distance, a soft ice cream cone. Most memorable was the large red and yellow tattoo of a bumble bee on the upper part of her left breast.

If the truth be told, a normal man couldn't look at the Queen Bee without being hooked by that tattoo. It had the ability to mesmerize. It almost seemed to be buzzing its wings.

Grady Jarrett possessed the tendencies of such a man, so between seven Babymakers--moonshine mixed with SunDrop in a red Solo cup--and nature itself, he was helpless when the bumblebee caught his eye. Grady was a big ol' boy, over 260, red beard and headband, windy as a sack full of farts when he drank, covered in tats himself and with a mean streak of his own. But for just a second or two that afternoon the only thing in his conscious world was that bumblebee.

"What the hell you lookin' at, Boy?"

It was the worst tone of voice Grady's hazed mind could imagine coming from one of the few people on earth he physically feared.

Grady peeked up, and there stood his worst nightmare. After careful consideration and in accordance with the extent of his vocabulary, only one thoughtful reply came to mind…

"Huh?"

Johnny Wayne repeated his question. "You heard me, Boy. What you think you're doin'?"

"Well, nothin', J.W., nothin' at all..." Grady was stammering.

Fulcher leaned into Grady's space. "I saw you starin' at Bee's tits, Grady. You disrespectin' me, Grady? Is that what you're doing, here at my house, disrespectin' me?"

Grady leaned back, holding his palms up. "Why no, J.W., no, not at all. I'm sorry if you think…"

Johnny Wayne projected himself as being crazy. It was one of his best weapons. "Now you're callin' me a liar, ain't you? What mother's child would do that, Son? Is that what you're doin', right here at my house, disrespectin' me and my woman and callin' me a liar? Is that what you're doin', Punk Boy?"

"Hey, J.W., it's me, Grady… you know better…" Grady voice had turned almost soprano. There was no getting away.

Johnny Wayne stood up, pulled out his carpet cutter, and looked Grady straight in the eye.

"Let's go outside, Grady. Don't say a word. Let's go outside."

Grady stood up slowly, fully believing his throat was about to be cut. Johnny Wayne followed as Grady eased out the door, crossed over the porch, and walked toward the motorcycles. Johnny Wayne threw him some rope.

The talking stopped and beers were held motionless waist high as Johnny Wayne and Grady approached the motorcycle. No onlooker dared get closer, but all eyes were cut in the same direction.

Fulcher issued a command. "Tie your ankles together, Grady."

Grady was hoping this was a dream. "Huh? What you talkin' about, J.W.? It's me. Grady."

Johnny Wayne clinched his carpet cutter and waved his fist at Grady.

"I'm going to cut your guts out and tie them around your ankles, you got that, Grady? You got that? Say another word and we'll get to guttin', you got that? I'll hang you in that tree like a pig after the first frost, and bleed you out… you hear me, Boy?" Fulcher actually smiled at the thought.

"OK, J.W., okay. I got you."

Grady sat in the gravel and tied the rope around his ankles. He did as he was told. He tied them tight.

"Ok, J.W., they're tied... Let's just say I tell you I'm sorry, that you were right, and we call it a night, huh, J.W.? I'll be clean out of here in no time, okay?"

"Give me the damn rope, Grady. Shut up and sit still."

Johnny Wayne tied the rope to his Harley's rear bar, just behind where Queen Bee rode. He kicked the bike stand and the last thing he heard as he took off was "I got you, J.W.! This situation has gone far enough, J.W.! You're right, J.W.! You win!"

Johnny Wayne and his Harley dragged Grady around the yard of the Fulcher farmhouse. This occurred in the presence of over 35 invited guests of the Fulcher household. Fulcher had made sure that everything he had done had been done in their presence and silently dared them to speak up or raise a hand.

The local emergency room personnel were compelled to call law enforcement after Grady had been triaged. He had arrived as a bloody pulp. His shredded clothes revealed multiple bruises and lacerations over every limb of his body.

Grady told deputies he simply could not remember exactly how or where he had been injured and did not see anyone who might have inflicted the injuries on him.

Neither could any of the guests. It simply hadn't happened.

Chapter 9

"Cocaine is God's way of letting you know you have too much money."

Unknown

Carlton Purvis's meetings with Dontrelle had been simple enough. Dontrelle would drive from Greensboro to Rockingham County and arrive at the OneStop Car Wash in Reidsville on Thursday and Sunday evenings at six o'clock. Within five minutes Carlton would arrive. Thursday was delivery day for Dontrelle to bring the dope and Sunday was payday when Carlton would return with the money. To assure that a proper inventory was kept and the correct amount paid, Carlton was to hand over both the money and any leftover drugs. It had to add up. Dontrelle would then pay Carlton his 25% up front and restock him with new drugs until the following Thursday.

Harley Ames had reminded Carlton that for the sake of his own health he needed to prioritize his wants and obligations. He needed not only to show up, but to show up on time. Otherwise, someone he wouldn't want to meet would appear at his front door looking for him. No matter what, Carlton Purvis and Harley Ames, or someone Harley would send, would see each other again in one way or another if the protocol was not followed. Carlton understood.

His initial transactions had been easy enough. Guys at He'sNotHere. Friends of the guys at He'sNotHere, both men and women. He invested in a paid-up phone so he could meet with trusted paying customers at any hour. He determined whom he could trust, and not trust, from a Darwinian intuition of who in the drug jungle posed a danger to the existence of his trade. The only unadmitted weakness that could quiver this drug lieutenant's knees and chip away at his protective armor was the above-average and crafty lure of offered, or even simply suggested, sex.

One night after proper and precautionary introductions, he met Samantha and Ebony in the parking lot of an old A & P Grocery store that had been converted into a bingo parlor. Both girls were 19, not in school or working, and pretty. Samantha's Plymouth Duster had seen better days and was littered with fast food paper and cups. Carlton gave the girls a telephone number that would be good for only a week. Two days later, after a call, Carlton cut his first deal with Samantha and Ebony in a $100.00 cocaine transaction that took place at the Dan River boat landing. Just before the exchange of drugs and money, the girls threw some cute talk and suggestive innuendo at Carlton, but Carlton had, at least on this occasion, a distinct memory of Dontrelle's reminder to keep all transactions on a business level.

The following Thursday evening Carlton received a call from Ebony. She sounded particularly cute and sweet that night and punctuated her speech with giggles. She spoke in girly talk. Could Carlton bring some Aunt Nora up to the bowling alley parking lot? Could he please do that, she sweetly asked. Carlton had already weighed and considered the possibilities when he drove up to find Ebony standing alone, without a car, next to a lamppost.

"Hey, Little Lady. You're looking nice tonight. Got the green with you?"

Ebony acted sheepish and cut her little girl voice on.

"Carlton, I gotta be honest. I thought I had enough when I got here. Turns out I'm running short. Real short. I want some blow, Carlton, so give me an idea. Use that brain that sits behind those pretty blue eyes of yours, Carlton... You're smart and you're cute, Carlton. How can we work it out so we can both get some tonight?"

And so the arrangement began. Over the next three weeks Carlton would pick Ebony up at the bowling alley, drive her to his home, enjoy whatever he wanted in the way of sex, and then give her a line or two when he dropped her back off.

Quid quo pro.

Chapter 10

*"Do not meddle in the affairs of wizards,
for they are subtle and quick to anger."*
J. R. R. Tolkien

Paul Gil Reed stood on Newt Newton's porch with his cap in hand. The 6:30 p.m. news had finished over an hour ago, and the yellow anti-bug bulb over Newt's door was doing its job when he knocked on the screen door.

Paul Gil Reed shared the first name of his father and half of the second of the well-known, at least to his father, actor named Gilbert Roland, who played the *Cisco Kid* in the 1940s movie and enjoyed a fan club consisting of a single member named Paul Reed. Naming his first born after himself and the actor who portrayed the *Cisco Kid* made perfect sense to a father who hoped his son would emulate heroes, and at an early age people called the younger Reed by both names in such a way not only to distinguish him from his father but also to make the moniker "Paul Gil" into a one-word given name.

Newt opened his front door and leaned his face toward the upper part of the screen door.

"Why, hello, Paul Gil. What are you up to this evening, friend?"

The un-oiled screen door hinges announced their presence as the door swung open. Newt motioned for Paul Gil to come into his den. Paul Gil's work boot crossed the threshold and he entered a room of warm, yellow light, overstuffed couches and chairs, and bric-a-brac. Family photos of grandchildren held on Santa's knees in Wal-Mart frames dotted the shelves, tables, and television console.

"Newt, I've come to ask for advice. I'm real worried, Newt, or I wouldn't have come here. I've come here about my daughter. Will you talk to me?"

"Of course, I will, Paul Gil. Of course I will. You know I will. Let's sit down, brother. Make yourself comfortable, Paul Gil. Have a seat."

Paul Gil Reed and Newt Newton had been brothers in the same secret organization since their early 30's. Paul Gil Reed's father and mother had raised him in the small community of Leasburg, located forty miles from the Rockingham County Courthouse in Caswell County.

Newt Newton was five years older than Paul Gil and born in Rockingham County. He had attended high school there but moved to Leasburg after falling in love with the raven-eyed daughter of the minister of the Pentecostal Holiness Church of the Fruited Vine in the nearby community of Frogsboro in Caswell County. It was at this minister's church that Paul Gil and Newt first met as young men. They were not yet close friends, simply distant acquaintances.

But as years passed and distinctions of age became less relevant, common political interests and shared values led them to enlist at different times in a secret fraternal organization that brought them into more frequent contact with each other. For over 25 years they drank coffee and loaned each other trailers, chainsaws, and tools. Both had hated Chief Justice Earl Warren and loved John Birch. They had regularly attended the fraternal meetings together, made similar vows, and participated side-by-side in what they considered to be acts of justice against both white and blacks not allowed within the bounds of the written law. Some of these acts resulted from racial hatred and a devout belief in state supremacy during integration, but most were against wife beaters, child abusers, and other miscreants who eluded formal justice in a courtroom. Skin color had no relevance to those matters.

"Newt, it's about my daughter, Ebony." Paul Gil had named his daughter Ebony not because he knew what it meant, but because it "sounded purdy" to him. Newt had seen her on occasion around town. She was a pretty thing, prone to donning Daisy Duke's.

"Newt, you probably remember me telling you about my daughter leaving home to move to Rockingham County to go to beauty school at the community college there. She's only 19. She's a beautiful young girl who favors her mama. Wanda and I have tried to raise her right. She don't come home no more, Newt. She stays away most of the time, but when we saw her last, she had lost a lot of weight and seemed sickly. She's quit school and lives with a girlfriend."

Newt simply listened to Paul Gil. He stared at the top of his hands.

"Wanda and I have gotten word that she's been getting illegal drugs from an older man in Rockingham County. Nobody's come out and said it, but I believe she's getting drugs in exchange for things of a sexual nature, Newt. I hate to say that about her. I'm deeply embarrassed. You know we didn't raise her that way, Newt. But that's my little baby Ebony, Newt. It's hard to think about it, much less talk about it. Wanda and I really need some help, Newt. We need it bad."

Newt's voice was tender.

"I'm so sorry, Paul. I'm so sorry. That happens to a lot of good folks around here. It's no reflection on you and Wanda, Paul Gil. Lord knows you've raised her right."

There was a pause. Newt's eyes firmed.

"Tell me, Paul Gil. Who is this older man?"

Paul Gil held out both hands and his head slowly swayed from side to side as he spoke.

"I want you to know this first, Newt. I went to the magistrate to find out if there was any legal recourse Wanda or I could take. I asked if there was some type of injunction, anything that could be done to keep this man away from our 19-year-old daughter. I told him it seemed like something could be done. The magistrate was very nice, Newt, but he said he had to be honest with me. If she's 19, and of legal age, Wanda and I couldn't step in to keep another person of legal age away, even if he's a lot older. Even if he's giving her drugs. He said it just can't be done as long as she's mentally competent. And she is mentally competent, Newt. The magistrate said it sounded like more of a family problem involving the mental health system, the church, counselors, or some type of intervention other than the legal system. I think he was suggesting you, Newt. I really do. So I came to you as a last resort, Newt. The law can't and won't help us, Newt. You're our last shot. We got no other place to go. We need help."

"All you need to do is give me a name, Paul Gil. That's all you have to do."

Paul Gil and Newt locked eyes. Paul Gil paused and cleared his throat before he spoke.

"His name is Purvis, Newt. Carlton Purvis. I know we both know him, Newt. You probably remember hearing his name, too, and might even know him better than I do. I hardly remember him. But he's been in and out of the Klavern over in Rockingham County, where you were raised. That's why I came to you first, Newt. I know he's not an official sworn member, but he's been in and out of the Klavern. So I thought it was best if I came to you first. I came to you first, Newt."

"Carlton Purvis. Yeah, Paul Gil. I remember Carlton. Couldn't rely on him at all."

There was a pause.

"Damn, Paul Gil, your daughter is mixed up with Carlton Purvis?"

"That's what Wanda and I hear, Newt. Maybe you could double-check for us... maybe you could do that and then do whatever you need to do to get him to stay away from her? Could you do that for Wanda and me, Newt? I'm asking you as a brother, Newt. It means a lot to me. It's the right thing to do, Newt."

Newt held a soft hand out to his brother, Paul Gil.

"Yes, Paul Gil, it is the right thing to do. Tell Wanda that you've taken care of little Ebony tonight, okay? She doesn't deserve the worry. You go home and sleep well, friend. Help is on its way, Paul Gil."

"God bless you, Newt. Thank you, Newt."

"No need for that, Friend. This is what God put us here for."

Unknown to Carlton Purvis, a tempest had been set into motion. And, unknown to Newt Newton the person who set the tempest into motion, namely Paul Gil Reed, had been an FBI informant for more than two years.

Chapter 11

"There are three kinds of people in the world. Those who can count, and those who can't."

Unknown

It was a Tuesday just before the late night news. Carlton Purvis was taking a drag from his cigarette when he heard a tap on his door. Squinting through one of the three glass panels, he made out the figures of three men standing on his porch. He recognized two.

He cracked open the door.

"Why hi, Edgar. How you doin'? What can I do for you this evening?"

Edgar Sills was in his mid-fifties, a working man whose cyclical seven-day clock demanded Wednesday and Sunday attendance at The True Gospel Church. He bore calloused hands and a deep voice. There was nothing effeminate about him. Carlton had known Edgar for years and was well aware of his prominence in the local secret organization he had flirted with on occasion.

"We need to talk to you, Carlton. It's about something important. Can we come in?"

Carlton swung the door open. He knew better than to refuse Edgar Sills.

"Why sure, Edgar. I know Buddy. It's Buddy Landreth! Hey, Buddy! Come on in. Who else you got with you tonight?"

"Carlton, say hello to Newt Newton from Leasburg. I believe you two have met in times past. He's come all the way from Leasburg about something we need to talk about."

Carlton shook Newt's hand. There was a familiarity about Newt. He waved them inside.

"Well, y'all come on over to the table and sit down."

Cans, newspapers, and a Kentucky Fried Chicken box on the table were pushed aside. Ashtrays were rearranged and all sat down.

"So, how can I help you gentlemen out? What can I do for you, Edgar?"

"Carlton, I'm going to get right to the point. You know who we are and what we stand for. We believe in God and family, Carlton. You know that. Now Newt here has received a visit from one of his local Knights, a man by the name of Paul Gil Reed. He's the father of a young girl we hear you know. Do you know a girl by the name of Ebony? Ebony Reed? Now be straight with me, Carlton, do you know this girl?"

Carlton wasn't about to lie. He knew who he was dealing with and knew men such as these did not bluff. He knew that they knew, and that they knew as a certain fact.

"Why, yes, Edgar, I do. I'd be less than honest if I said I didn't. You know I'd never lie to you, Edgar. But you've got to understand that since Iola died, I get lonely. Real lonely. You don't know how hard that is, Edgar. I'm sorry, fellas, but it gets really quiet here, and well, I..."

"No need to explain, Carlton. We're just here to tell you one thing. Now listen good. Real good, Carlton. I'm going to tell you something, and I'm only going to tell you one time. So here it is. Are you listening to me, Carlton?"

"Well, sure, Edgar, sure, I…"

Edgar pointed with two fingers toward his own two eyes.

"You look straight into my eyes, Carlton. You look right here." He continued to point at his own eyes. He waited for Carlton's return gaze and allowed a decided pause before speaking. Carlton knew the man was serious.

"You are not to be around or call or associate with the daughter of Paul Gil Reed. Paul Gil Reed is a fellow brother of Newt so that makes him our fellow brother, too. Let Ebony Reed's daddy deal with her problems, Carlton. You got that? This is a family situation. We're not asking you, Carlton. We're telling you. No more Ebony Reed. Do you understand what I'm saying, Carlton? Keep looking straight into my eyes and tell me you do so there will be no misunderstanding at all. You only get this one warning, Carlton, so let's make sure you value what I'm not asking—but telling—you."

"I got you, Edgar. I didn't know."

"Then say it, Carlton. Say it. Say you know what I'm telling you and that everything is crystal clear."

"I understand. No more Ebony, Edgar. None. I've got that. None. And Mr. Newton, I'm sorry. Please tell Mr. Reed I'm sorry, too. Real sorry. You gentlemen won't have to worry about me no more. I didn't know."

Edgar Sills' stare never left Carlton's eyes. "That's all right. We'll all look around this room at each other and pretend you didn't know. But now you do. You get this one nice warning, Carlton. Not two. One."

Now he did know. Now he did, indeed.

Chapter 12

"The best laid plans of mice and men often go awry."

John Steinbeck

U.S. Attorney Timothy Herndon for the Western District of Virginia sat in his office overlooking the streets of the City of Roanoke. It was after hours, and evening traffic had slowed on the four-lane Highway 220 visible from his office window. If he looked up, he could see the 88½ foot-tall neon star visible to others from 60 miles away sitting atop Mill Mountain that had caused Roanoke to be designated for promotional tourism and business purposes as The Star City.

Herndon was 41 and had worked in the federal system for more than 15 years. He was polite, professional, and thorough.

For three years he had headed an investigation without concrete success into crimes instigated by kingpin Ricky Dean, crimes that snaked through the Commonwealth into the mountains of western North Carolina and from there to

Tennessee. This operation was more than organized crime, Herndon believed, because the very foundation of law--its enforcement--was being compromised and corrupted. Sworn law enforcement officials and officers, duty bound, were being bought and sold. It was a frustratingly tough, if not seemingly impossible, nut to crack.

Ricky Dean had been diligent and taken huge risks to attain his protected status. Eleven sheriffs in three states were in his back pocket. Starting at a truck stop/motel in Bath County, Virginia, prostitutes working two-week shifts would travel to the next stop in Montgomery County, Virginia, for two weeks, and then move on to another truck stop in Patrick County, Virginia, and roadside motel in Tightsqueeze, Virginia, for two weeks, and then cross the North Carolina line to work for another two weeks at The Train Stop. And on and on until a total of 13 stops, encompassing six months, had been completed in Claiborne County, Tennessee.

When one shift of prostitutes moved to their next post a new shift would follow to replace them. With the prostitutes came cocaine from Virginia ports, moonshine from the North Carolina mountains, and methamphetamines and marijuana from Tennessee. It was a tremendously complex operation, involving complicated logistics, detailed accounting, secrecy, clouded and distanced relationships to assure deniability, and the payment of large sums of money in salaries and payoffs. And, most importantly, its success depended on a disciplined understanding among all involved, including those in law enforcement, that Ricky Dean was to be feared above any arm of the law.

Loyalty to Ricky Dean was predicated on more than fear. Those who lived by the common understanding and performed their duties were paid, and paid well. No one knew or dared ask how much Ricky was raking in each year.

Herndon gave an assignment to his clerk.

"I've got a subpoena I want you to issue for the grand jury. Here's his name and address."

Jamie Watson, 24 years of age and fresh out of the Washington & Lee's School of Law, read Carlton Purvis' name and address. Jamie had been inwardly fighting the timidity of a young girl thrust into a man's world of criminal law enforcement. Despite her wardrobe of professional suits and glasses, her long legs, straight blonde hair, and girlish voice, she gave the outward impression of being out of her true element. Her strengths included her abilities to listen, learn, and follow through. She possessed an inherited stubbornness passed down from her mother.

"So what's Carlton Purvis all about?"

"It seems the FBI believes that our informant Mr. Paul Gil Reed down in Leasburg, North Carolina can give us a final link in the transportation setup for Ricky Dean's girls and dope in Rockingham County, North Carolina. So far everything Mr. Reed has told the Bureau has been dead on so far, from who's in the Klan right down to what they eat for breakfast. Mr. Reed knows Carlton Purvis."

Jamie looked at the address on the subpoena. "And?"

"Paul Gil Reed is telling us that his associates are in constant contact with Carlton Purvis. Purvis has dealings with the folks in the Klan and works for Ricky Dean. Not directly, but under Harley Ames, the manager of a restaurant and café in Rockingham County called the Train Stop."

Herndon was connecting the dots for Jamie.

"Paul Gil Reed has been what we call a Busy Boy. He knows where Carlton Purvis lives, what he eats, what he thinks, and what his role is when he's working for Ricky Dean's local operation manager in Rockingham County. He's telling our agent that Harley Ames is the name of Ricky Dean's local operation manager in Rockingham County. And, in turn, Carlton Purvis is Harley Ames' right hand man. Purvis works for Ames, and Ames reports to Dean. Those are the connections of the Ricky Dean crime organization in Rockingham County."

Jamie wasn't convinced.

"What makes you think Purvis will testify, Mr. Herndon?"

Herndon's inner fox knew its prey.

"The only things we have to go on are logic and what Reed is telling us, Jamie. Paul Gil Reed is insisting to our agents that if we subpoena Carlton Purvis, he'll cave in and give us the links all the way to Ricky Dean. He's got weak knees. Our agents can convince Purvis that, no matter what, the simple fact that he's been subpoenaed will convince Ricky Dean that Purvis has flipped to our side. Purvis will need our protection to see the light of tomorrow's day."

Jamie nodded. Herndon went on.

"Think about it: Dean would have no choice but to take Purvis out if Purvis testifies before the Grand Jury. We know enough about Dean to know that he couldn't risk not doing it. There's no doubt Carlton Purvis knows the same thing. So we just subpoena Carlton Purvis, and then he's dead meat to Ricky Dean without our protection. He has no choice but to testify."

Jamie understood. "You're right. He'd be in between the rock and the proverbial hard place."

"Paul Gil Reed says Carlton Purvis is deeply involved in what's going on down there, that he knows in detail who's coming in and with what. He insists Purvis is spineless and will cave when put under pressure. So we need to turn the knobs up on this guy, Jamie. It's that simple. Let's put it to Carlton Purvis. Get the subpoena issued for the 26th, got it?"

"What makes you think Purvis will testify truthfully, Mr. Herndon? They've kept their cards close to the chest so far."

"I'm about fed up with this bunch, Jamie. Keeping their mouths shut and winking at us. Everybody wants to sit back like monkeys in the stands and not step up, not be seen, not testify to what's going on. If Carlton Purvis wants to play that game, to hell with him."

Herndon's voice got firm. He rested a fist on his desk.

"I'm changing the rules, Jamie. If Carlton Purvis doesn't willingly tell the truth, and the whole truth, I'm going to have him indicted for perjury or obstruction of justice and get the magistrate to set a high bond for Dean's little runner boy. Dean won't be able to match a high bond without coming out from under the covers."

Herndon was confiding in Jamie. He was guarded about sources and strategies because of the high stakes involved in his prosecution of upper crime level figures. This caution extended to conversations with his staff. Each worked on a strict need-to-know basis. Herndon was confiding in Jamie that she had risen from a novice staffer to a trusted aid, a near equal. He dropped a minor bombshell.

"I've discussed all of what I've told you with the Attorney General of the United States himself."

He paused for effect. Jamie eyebrows were raised. She was surprised. Impressed.

"If Carlton Purvis doesn't willingly roll and I have to have him indicted, I'm going to have him sent down to our Atlanta facility, where he'll await trial as the only white American male among 2500 Spanish-speaking, sex-starved, mean-as-hell Marielito murderers and rapists from Cuba who've been waiting for extradition back to Cuba since Castro emptied his prisons and sent them to us a few years ago. Can't think of a worse place on this earth. The Gulag isn't crap compared to Atlanta, Jamie. It's not crap."

Herndon balled up a piece of paper and tossed it toward the waste can. He missed.

"We've got rats in Atlanta who are always looking for ways to suck up and do us favors. It's just a matter of what we'd want to ask them to do—short of killing him--to Purvis."

Jamie said nothing.

"He'll be squealing in Spanish to tell us what he knows by the time they're through with him. In the meantime, I'll get word to Ricky Dean that Carlton Purvis is singing like a bird, whether Purvis is talking or not. Purvis won't have any place to go by then, Jamie. Witness protection based upon truthful testimony will sound like a honeymoon to Purvis compared to what Ricky will do to him for working with us."

He paused, picked up and tapped a pen on his desk, and looked through the window up toward The Roanoke Star gazing down from Mill Mountain.

"So get that subpoena going, okay, Jamie?"

"Yes, Sir, Mr. Herndon. It's done."

Herndon shook the change in his pants pocket.

"You know what, Jamie? I never thought I'd say it, but God Bless the Ku Klux Klan. Carlton Purvis wouldn't be about to have the fear of God placed in him if it weren't for the Invisible Empire.

Paul Gil Reed would have smirked. Carlton Purvis had been teed up. Whether it was by the hand of Newt Newton and associates, by the reach of the FBI, or by the arm of one of Ricky Dean's thugs, his problems with his little Ebony caused by Carlton Purvis were going to be solved.

Chapter 13

"Excuse me. Here's your nose. I seem to have found it in my business."

Unknown

Any young court reporter of promise learns early in the game that they are viewed as instruments to be played by the legal community, both prosecution and defense. Reporters' questions about prosecutions or defenses are answered with the sole consideration of how responses will read in print and be most effective in swaying a potential jury outside the courtroom. It is an unwritten, and accepted, violation of judicial ethics that decrees that only evidence duly and properly admitted in an open courtroom should be considered by a jury, unless, of course, jurors secretly read it in the newspaper.

Abby Trimyer of the Roanoke <u>Times</u>, 26, cute and insecure enough to be out to prove herself, had learned that U.S. Attorney Timothy Herndon was of little help in her writing stories that appealed to readers. Her smiles and appearance were worthless and ineffective as far as

Herndon was concerned. Nevertheless duty bound to ask, she had learned that Herndon stubbornly preferred to stick to the book and most often replied that he was sorry, but no comment.

The Dean story had been a slow one. Difficult to investigate because everyone, both cowboys and Indians, kept closed mouths. The territory covered was large by Abby's usual standards, and multiple witnesses involved in different aspects of the investigation were difficult to locate. It was a large story encompassing a huge area and thousands of witnesses that dwarfed a young reporter's capabilities.

Abby was forced to relegate the Dean story to her sidelines. She continued to write about local break-ins and murders and kept a watchful eye on the Federal court calendar in the event something newsworthy arose. But as a practical matter, Federal matters, which typically involved arcane offenses such as tax evasion or securities fraud, were less interesting to Roanoke Valley readers than a local apartment break-in or parking lot shooting.

It happened to be on the Monday before Carlton Purvis's grand jury appearance that Abby dutifully stopped by Timothy Herndon's office for a quick inquiry into progress in the investigation. She made it to Jamie Watson's desk to ask if Mr. Herndon was available. Instead of giving Mr. Herndon a phone buzz in front of Abby, Jamie thought it would be more prudent if she warned Mr. Herndon of Abby's presence.

As Jamie walked toward Mr. Herndon's office, Abby eyed a subpoena on Abby's desk. She couldn't help but see it.

Particularly if she leaned forward for a closer look.

"Ricky Dean. Carlton Purvis. Rockingham County. Thursday, August 26th. Grand Jury."

Jamie returned. Abby rose and checked her wrist as if she had been studying her watch. Neither Tim Herndon or Jamie Watson saw any benefit to their investigation that could result from talking to anyone in the press at this point, particularly without a prepared text that specified exactly what limited information should be released and probably had no relation to any questions that the press might have asked. Control of the floor had to remain with them.

"I'm really sorry, Abby, but Mr. Herndon is in the middle of a brief that's due by the end of the week. Would you like to check back next week, maybe on Wednesday? I'm sure he'd be glad to see you then."

There was no need to push the issue. Abby had her story.

"Oh, that's just fine, Jamie. Thanks so much for asking."

Abby was out of the door.

"Finally."

Abby finally had the name of a witness in the Ricky Dean Case. Carlton Purvis.

Her editor was going to be proud.

Chapter 14

"One timely cry of warning can save nine of surprise."

Joshua Thompson

Sheriff Bailey had settled into his office after lunch when Juanita buzzed him.

"Sheriff, there's a Deputy from Virginia out here to see you. The gentleman asks me to tell you that he's an employee of Sheriff Dudley Davis up in Giles County, Virginia."

"Thank you, Juanita, I'll be right out."

The good Sheriff rose from his desk and stepped into the lobby. A uniformed Virginia deputy, around 29 years of age, thick-fingered and somewhat corpulent from his hometown diner's food, stood with his hat in hand.

"Hello, Sherriff, I'm Deputy Earl Cayton from up in Giles County. It's really nice to meet you, Sir. I've heard wonderful things about you, Sir."

"Welcome to Rockingham County, Deputy. How's my friend Dudley doing?"

"He's just fine, Sir. Just fine. I was passing through Rockingham County on my way to pick up a prisoner on extradition and thought I'd just stop by to pay my respects, Sir. You should know that Sheriff Davis has an abiding respect for you, Sir, and that he asked me to stop by and give you his personal regards and express a concern to you."

"Well, he's a good man, Deputy. A really good man. So, come on in and have a seat."

Within moments the two were alone in the Sheriff's office. Efron Bailey knew this call wasn't social. It concerned business.

"Sheriff," Cayton began, "there was some news in this morning's Roanoke newspaper that Sheriff Davis thought you should know about right away. We don't know if you get the Roanoke paper down here, Sir, and he thought it was important that you know."

"Go on, Deputy."

"Well, Sir, there was a short story about the Mickey Dean investigation. It was written by a young lady by the name of Abby Trimyer. Page five of the Roanoke <u>Times</u>. Not much writing in it, but it did say that the U.S. Attorney is continuing the investigation."

"And?"

Efron Bailey's mind was already considering the ramifications of what he was hearing. No press coverage involving the ongoing investigation had ever included good news.

"Well, Sir, the article said that someone by the name of Carlton Purvis had been subpoenaed to testify, and that Carlton Purvis was from right here in Rockingham County. He's supposed to appear before the Federal Grand Jury on August 26th, Sheriff. That's within the next two weeks. We don't know what he might be testifying about, Sir. We just know he was subpoenaed. We thought you should know that, Sir. Sheriff Davis thought you might be concerned about, uh, Mr. Purvis's safety so that's why I came."

"Okay."

Efron Bailey's business practices included keeping his mouth shut as much as possible and, when he did speak, choosing his words carefully when news was being conveyed to him. After all, even this Deputy could have been carrying a recording device.

"And, Sir, we don't know if you know this gentleman or know anyone who knows him. We don't know anything, Sir. We just thought you'd like to know."

Both knew neither of them was involved in enforcing the laws they had sworn to uphold. It was their mutual tacit understanding that common interests were being threatened.

"Is there anything else, Deputy?"

"Well, no Sir, there's nothing else. That's about it."

Deputy Cayton had carried out his assigned duty. The Sheriff reached to shake his hand.

"Then Deputy, all I would like to say is thank you. Thank you, Sir, for stopping by and conveying Sheriff Davis's warm regards. And would you please, on my behalf, Sir, kindly relay to the High Sheriff that his feelings are reciprocated and possibly exceeded. He is a wonderful gentleman, Sir, and, from meeting you, I can see he retains employees of similar high standards. Yes, Sir, your parents have sown their seeds well, Deputy Cayton, and I know that they are justifiably proud of you. Would you do me the honor of returning for a visit and allowing me to treat you to a barbecue dinner on another occasion, young man?"

Efron was thinking of a possible recording device on the Deputy. The Deputy was thinking that the Sheriff must indeed be one hell of a politician.

"Why thank you, Sir. It would be a pleasure. Thank you for your time, Sheriff."

"Drive safely, young man. And God bless you. And may He bless your family also."

As soon as the deputy left, Efron Bailey turned to Juanita and asked, "Juanita, could you please do me the favor of having Arnie Robertson meet me at my car in ten minutes?"

The Sheriff was, as usual, calm. This was, after all, just another ordinary day of business.

Chapter 15

"Half the lies they tell about me are not true!"

Yogi Berra

Arnie Robertson had known the Sheriff for over 30 years. He had been in law enforcement for just about as long.

Arnie had lost his first job along with Efron Bailey as a deputy years earlier when their boss--Sheriff Jim Priestly--lost his re-election bid to Abel Fulp. Out of real work, with children to raise, and possessed with an exuberance for revenge for the travails his unemployment had brought upon him and his family, Arnie dedicated the nine months of his life before the next Democratic primary--tantamount to election in Rockingham County--to the election of his friend Efron. Every dollar, every paid poll worker, every rumor, every slur, went through Arnie. And, when Efron Bailey won the primary by 78 votes and Arnie was named as his Chief Administrative Assistant, one of his missions in life became never to be fired and unemployed again, no matter what. Arnie Robertson was, by every definition of the word, a dedicated Sheriff Efron Bailey man.

Arnie spotted the Sheriff waiting in the Ford LTD patrol car with the air conditioning running. Something must be up. He had met Efron in his car before when other fires were in need of being put out.

When Efron was particularly concerned, he might use the catchphrase that he had been "losing sleep" over someone or something that was bothering him. That's when Johnny Wayne Fulcher sometimes factored into a solution.

Arnie opened the door and started in.

"Afternoon, Efron, how ya' doin'?"

"Ok, Arnie. I'm okay. Listen, I just heard something really sad."

It was the tone in his voice that clued Arnie in. The High Sheriff was going to be speaking in a code.

No one was to be trusted when serious business was at hand, not even Arnie. Deniability and shut doors were paramount. Double entendres were used and understood. It was the "spoken, unspoken" code that was used, just in case anyone participating in the conversation happened to be wired.

"I just got word that the newspaper in Roanoke is writing that our local fool Carlton Purvis has been subpoenaed to testify before the Federal Grand Jury in

Roanoke on the 26th over the Dean investigation. You know Carlton, don't you? Fat wife who asphyxiated in her bed on her own reflux caused by too many chicken wings? Only three fingers on his right hand?"

"Sure, Efron, everybody knows Carlton."

"Look, Arnie, you and I both know that we got nothing to do with that investigation. We both know they're on some kind of witch-hunt because we don't always hold the Feds' hands when they come into this county. No telling what old Carlton's going to say. I've heard here and there that he's been working some side jobs for Harley Ames over at The Train Stop, but that's just what I hear and nothing more. It'd be a shame for Carlton to go up to Roanoke and spread a bunch of lies, wouldn't it? I sure would hate for any misunderstandings between us and the Feds to reflect poorly on our county, do you know what I mean, Arnie?"

His tone made it clear to Arnie that he was demanding action over a serious matter.

"Yeah, Efron, that just wouldn't be right."

"You're right, Arnie, that just wouldn't be right. To be honest with you, Arnie, I'm so upset about this I might just lose sleep over it tonight, you know what I mean? Ol' Carlton Purvis has got me upset. I'm concerned. You know what I'm sayin', Arnie? I don't know if I'll sleep good tonight because I'm so tore up."

"I understand, Sheriff. I hear what you're saying. Now, just do me a favor, will you? Go on home tonight and go to bed and go to sleep. You should sleep like a baby tonight, okay, Efron? You understand that? Sleep good."

"Thank you, Arnie. I appreciate it. I really do. Now I'm going to head over to see Earl Mabry's family over at the funeral home, but I do hope God blesses you, Arnie. He already has in the past, and I'm sure he'll keep doing just that. God bless you, Arnie."

"And God bless you, Efron."

Arnie stepped out of the Sheriff's patrol car and into his own. He drove directly to a payphone in the Winn-Dixie parking lot and dialed the number of the man who had brought Carlton Purvis into the Sheriff's circle.

"Harley, you get your skinny ass to the barn at nine tonight. You got that? Nine o'clock or you're gonna get whupped like a rented mule. You hear me? The barn. You hear me, Harley Ames?"

Harley Ames sounded confused.

"What's this all about, Arnie?"

Click.

Chapter 16

"Between two evils, I always choose the one I never tried before."

Mae West

Carlton had just settled down and finished his fifth beer when the phone rang.

"Hey, baby..." the voice cooed.

Carlton immediately recognized Ebony's girlish inflection.

"Listen, Ebony, I ain't got no more time for you. You need to go someplace else, you hear? Your Daddy's onto you and mad as hell at me. To be honest, I don't really blame him. And I don't need to be in the middle of that."

Ebony knew what she was after. She turned up her usual routine a notch. Her voice turned cute, wanting. It usually worked.

"I hear you, Carlton. I hear what you're saying. So whatcha' doin' all by yourself tonight, Carlton? Don't it get lonely in there? All alone, just your TV and nothin' to do? No one to talk to?"

"I'm doing just fine, Ebony. And no, I ain't going to come pick you up nowhere."

"You don't need to come pick me up nowhere, Carlton. You don't need to drive nowhere at all. Check out your front window, Carlton. I'm sitting out here in Samantha's Neon right in front of your house. All by myself, Carlton. All by myself. She loaned me her car. Sure is hot out here in all these clothes, Carlton. Samantha said for me to take my time. So I've got nothing to do, Carlton, nothing to do at all. All the time in the world. Nobody knows where I am, and I ain't got nothing to do..."

Carlton used one finger to spread the window curtain and saw nothing but the Neon.

"Carlton, couldn't I just come in and have one little beer? Just one? I won't stay long, I promise, Carlton. Just one little beer and I'm gone. I won't stay long, Carlton. I won't. I swear to it, Carlton."

"Damned if I do, and damned if I don't," Carlton thought.

He slid the latch of the lock on his door.

Chapter 17

"A good friend will bail you out of jail. A best friend will be sitting in the cell right next to you, saying, 'Damn, that was awesome!"

Anonymous

Harley Ames arrived at the tobacco barn at 8:45 p.m. That was 15 minutes early. Located at the end of a dirt farm road and in the middle of the 120-acre Simpson farm, this particular barn, 25 feet by 25 feet square, was made of pine logs chinked with mud and had been used to cure tobacco on a yearly basis for nearly 80 years.

This remote, quiet barn had been a hub of activity in seasons past. The process of curing tobacco in this barn had been laborious. Once the tobacco was picked, it was strung on four-foot long sticks, hung in rows in the barn, and then cured using the dry heat of log fires. After a day of curing, the leaves became stiff and brittle. Workers then let the fire die down and threw buckets of water on the floor of the barn. They followed this process by sealing the barn doors to trap the wet heat. Within hours the leaves were re-hydrated and appeared to the eye to be in the form of paper-thin leather. Once taken down from the racks and unstrung, the leaves were packed in large bales for delivery to market as the Golden Leaf. But that was then.

Tonight, all was quiet. Harley didn't have the motor running. The radio was quiet. He didn't smoke. He knew he had done something, but he didn't know what. He waited. Wondering.

Headlights appeared in his rearview mirror. The car stopped within two feet of his rear bumper. Harley tensed up, both hands on the wheel, and waited to be told what to do.

He heard Arnie's voice.

"Harley, get your stumpy ass in here."

Harley swung his door open, stepped out, and smiled as if he was about to cry. False bravado was put on display.

"Sure, Arnie, I'm comin'. How ya' doin', Arnie? What's goin' on?"

Arnie wasn't in a sociable mood and stuck his head out of the driver's window.

"Get in the car, sit down, and shut the door, Harley."

Harley did exactly as Arnie directed.

"OK, Arnie. What's going on, Arnie?"

Arnie was silent. And uncontrolled fear began to set in on Harley.

"I don't know what's goin' on! Am I in trouble?"

Arnie knew the first thing he needed to do was to assure Harley that in no way whatsoever was Harley his equal. Not in intelligence, not in rank, not in the human order. Arnie was in charge and Harley was to do exactly what Arnie directed.

"Shut up and listen, you little shit. Your world is messed up, Harley. You need to know that, your world is seriously messed up, in a bad, bad way."

Harley became an instant soprano.

"What's going on, Arnie?"

"It's about your friend Carlton Purvis."

Arnie's head jerked toward Harley.

"Yeah, your friend three-fingered Carlton…it seems he's going up to Roanoke to testify before the Federal grand jury on the 26th. You got that, Harley?? Your boy Carlton's got a mouth big enough to eat a banana sideways and now he wants to go to the top of the mountains in Roanoke next week and sing to the whole damn world."

Arnie's voice lowered to a growl.

"You hired that stupid SOB, and now he's become the Sheriff's problem. That's a mortal sin in the world we live in Harley. You understand that, Harley? You got that, you Puss Bubble?"

"Carlton wouldn't..." He had almost squeaked in his reply. Harley was hoping against hope.

"You're about as sharp as a marble, Harley! Carlton would and Carlton will, Harley!"

Someone was to be held responsible for the desperation of the situation, and Arnie laid it squarely at the foot of Harley.

"And who does the world have to thank for this turn of events, and who gets the credit? Well, whatta ya' know, World, I'm sittin' right next to the son-of-a-bitch who put this all together? You're the one who hired Carlton Purvis, Harley, and you're the one who's responsible for any and all trouble he might be bringing. Can you imagine that? Me, Arnie Robertson, sitting right next to a damn idiot-savant ingenious enough to create this mess, right next to a suicide victim, right next to the walkin' dead!"

Harley reflexively fumbled into his shirt pocket for a cigarette. "Wait a second, Arnie..."

"No, you wait, and you shut up, you pot-bellied, mealy-mouth buzzard bait. It don't matter that I might be upset. It don't matter at all in the scheme of things. The world's gonna keep turning around. The big problem for you-and not for me, Harley-is that the Sheriff is worried that he's going to have trouble sleeping over this. You hear what I'm telling you, Harley? The Good Man might lose sleep simply because he trusted a numb-nut like you."

The Code was being spoken. Harley knew Arnie was speaking for the Sheriff himself. And for those the Sheriff associated with. This was bad news. Bad. Harley's hand trembled as he reflexively reached for a cigarette in his shirt pocket that was not there. His voice lowered.

"Oh damn, Arnie."

"Yeah, Oh, damn, Harley."

Arnie gripped the steering wheel with both his hands. He stared straight ahead. Harley sensed that Arnie acted as if he didn't want to look at him, that there was an attempt by Arnie's to distance himself from Harley as a person. They were, at this moment, no longer social beings. They had become animals engaged in a deadly business.

The instructions began. Arnie continued to look forward. He spoke with absolute authority.

"You need to make sure the Sheriff's constitution isn't upset any more over Purvis, Harley. You need to do that right away. I mean quick. Pronto! If something isn't done before Carlton goes to Roanoke or before he's put into protective custody, Harley, and if the Sheriff loses sleep, well, you really don't want to be responsible for that, Harley. It could be really, really bad for your health, Harley. We all enjoy breathing air, Harley. It's habit forming, ya' know? You want that habit broken, Harley? You want it broken?"

"No, Arnie, I wouldn't. I really wouldn't." Harley had switched to survival mode. He had no choice. He knew the instructions were coming.

"So I'm going to leave it right there, Harley. Figure out a solution all by yourself, Harley. And make sure you get all of this stress out of the air right away and not later. You got that, Harley?"

"Sure I do, Arnie. I will, Arnie, I swear I will." He wasn't sure where or how he'd start to solve the problem.

"Ok, Harley, now get the hell out of my car. Go figure it out, right away, you got that? Do it quick. He's supposed to be in Roanoke late next week if they don't pick him up earlier. There's not much time. Now get your ass in gear and out of my car."

"Sure thing, Arnie. Sure thing." Harley reached for the door handle.

"One more piece of advice, Harley..."

"What's that, Arnie?"

Arnie planted his seed.

"You seen Johnny Wayne Fulcher lately? I was just wondering how he and the Queen Bee were doing? They've been on my mind for some reason or another. You seen them? You might want to go see Johnny Wayne just to see how he's doin'; that is, if you want to."

Harley winced at the mere mention of Johnny Wayne Fulcher. The first words in his mind were simple: Johnny Wayne. God help me.

"That's a good idea, Arnie. I'll do that right away..." Harley gulped. "Thank you, Arnie. Thanks."

Harley had been told what to do. Carlton had to be shut up. Johnny Wayne Fulcher was the perfect person to do it.

Harley Ames, the Good Sheriff's courier, immediately set out to find Johnny Wayne.

Johnny Wayne Fulcher had been summoned to do another job for the People's elected official.

Chapter 18

"I know that you believe you understand what you think I said, but I'm not sure you realize that what you heard is not what I meant."

Robert McCloskey

Saturday, August 12th

It was just after 9 p.m. when Edgar Sills' wife called him to the phone.

"Hello, Edgar, this is Newt."

Edgar Sills and Newt Newton hadn't spoken since their visit to Carlton Purvis's house on Paul Gil Reed's behalf the month before.

"Oh Hey, Newt, how you been doing?"

"Well, Edgar, I guess you could say I have done better. I guess you could say that."

Edgar's voice changed from welcoming to one of concern. He leaned forward over his counter, holding the telephone in both hands.

"What do you mean, Newt? What can I do for you?"

"Well, first of all, Edgar, I want to thank you for having me over last month. I really enjoyed that. I really did. I asked for some help on behalf of my friend Paul Gil Reed, and you and Billy were there for us. So thank you again. I hope I can do the same for you some day."

"Don't think nothing of it, Newt. That's what we do around here. That's what we're here for. If we're not in this friendship together, we're not in it at all, are we?"

The form and structure of their speech patterns, along with the meanings of words, altered as the two men began to communicate in the distinct language of their fraternal Order.

"No, I guess not. I guess not at all."

"So what's on your mind, Newt?"

Newt transitioned into the mutually understood code. Wiretaps, although factually scarce, were feared within their circle.

"Well, do you remember when I came to visit and you and Billy and me told that neighbor's dog to stay out of my friend Paul Gil's front yard? Do you remember looking that dog straight in the eye and telling him in the most polite and respectful way to stay out of that yard?"

"Yeah, 'course I do, Newt. I remember that."

"Well, I got word today that my friend's yard's been trespassed on by that dog again. I was there when you told that dog, Edgar, and I told him, too. He's been trespassing again, in the worst way and degree, and my friend is really, really upset about his yard. You can take this man's word on it, Edgar. He's got a good word. He's a good man. I gotta help my friend, Edgar, so I'm calling on you."

"Do you want the dog put down, Newt? Is that what you're asking?"

Newt's voice was appreciative.

"No, my friend, I won't ask that of you. He doesn't need to be put down yet. I know you'd do that for me if I asked, and you know I'd do the same for you, but I don't think that's going to be necessary quite yet. If you could just give him a more, shall we call it, *forceful* warning, I'd appreciate it. I'd appreciate it very much. And so would my friend."

"I'll see what I can do, Newt. Just keep your ears to the ground, okay?"

"Thank you, Edgar."

"No problem, Newt."

It had been nice for both to speak with a friend trusted even more than their spouses.

The trigger had been pulled.

Chapter 19

"If a stripper changes her life she's still a stripper. If a drug dealer changes his life, he's a business man, an entrepreneur."

Unknown

Tuesday, August 15th at 7:30 p.m.

Johnny Wayne and the Queen Bee had the pickup loaded. Eddie Rabbit was crooning "I Love A Rainy Night" on the truck radio. It was time to go. A cooler the Bee had stuffed with bread, baloney, mustard, a quart jar of pink pickled eggs, a can of potted meat, crackers, and beer sat at a makeshift console in the front seat between the driver's and passenger's seat. Three rods, a tackle box, blankets, a flashlight, and a tub of Johnny Wayne's secret carp bait sat in the bed of the truck.

The carp bait had been made from a number of ingredients including flour dough encased in Kellogg's Sugar Pops, lime Kool-Aid, and Rice Krispies, the idea being that the carp would smell the Kool-Aid, vacuum the Rice Krispies, and work its way up to the barb which had been elevated from the bottom by a single Sugar Pop. It worked. Johnny Wayne had won thousands of dollars at carp-fishing pond contests in the vicinity of Rockingham County. All carp fishing competitors had their own mysterious recipes for carp bait, but Johnny Wayne Fulcher's private recipe was as dear to him as the deadly secrets he kept.

Only one thing was missing for the night's fishing trip. They'd get it on the way.

The pickup truck slid into Carlton Purvis's driveway and settled into mud in a swale that was supposed to avert water from his house. When Johnny Wayne got to the porch, he knocked once, turned the knob, walked in, and announced his presence. The TV was on, but Carlton was nowhere to be seen.

"Carlton, it's me. Johnny Wayne. Where the hell are you?"

"I'm back here, J.W. Be right there." Carlton was zipping up when he stepped out of the bathroom and came into the den wiping his hands on his blue jeans.

"Hey, J.W. What can I do you for?"

"Need some smoke and a little blow, Carlton. Goin' fishing up at the lake."

These words were more of an order from Johnny Wayne than a request. Carlton didn't flinch. It was an ordinary demand Carlton understood should be met not just because it was Johnny Wayne Fulcher himself who was standing in his den, but also because of an unstated understanding drugs were a perquisite Johnny Wayne earned for his clandestine role within Sheriff Bailey's department.

"How you been doing at that lately, J.W.? Been making any fish money?"

"I picked up over $4500 in the fishing contest over at Pickerel's pond three weeks ago. Got a good space to throw from, and my bait keeps doin' its thing. Hey, Queen Bee's waitin'. Get your ass moving, Carlton."

"Sure thing, J.W. Be back in a minute."

Carlton left the house and stayed gone for about five minutes. He walked back in grasping two sandwich bags, one with buds of "green vegetable material" and another with white powder.

"Here you go, J.W."

"I'm outta here, Carlton," Johnny Wayne said as he grabbed the bags. "You're a good man, Carlton, a real good man. Always a pleasure doing business with you. Catch you later."

The fish were waiting. Johnny Wayne held up his hand in a wave, swung around, opened the door, and walked across the porch to the truck.

Carlton never asked for the money. He knew better.

It was a matter of professional courtesy.

Chapter 20

"I'd rather hang out with the losers who would sit and smoke a cigarette than the ones who wanted to throw a baseball."

Kurt Cobain

Tuesday, August 15th at 11 p.m.

Harley Ames drove down the path to the Fulcher farm. He was on Arnie Robertson's mission. When he came to the edge of the clearing, he stopped, kept his lights on dim, and got out and yelled.

"Halloo! Anybody home? It's me. It's Harley Ames! I come to see Johnny Wayne! Is J.W. there! Halloo!" His voice echoed across the field.

Harley didn't want to get shot. He knew better than not to announce himself before coming onto Johnny Wayne Fulcher's premises. Johnny Wayne had a couple of Blue Tick hounds used for raccoon hunting that slept under his porch and usually bayed when strangers showed up, but the dozen or so guinea hens that scratched around the yard served as better watchdogs.

"Is that you, Harley? Harley Ames from The Train Stop?" yelled another voice from the porch. It wasn't Johnny Wayne. This voice had a peculiar twangy and unattractive screech to it.

"Yeah, it's me," came the reply. "It's Harley. Harley Ames. Can I come on in?"

"Yeah, that's fine, Harley" the voice called back. "Drive on up."

Harley drove toward the edge of the porch and cut off his motor. The dozing dogs barely acknowledged other than by simply raising their heads, but the guinea hens gave Harley their full attention. Harley had another reason to know the figure he had been yelling to wasn't Johnny Wayne. Johnny Wayne Fulcher would have asked more questions. And sounded a lot scarier.

As it turned out, command of the Fulcher farm had been left to a lowlife by the name of Cheech Mann.

Harley knew Cheech Mann from The Train Stop. He had a slimy complexion, greasy hair, and bore a striking resemblance to Charles Manson without the swastika between his eyebrows. Brown residue from smoking tobacco stained his fingers, and his teeth were a luminous, fuzzy yellow. He smelled. He was possessed of a wet handshake. His sagging pants revealed an apparent lack of ass and the identity of the NASCAR driver on his Kmart T-shirt could no longer be distinguished. Few regulars at The

Train Stop could bear to sit in his vicinity, much less listen to his disgusting mouth.

Even by Harley's standards, Cheech Mann was one of the lowest of the low.

Cheech was one of those people you just didn't want to know too much about. And, once you knew about him, you wished you hadn't.

To best understand Cheech Mann, one would need to start with his conception.

Jess Mann was the grandfather of Cheech Mann's mother. Incapable of regular employment because of inherited alcoholism and an afflictive revulsion for employment, Jess relied upon cutting firewood, gathering collards and other wild edibles, theft, and hunting squirrels, rabbits, possums, and other wild game for his subsistence. Although unschooled in the ancient Egyptian practice of incest, he had followed family tradition that accepted interfamily relations without comment or moral judgment. At age 15, Cheech's mother had voluntarily engaged in relations with her 35-plus years grandfather Jess simply for the sake of fun. There were two results from these engagements: the conception of Cheech Mann within the belly of his mother and the onset of painful and recurring symptoms of syphilis in the abdomen and private parts of Jess.

A visit to the Rockingham County Health Department and the subsequent referral to the local urologist resulted in a prescription of mega-doses of anti-biotics and the insertion one of the new "Double J" stents into Jess's privates to keep the passage open and fight the spread of infection. Just to make sure it was easy to remove, the Doc had tied a string to the stent and taped it to Jess's inner thigh. Sure enough, during the anticipated recovery, Jess was home, wearing nothing but a flannel bathrobe and sitting in his Lazy-Boy popping Percocets, drinking Vodka mixed with SunDrop soda against doctor's orders, to the drone of "Let's Make a Deal," when his old cat Stumpy strolled by. As fate would have it, Stumpy noticed a string hanging from the Lazy-Boy. The next thing Jess knew the cat took off with both the string and the stent. Jess' most favorite thing had almost been disemboweled. No one was sure what caused the coronary. It could have been Jess's simply being pissed off or the strain from the trauma. But a mostly naked Jess, dead and bloody in the crotch, was found on his front stoop along with his pocket pistol and poor old dead Stumpy, shot right through the gut with the .38.

So Cheech had started life as the orphan of his father/great-grandfather. He was raised in a shotgun house on the edge of the cotton mill property. There weren't too many things Cheech was proud of, but the things he was proudest of were repulsive to most people.

True to family form and disgustingly enough, he had fathered a little girl by his own mother when he was 17 and she was 33. Even worse, years passed and he sired yet another daughter-by his own 14 year old daughter born of his mother. Or his sister. Or his Aunt. You decide.

Cheech Mann didn't have a family tree. He had a family wreath.

Such was the man Harley Ames spoke to that night in the darkness. Harley noticed that Johnny Wayne's pickup was gone.

"I need to talk to J.W., Cheech. Where'd he go?"

"Oh, he went up to Bassett to go carp fishin' up at Philpot Lake, Harley. Took his truck and lantern and The Bee and headed up. Said they're going to sit on the bank all night."

Cheech Mann was scratching his chest, adjusting his pants, apparently high on something.

"Should be back in the morning, but you know how he is, Harley. He could be back in the morning, tomorrow night, or in five minutes. You just don't know about J.W."

Mann turned as if he was going back into the house. He was losing his concentration.

"And he can get right ornery if he's been up all night drinking and not sleepin', so you might want to check back tomorrow. I'll tell him you stopped by just as soon as he gets back."

Philpot Lake was 40 miles away and had a 100-mile shoreline.

Harley was desperate, and Mann was his only lifeline at that moment.

"Listen, Cheech. You got any idea where on the lake I could find him? I need to talk to him real, real bad, and real soon. It's about some money somebody owes me."

"He didn't say, Harley. Could be up at Powell's Bridge, maybe near the dam, maybe at Goose Point. I got no idea."

Harley had to coax Cheech as if he was a child, knowing it was a long shot that Cheech would be of any benefit.

"Okay, Cheech, I'm gonna go up and try to find them. But be sure to have Johnny Wayne call The Train Stop just as soon as he gets in, got it? Just as soon as he gets in. I'll check with them to see if you've called, okay?"

"Ok, Harley, I'll try to remember. I'll try real hard, but my head's hurtin', and some green salve would certainly help me remember, if you know what I mean..."

"Look, Cheech, would $20 help you remember? Would $20 help?"

"$30 might do it, Harley. $30 sounds about right."

Harley yanked out his wallet and fumbled for the $30.

"Here you go, Cheech...here's 25."

"Hey, Harley, can I ask you something? Just one thing?"

"Go ahead, Cheech."

"You got any extra cigarettes, Harley? You got any at all?"

Chapter 21

"Beware of the fury of a patient man."

John Dryden

Early morning, Wednesday, August 16th

It had been over a week since Ebony had stopped by for another one of her short two-hour visits. No one had seen her come, and no one had seen her go. Or so Carlton thought.

Both had been satisfied when she left.

Carlton settled in for the night on his couch after a celebratory bowl of beans and onions. It was around 1 a.m. when his hound bayed and he heard a knock on the front door. He stood in his underwear and made it to the door. Looking through one of the glass panes, his neck jerked when he saw two figures standing within feet of the window, both wearing hooded garments. He hadn't heard a car or truck pull in and none were in the yard, but he knew who they were, who they had come for, and why. And he was savvy enough to know there was at least one more at his back door.

"Open up, Carlton. You know why we're here."

There was a noticeable silence from within the house. It was *too* quiet. The voice boomed louder, and the knock became a fearless bang.

"Open up. We're not going to kill you, Carlton. Now open up the door."

It was the voice of Edgar Sills. Carlton knew better than to say his name. But hoods, he thought as he ran his fingers through his hair. "Hoods. And robes. Oh hell."

Carlton had no choice but to answer the call.

"Yes, Sir. I'm opening the door."

Carlton began to plead before the screen door swung open.

"Now please don't take me away nowhere. I swear to God on everything that's holy you won't have to come back here. I really, really get your message this time, Sir. Ain't no way I'll even talk to that girl again, I swear it."

The two men walked in, standing ramrod straight and with authority. All in the room knew each other, but the hoods and robes brought the presence of another force. It signified representation. Representation that the two men were acting with the authority of a much larger, more powerful group.

Carlton's eyes widened. They were wearing gloves.

"Carlton, could you unlock the back door and let one of our brothers come in from the back porch? And Carlton, there's more than three of us here. And no reason to try to run. Even if you got away, you know we'd be back. There wasn't even any need for me to tell you that, now was there, Carlton?"

Carlton simply looked down, noticed that he had put on his boxer shorts backwards, and shook his head. He knew this night was turning out to be just shitty. He turned, each arm dangling limply by each side, and shuffled his way to the back door. After unlatching the back door a third hooded man came in. He also wore gloves.

Only Carlton and the hooded Edgar spoke.

"Carlton, the first thing I want to ask you is a simple question. Is there anyone else in this house?"

"No, Sir, there's not." Carlton answered truthfully. Meekly.

"Then I want you to stand up straight, look at me, and open your mouth."

"Open my...?"

Edgar cut him off. He wasn't asking. He was ordering. The syntax of his speech was simple, direct. Nothing could be misunderstood.

"Open your mouth, Carlton. Look straight at me and open your mouth."

Carlton heard and understood he had no choice. He opened his mouth. A second hooded figure reached into a gunny sack pulled out a sawed off shotgun less than three feet in length. He handed the shotgun to Edgar.

Carlton started to collapse. "Oh my God. Please, I didn't…"

Edgar asserted himself.

"Did I tell you to speak, Son? I told you to shut up, stand there, and open your mouth. You hear me, boy? Open your mouth, Carlton. Open your mouth and don't say a word. Not a word. And keep your hands by your side."

Carlton emitted a whimper, a pitiful, childlike whispered squeal bereft of any hint of manhood. He re-opened his mouth. Edgar inserted the barrel of the sawed off shotgun past Carlton's lips and teeth. His arm was outstretched, his finger on the trigger.

Carlton faced forward, seeing nothing. Too afraid to cry, a convulsive shake pulsed through his body. His eyes bulged. But his head remained still. He gave no thought to anything but the moment, with no words coming to mind but "Oh, God. Oh, God. Oh, God."

Edgar got to the reason for the visit.

"Now don't try to say a word or move, Carlton. Just hold both of your arms down and don't move them. Don't move them at all, Carlton. I've got a steady hand, Carlton, but I can't vouch for the trigger on this gun. So be real still and just listen, Son, and don't move at all."

Carlton held his arms down. The third figure then reached into a gunny sack and brought out what turned out to be his first roll of duct tape. Silver duct tape. Both of Carlton's arms were wrapped and, once so bound, the duct tape was threaded around Carlton's torso, and then each of his legs.

Within 5 minutes Carlton had been mummified in duct tape.

"Now Carlton, we're going to pull the barrel of that gun out of your mouth, you hear? And then we're going to put duct tape over your mouth and head but not your nose so you can breathe."

It struck Carlton that Edgar had not blown his head off. He was by the grace of God alive. Nothing else mattered. He'd do whatever they asked. His main concern was the barrel of the shotgun. He didn't want another taste of it. His breathing was forced and labored, and tears slid into the crevices of his cheeks groomed from the excessive consumption of alcohol and cigarettes.

Edgar went on.

"And I want you to know, Carlton, that you should thank us for all of that tape. You see, Carlton, that tape is going to keep your bones from breaking while we beat the living hell out of you, you understand? I hope you can hear me fair and good this time, Carlton, because you apparently couldn't hear that fair and good last time we talked. It's been just over a month, Carlton, and you forgot right away.

A warning just to do the right thing, Carlton. You just didn't hear. You just didn't listen."

Carlton's head rose up and down in agreement. Edgar should know he was contrite. He started to speak, but Edgar cut him off.

"No, Carlton, don't you say anything unless it's to thank us. We're going to beat the hell out of you. I didn't say we were going to kill you. I said beat the hell out of you. If I told you we were going to kill you, you could rest assured that would have already happened."

Edgar circled toward Carlton's left ear. Carlton didn't dare make a move. He was at their mercy.

"We're not going to kill you, Carlton. We're not. Unless you resist. You have my word. Do you understand what I'm saying to you, Carlton? Nod if you do, Carlton."

Carlton nodded. Vigorously.

"If you believe I'm an honest and sincere man who keeps his word, Carlton, then you will believe what I'm going to say. You've been warned once without penalty. You're being warned again without being killed. There will be no more warnings after tonight, Carlton Purvis. Do you believe me, Carlton? Nod if you do, Carlton."

Carlton nodded again.

"Then on behalf of the Holy Brotherhood, I say to you that recompense is hereby being collected for your trespass upon that which we deem of true worth."

The third figure again reached into the gunny sack and brought out two Louisville Sluggers baseball bats. Passing one to his cohort, a ten-minute beating of Carlton Purvis began. A beating in which horrific bruises would be inflicted, but no bones broken. A beating intended to be followed by weeks of painful recovery when properly administered. All precautions had been taken to make the event as painful, yet not lethal, as possible. By the time the three left, all considerations had been kept in mind as the wooden bats rained upon Carlton's arms, legs, and torso, leaving him limp and seemingly lifeless on the floor of his Clayton home.

Everything had been taken into consideration. Everything.

Everything but the clot.

The clot shot directly from Carlton's crumpled right leg to his left lung thirty minutes after Edgar and his group left. The clot, caused by the beating, killed Carlton Purvis.

The same Carlton Purvis who was described as "a self-employed handyman" in his obituary.

Chapter 22

"There is nothing in the world more stubborn than a corpse:
you can hit it, you can knock it to pieces,
but you cannot convince it."

Alexander Herzen

Friday, August 18th at 3:00 p.m.

U.S. Attorney Timothy Herndon had taken the advice and recommendation of a colleague from the Federal Middle District of North Carolina. He had retained a wily and resourceful private detective by the name of Anita Mills to deliver Carlton Purvis's subpoena.

Anita was almost evil in her abilities. She could pass for a bag lady in Wal-Mart or an executive's wife on a tennis court and slip into, and thrive in, almost any social environment.

Anita had come from Greensboro and made her first stop at He'sNotHere, but no-one had seen Carlton in at least two days. The next stop was the Purvis homestead, where she was greeted by Carlton's howling hound and the scattering of his chickens. And, luckily, Carlton's pickup was parked just in front of the dwelling.

At first the detective thought the odor she detected was one of simple filth. The residence was obviously unkempt and occupied by someone of lowly standards. Trash and beer cans lay around garbage bins and in the yard; old batteries were stacked on the porch; and a couple of cars used for parts were parked to the right of the dwelling. A hound was tied to one of cars with an overturned 55 gallon drum barrel next to it for the dog to sleep in.

When there was no response to knocks at the door, Mills took a peek in one of the three horizontal glass panes. That's when she saw it.

On the floor lay a body, clad in silver, obviously dead, swollen, and with burgundy fluid seeping out of the right side of the corpse's distended mouth. The corpse's tongue was obviously swollen. Reaching reflexively into her pocketbook for her pistol, she retreated to her car, not in a panic, but with a determination to get immediate assistance. Arriving at Stone's Store a little more than a mile away, she told the store clerk of the circumstances and was handed the telephone on a stretched cord to contact the sheriff's department.

After giving details to the dispatcher, Mills told the store clerk she needed to make an urgent long distance call. Tossing a ten dollar bill on the counter, she dialed "0," gave the operator the number, and was rewarded by an answer from Timothy Herndon's office.

"Is Mr. Herndon in?"

"No, I'm sorry, but he's been called into the courtroom. May I help you? My name is Jamie Watson, and I'm Mr. Herndon's administrative aide."

"Miss Watson, if you're Mr. Herndon's aide then you've probably heard of me. My name is Anita Mills, and I was retained by your office to serve a subpoena upon a Mr. Carlton Purvis in Rockingham County, North Carolina."

"Yes, I know who you are, Ms. Mills. I prepared that subpoena and contacted your office myself. How can I help you?"

"Call me Anita, Jamie. Apparently Mr. Purvis is dead, Jamie. I just left his house, and there's a body inside. Smells like hell and looked really strange, even from outside. Odds are it's him. It's bloody and messed up in there, Jamie. Can you let Herndon know that as soon as possible? I'd guess that Carlton Purvis is dead. I'll call back before the end of the day, but right now I need to get back to the house to make sure it's him. The sheriff's department has dispatched deputies so they're on the way."

"I'll let him know." There was a pause. The thought of having just typed the subpoena for Purvis was on her mind. "Wow, Anita, it's so…what happened?"

"No idea, Jamie. That's what I'm going to try to find out." Jamie heard a click as Anita ended the call.

By the time Anita returned, four sheriff's patrol cars were parked over one hundred feet from the house. An ambulance was closer. She could see that yellow barricade tape surrounded the house. A deputy seated behind the steering wheel of his patrol car directed Anita to stop where she was and to proceed no further. When Anita displayed her private detective shield, the deputy motioned her to a spot to park.

Exiting the car, the deputy approached and asked for identification.

"You can't cross that line, ma'am. They're in the midst of doing an initial investigation, and the area is closed. You're not family, are you?"

"No, Sir, I'm not. So who is it, Deputy?"

"I'm not allowed to say anything, ma'am. Now, if you'll..."

Anita Mills persisted.

"I'm the one who called. I'm the one who saw the body from the front porch window and called the sheriff's department from Stone's Store. That's how you know about this. So who's dead? I saw him lying there, and something was on him. Something silver. What was it?"

The deputy eased up.

"Well, ma'am, I'm sorry to tell you if you knew him, but it was Carlton Purvis. Did you know him?"

"No, Deputy, not personally. No, I don't."

The deputy's voice was somber.

"Well, he's dead. But it's the dog-gondest thing I've ever seen, ma'am. He was wrapped in duct tape. I know that sounds crazy. But that's what you saw that was silver. Duct tape."

Anita's mouth opened and a hand rose to rest on her chin. The deputy's description mesmerized her.

"He was wrapped tight as a tick, except for the top of his head. You saw it. I've never seen nothing like this, ma'am. Wrapped him up in duct tape either before or after he died. Don't know whether it was violent or one of those sex things… It's weird..."

The deputy then made a face as if he had eaten something sour.

"And smells like hell. It'd make a maggot gag. Nasty it is. First degree nasty."

Mills could see two deputies working around at the indentions apparently left by a vehicle in the yard. One was mixing Plaster to pour into them.

A gurney sat on the porch, waiting to be used to transport of the body once the crime scene photographs and other procedures took place. One procedure involved a deputy brushing the outside doorknob for fingerprints. Presumably the same would be done for the inside doorknob, with the whole doorknob assembly being then removed and checked into evidence.

"Are you sure it's Carlton Purvis, Deputy?"

"Yes ma'am, I knew Carlton." He shook his head. "Most people did. It's Carlton."

"Thank you, Deputy. I hope you find out who did this to your friend."

Chapter 23

"Look like the innocent flower

But be the serpent under it."

From William Shakespeare's "Macbeth"

Friday, August 18th at 4 p.m.

Juanita punched "1" and picked up the telephone receiver after the third ring. "This is the office of Sheriff Bailey. How may I help you?"

"Hello. My name is Thomas Herndon, and I'm calling from Roanoke, Virginia. I am the U.S. Attorney for the Western District of Virginia. Is Sheriff Bailey in? I'd like to speak to Sheriff Bailey if he is available."

"I'm not sure if he's tied up or not, Mr. Herndon. I'm going to ask you to wait on hold while I check, if you will." Juanita placed her on hold and buzzed the Sheriff. Sheriff Bailey said he'd take the call. He was thinking that this was going to be fun. The Sheriff picked up the receiver and poured sunshine into the microphone.

"Good morning! This is Sheriff Efron Bailey hoping you're having a blessed day. How may I help you?"

"Good morning, Sheriff Bailey. I'm Tom Herndon calling from Roanoke. Formally speaking, I'm the U.S. Attorney for the Western District of Virginia. You may have heard of me?"

The good Sheriff chuckled. "Oh, I've heard a lot of things about you, Mr. Herndon. It is a distinct pleasure to finally make your acquaintance and hear your voice. Is there anything I can do to help you today?"

"Sheriff, I've just received word that a witness who we had subpoenaed to testify in a very important matter up here in Roanoke has been reported to be deceased. We've heard that just this morning, Sir. His name was Mr. Carlton Purvis, age 45 or 46, and he lived just outside of Lawsonville. Is there anything you may have heard about this, Sheriff Bailey?"

"Mr. Herndon, everyone in this county knows Carlton Purvis. Or knew him. He didn't amount to much in this life, Mr. Herndon. Known for his gambling, drinking, fighting, drugs, you name it. He's dead, Mr. Herndon. My boys found him this morning and noticed some bruising. Looks like he might have been beat to death."

"So, do you have any suspects, Sheriff Bailey?"

The Good Sheriff intended to seize control.

"Don't get ahead of yourself, Mr. Herndon. Let's me and you get straight with each other, and let's just do that right now, if you don't mind."

Sheriff Bailey leaned back in his desk chair and propped a foot up on his desk. He began a paternalistic, condescending lecture.

"Let's recognize a few facts here, Mr. Herndon. You're up in Virginia, and I'm the duly elected Sheriff here in Rockingham County. Rockingham County is not in Virginia, Mr. Herndon. It's in North Carolina. Are we clear on that, Mr. Herndon? Rockingham County is in the Great State of North Carolina. It is not in the Commonwealth of Virginia. My duty is to my constituents here in Rockingham County, North Carolina, and you are not one of them. You do not reside here. You have never voted here. You are not one of my constituents. Do you understand me, Mr. Herndon? Are we communicating?"

Herndon gave no reply.

"This is in my jurisdiction and your name and title don't amount to a pinch of puppy shit down here. It's none of your official business whatsoever, whether or not I have any suspects because this a state matter within the bounds of the Great State of North Carolina. You are welcome to watch television or read whatever news there is pertaining to this situation in the newspaper just like everyone else. Am I making myself clear, Sir?"

"Crystal clear, Sheriff Bailey." Herndon mentally refused to stoop to the Sheriff's level of conversation and instead maintained a cool professionalism.

But Herndon did want to remind the Sheriff of the extent of his authority.

"Sheriff, Bailey, I am sure you know that it is very much my business if someone has been threatened or murdered to prevent, or in retaliation of, testimony whether already given or subpoenaed to be given in the Federal Judicial system."

Sheriff Bailey refused to surrender the offensive. He was compelled to throw in a dig at Herndon's office.

"Well, Mr. Herndon, I reckon' both of us are smart enough to know that any subpoenas issued by any competent U.S. Attorney are usually kept secret just to prevent that kind of thing, aren't they? And you, Mr. Herndon, consider yourself to be more than competent, don't you?"

Once again, Herndon remained silent. The Sheriff was ready to end the conversation.

"I have important matters to attend to, Sir, so let's just leave it like this. We have a lot of people down here who might have liked Carlton Purvis dead, whether over a grudge or on a whim. That's how a lot of folks down here simply are. Either they ponder and pray over their needs and concerns and sleep on them, or they act impulsively and just go and do whatever fulfills their immediate desires. It doesn't matter who or what they hurt. Their only concern is for themselves and what they want at that moment. "

Bailey planted both feet on the floor and leaned over his desk. The first finger on his right hand was going from left to right while his other hand choked the telephone receiver held to his ear.

"Truth be told, Mr. Purvis had a talent for making people mad and running with the lowlifes. He could've been killed over a woman, over a gambling debt, over a drug debt, or just for fun, or for no reason at all. Maybe just for sport. For gracious sakes, for all we know he tied himself up with all of that duct tape and beat himself to death. Yep, it could have been a suicide. Wouldn't surprise us a bit down here if that's how it went down. I don't know at this point."

The Sheriff spoke down to Herndon.

"But that's for me and my honest and capable staff to find out, isn't it, Mr. Herndon? It's not any of your business at all. You might as well be from China or from the moon as far as we're concerned."

Herndon had heard enough.

"I'll let you go, Sheriff Bailey."

But the Sheriff wasn't quite through.

"Two more things, Mr. Herndon. You probably don't want to waste your time checking for confidential information about our investigation and witnesses in the newspaper down here. I understand you might have problems of that nature in your office, but down here we're good about being professional and keeping such things confidential, you understand?"

"That son-of-a-bitch," Herndon thought. He swung his chair toward the window, and the green H & C Coffee sign perched on the roof of a nearby building.

"And second, earlier I let a profane word slip into this conversation. I was wrong to do that, Sir, and for that, I apologize. I know I will answer to my Maker for such talk when I meet Him in His Glory, but until then I must ask for your forgiveness. Could you do that for me, Sir? I feel I may have offended your sensibilities."

Herndon later said he felt like throwing up.

"Have a good day, Sheriff Bailey," Herndon said, forcing himself not to slam the phone back in its cradle.

Chapter 24

"Dont let cha mouth open up cuz you dont wanna see the handgun open up,(no)dont let cha mouth open up cuz you dont wanna see the automatic open up."

From L'il Wayne's "Snitch"

Friday, August 25th at 11: a.m."

The chief jailer had contacted Deputy Arnie Robertson to advise that one of the inmates was desperate to speak with him.

It wasn't uncommon for a disgruntled inmate to snitch on another person for some advantage and, as a general practice, dealing with such miscreants often provided leads or information impossible to obtain using by the book methods.

Robertson directed the jailer to have the jail nurse retrieve the snitch and bring him away from the cells and to her station under a pretense. He'd meet with him there.

When Robertson walked in, little Cheech Mann, all 125 slimy pounds of him and with all the stench he emanated to permeate the room, greeted him.

Robertson knew better than to grant Cheech Mann undeserved respect in any shape, manner, or form. That wasn't how you dealt with Cheech. Cheech understood dirt. You treated him like dirt and dirt you got in return.

"What's this about, Cheech? I understand you tried to lift two cartons of cigarettes from the grocery. Is that what you did?"

Arnie was already leaning toward Cheech, on the attack. Cheech, forever used to such treatment, cast the same penitent look downward he had used thousands of times before. Still, Arnie went on…

"Don't you ever get tired of stealing, Cheech? You gotta be good at what you do, Cheech. But you're just not good at stealing. You ought to know by now that you are one sorry-ass crook, Cheech. You're dumb as a sock full of hair, you know that? You can't even figure out whether you should check your ass or scratch your watch."

Cheech had difficulty listening and thinking at the same time. He stood with a limp smile on his lips. Arnie Robertson kept on.

"Time to find something you're better at, Son. Last time you got six months just for lifting a six-pack. The judges know you better than they know their own dogs, Cheech. They like sending you off just so they don't have to see or smell you. Must be because you like it, Cheech. Three hots and a cot and all the sex you want... Sounds right up your alley, except you're gonna to have to commit adultery on your Mama and Sister with your fellow inmates--a real moral dilemma for you, I'm sure.... You're a livin', breathin' one-household Juan Nightstand, Cheech, you know that?"

Cheech was nonplussed, with such low esteem he was incapable of suffering an insult.

"Come on, Mr. Robertson, I'm feeling bad about something and just thought you should know... kind of a matter of conscience, you know..."

His feigned attempt at sincerity never had a chance. Arnie Robertson pounced.

"Well, I'll be! Cheech Mann has had one of those E-piph-a-nys! A new beginning. Lord help me! It's really happened!"

Robertson's voice was bouncing in echoes within the confines of the cement walls and tile floors of the small nurse's station. He dug a cigarette from his left shirt pocket and in one motion clicked and struck a flame from his brass Zippo lighter. Wooden chair legs screeched as he pulled the chair across the floor and plopped himself down.

"Conscience? Did you say conscience, Cheech? What you gonna do, Cheech, borrow one? And then you're going to be a good citizen, step forward, and help the law and ask for nothing in return? And why? Because it's the right thing to do? Miracles do happen! So, Cheech, you gonna get your own religious TV show, Cheech, and get people to send you money and, heck, maybe even cigarettes? Buy yourself a bouffant and a blue polyester jump suit and be on The Cheech 'n Preach TV Club? Is that what you're going to do?"

"No Sir, Mr. Robertson. I'm not." Cheech had surrendered any pretense of a challenge to anything Robertson might throw at him. What he wanted from Robertson was more important, so he tried to get to the point.

"If you're done with me, maybe we can talk..."

"What's wrong, Cheech? You nervous about something, son? You're shaking like a dog pooping a peach pit, boy."

Arnie Robertson had enjoyed his fill of taunting for the moment and decided to listen.

"OK, Cheech, what in the name of Captain Kirk's Nipples is important enough for me to learn from you to miss 'The Guiding Light'? What did you send for me for? This better be good, Cheech. I ain't got no time to fool with you."

Cheech was tentative, careful with the few words in his limited vocabulary to protect his bargaining position.

"It's good, Deputy Robertson, Sir. It's real good, Sir. I might have heard something about that Carlton Purvis killing that might help ya'll figure out who done it, Sir. I might have heard something for sure, Sir, if I can remember what it was."

"Cheech, what are you getting at?"

Cheech Mann instinctively milked every moment for anything he could garner to his advantage from this meeting.

"I just can't think clear, Deputy Robertson. I'm having trouble thinking 'cause it's been over two days since I had a cigarette. Can you give me a cigarette so both of us can get me to remember what I might know?"

Robertson upped the ante by standing as if he intended to leave the room as a waste of time.

"Dammit, Cheech. Is all this talk about a stinking cigarette? Is that why you called me over here?"

"Oh no, Sir, Deputy Robertson. No Sir, it ain't over a cigarette. But if you could just find it in your heart to give me a cigarette..."

Arnie turned toward the door and reached for the knob. A few more insults were in order.

"Cheech, I'm getting back to work. Anybody ever tell you that you stink? Better yet, anybody ever tell you that you don't stink? You could knock a dog off a gut wagon, Cheech. I'm not being paid enough to have to see and smell you, Cheech. I'm outta here. Go stand in the rain when you get outta here, okay? Have a good year or two..."

"Wait. Wait, Deputy Robertson."

Cheech extended his hands in the direction of Robertson.

"I think Purvis owed some money to the wrong people."

That remark caught Robertson's attention.

"What did you say, Cheech?"

"I can't remember too much more right now, Deputy Robertson. I'm too worried. Worried. That's what I am. I'm worried about my family, Deputy. They need me, Deputy Robertson."

Robertson couldn't contain himself. He was laughing inside at his own smart remarks before they even left his lips. He was smiling. Cheech had actually said he was worried about his family. The door was open a mile wide.

"Worried? About what, Cheech? Is your daughter expecting again? That means you'd be a Daddy again! And an uncle! And a granddaddy! And have a new little brother! All of the above!"

Cheech dropped the subject of his family. He knew he couldn't win that one. Besides, he was there to conduct a business transaction which, in this case, simply meant doing what was necessary to get out of jail.

"Deputy Robertson, Sir, if I could tell you who was going to see Carlton Purvis on the night he was murdered, and that Carlton Purvis owed money to the people I tell you about, do you reckon' you might be able to get me home with my family?"

Cheech Mann lowered his voice. Fear permeated his words.

"We're talking about life and death here, Deputy Robertson, not some jackoffs. Serious situation that could involve me being taken out just for talking to you. I'd be taking a big chance here, Deputy. That is, Sir, if I can remember who it was..."

Robertson bit.

"So, who was it, Cheech?"

Cheech had slowly but effectively turned the table of power. He and Robertson had suddenly become equals dancing in a primitive trade of information.

"I just can't recollect' right now, Deputy Robertson. For the life of me, I can't recollect. Now, if you'll have the district attorney talk to my lawyer and come up with something so I can go home right away with the understanding my charges will be dropped, I'll pay for those two cartons of cigarettes I'm accused of stealing and probably remember enough to help you find out who the last people to see poor old Carlton were. It'll jar my memory if you'll do that, Sir."

Robertson had forgotten the fun of his bullying. And Cheech Mann had seized control of the topic of conversation.

"Did you say 'people', Cheech?"

Mann silently reveled in his newfound authority. Arnie Robertson was curious, and Cheech had the answers. He was keeping his cards close to his chest. Mann suddenly seemed to notice a hangnail, belittling the presence of Arnie Robertson.

"Oh, did I say that? I don't remember if I said that or not, Deputy Robertson. People? Person? I just don't remember for sure, I don't. But I'll go to work on it on my end if you'll go to work on your end, Deputy Robertson."

"Ok, Cheech, I'll see what I can do. Keep your mouth shut, got it? And we haven't talked, understand?"

Arnie Robertson signaled the guard with a wave as he stood in the doorway.

"I hear you, Sir. But there's something else."

Robertson was looking toward the approaching guard, refusing to dignify Cheech further with a glance.

"What is it, Cheech?"

"Deputy Robertson, Sir, could I have that cigarette now? Could I, Sir? Or maybe two?"

Chapter 25

"I've never had a problem with drugs. I've had problems with the police."

Keith Richards

Friday, August 28th at 10 p.m.

Harley Ames was perplexed when Arnie called him back to the tobacco barn. He assumed some other source had been sent out to take care of the Carlton Purvis problem and that the matter had been resolved before he had time to do it himself. He didn't care who or how and, for that matter, he didn't want to know.

Once again, Harley arrived at the barn earlier than Arnie and, once again, after Arnie drove up, Harley left his car and sat in Arnie's.

"You screwed up, Harley. You really screwed up."

"What's that, Arnie? I screwed up? How?"

"You told Cheech Mann. You told that no-good sawed-off little worm that you and Johnny Wayne killed Carlton. And there's no telling who Cheech has told in the jail."

Harley knew his continued living existence depended upon Arnie Robertson believing him. His voice was insistent. Pleading.

"What? What are you talking about, Arnie. No, I didn't! I swear, Arnie. That didn't happen! You're believing Cheech? What in God's name are you talking about, Arnie?"

Arnie slowly tightened a proverbial noose around Harley's neck. He looked straight into his Harley's eyes.

"Listen, Harley. It's too late. Cheech has worked out a deal with the DA. You need to know all about it. They found Johnny Wayne's prints in Carlton's house. On the table. On the doorknob. Inside and out. And his truck was there. Plaster casts of Johnny Wayne Fulcher's truck tires, Harley. All the morning of the murder."

Harley acted perplexed. He knew that somehow he had screwed up. There was no other explanation for Arnie's presence.

"So what, Arnie? What's that got to do with me?"

"The Feds are already sniffing around, and the murder has led to Johnny Wayne. No telling what Johnny Wayne will tell the Feds about you and him. Cheech Mann has already cut a deal. What's to keep Johnny Wayne from cutting a deal, Harley? What's to keep him from doing that?"

Harley held his hand up.

"Wait a minute, Arnie! Wait a minute! Me and J.W. ain't talked about doing nothing to Carlton for you or the Sheriff or anybody else! We ain't talked about a damn thing! I swear to God we haven't."

Arnie liked part of what he had heard. Harley was saying he hadn't done anything to Carlton for the Sheriff or him. That was good.

Harley's mind was spinning. Had he been set up? Who was after him? And why? Surely they knew he wasn't involved. What was happening?

"Arnie, I swear to God that's a boldfaced lie. I didn't have nothing to do with beatin' ol' Carlton to death. That dog just don't hunt, Arnie. It's a damn lie."

Harley's voice rose to a screech. "Shit! You're believing Cheech! Have you gone crazy?"

Arnie stayed on track for the purpose of this meeting.

"Simple question. Did you see Cheech that night? Look me in the eyes, and tell me whether or not you saw Cheech that night, Harley."

Arnie Robertson was pointing to his eyes. Harley responded by staring back.

"I ain't gonna lie, Arnie. I went to J.W.'s house looking for him. Cheech was there, and J.W. and the Bee had gone fishing up at Philpot. They wasn't there. I drove all around the lake, but I couldn't find J.W. I was up most of the night. Cheech was supposed to call The Train Stop if J.W.

got home. He never called like he was supposed to. I ain't seen J.W. or the Bee since then. That's the truth, Arnie. I swear on all that's holy that what I told you is the truth, so help me God, Arnie."

At that moment, both had different agendas. Harley wanted to go home as if the conversation had never happened. Arnie had his orders and a job to carry out.

"Well, Johnny Wayne's getting ready to be put into custody and you know he'll be denying everything. Cheech says he'll be claiming he was fishing, just like you said. That's what they call an alibi on TV, Harley, and alibis usually don't work on TV, do they?"

Harley was silent. It was dawning on him that he was in deep trouble and would have to do as he was told.

"And Cheech has told us that you were looking for Johnny Wayne because Carlton owed you some money, and then Carlton's beaten to death in a matter of hours. Johnny Wayne's prints and truck. You and Johnny Wayne. It don't look good, Harley. You could get the death penalty for that."

What was undeniable in Arnie's own mind was his earlier direction, however unspoken, for Harley to "take care of" Carlton. That, coupled with Carlton Purvis's death, Johnny Wayne's prints in Carlton's house, and Cheech Mann's verification that Harley had been with Johnny Wayne on the night of the killing had Arnie convinced his instructions had been carried out and that despite his insistent denials Harley had helped kill Purvis.

Arnie and the Sheriff needed distance from the killing. He told Harley what Harley was going to do.

"Listen, Harley, it's going to go down my way. You've got no choice. Forget democracy because you've got no vote, you got that? So you get that stupid look off your face and do what I'm telling you, you understand?"

Harley started to whimper.

"But Arnie..."

Arnie had listened enough. He reached for his holster and pulled out his pistol. The mechanism clicked just before he pointed it toward Harley's face.

"For God's sake, Arnie."

Arnie Robertson was serious. He would do whatever it took to keep him and Efron Bailey from being dragged into federal court in Roanoke because of the moron at the end of his gun barrel.

"You shut the hell up, Harley. We got two ways to go, so shut the hell up. Which way you want to do this? Your way or my way?"

Harley had leaned his head as far from the pistol as possible.

"Your way, Arnie, your way. Now please, for God's sake, put that thing down. Your way, Arnie. Your way."

Arnie lowered the pistol.

"This is what happened, Harley, so you listen carefully, you hear me?"

Harley nodded.

Arnie Robertson began his instructions.

"Okay, Harley, here's what you're going to do, so listen good. And I'm not speaking on behalf of myself, Harley. You know that. This is coming from up top."

Arnie held the floor. Harley was silent. He was being told, not asked, what to do. This was business.

"I know we had our earlier talk about Carlton, and I mentioned Johnny Wayne. In my mind you did it. But it's possible just to make double sure or to cover some tracks somebody other than you had Johnny Wayne took care of Carton Purvis. I guess it's possible somebody else had to make sure Carlton didn't testify before the Federal Grand Jury up in Roanoke."

Even Arnie wasn't convinced how the killing had occurred.

"But I believe in my heart, Harley, it wasn't somebody else at all. I think it was you who contacted Johnny Wayne and it went down one way or the other, and you're sitting there looking me straight in the eye and denying it."

Arnie paused for a moment.

"I understand you'd have to do that. That makes sense. I don't blame you."

Arnie Robertson placed his wrist on the steering wheel.

"But the bottom line now is Johnny Wayne's getting indicted, and he might start running his mouth about all kinds of things. Both present and past."

Harley didn't interrupt.

"Look, Harley, Johnny Wayne's going to be in jail wating to be tried. He shouldn't be. He ought to be home and no risk to anyone. But he's not home, and like it or not, you're being held responsible. You gotta fix this thing. And you got no choice."

Harley raised one finger.

"Can I say something, Arnie?"

Arnie was in no mood to discuss it further with Harley.

"No, Harley. Not a word. You're here to listen and do what I say. You got that? Nod if you got that, Harley."

Harley nodded. Arnie began.

"Looks like Johnny Wayne did it, but he screwed up and left finger prints and tire tracks. He'll be in custody, and God knows what he's going to start talking about to get out. So you're going to make sure that when Johnny Wayne killed poor ol' Carlton, it had nothing to do with the subpoena, you got that? Nothing to do with any subpoena."

Arnie Robertson spelled the story out slowly and with deliberation.

"The DA wants Johnny Wayne bad, Harley. He wants him bad. But think about what they have without your testimony at the end of the day. The DA ain't got nothing any half-ass defense lawyer couldn't shoot down. Prints and tire tracks. Stinkin' Cheech. There's no proof Johnny Wayne did a thing. How's Gerry Wiles going to get a conviction with just that? How's he going to do that? You tell me that, Harley. You tell me."

Harley didn't respond. He was looking straight ahead, listening.

"I can tell you how they're going to get a murder conviction, Harley. I can tell you how Johnny Wayne Fulcher's going to be found guilty of murdering poor ol' Carlton. I can tell you how it's going to happen. So listen good. Here's how it's going to go down."

Arnie waited for effect.

"You're going to nail Johnny Wayne's coffin shut, Harley."

Harley simply looked at the palms of his hands.

"Ain't nothing wrong with what you're going to do, Harley," Arnie said. "It ain't illegal 'til you get caught, you know."

Both nodded their heads. Arnie went on.

"It was over a debt, Harley. Over money. Whether you know it or not, you and Johnny Wayne killed Carlton. Carlton owed you some drug money, Harley, and you got

Johnny Wayne to help you get it back. This didn't have a thing to do with the Feds. You went to Johnny Wayne's and Cheech told you where he was. You found him up at the lake and you and Johnny Wayne then went to Carlton's house. You got that so far? You got that?"

Harley slowly bobbed his head. "I got you, Arnie."

"So the next thing that happened was you and Johnny Wayne taped him up in silver duct tape just to send him a message, and you beat him with 2 X 4s you got out of the back of Johnny Wayne's truck, understand?"

Harley was staring in the direction of the glove box as he listened. He gave a slight nod.

"And you got only part of the money and left. Didn't know if he was dead when you left. Got that, Harley?"

Harley looked at his shoes and nodded.

"Harley, you helped Johnny Wayne kill Carlton Purvis. I've assigned Bunk Blanchard as lead detective, and me and Bunk are going to see Gerry Wiles and tell him that you need to be granted immunity for telling the jury you went with Johnny Wayne and helped kill Carlton. Carlton owed you a drug debt or some money over something else, and you got Johnny Wayne to help go collect it. And everything just went all wrong, Harley, and Johnny Wayne went too far and killed poor old Carlton. You saw the whole thing. It's horrified you and worked on your conscience, and that's why you stepped forward."

Robertson wagged a finger toward Harley.

"And you're going to convince 12 people that's what happened, Harley, you got that?"

Harley didn't answer. He had reached into his pants pocket and was jingling a key chain.

"I asked you a question. Think about who you're dealing with here, Harley."

Arnie listed Harley's alternatives. None were good.

"Word is going to be sent to Johnny Wayne that you're working with us. So he either goes away for good or gets released and goes, shall we say, Harley Hunting. Or it could work out that both the DA's Office and Johnny Wayne get together and cut a deal that drags you into this anyway. You're in a heck of a mess, Harley. No, a hell of a mess. Your only way out is to make sure Johnny Wayne goes down. Do you understand what you're going to do to get that done, Harley, and what we're going to do for you?"

Harley finally spoke up. "Yes, Arnie, I've got it." He was quiet. "Me and Johnny Wayne killed Carlton. I walk out of the courtroom."

Arnie started to smile.

"That's right, Harley, you walk out of the courtroom. You go home at the end of the day. But let me remind you of something. You look at me when I tell you this, Harley. You look at me."

Harley looked up at Robertson.

"You'll walk out of that courtroom. You'll do that. But if you don't convince those 12 people what happened, and convince them real good and beyond a reasonable doubt, Johnny Wayne's walking out of that courtroom right behind you."

The two were quiet. Arnie finished up.

"And if I was you, I really wouldn't want Johnny Wayne walking out of that courtroom behind me, Harley. I really wouldn't want that. That would be the shortest day of your life. You might make it to supper. But then again, you might not."

Arnie's logic was irrefutable.

Chapter 26

"If we wait until we're ready, we'll be waiting for the rest of our lives."

Lemony Snicket

Detective Lawton "Bunk" Blanchard asked for a meeting with Assistant District Attorney Gerry Wiles. He wasn't fully convinced he was prepared, but time was a luxury he couldn't afford. He needed to see Wiles, and soon.

Blanchard had the moniker "Bunk" bestowed on him by high school football teammates who had endured listening to his imagined exploits in the areas of hunting, fishing, and girls. Prone to plaid suits, white ties, and Marlboro cigarettes, Blanchard was raised on a tobacco farm in Rockingham County and began his career in law enforcement as a city policeman in Reidsville, North Carolina, population 12,183, after obtaining an associate's degree in law enforcement from Rockingham Community College. After six years on the street, he had applied for and received a job as a detective in the Reidsville Police Department when a senior officer retired

The usual extent of investigations typically assigned to Blanchard, such as breaking and entering or sex offenses, consisted of determining a suspect, bringing him or her to his office without the use of handcuffs ("You're not under arrest, and I won't arrest you unless you refuse to come with me and no, you're not entitled to an attorney because you're not under arrest."), and then threatening or cajoling a confession that closed the case. Those who insisted upon their innocence, clammed up, or obtained counsel before charges were instituted were generally too much trouble for Bunk Blanchard. It was simpler either to obtain a confession or to put a case on the back burner until someone talked rather than to act as a gumshoe and professionally investigate a case.

As a first-time candidate for sheriff Efron Bailey had found a hard-working and loyal supporter in Bunk Blanchard of the Reidsville Police Department. Many officers on the police and sheriff's departments had shaken Bailey's hand, smiled, and wished him well in his campaign, but few were willing openly to support a candidate opposing the powerful incumbent sheriff. Employees of the incumbent Sheriff himself and the Sheriff's friend--the Chief of Police, who was hired by the Reidsville City Council--knew that support for Bailey endangered their job security.

After the election returns proved an upset in Bailey's favor, Bailey remembered those few who had openly supported him, and the many who had not, and divvied up his campaign spoils accordingly. One of those richly rewarded for selling raffle tickets, for putting up yard signs, and for acting as a poll worker was Bunk Blanchard of the Reidsville Police Department, who was hired by newly elected Sheriff Efron Bailey to replace Detective Omar Utley, loyal supporter of the losing candidate and now an unemployed detective with 12 years experience.

By the time of the Carlton Purvis murder, Blanchard had been lead investigator in four death penalty cases. He had learned to stay in close contact with the district attorney's office when murder investigations began. In his previous three death penalty cases, each defendant had, with the help of Blanchard, eventually fully, clearly, and tearfully confessed to murder in the first degree. And in each case, each defendant had acted alone. All three cases had ended in verdicts of guilty of murder in the first degree, with only one of the three resulting in the death penalty.

The case Blanchard wanted to talk to Assistant District Attorney Gerry Wiles about was different from the previous three.

First, Blanchard had not sought out Harley Ames to give a statement. Instead, Harley Ames had been brought to his office by Arnie Robertson, which was strange in itself.

Everyone knew that Arnie Robertson was not, nor had he ever been, an investigating officer. Investigations were not, nor had they ever been, within his job description. Arnie Robertson was simply a courier for the Sheriff himself. He enforced the Sheriff's spoken and unspoken wishes. When the duo of Harley and Arnie entered the detectives' office, the furthest thought from Blanchard's mind was that Arnie Robertson was somehow involved on an official level in the investigation of the murder of Carlton Purvis.

Second, Arnie Robertson clearly had not entered Blanchard's detective office with the intention of working on the investigation with Blanchard. He had bullied his way through the Harley Ames' statement and how it had taken place. Arnie Robertson simply instructed Harley Ames to remain quiet until he was told he could speak.

"You got that, Boy?" he had asked Ames. Ames simply nodded.

Arnie Robertston then told Detective Blanchard that Harley Ames was going to give a statement implicating himself and Johnny Wayne Fulcher in involvement in the murder of Carlton Purvis. He stated that without Harley's testimony a conviction of Johnny Wayne Fulcher would be an impossibility.

Robertson attempted to reassure Harley. He looked at Harley, then at Blanchard, and pointed his finger at Harley as he spoke.

"Detective, you need to know how the Sheriff feels about this situation. The Sheriff thinks Mr. Fulcher needs to be put away in prison and that our good friend Harley should get a little something back for helping us do that."

He advised Detective Blanchard that it was the wish of the Sheriff--Blanchard's boss and employer-- that Blanchard strongly recommend to the district attorney that immunity from prosecution be granted Harley Ames conditioned upon Ames' full and honest cooperation with the State or, at the least, that a suspended sentence be imposed on Harley upon a plea of guilty to being an accessory after the fact to manslaughter.

"Are we on the same page, Detective Blanchard?," he asked.

"I think I understand. I'm to tell the DA's office that Harley has co-operated fully and that I recommend that he's got to have the charges dismissed or to be allowed to plead to accessory after the fact if he testifies truthfully, right?"

"That's right, Detective. Bingo. Ok, Harley, you can talk now."

It was only after Blanchard's assurances of his agreement with this understanding that Harley Ames was allowed to speak by Arnie Robertson. Blanchard had sensed that Robertson was acting as a de facto attorney for Harley and knew that, for whatever reason, some kind of deal had been struck between Harley Ames and, through Arnie Robertson, the Sheriff himself. He did not dare ask the reason.

The third difference for Detective Blanchard was that this case involved two perpetrators to a single murder. Like the other three, there had been an admission of guilt by a person who had participated in the murder. Unlike the other three, there was a denial of responsibility by a perpetrator. According to Harley Ames, Johnny Wayne

Fulcher would never, under any circumstances, admit to any culpability in the murder of Carlton Purvis. It simply was not in his nature to do so. For Blanchard, this meant that for the first time in his career, he would be required to supply evidence to the district attorney and would actually have to prove beyond a reasonable doubt the guilt of a defendant in a first-degree murder trial. This was totally new territory for Detective Blanchard.

The evidence Detective Blanchard would have to provide the assistant district attorney would have to prove beyond a reasonable doubt two vital matters.

The first requisite to be proved beyond a reasonable doubt would be that Johnny Wayne Fulcher had committed every element of the offense of first-degree murder.

The second would be an "aggravating factor" specified by the North Carolina General Statutes. The gravity of an "aggravating factor," such as extreme cruelty or torture, would have to outweigh any "mitigating factors," such as mental defect, before a jury, and not the judge, would be authorized to sentence Johnny Wayne Fulcher to death.

The death penalty procedure Blanchard faced in North Carolina had evolved since the dawn of man. From time immemorial, the death penalty had been rendered for offenses ranging from blasphemy and counterfeiting to murder, carried out in North Carolina by means that have included, but were not limited to, burning, hanging, electrocution, lethal gas, and lethal injection.

By 1868 North Carolina had reduced the number of crimes punishable by death to four: murder, arson, rape and burglary. Within 25 years, the crime of murder was divided into two degrees with only first-degree murder being punishable by death. In 1909 hanging was outlawed as a means for carrying out the death penalty, and electrocution became the official means of execution in North Carolina. In 1935, following the six-minute electrocution of a defendant by the name of Rufus Satterfield, the North Carolina legislature substituted lethal gas as a more humane method of carrying out the death penalty. Death row inmates later were given the option to choose between lethal gas and lethal injection, and, even later, lethal gas was ruled out as a means of execution leaving lethal injection as the only means of execution.

In 1976 in the case of Gregg v. Georgia, U.S. Supreme Court Justice Lewis Powell described the death penalty as an "expression of society's moral outrage at particularly offensive conduct" and wrote an opinion in which the U.S. Supreme Court imposed strict limitations on how the death penalty could be administered.

The U.S. Supreme Court also established a set of rules and procedures that were to be followed before a death penalty could be imposed. In 1976, the same year as the Gregg case, the U.S. Supreme Court ruled in the case of Woodson v. North Carolina that *mandatory* death sentences were unconstitutional. It further held that juries must first find that a defendant is guilty of first-degree murder. And *juries*, and not *judges*, had the *option* to choose between death and imprisonment *after* weighing aggravating and mitigating circumstances that has been presented as evidence.

So Blanchard faced what came to be described as a *bifurcated* trial procedure.

"Bifurcated" simply means that a **judicial proceeding is divided into *two stages* with different issues being addressed separately.**

In this situation Blanchard was required to supply the district attorney with proof that would convince a jury beyond a reasonable doubt that Johnny Wayne Fulcher had committed each and every element of murder in the first degree. That would be the *first* stage.

Assuming the jury had rendered a verdict that Johnny Wayne Fulcher had, in fact, committed each element of murder in the first-degree, it would then be time to move to the second stage of the proceeding. In the *second* stage the State would be required to convince a jury to find beyond a reasonable doubt that Johnny Wayne Fulcher had committed the crime under specific circumstances listed in the death penalty statutes that *aggravated* the murder before it, the jury, could impose the death penalty.

For Detective Bunk Blanchard, formerly of the Reidsville Police Department and now of the Rockingham County Sheriff's Department, this situation was complicated. He had no confession from Johnny Wayne Fulcher and actually would have to work to earn his paycheck and obtain evidence to prove Fulcher's guilt.

Between Harley's statement and the initial crime scene investigation, a verdict of guilty of murder in the first degree was possible. But what about the death penalty? Could he really be the one to round up evidence that would lead to a needle being stuck in Johnny Wayne Fulcher's arm? Were there any factors in this particular case that would--he wrote it out--lead a jury to be "morally outraged" at "particularly offensive conduct"?

Three aggravating factors might come into play. *First*, the jury could find as a factor in aggravation of the murder that Carlton Purvis had been tortured by being taped up and beaten, and that torture led to his death. *Second*, the jury could find Carlton Purvis was murdered in what was, in essence, the commission of a robbery. Not only had Johnny Wayne and Harley gone to Carlton's house with a gun demanding what may or may not be money owed from a loan, they had demanded that Carlton give them another $150. That was robbery, Blanchard thought. *Third*, Carlton Purvis had been beaten and tortured for monetary gain. It was all about the money.

Taking his notes, statements, and law, Blanchard turned to his typewriter and began his investigative report to the district attorney's office. It began with his initial call to the crime scene and ended with the statement Harley, with Arnie Robertson's assistance, had given him. He outlined a potential death penalty scenario against Johnny Wayne Fulcher. His report ended with a glowing account of Harley Ames' waiver of his *Miranda* rights and his unconditional cooperation. Blanchard finished with the reminder that the prosecution's case against Johnny Wayne

Fulcher rested on the shoulders of Harley Ames, and recommended that no charges be filed against Harley Ames at the present time, it being subtly understood that Harley would walk free if Harley continued his full and honest cooperation and Johnny Wayne was convicted.

When Blanchard finished his investigative report, he called the District Attorney's office and asked for an immediate appointment with Assistant District Attorney Gerry Wiles. The next morning he took the investigative report, put it in his briefcase, and walked to the district attorney's office. Once he arrived, he met with Gerry Wiles and spelled out his evidence in detail, orally, in writing, and with photographs of the crime scene.

Wiles was satisfied with the evidence Blanchard had accumulated. He knew the odds favored his getting a conviction of second or maybe even first-degree murder. But the death penalty? Wiles couldn't wait indefinitely to see if more or better evidence arose before he began the death penalty procedure. To preserve that option, Wiles chose to begin the death penalty process, even if he really wasn't ready.

What made the gamble worthwhile was the subject of the investigation--Mr. "Johnny Wayne 'J.W.' Fulcher." He would gladly throw ten Harley Ames' back into the pond just to hook one Johnny Wayne Fulcher.

Chapter 27

"If you want to hit a bird on the wing, you must have all of your will in focus. You must not be thinking about yourself, and equally, you must not be thinking about your neighbor. You must be living in your eye on that bird. Every achievement is a bird on the wing."

U.S. Supreme Court Justice Oliver Wendell Holmes

Judge Amos Burgwyn parked his Buick in his courthouse reserved parking space after driving from the Holiday Inn in Reidsville. He had returned to Rockingham County from his home in Jackson County after a four-hour drive the Sunday evening before to preside over Superior Court for the week. He walked into the lobby of his chambers, greeted the secretary, and retreated to his own office for another morning smoke. Bookshelves of brown and gold-bound North Carolina Supreme Court decisions were within easy reach of his burgundy office chair. There was a cleared space surrounded by pens, miscellaneous papers, a photograph of his wife and children, and books in the middle of the top of his desk. It was there that he laid folders or papers for his examination.

Judge Burgwyn had been raised poor and took great pride in the education his parents had encouraged. Whenever he was assigned by the Administrative Office of the Courts to preside over a district's court for a six-month stint the first items he unpacked in his office was an aging framed photograph of his wife and six children and his diplomas from Mars Hill College and the University of North Carolina School of Law, along with the license to practice law bestowed on him by the North Carolina State Bar. These objects defined Judge Burgwyn and, upon his kind request, every bailiff in each county he served regularly and carefully hung them in a prominent place in his chambers.

One of the first visitors to tap on his door that Monday morning was Gerry Wiles.

"Good morning, Gerry. How's it going? Come on in and have a seat." Judge Burgwyn pointed toward the two leather chairs in front of his desk.

"Thank you, Your Honor, but we both have just a minute. I wanted to give you a heads up on something."

"And what's that, Gerry?"

Judge Burgwyn pulled his pack of Marlboro cigarettes from his coat pocket, removed one, and tapped the unfiltered end three times on the glass-top of his desk. His Zippo made its familiar click as he opened it and lit his third cigarette of the day.

"We have a capital case that's going to come up. A man was beaten to death, and we've charged someone who I think is a particularly bad and dangerous person." Wiles paused to measure the Judge's reaction. "Out of the ordinary. He's in the process of being arrested by one of Sheriff Bailey's detectives as we speak."

"All defendants are bad to you, Gerry." The Judge leaned toward the green ashtray on his desk and flicked his ashes. "All bad and going to hell. Tell me the truth, Gerry, have you ever had one that you didn't think was the worst person in the world?"

"Okay, Your Honor, I'll confess that I do try to be an advocate, but I'd wager this defendant is pretty rough even by your standards. You'll hear more about that during his first appearance this morning. He has a reputation here in Rockingham County, Judge Burgwyn."

Wiles got to the point.

"The reason I'm here is that he's going to need court-appointed counsel. Once again, it's a capital case, and we're going to ask to have him put to death for this one."

Wiles didn't want to recite any of the specific circumstances of the murder. He could do that in an open courtroom. To do that in closed chambers with the judge might lead accusations of an unfair attempt to prejudice the judge in the State's favor. Both he and Judge Burgwyn knew that they were to avoid the subject of how the killing occurred.

Wiles talked about the defendant Fulcher's financial situation and his ability to retain counsel.

"He's got no job and an old farm he inherited and a truck or two, but those are certainly not sufficient assets to turn into money to take care of hiring lawyers on a capital case."

"No problem, Gerry. Just have the Clerk pass up the list of attorneys on the capital case court-appointed list to me on the trial bench. I'll pick one."

"And that's what I wanted to talk to you about, Your Honor." Wiles readjusted his seat and placed both hands on the ends of the armrests.

"We've got several attorneys on the Capital list, but I want to bring Bob Lee Pender up with you, Judge."

Judge Burgwyn tapped the end of his Marlboro into the ashtray to snuff out the cinders. He leaned toward Wiles.

"What about Bob Lee, Gerry?"

"Well, as I said, Judge, I think this defendant is going to be shown to be exceptionally deserving of the death penalty by the time all of the evidence comes out. I don't want to say anything that might prejudice you in anyway, Your Honor. But we think we have a pretty good case and good odds of nailing him."

"And Bob Lee?"

"Judge, you and I both know Bob Lee runs a tough and clean case. He knows the Rules of Evidence, and he fights. That's okay. That's just fine because so do I. Bob Lee's tried a number of capital cases and has won some and lost some. He's been back and forth to the Court of Appeals and Supreme Court. I'm here to ask you to consider appointing Bob Lee."

Gerry Wiles sounded earnest in his request. Judge Burgwyn gave a slight cock to his head and chuckled during his reply.

"You want me to appoint Bob Lee for this guy? Seems like you're putting yourself through a lot of extra work, Gerry. It's your life, though."

Wiles didn't smile back. There was good reason for his visit to Judge Burgwyn that morning.

"Maybe so, Your Honor, but I don't want this defendant to end up with a young lawyer learning how to try a capital case. I don't want for me and my office and our investigators to bust our guts, get a conviction and death sentence, and then have it sent back by an appellate court because some inexperienced defense lawyer has made a stupid mistake or because of an allegation of ineffective counsel."

Wiles pressed harder. His voice raised an octave.

"Think about it, Your Honor. If I'm trying this case against someone cutting their teeth or who doesn't keep their guard up, I might have to object to my own questions simply to keep the case from being bounced back down from the Supreme for another retrial because they deem him or her ineffective."

Judge Burgwyn was listening and wanted the assistant district attorney to know it.

"I'm following you, Gerry."

Wiles made one more pitch on the practicality of his request. He leaned back in his seat and stared directly into Judge Burgwyn's eyes.

"No, Your Honor, I'm willing to work hard and go up against the best. Bob Lee's a good man; he works hard; and he's thorough. The Supreme Court knows him and his work. To be honest, he'd be the first lawyer I'd hire around here if I got into my own jam. But I want to convict this murderer and leave as little room as possible for him to squirm out of it after he's been convicted and waits for the needle."

Judge Burgwyn was convinced. Everything the assistant district attorney had said was logical and served good purposes. And justice.

"Ok, Gerry, makes sense to me."

The judge's signature smile returned.

"Let's make sure this innocent defendant has the best counsel available."

Gerry Wiles smiled and nodded. He stood from his seat and, instead of reaching for a handshake, maintained eye contact and slightly bowed his head.

"Thank you, Your Honor." The bulldog in Wiles slightly reared its head, but with a smile. "We'll see how innocent he is at the end, though."

Judge Burgwyn also rose as a sign of respect.

"I'm sure Bob Lee will have something to say about that, Gerry. I'm sure he will."

Both parties had forgotten to mention one detail. The Judge brought it up.

"By the way, Gerry, what did you say the defendant's name was?

"His name is Fulcher, Your Honor. Johnny Wayne Fulcher. Sometimes goes by his initials—'J.W.'"

Gerry left the judge's chambers with his thoughts lasered on one simple concept: Johnny Wayne Fulcher wasn't going to escape the needle because Gerry Wiles hadn't done everything possible and expended every effort to prevent that from happening. The facts were on his side. He had determined that Johnny Wayne Fulcher was going down simply because he was going to will it so by honest, uninterrupted, clean, thorough hard work.

Chapter 28

"You can tell a lot about a woman by her hands. For instance, if they're placed around your throat she's probably slightly upset."

Unknown

The Queen Bee had smoked a joint of The Devil's Lettuce and was slurping her third beer when she noticed Johnny Wayne's wallet. It was three in the afternoon, and she was sprawled on the bed, thumbing her newest Atari game. Johnny Wayne was in the back yard, tools spread around his feet and on fenders, beer on the hood, humming and singing along with Kenny Rogers to the tune of "Lady" while replacing the master cylinder on his rusted dump truck.

She had known Johnny Wayne since the age of 15 years. Back then her white blonde hair, blue eyes, pink lipstick, skinny legs, and tiny ass, coupled with ample tits beneath a braless blouse and the fire engine red mini skirt she favored on Fridays nights, made any guess of her age questionable.

Illegitimate with a usually absent mother, young Misty was advanced beyond her years at age 15. Flirting with a man 10 years her senior at the Carolina Cafe--and having the sexy Bad Boy favorably respond--accomplished several things for Misty. None of them were sexual. She had appeared more attractive than the competing girls in the café; she had crossed over a line into dangerous and adventurous world; and, most importantly, she had garnered an affirmation of worth, however shallow.

Misty's deflowering by Johnny Wayne the same weekend, although uneventful to Johnny Wayne, was followed by numerous loveless, but fun and physical, "pokes" with various men over the next few years. Misty did not discriminate—age, girth, height, race, education, and every other conceivable attribute or trait that factored into appeal were simply unconsidered. Misty simply liked sex. She couldn't cook or clean or answer questions asked on game shows or driver's license exams, but she was Olympian at sex. Her abilities in that regard did not extend to sufficient birth control, and by age 17 she became pregnant.

Uneducated after having quit school, with an infant child, and unemployable in large part because of her engagement in daytime television soap opera plots, Misty and the baby resided with her mother. She signed up for and received monthly stipends in the forms of Medicaid and child support as wards of the state. Her child Britney would join five other classmates of the same first names, or one of its variants, when she was enrolled in kindergarten at age five.

Then, almost 10 years after they first met and Britney had reached 7 years of age, the foundation of a new life was set for Misty when she said yes to Johnny Wayne's demand for a dance at the TapATop Lounge. He hadn't remembered who she was until she reminded him.

Within two weeks Johnny Wayne had tossed out his older regular girlfriend and moved Misty in. Britney joined them from her grandmother's house within the month.

Nine years later and at 35 years of age, 40 pounds heavier, still uneducated, able to start an argument in an empty house, unemployed, dependent upon monthly welfare and Johnny Wayne's wiles as means of support, with hair tinged in pink and stacked atop her head like a Totem, Misty had developed into a tough, attentive, protective, and instinctive partner for Johnny Wayne in a relationship based upon a mutually shared lack of ethics. This loyalty did not reciprocate in regard to sexual partners. These were allowed for Johnny Wayne. Misty, who eventually became known as the Queen Bee, was not granted the same liberty.

In this particular afternoon Misty's eye caught sight of Johnny Wayne's wallet as it lay on the floor just beneath the corner of the bedroom dresser. She reached to retrieve it and the corner of a crumpled photo pushed between small bills became apparent. Curious, she took the wallet into the bathroom and shut the door. Within moments she was immersed in its contents. A photo of a nude. A small, crumpled note that simply read, "I love you, Honey." A receipt from a jewelry store. Another from a motel in Winston-Salem. And another note.

The nude photo was of Misty's daughter Britney. The notes were in Britney's handwriting.

Johnny Wayne was poking her daughter Britney. He had crossed an unforgivable line.

The Queen had admitted to herself that she had neglected her appearance and Johnny Wayne's needs. She had rolled over and snored too many times and accepted her changing role in Johnny Wayne's life. She had no objection to his messing with the girls who came and went on the farm during visits and parties. After all, why should she get mad at her dog for messing in the neighbor's trash when she wasn't feeding it at home?

But her Britney was another matter. That was unacceptable. Unnatural, even to her. Should she leave him? But where would she go? Should she kill him? She'd have to be careful and, then again, where would she go?

An hour had elapsed when she heard car doors slam. In unison. Misty fingered a blind and tucked her head sideways for a look. Four patrol cars were in the yard.

Johnny Wayne came around the house and asked what the hell they wanted. Blanchard told Johnny Wayne that he needed to come to the sheriff's department because some papers needed to be served on him. When Johnny Wayne asked what kind of papers, Blanchard lied.

"I couldn't tell you for sure, Johnny Wayne. The magistrate's got them. You didn't forget to appear on a traffic ticket or anything like that, did you, Johnny Wayne?"

Johnny Wayne was in no mood to leave the dump truck.

"Dammit, Blanchard, just bring the damn papers out here." He jerked a rag out of his pocket and turned toward the house. He didn't look back when he spoke to Blanchard.

"I'm here. I ain't going nowhere. Just get one of your peckerheads to drive the damn papers out here."

Johnny Wayne paused, turned around, and took a step back toward Blanchard. He pointed to Blanchard's backup.

"And what the hell is it that made you bring four cars out here?"

Blanchard stuck with his story.

"Johnny Wayne, I've got something else going on, and I radioed these guys to meet me here. I'm supposed to send them over to the Ruffin community about a break-in. But I've got some papers here that tell me I'm supposed to bring you to the magistrate's office."

Blanchard sounded earnest.

"Don't get me in a mess with the Sheriff, Johnny Wayne. Come on, man, work with me. I'll bring you right back, okay? I've got a lot more to do than argue with you, Johnny Wayne, and I really do hate this, but let me get you to the courthouse and back so you can finish on your tractor, okay? I know you don't want to get me in trouble with the Sheriff. You're a better man than that, Johnny Wayne. And it won't take long, I promise."

"OK, Blanchard. Just get me right back, okay?"

Blanchard had him. He kept his distance and addressed Fulcher in a respectful tone.

"You got it, Johnny Wayne. Now you know when I bring folks in, I've got to handcuff them, so let me get them on you real loose, and we'll get you in the back seat and down there real quick, okay?"

Blanchard hadn't reached for the handcuffs hooked to his side belt. He waited for Johnny Wayne's reaction.

"All right, Blanchard. All right. Let's get this over with."

Blanchard reached for the cuffs and stepped forward. Johnny Wayne turned around and connected his wrists behind his back. Blanchard's tone of voice was friendly.

"I think all of this trouble is just over something like a traffic ticket, Johnny Wayne, I really do."

Johnny Wayne checked out the mud on his boot and kicked one of his heels into the ground to disengage it.

"Damn if I remember anything like that, Blanchard. I ain't got a ticket in a while. I'm not sure if I paid all the fines and costs, though, to be honest. Maybe it's that."

Blanchard ran with that.

"That's probably it, Johnny Wayne. Judge gave you some time to pay, and you just forgot. You'll be home for dinner before the magistrate, Johnny Wayne."

Blanchard kept a light hand on Johnny Wayne's left elbow as they approached the patrol car.

"You got $100 bail money on you just in case, Johnny Wayne? Hell, I'll loan it to you if I have to. I know you're good for it, Johnny Wayne."

Johnny Wayne welcomed Blanchard's concern.

"Nah, Blanchard, I got some money in my pocket. But thanks. I appreciate it."

Blanchard helped Johnny Wayne into the back seat of the fourth patrol car. A deputy sat in the driver's seat. He shut the door and walked around to the front passenger's side, opened the door, and sat in the front seat. He turned around and faced Johnny Wayne through the cage between the seats.

"Johnny Wayne, just a formality. I'm supposed to read you your Miranda rights. I do that for everybody, so just listen up, and I'll get this over with."

Johnny Wayne didn't understand. "Rights? What the hell are you reading my rights for? For a traffic ticket, Blanchard? What the hell is going on?"

Blanchard didn't hesitate. "New Supreme Court decision, J.W. The Supreme Court says we gotta read these things every time we put somebody in a patrol car, whether it's for killing the president or a parking ticket. So here goes."

After the rights were read, Blanchard looked up and turned to face Johnny Wayne.

"Johnny Wayne, just a couple of things before we take off. We have word that you might have been up at Carlton Purvis's the night he was killed. Were you, Johnny Wayne? Were you up there with Harley Ames?"

Johnny Wayne realized he had been duped.

"Is that what this garbage is about, Blanchard?"

Johnny Wayne's voice rose. He was irritated not only because of being inconvenienced by a made-up charge, but because Blanchard had played him.

"Hell, no, Blanchard, I wasn't there. Me and The Bee were fishing up at Smith Mountain Lake. Just ask her…go ahead, just ask her. "

Johnny Wayne waited for a reply. Blanchard didn't answer. This irritated the hell out of Johnny Wayne, so he pointed toward his house.

"Dammit, Blanchard, go ask the Bee!"

Blanchard pushed on.

"One more thing, Johnny Wayne. You wouldn't mind if we took a look around your place while we're here, would you? We'd like permission to do that, if we could."

Fulcher glared back at Blanchard.

"What the hell you talking about, Blanchard? You've got me handcuffed in the back of a patrol car taking me to a magistrate 'cause I didn't pay a pissant fine, and now you want to search the place? What the hell's going on?"

Johnny Wayne was getting loud.

"Nothing's going on, Johnny Wayne. We were just out here and we like to check out places because..."

Johnny Wayne cut in. His red face was contorted and random spittle was cast toward the cage and Blanchard.

"You know what, Blanchard? You know what? You're a prick, Blanchard. Hell no, Blanchard. Get the hell off my property. You and your monkey ass little helpers get off my land, you hear me? You kiss my ass and get off my land."

Blanchard knew he had another angle to try. Johnny Wayne was handcuffed and trapped safely in the rear cage of his patrol car.

"Okay, Johnny Wayne, okay. Just calm down. No offense meant. Now this officer's going to take you to the magistrate so work with him, okay, Johnny Wayne? He'll try to get you home as soon as he can."

Johnny Wayne had the last word. He always had the last word.

"I ain't forgettin' you double-crossed me, Blanchard. I ain't forgettin'."

Blanchard left the car. He resumed his acting role as investigator and friend of the Johnny Wayne Fulcher household.

Detective Bunk Blanchard of the Rockingham County Sheriff's Department politely and dutifully approached the porch and asked the Bee if she would kindly allow him to have a few words with her.

Blanchard explained he was obligated by virtue of his position to investigate the murder of Carlton Ray Purvis and asked if she would be patient enough to answer a few questions for him. He admitted Johnny Wayne had not been taken away over an unpaid traffic fine and apologized for using that as a means of avoiding a violent confrontation.

"You see," he explained, "Harley Ames had given a statement stating that he came to this house on August 16th at 4 a.m. in the morning and left with Johnny Wayne to collect some money Carlton owed Harley. Johnny Wayne wanted to drive both of them in his own truck, according to Harley."

The Bee didn't say a word. She reached under her t-shirt, scratched between her breasts, and chewed her Doublemint with her head cocked in Blanchard's direction.

Blanchard continued to explain that Harley also told them that Johnny Wayne had brought him back to his own vehicle--and this house--just before six a.m. Blanchard told the Bee that she also probably knew Johnny Wayne had refused to talk to them except to say he had been with her all night at Smith Mountain Lake."

Blanchard played with the keys in his left pocket and picked at his right eyebrow. He spoke as if he was appealing to an existent person of conscience.

"Ma'am, could you please help me straighten this situation out?"

The Bee's mind went into fast forward. She had heard only part of what Blanchard had said because her inner voice had taken over, saying, almost screaming. "So go straight to hell, J.W., and don't let the door bump you in the ass." The son-of-a-bitch had messed with Britney.

Yes, the Queen Bee explained to the detective, she certainly could. Johnny Wayne was a damn liar.

She set out to nail Johnny Wayne Fulcher in any way she could.

"It's just like Harley Ames said, Detective. Just like he said. I don't know first hand what happened once they left, but I do know Johnny Wayne came home and said he had taken care of some kind of business over some money that was owed somebody."

Did he say who owed the money? No, she said, he didn't.

"And Carlton was bound up with duct tape and beaten," the Detective continued.

Did she ever know Johnny Wayne to have silver duct tape?

The Queen was enjoying the moment.

"All the time, Detective. He uses it for everything. There might be some in the box in the back seat of the truck over there for all I know. Look in there if you'd like."

She pointed to the truck. She couldn't help herself. She had to pour it on.

"He keeps it locked up, but I believe J.W. had the keys with him when your deputy just drove him off. You can get them from the jail."

Blanchard asked if the Bee would please excuse him for a moment. He went to his patrol car and radioed the jail. The keys were on the way.

The Bee had followed Blanchard toward the patrol car and stood with one hand on the front quarter panel and another on her hip, acting all the while as if she weren't listening to Blanchard's radio transmission. When he was through, she walked toward the door of the patrol car and looked down toward Blanchard.

"I gotta ask you, Detective. I'm scared of that man. If he knows I talked to you I'm a goner. Is he going to get out on bond anytime soon? 'Cause if he does, I'm dead meat for talking to you. He's a killer."

Misty pointed toward a well house several hundred yards from where they stood.

"If you don't believe me, just check that well house down at the edge of the field over there. He tells me he's thrown people he's killed down in that well and says he'll do the same to me when he gets mad or drunk, or both. He won't let me in the well house. He keeps it locked up, but I know where he hides the key. He don't know that I know where the key is, but I saw him hide it and I can show it to you. All I know is what he told me. Just check it out for yourself."

Blanchard found it difficult to suppress emotion over what he had just heard. People? Thrown in the well? He wanted to cover his bases.

"So, ma'am, I just want to be clear on a couple of concerns here. Do you live here?"

The Bee was in cooperative mode.

"Why yes, I do, officer. I've lived here for almost nine years."

Blanchard followed up.

"And, as a resident of these premises, you're giving us permission to search these premises? Before you answer, you should know that J.W. has told us we cannot search the premises."

The Bee hardly let Blanchard finish his question.

"Hell, yes, Mister. You fellas go wherever you'd like. I live here, too. You can look wherever you'd like. You or one of your cohorts just check under that rock at the right corner of the well-house. The keys right under it. That's where he hides it. He don't know I know it's there, but I saw him from the window about a month or so ago hide his key. It's right under that rock at the right corner."

By 7:00 p.m. the Rockingham County Sheriff's Department had discovered the remains of four victims in the well.

Forensics later identified the remains as those of a middle-aged male and three teenage females. Each of the skeletons had bones broken by acute trauma from an undetermined blunt object. Two had additional knicks from cuts with a sharp object.

At 10:00 p.m., Bunk Blanchard called Arnie Robertson.

"I'm sorry to bother you at this hour, Arnie, but I've got some news you need to know. We just left Johnny Wayne Fulcher's farm. The Queen Bee dropped word we ought to check out the well. Found four bodies. We think one of them might be that pervert the Sheriff was after who disappeared. He was a Jenkins, remember him? Other three look like young people. Oh, and Queen Bee says Harley Ames found them at the lake and dropped her off so Harley and Johnny Wayne could go somewhere. That's what she's saying."

Johnny Wayne Fulcher was indeed a killer. He had a pattern of murder.

Chapter 29

"With time I've grown older and wiser. If I drop a quarter and bend down to pick it up, I'll stop while I'm squatted down there for a moment and ask myself, 'Now, is there ANYTHING else I might need to do while I'm down here?'"

Jerry Martin, owner of Megasuds Car Wash, Eden, NC

Bob Lee Pender had just finished his lunch break in his law office on 2nd Avenue in the small town of Mayodan.

Mayodan overlooked the Mayo River near its confluence with the Dan River (hence "Mayodan") and was just 14 miles from the Rockingham County Courthouse. Its main business district clustered around the T-intersection of NC Highway 770 (Main Street) and US Hwy 220 (2nd Avenue, which snaked above the banks of the Mayo River).

One of Mayodan's two stoplights was located at the T-intersection, and from the intersection going up the east/west sidewalks of Main Street was a Shell gas station, a few small retail proprietorships, a drug store, Lefty's Grill, and Howell's Hardware Store. By looking northward up 2nd Avenue from the steps of Mayodan's Episcopal Church of the Messiah, one could spot Kellam's Grocery, Gravely's Radio Shop, two insurance agencies, the local optometrist's office, and a few offices that were as often vacant as occupied. Below 1st Avenue ran a line of railroad tracks trailing the Mayo River owned by the Norfolk and Southern Railway that had spined northward from Greensboro. This rail line, once owned by the Atlantic and Yadkin Railroad, ribboned northward from Mayodan across the North Carolina/Virginia state line to Martinsville and beyond to deliver Mayodan's textile production worldwide. A small railroad station painted in two shades of green with the word "Mayodan" adorned each end of the building. On one corner of the intersection of Main Street and Second Avenue—the "town square"—stood a poster board that announced local events and where over a century earlier the local populace had learned the fates of wounded and dead loved ones at too regular intervals during the American Civil War.

Pender's office was small but efficient. The waiting room was furnished simply and for utility with an overstuffed couch and two oak chairs. There was the secretary's office, a conference room surrounded by hundreds of volumes of the Reports of the North Carolina Court of Appeals and the North Carolina Supreme Court, and two small bathrooms. Down the hall from the conference room was Bob Lee's office, which was a conglomeration of utility and collected knickknacks: Law books and Indian arrowheads, a Smith-Corona typewriter, academic degrees on the wall, and a dried gourd turned into a birdhouse from his farm.

Bob Lee preferred not to eat at Lefty's Grill on a regular basis because of incessant "Hellos" from folks who didn't want to interrupt his lunch (but did) and wanted to ask "just one question" (or 10) about a legal matter which, if Bob Lee gave an answer they didn't particularly like, resulted in an interruptive and whiney debate through his meal. Bob Lee was growing weary of such inconsiderations.

No different from most days, Bob Lee had seated himself behind his desk and shared a banana sandwich with the one devoted creature who never disagreed with him, his beagle Booger. Booger was such easy company that--whether it be steak, peanuts, pickles, or any other food--he would eat whatever Bob Lee ate and then compete with Bob Lee's snoring during the twenty-minute power naps on the couch in the office. On this day it just so happened that Booger liked banana sandwiches. Bob Lee had set his Cheerwine bottle on the desk when his secretary poked her head in the door.

"Bob Lee, I've got some news for you."

Ida Strader would call Mr. Bob Lee Pender by his first name out of the presence of clients because he was a youngster to her. At 71 years of age, she had been in the law business longer than anyone in the county. Ida quit school at age 16 and expected to work second or third shift at Mayo Mills since first-shift jobs were often based on seniority. While waiting for an opening at the mill, Mr. Garson Fulp, Esquire, of the law firm of Fulp and Gainey bent to his own secretary's entreaties and agreed to allow the young girl to type envelopes and run errands for a reasonable stipend until an opening in the mill arose. Ida evolved from a novice secretary into a hard-driving, no-nonsense paralegal and then to a slower, but wizened, counselor and assistant to Bob Lee Pender.

Bob Lee had joined the law firm after his graduation from law school and maintained the law firm as a sole practitioner after the deaths of his senior partners with Ida as his true partner. Ida was indispensable, fiercely loyal, and possessed a higher IQ than her employer.

By the time Bob Lee had burped and tossed his napkin and wax paper into the trash can, the mill had been waiting for Ida to show up for work for more than 55 years.

"You've been handed the Fulcher case, Bob Lee."

Bob Lee leaned back in his chair and barked, not at Ida, but at the situation that has been presented. He had heard on the 6 o'clock news the night before that Fulcher had been charged with the Carlton Ray Purvis murder.

"Oh, hell, Ida. Do we really want to deal with that? I thought I had asked you to get me off the Capital list. Did you get me off the list or not? We really don't need that headache, do we?"

"Bob Lee, you told me you were thinking about getting off the list, not to get you off it. So yes, you're on the Capital list, Bob Lee. You're on the Capital list. You've been appointed to represent Johnny Wayne Fulcher. Also goes by his initials 'J.W.' He had his first appearance before Judge Burgwyn and Burgwyn's handed him over to you. And bond was denied for the time being."

Bob Lee shuffled his feet, picked up a pen from his desk, and threw it back down.

"When am I supposed to be in Court with Fulcher, Ida?"

"The preliminary hearing's set for a week from Thursday, but the Clerk let me know they're going to go ahead and indict him before that so there won't even be a prelim on that Thursday. Looks like the first time you'll be up will be in Superior Court over the bond issue."

Bob Lee mechanically clicked in his mind the process he would be facing. Naturally, he thought, the district attorney had to obtain a bill of indictment from the Grand Jury. A preliminary hearing would simply establish whether or not the State prosecutors had presented sufficient evidence to bind the murder charge over to Superior Court for a jury trial and allow the defendant to be held in jail or released on bond while awaiting trial. But regardless, whether such evidence was proffered at a preliminary hearing or not, North Carolina law dictated that before a felony could be tried by a jury an indictment had to be obtained from the local Grand Jury. And, in reality and practicality, an indictment simply consisted of charges presented only by the prosecutor and rubber-stamped by a Grand Jury.

Bob Lee presumed that Sheriff Bailey's detective division wouldn't have charged Johnny Wayne Fulcher with murder unless they had at least one spade up its sleeves. He acknowledged in his mind that unless a magic rabbit could be pulled out of a hat that the issue of bond was, in all probability, moot. Bond would be denied either explicitly or in effect by a large dollar amount. It was, after all, a capital case. They intended to try to kill Johnny Wayne Fulcher.

"Ida, am I through seeing folks after four? What's on the book this afternoon?" Bob Lee was moving papers on this desk in search of his appointment book. He finally fumbled it out from under a stack of papers next to his telephone.

"Take a look for yourself, Bob Lee. And yes, you're free after four unless you want to prep for tomorrow."

Ida turned to leave the office, but Bob Lee gestured in his direction anyway.

"Nope, Ida. Put a legal pad in my briefcase. I need to go see the innocent Mr. Fulcher."

Chapter 30

"Chance favors the prepared mind."

Unknown

The Rockingham County jail was annexed to the Rockingham County Courthouse so the two made one large building. The fact that the jail's construction postdated the courthouse was readily apparent. Built during the 1960s to replace an older jail, a different, redder brick had been used for the new jail. Its lines were more direct and its architecture more basic and less elaborate than the older courthouse. Both sat beside what was once a stagecoach road that pre-dated the American Revolution.

The old jailhouse building, located directly across the road from the courthouse, currently housed Rockingham County's Board of Elections. It was within the old jailhouse's wall, and not in front of it, that the last execution by hanging took place in Rockingham County. In 1903 administration of the death penalty was a county matter and remained so until the State of North Carolina took over this responsibility in 1910.

A 16-year-old black male named John Broadnax was arrested for the shooting murder of an esteemed farmer named Sydney Blair and the burglary of his homestead during evening dinner on March 19th, 1903. To inflame the community further Mr. Blair's schoolmarm niece, Miss Sallie Walker, had also been shot but miraculously escaped, wounded and in the dark, to get help.

The accused Broadnax had been arrested rummaging through the victim's home place; a confession had been obtained; a trial before 12 of 16-year-old black Broadnax's white "peers" had taken place; a guilty verdict had been entered; a sentence of death by hanging had been entered; and a date for execution set and carried out---all between March 19th and May 20th, 1903, or 62 days. Word of the hanging event spread and a large portion of the Rockingham County community of men, women, and small children gathered outside the county jail on that Spring noon to observe and participate in the administration of justice. The actual execution took place inside and out of public view in the presence of approximately thirty witnesses and guards as permitted by Sheriff Pinnix.

After a tearful expression of regret and plea to his Maker for forgiveness, the teenager was led up the steps of the scaffold. A hood was placed over the young man's head; a noose was fitted around his neck; and he was dropped from such a height that his neck audibly snapped upon impact. Urine dripped from the denim leg of the hanging corpse. Twelve minutes later and following verification of the prisoner's demise by the elected County Coroner ("Yep, he's dead."), the Sheriff emerged from the front of the jail and announced to the crowd that the execution had occurred and that the prisoner had met his premature, but deserved, demise.

"That's good."

"He deserved it."

"Don't you just know he's burnin' in hell right now?"

The remains of 16-year-old John Broadnax were then placed in a coffin and taken from the jail outside for the spectators and their children to see.

"Don't you look away! Take a good look, you hear? See what happens, son?"

"May God have mercy."

"Justice."

After similar murmuring comments among the people, the mass parted as each made his or her way home.

The body was then handed over to Drs. Matherson and McGehee of Madison who had paid $3.00 for the body to the county (it was now, after all, considered Rockingham County's personal property), ostensibly to study the brain of the deceased.

The sale of John Broadnax's remains varied from the typical disposition of an executed criminal's body. Usually within an hour the murderer's or rapist's or burglar's or arsonists remains were wrapped in a jailhouse blanket, placed in a pine box stored among others in the courthouse attic, and transported a mile by a mule-drawn wagon to Rockingham County's Home Cemetery, which was situated across the road from the county "Poor House." Here the body was interred without the benefit of comment by clergy among hundreds of unmarked graves of the county's most pitiful and forgotten poor, disabled, feeble, and insane dating back to 1828.

The "new" jail across the street had been built for expansion and modernization because the "old" jail had simply become too small to accommodate a growing jail population. The numbers of prisoners had increased not because of the increased local population or more effective law enforcement, but because a more modern culture promoted the idea that people begin reaching less for their guns and instead avail themselves of the services of a magistrate to issue criminal warrants for arrest when disputes arose.

Bob Lee parked his car, reached for his briefcase, and entered the lobby of the jail. He was greeted by a deputy attendant who waved and reached for enormous brass keys to unlock a massive iron door that opened up into the stifling, suffocating world of the imprisoned.

Bob Lee walked into an alcove facing the closed brown doors of an elevator 25 feet away. The iron door clanged and clicked shut behind him. Conversations echoed among the steel, cement, and thick glass of the room. The deputy telephoned the jail attendant upstairs, and the iron elevator doors opened with German precision to accommodate Bob Lee.

On the second level, the opening elevator doors revealed veteran Chief Jailer Jack, standing in front of the bullpen with a clipboard in hand. He asked Bob Lee who the hell he wanted to see. Jack was a veteran of the U.S. Navy and linguistically gifted in the profanity and insults of that particular branch of the armed services. He was irascible, always crabby, and loved for it. Bob Lee smiled and told Jack he needed to see Johnny Wayne Fulcher.

"Oh, Hell, Bob Lee and Johnny Wayne!" Jack was tapping his clipboard on his right hip. He was hoping for some return banter from Bob Lee. "This is gonna be good! A veritable Battle Royale! Don't worry, Bob Lee, I like you just fine…it's just that ninety-nine out of a hundred lawyers give the other one a bad name, you know? Judge mad at you, Bob Lee, or you doing penance?"

"Jack, Johnny Wayne might be guilty or not guilty… who knows? There's one thing we'll always, know, Jack. You're always going to be ugly, Jack. And how's your suffering bride, Jack? How's your pretty Tootie?"

Jack had won. Bob Lee had tossed a returning insult.

"She remains tolerant, Bob Lee. Lemme get that murdering son-of-a-bitch for you, okay? I'll get him for you right away," Jack said, reaching for the brass keys on his belt. He turned toward the iron bars leading to the cell block.

Bob Lee sat on a molded plastic chair behind a small table in one of the two attorney rooms. Each room was eight feet by eight feet in dimension, had a heavy steel door, two mesh windows, and, of course, a cement floor. Sound, in the form of speech, chair legs scraping across the floor, and the opening and closing of briefcases, reverberated from wall to wall.

Jack escorted Johnny Wayne to the door and told him to go in. Bob Lee rose, greeted his new client with a handshake, and told him to have a seat in the chair farthest from the door. Fulcher accepted the handshake and reached beneath his crotch to pull the chair under his sagging pants.

Bob Lee began.

"Johnny Wayne, let me formerly introduce myself. I'm Bob Lee Pender, and I've been appointed by Judge Burgwyn to represent you in the charges that are pending against you."

Johnny Wayne shook his head from left to right, and then looked up at the ceiling with both his hands raised as if seeking supplication from God.

"I know who you are, Bob Lee. We've seen each other for years around here. We know each other."

"I understand that, Johnny Wayne, but everything here has got to be done by the book. You now know you have a lawyer and who he is. You now know you have attorney-client privilege, and now I'm going to tell you about the charges against you. Bear with me, Johnny Wayne."

Bob Lee opened his manila file and pulled out a single sheet of pink paper. The criminal warrant contained the charges lodged by the State of North Carolina against Johnny Wayne Fulcher.

"Ok, Bob Lee."

"Johnny Wayne, the charge against you is for the first degree murder of Carlton Ray Purvis. The State is saying you killed him unlawfully with malice and with premeditation and with deliberation. That means not only did you kill him, but there was no legally justifiable reason for killing him. It means you had intended to kill Carlton and that you were fully aware your actions would lead to death or--and here's the catch--serious injury. They've proved malice if they prove you used a deadly weapon, in this case a stick or board or baseball bat."

Johnny Wayne wasn't listening. His concentration was focused on a hangnail. Bob Lee pushed on.

"Malice doesn't necessarily mean you hated Carlton, Johnny Wayne. It simply means that you intended to commit an unlawful act without just cause or provocation. If a money deal goes bad, if someone's trying to rob Joe and they hold up Jim by mistake and things go bad, well, Johnny Wayne, that's illegal to begin with, and if somebody dies, then malice has been proven. Do you understand that, Johnny Wayne?"

Johnny Wayne was impatient and getting irritated. "Yes, Bob Lee, I understand that," he mumbled.

Bob Lee raised his voice, growing impatient with the seeming indifference of the seriousness of the charges by Fulcher. Fulcher's mentality was more short sighted and immediate and was directed toward posting bond, getting out of jail, and going back to the farm and The Bee. Bob Lee's focal point was trying to save Fulcher's life.

"They're going to try to put you to death, Johnny Wayne. By the needle, Johnny Wayne. To death. The Capital List is a list of attorneys who are willing to try death cases, Johnny Wayne, and I'm on that list, so I think that's where we're headed. Are you following me, Johnny Wayne?"

"Hell, I know all of this, Bob Lee. But I ain't done nothin'."

"Just give me a minute, Johnny Wayne. To put you to death, the State has got to prove to a jury that you should be put to death because there are what is known as 'aggravating factors' involved. To put it another way, they've got to show what you did was so bad for specific reasons they have to prove you should be put to death. They've got to tell us those specific reasons before trial, Johnny Wayne, so I don't know what they are right now. Do you have that, Johnny Wayne?"

"Yeah, I got that, Bob Lee, "Johnny Wayne said, seeming more interested in what Bob Lee had to say. "Now, can I say somethin' here? Can I speak?"

"Go ahead, Johnny Wayne."

"Bob Lee, I ain't done a damn thing. Nothin'. I was carp fishing up at Smith Mountain Lake with the Queen Bee. She'll back me up."

"Queen Bee?"

"Misty, my girlfriend. Misty Street."

Bob Lee had a blank look on his face. Everyone in the legal community, whether involved in law enforcement or the legal profession, knew Misty Street, a/k/a "The Bee."

Johnny Wayne had listened to Bob Lee, and now it was his turn to take the floor.

"Her Mama knows you. We've been together for nine years or so. I'm a carp fisherman, Bob Lee. It's my hobby. I've won a lot of money in the carp ponds, and it's what I do."

"So every day you make it a point to 'carpe diem'?", Bob Lee asked, smiling.

"Huh?," Johnny Wayne asked. He had no idea what Bob Lee was talking about.

"Never mind, Johnny Wayne. Tell me what happened."

Johnny Wayne leaned back in the chair and watched his hand as it spun a pencil in slow rotations on the table. He felt uncomfortable making eye contact unless he was in total control of the environment.

"Me and Queen Bee were up at Smith Mountain Lake just fishing. That's all we was doing. In Davis Cove. "

Bob Lee's mind performed the dual function of listening to Johnny Wayne's present recitation of what had occurred and picturing past recollections of "The Bee." He remembered Misty Street's formal name from court dockets and her appearance from behind defense tables in courtrooms. Eyeballs yo-yoed from the mountainous platinum bee-hive hairdo down to the intentionally presented cleavage and back up again. How could anyone forget having seen Misty at one time or another?

Bob Lee interrupted Johnny Wayne to get to the specifics.

"What time did you leave for Smith Mountain Lake, Johnny Wayne?"

"Just before dark. I did see Carlton before we left, Bob Lee. I ain't going to deny that. Me and the Queen Bee drove over to his place, and I picked up some smoke and a line or two of coke for the fishing trip. When I left his place, Carlton was just fine, Bob Lee. Just fine."

Johnny Wayne's face lit up as his witness for his alibi came to mind. His left thumb pointed toward the door, toward home. His voice rose.

"Queen Bee will back me up on that. I wasn't there for five minutes. He was just fine."

"Where did you go after you left Carlton's, Johnny Wayne?"

"I told you that. Davis Cove," Johnny Wayne answered, pushing back to assert some of his manhood.

"Did you stop and get gas? Stop to eat? Did you see anyone between Carlton's and Davis Cove? Did you use a credit card?"

"No, Bob Lee. We drove straight to Davis Cove. Had a full tank and everything in the bed of the truck."

"And what time did you leave to come home?"

"Around seven in the morning, Bob Lee. Ask the Bee."

"Anybody stop by during the night? Talk to any other fishermen? Anyone stop by?"

"No, it was quiet. Just me and the Bee."

The palm of Johnny Wayne's hand slapped the table. It was simple to him. He was with The Bee. The details being asked by Bob Lee were not only unimportant, they were also irritating. Johnny Wayne wanted one thing, and that was to go home. Now.

"Look, we're wasting time, Bob Lee. Tell those peckerheads just to go to the Bee, and she'll get this straightened out!"

Johnny Wayne suddenly stood up. His mercurial nature was on display.

"I was fishin', goddammit!"

Bob Lee challenged Johnny Wayne. It was important that Johnny Wayne understands that under the present circumstances Johnny Wayne Fulcher was not in charge.

"Johnny Wayne, sit down. Sit down, or I'm going to walk out of here and come back when I'm good and ready. I don't have time for this. Now, sit down!"

Johnny Wayne gave the leg of the chair a slight kick and plopped himself down. Bob Lee continued.

"Just listen, Johnny Wayne. Did you get any gas, or stop for a sausage biscuit, or talk to anyone on your way home?"

"No, we just went home. Why the hell have they charged me, Bob Lee? I was fishin'! They ain't got nothin' on me. I didn't do nothing to Carlton. I was fishin'. Just please tell those Skidmarks to go talk to the Bee. She'll tell 'em. I was fishin."

"I don't know what they have, Johnny Wayne. But I can find out. Under the Rules of Criminal Procedure the district attorney is required to give me the results of the investigation. They have a lot to prove. I just wanted to stop by, talk to you, and hear what you had to say about all of the information I've put together so far. I will be back in touch with you, Johnny Wayne, but I'm going to tell you one thing before I go, so you listen to me, and you listen real good."

Johnny Wayne had leaned his neck back and stretched out his feet. He faced the ceiling.

"Are you listening to me, Johnny Wayne?"

"I hear you, Bob Lee." He never looked at Bob Lee. He focused on the blankness of the ceiling.

"Don't you say a word about your case to anyone, do you hear me? Not a word."

Bob Lee waited for a reaction.

"Look at me, Johnny Wayne. What I am saying is important."

Johnny Wayne turned his head in Bob Lee's direction. For one of the few occasions during this visit their eyes met.

"Don't admit it; don't deny it. Don't discuss it. It's best that you don't make any friends or talk to anyone. This place is full of people wanting to snitch and twist and make things up to get a break with the DA, so don't say a word, no matter what. Do you get that?"

Johnny Wayne's tone of voice indicated that he did not like to be lectured.

"I get that."

"Don't talk to a cellmate, to anyone during supper, to anyone in the bullpen. No one."

Johnny Wayne had heard enough. He wanted to go home.

"I told you I heard you." His speech sped to a rat-a-tat-tat cadence.

"When do I get out of here? When do they talk to Bee so I can go home? I ain't done nothing! I shouldn't be here. I was fishin', for God's sake. What about bond?"

"I don't know about the Bee, Johnny Wayne. I'll try to run her down myself real soon. You have a bond hearing on Thursday, but don't hold your breath on that, Johnny Wayne."

Bob Lee hesitated, waiting for an expected reaction from Johnny Wayne. Johnny Wayne tapped his index finger on the table. Bob Lee continued.

"Don't hold your breath. This case is a capital murder one, so don't expect a judge to give you a low bond, if any bond at all."

"Well, I'll be god dammed. I've done my share of things in the past, Bob Lee, but I swear I didn't do this one."

Johnny Wayne kicked the floor with the balls of his feet, and then slid his chair back until it hit the wall. His voice was quivering in outrage. The frustration of not being in control was overwhelming. He became demanding.

"I was carp fishin'. I'll be god dammed. Get their asses to the Bee so I can get out of here, will you? Get this straightened out. I ain't asking you, Bob Lee, I'm telling you. Do it! I ain't done nothin'!'"

Johnny Wayne was getting louder and louder. It was time for Bob Lee to go.

"I'll see what I can do, Johnny Wayne."

Bob Lee could not get out of the conference room fast enough. As soon as the elevator doors shut and the whir of the descending room was heard, Bob Lee wiped his brow and thought, "Hell of a way to make a living. Hell of a way..."

Chapter 31

"The courtroom is a quiet place, Judge Roberts, where you park your political ideology, and you call the balls and you call the strikes."

Senator Lindsey Graham of South Carolina

By Thursday the duly impaneled Grand Jury of Rockingham County had rubber-stamped the district attorney's request for an indictment of Johnny Wayne Fulcher for the first degree murder of Carlton Ray Purvis. The case was therefore elevated from the District Court level to the Superior Court level. Assistant District Attorney Gerry Wiles had, as expected, been assigned to prosecute the case on behalf of the State. Gerry Wiles and Bob Lee Pender touched base with each other and agreed to have several matters resolved by Judge Burgwyn the same day.

The courtroom contained Judge Burgwyn, properly seated at his bench, the two attorneys, a clerk, a court reporter, two bailiffs who stood with right hands on belted hips and left hands on pistol handles, two local newspaper reporters, and Johnny Wayne Fulcher.

The only other person present was U.S. Attorney Timothy Herndon's aide, Jamie Watson, who sat conspicuously alone in the third row taking notes. After noticing her attire and appearance a bailiff had politely obtained her identity. This fact would be reported to Sheriff Bailey.

Johnny Wayne had been shuffled into the courtroom accompanied by two deputies who closely escorted him to his seat and left him in the physical custody of the bailiffs. His handcuffs had been removed at a side door that opened from a cement hallway between the jail and courtroom but shackles remained on his ankles. He wore nothing but an orange jumpsuit and plastic slippers. All participants were properly located, with both attorneys dutifully standing behind counsel tables when addressing the court and seated when not. Every word was recorded by the court reporter.

The first issue to be addressed concerned the charges themselves.

Gerry Wiles addressed the Court.

"Your Honor, we appear before the Court today in the case of The State of North Carolina versus Johnny Wayne Fulcher. Your Honor should have the file before you."

"I do, Mr. Wiles." responded Judge Burgwyn.

Gerry Wiles became methodical and mechanical at this point, reading from notes to assure that every "i" was properly dotted and a careful record of what was required was more than adequately taken.

It was important that every step in a capital, or death penalty, murder case be done with precision.

Once again, capital cases in North Carolina utilized a *bifurcated* process. That is, a jury of 12 was required to first decide whether a defendant had committed every element of the charge of first-degree murder. If the answer was "no," the defendant was either acquitted or convicted of a lesser charge, such as manslaughter. If the answer was "yes," then the first stage of the process ended. Then the second stage, with the same jury, began.

In the second stage the prosecuting district attorney was required to present evidence of factors that aggravated the circumstances surrounding the murder. All "aggravating factors" were specifically listed in statute and, if the jury found one or more such factors existed, it was then allowed to return of a verdict of death if it determined the aggravating factors "outweighed" mitigating factors presented by the defense.

The assistant district attorney stood from behind his counsel table holding a single piece of paper with both hands and addressed the Court.

"Your Honor can see in the file that the Rockingham County Grand Jury has indicted Mr. Johnny Wayne Fulcher for the murder of Mr. Carlton Ray Purvis with premeditation and malice aforethought on the night of August 12th of this year. I announce today, Your Honor, that the State will seek to have the death penalty imposed in the case as by law provided. For the record, Your Honor, I announce that the specific factors in aggravation of the unlawful killing are as follows":

Assistant District Attorney Wiles paused as he examined his notes. Bob Lee and Johnny Wayne Fulcher remained seated. Bob Lee listened attentively while doodling straight lines and stars on his notepad. Johnny Wayne Fulcher stared at the court microphone situated in the center of the defense table.

"First, Your Honor, the State will prove beyond a reasonable doubt that the murder of Mr. Carlton Ray Purvis on the date aforesaid was especially heinous, atrocious, cruel, depraved, and involved torture. Specifically, Your Honor, that the victim Carlton Ray Purvis was bound with duct tape and repeatedly beaten with an object over an extended period of time directly causing his death."

There was another pause. Johnny Wayne shook his head reflexively.

"Second, Your Honor, the State will prove beyond a reasonable doubt that the murder of Mr. Carlton Ray Purvis on the date aforesaid was committed during the commission of, or attempt of, a specified felony. Specifically, Your Honor, the murder of Mr. Carton Ray Purvis on the date aforesaid was committed during the commission of a felonious robbery by the Defendant and was also committed during the commission of the felonious assault and battery upon Mr. Carlton Ray Purvis by the Defendant, either or both of which may apply."

Bob Lee had yet to receive the formal discovery from the district attorney's office but was not particularly surprised to hear such an allegation. Johnny Wayne emitted a loud breath. Judge Burgwyn noticed it and only glanced quickly in Fulcher's direction.

"Third, Your Honor, the State will prove beyond a reasonable doubt that the murder of Carlton Ray Purvis by the defendant Johnny Wayne Fulcher was part of an illegal and heinous course of conduct in which the Defendant Johnny Wayne Fulcher engaged. Specifically, that the Defendant Johnny Wayne Fulcher has engaged in the course of conduct of murder by the physical beating to death with premeditation and deliberation on at least four prior occasions of one middle-aged male and three young females whose specific identities will be revealed at trial if identifiable."

Johnny Wayne stood up and erupted.

"WHAT? WHAT THE HELL? SON-OF-A!" Bob Lee grabbed his shoulder. Both bailiffs' hands tensed on their gun handles, with the closest one taking two steps toward Bob Lee and Johnny Wayne before stopping.

"Sit down, Johnny Wayne, Sit down and just lisen." Bob Lee insisted.

Johnny Wayne cocked his head and with one hand on the defense table jerked his shoulders away from Bob Lee.

"What the hell, Bob Lee?"

"SIT DOWN AND SHUT UP!"

Johnny Wayne slithered back into his seat but had to have the last words, even if it was muttered.

"Damn kangaroo court."

When Judge Burgwyn noticed Bob Lee had taken control of his client, he addressed Bob Lee. The reporters wrote furiously.

"Mr. Pender, I am advising you and your client that any further disruption will involve your client being gagged to assure that this proceeding takes place with proper decorum. I am admonishing you, Mr. Fulcher, that any further outburst will result in your being held in direct criminal contempt and your being gagged. Do you understand me, Mr. Fulcher?"

"So what are you going to do, Judge, put me in jail?," Fulcher sneered. He had crossed both arms on the defense table and leaned forward, toward the Judge.

Bob Lee stood before Judge Burgwyn could respond.

"He understands, Your Honor, he understands. These extremely unnerving circumstances are affecting my client, Your Honor, and I assure the Court I will have a word with Mr. Fulcher in due time about court decorum."

It was important that some of the dust settle. Bob Lee paused for a moment for at least a portion of the tension to dissipate.

"For the time being, Your Honor, I would remind everyone in this courtroom, including my client, of the respect and etiquette this courtroom demands and deserves."

Bob Lee was stalling, waiting for the tension in the courtroom to subside. He purposefully dropped his pen on the floor and slowly reached down to pick it up before saying another word. Everyone needed a breather, especially Johnny Wayne and the Judge.

He softened his voice and spoke lowly, seeking understanding.

"My client is justifiably, from his perspective, upset over the nature of allegations that he fully denies."

Bob Lee gently placed his right hand on Johnny Wayne's shoulder, conveying the silent messages to Johnny Wayne that he empathized, that he was there to advocate for him, and that Johnny Wayne should remain silent and still while he spoke.

"He hears me now, Your Honor, when I convey to this Court his unqualified apology. So if we can proceed, Your Honor, I am sure Mr. Fulcher will cooperate so we can all complete this Court's business with all due speed and the thoroughness it deserves."

Bob Lee placed both hands on the counsel table before him and sat.

This short speech gave Johnny Wayne time to deflate enough to hear Bob Lee murmur, "For God's sake, Johnny Wayne, button up, will you? Let's get through this together, okay? I'm on your side, Son. You can do that for me, can't you?"

Johnny Wayne nodded.

Gerry Wiles stood.

"May I continue, Your Honor?" He looked in the direction of Johnny Wayne, fully enjoying the trapped rat's misery.

"Go ahead, Mr. Wiles."

"Fourth, Your Honor, the State will prove beyond a reasonable doubt that the murder of Carlton Ray Purvis on the date aforesaid was committed by the defendant Johnny Wayne Fulcher for pecuniary gain or pursuant to an agreement that the Defendant would receive something of value. Specifically, Your Honor, that the Defendant was hired by a third party to commit the felony of felonious assault and battery and/or felonious armed robbery against the person of said Carlton Ray Purvis, now deceased, in expectation of pecuniary gain in the form of payment of money, which he did in fact receive."

Fulcher heard none of this. His mind was racing.

"Fifth, the State will prove beyond a reasonable doubt that the Defendant Johnny Wayne Fulcher has committed at least one prior murder individually, and, in fact up to four in total. That is, Your Honor, as mentioned previously, that the Defendant has committed the felony of murder on one middle-aged male, identity presently undetermined, and three females, identities also presently undetermined."

Johnny Wayne's hand slapped the table loud enough to draw the eye of Judge Burgwyn, who then saw Bob Lee, with upheld left palm, leaning toward his client.

Bob Lee grabbed Johnny Wayne's wrist.

"Calm, Johnny Wayne. Calm."

"That is all, Your Honor." Wiles sat.

"Is there any other business before the Court?" Burgwyn asked as he began gathering the papers and files resting before him.

Bob Lee rose. He pulled his reading glasses from the front pocket of his dress shirt and unfolded them. He deferred speaking until Judge Burgwyn looked up.

"Your Honor, there are two matters."

Bob Lee reached for papers of his own, all involving Johnny Wayne Fulcher's prior criminal record.

"The first involves bond, Your Honor. You are aware that a $2 million dollar bond was set by the presiding District Court Judge shortly after Mr. Fulcher was arrested. Your Honor, my client is 46 years of age and has a prior criminal record that I am sure will be presented to the Court by Mr. Wiles. The Court can see from this record that it consists of a number of pages of paper that, in actuality, reflect a minimal number of convictions. And these convictions are for minor offenses, Your Honor. Trespass. Breaking and Entering. A number of misdemeanor marijuana charges that were simply paid off."

Having finished laying out the facts, Bob Lee got to his first point about the size of the bond.

"I argue to the Court that $2 million dollars is unreasonable in its amount. It is prohibitively high and violates the Equal Protection clause of the Constitution in that the bond is set in such an unreasonably high amount that it would be impossible for a typical citizen with income and assets comparable to Mr. Fulcher who maintains his or her innocence to raise."

Bob Lee moved on to the practicality of the amount of the bond. He had to cover all bases if, for no other reason, than to protect the written record—and himself. After all, in the event Fulcher was convicted, an incarcerated Fulcher wouldn't hesitate to base an appeal for a new trial by alleging that Bob Lee Pender had failed to provide "effective counsel." And while Judge Burgwyn would in all practicality never do Johnny Wayne Fulcher any favors, there was a slight, ever so slight, possibility that he would consider as a professional courtesy making Bob Lee Pender's trial preparation a bit simpler by granting him easier access to his client.

So Bob Lee made his mandatory—and knowingly fruitless—pitch to Judge Burgwyn.

"Secondly, I also ask the Court to consider the situation in which I, as Mr. Fulcher's counsel, am being placed. This capital case, Your Honor, requires access. I need Mr. Fulcher released so he can assist me in providing a defense. I need to be an effective counsel, Your Honor, and I argue to the Court that it is virtually impossible for me to be an effective counselor unless I can have unhindered, open, and regular access to my client."

Bob Lee Pender held his reading glasses by both hands. His voice was earnest.

"He needs my assistance, Your Honor, and I need his. He has no regular source of income, Your Honor, and owns a small farm. Please consider his circumstances. My circumstances. The gravity of this case. Please determine a more reasonable bond so justice can be served."

Bob Lee sat. Gerry Wiles stood.

Gerry Wiles knew the disgust already held by Judge Burgwyn for the lowlife sitting beside Bob Lee Pender. He decided to throw a little gas on the fire. There was indignation in his voice.

"Your Honor, you have heard the allegations of the State in addition to a charge of first-degree murder against this Defendant. Other murders. Four that we know of that we are going to prove beyond a reasonable doubt. The State is going to submit evidence that indicates that our investigators discovered four bodies on the very farm referred to by counsel for the Defendant."

Bob Lee didn't know all the details about the bodies. Once again, discovery from the State was still pending.

"And if the Court will review the Defendant's criminal record, the Court can discern a pattern of assault and battery cases against male victims, and a pattern of assaults on a female against female victims, being regularly dismissed by the State because of an unwillingness on behalf of those victims to testify."

Gerry Wiles knew he was preaching to the choir. Burgwyn was nodding his head in a barely perceptible way not just because he sat in agreement of Wiles' argument. The Judge also appreciated that Wiles was providing verbal affirmation of the negative first impressions he had garnered when he first laid eyes on Johnny Wayne Fulcher.

Assistant District Attorney Gerry Wiles held Johnny Wayne Fulcher's voluminous criminal record in one hand and waved the finger of his other hand toward it.

"The records speak for themselves and this Court can make its own determination, but I argue to the Court that if it will consider the gravity of the charge of first-degree murder, coupled with both the pattern of dismissals of assault cases because of the persistent refusals of victims to testify and the Defendant's uncontrolled outburst in Court today, there is the real risk that other lives will be placed in peril. I argue to the Court today, Your Honor, that Mr. Johnny Wayne Fulcher is a mad dog killer who needs to be penned up as a clear and immediate risk to society until justice is properly administered."

Wiles sat.

Judge Burgwyn tapped the end of his ballpoint pen on the bench and leaned over the microphone sitting before him.

"Gentlemen. The Court has considered the $2 million dollar bond. This Court considers such a bond to be unreasonable under these circumstances. "

The Judge paused. There was no movement, except for Johnny Wayne raising his head and faintly smiling in relief.

"The bond is unreasonable in that it is unreasonably *low*."

Judge Burgwyn honed in on the eyes of Johnny Wayne. There was the sense of a bully playing with its prey.

"No bond will be allowed for Mr. Fulcher. None whatsoever."

Johnny Wayne looked back down. His shoulders sagged.

"Is there anything else, Counsel?"

Bob Lee stood.

"Your Honor, I'm unaware of whether or not the court has assigned me co-counsel to assist in Mr. Fulcher's defense. If not, I ask that such an assignment be made. Mr. Fulcher's life is a stake, Your Honor."

Bob Lee wanted all the help he could get. Murder cases are time consuming.

Judge Burgwyn wheeled to his left and addressed a portly lady seated behind a desk lined with files and lists of defendants being held in jail and pending cases.

"Madam Clerk, who is next on the Capital list?"

The Clerk scanned a written list before her, and after a short perusal, answered.

"That would be Edward Griggs, Your Honor."

Both Bob Lee Pender and Gerry Wiles knew and liked Eddie Griggs. He was locally raised, a graduate of the University of North Carolina School of Law, and he had passed the bar examination eight years ago. This case would be his first death penalty trial.

"Then it is so ordered."

Judge Burgwyn was ready to finish the day. "Once again, counselors, is there anything else?"

Bob Lee remained standing.

"Yes, Your Honor, there is. You have ruled that my client will remain in custody without bond at least for the time being. He will be unable to assist me outside of the bars of our jail in his defense. I need such help, Your Honor. I ask the Court to assign sufficient funds for me to retain a private investigator in this case, Your Honor. The good assistant district attorney has at his disposal the competent Detective Division of the Rockingham County Sheriff Department. He has the State Bureau of Investigation, along with its laboratories and experts at his disposal. I have no one."

Bob Lee placed his right hand on his client's shoulder. He then made his request.

"I'm not an investigator, Your Honor. I don't know how to do that. Mr. Fulcher deserves a fair shot, and he can't possibly get a fair trial being in jail without the assistance of a private investigator. I ask the court to provide us with sufficient funds to retain a private investigator."

"Do you have a response, Mr. Wiles?" the Judge asked.

Wiles knew it was common practice for a defendant to be awarded the assistance of a private investigator in such cases. He was mindful of the necessity for Fulcher's conviction not being overturned because of an ineffective defense. He would pick his battles, and this was one fight he needed to lose.

"Your Honor, the State would stand moot on Mr. Pender's request, except to say that it is our sincere desire that Mr. Fulcher be able to put forth each and every defense in his favor. If the Court feels that a private investigator would assist in that goal, we would certainly not object to it."

Wiles sat.

"Motion for the investigator is granted. Anything else?"

"One more thing, Judge."

Johnny Wayne had spoken up. Bob Lee's head swung toward his client. Judge Burgwyn turned his attention to the defendant. The Judge held up his right hand, palm facing Gerry Wiles, as he motioned to Bob Lee an "It's okay." He addressed Fulcher.

"Go ahead, Mr. Fulcher. What is it?"

Fulcher looked directly into the eyes of Judge Burgwyn and raised his voice.

"You can kiss my sweet hairy ass, Judge."

Judge Burgwyn didn't miss a beat. He ruled without emotion and matter-of-factly.

"Motion denied, Mr. Fulcher."

Court was adjourned.

Chapter 32

"A lucky man is rarer than a white crow."

Juvenal

Paul Gil Reed could not believe his good fortune. Having Federal heat put on Carlton Ray Purvis for messing with his little Ebony by squealing on Carlton as being one of the lower links in the Ricky Dean crime syndicate would have been a feat in and of itself. But having Carton Ray Purvis publicly subpoenaed to appear before the Grand Jury in Roanoke, causing a couple of visits by the Knights, and having Purvis unexpectedly and inexplicably die from a Knights' beating originally intended only to send a warning exceeded every bad wish Reed could imagine for Carlton Ray Purvis. The lowlife, dope-dealing bastard was receiving everything he deserved in white-hot hell.

But to Paul Gil Reed, only faith in Providential blessings could explain how Johnny Wayne Fulcher, and not a single Knight, had been charged in the murder.

God had led the dogs to follow the wrong scent.

It was almost a dream come true. Paul Gil felt as if he had won a lottery. He had batted .1000.

Paul Gil Reed knew he would have been implicated and his cover blown had the investigation led to the Knights. A quick death or witness protection for himself and his family would have taken place. For some baffling reason Harley Ames had stepped forward, falsely admitted to his participation in a murder, and implicated scum in the form of Johnny Wayne Fulcher. Ames had even explained the duct tape!

Reed did not dare to question his FBI contact. All that mattered was that everyone was perfectly happy, if not accepting, to have Johnny Wayne Fulcher held accountable.

The U.S. Attorney Herndon had understandably suspected Fulcher acted at the behest of Sheriff Bailey. He had caused another investigation to be opened and every proceeding in the prosecution monitored by a member of his staff. In the meantime Herndon was content to have Johnny Wayne behind bars faced with the possibility of a death sentence.

From Paul Gil Reed's standpoint, his little Ebony was finally safe from Carlton's influence. Carlton was suffering in eternal damnation. Paul Gil was in no way suspected of influencing any of the fortuitous events. And, most importantly, his sense of revenge had been fulfilled.

The whole affair was a magnificent circus with more wonders and actors than the mind and eye could readily behold, and with more than three rings. And good citizen Paul Gil Reed had been the unseen ringmaster of it all.

Yes, everyone seemed to be perfectly happy.

Everyone, that is, but Johnny Wayne Fulcher.

Chapter 33

"The whole purpose of education is to turn mirrors into windows."

Sydney J. Harris

The North Carolina Rules of Criminal Procedure dictated that a district attorney reveal to the defense results of law enforcement investigations in felonious prosecutions. This ongoing responsibility extended to the trial and applied not just in condemning, but also to exculpatory evidence.

Assistant District Attorney Gerry Wiles did not wait for Bob Lee to file a Motion for Discovery to obtain this information. It was Game On for Gerry. He intended to be aggressive.

Wiles had known Johnny Wayne Fulcher from years in the courtroom and could not abide the man. Dismissal after dismissal because of intimidation, witnesses' dogs poisoned, continuance after continuance at Fulcher's behest for pressure to increase, and other threats to be made or carried out. Even witnesses disappearing, at least two of them young women in separate cases.

So Wiles had a box of documents containing witness statements, the coroner's report, and forensic reports hand delivered to Bob Lee's office with receipt acknowledged by Ida.

The first statement Bob Lee scrutinized was Harley's. Scribbled in poor handwriting by Harley himself, the statement was a broad overview of Harley's version of events. Bob Lee's intuition led him to the correct conclusion that a detective had assisted and overseen the feebly educated and not- too-bright Harley organize and spell the statement. It read as follows:

"Carlton Purvis owed me $1,500 over a pickup truck. Carlton had a bad reputation for dealing in drugs, so I asked Johnny Wayne Fulcher to help me collect. We also call Johnny Wayne Fulcher by his initials J.W. J.W. and me agreed that J.W would get $150. 00 for helping me get my money and that Carlton should pay that, too. We would either get the money or give Carlton a beating and get the money later. We agreed to meet early on the morning Carlton died. Earlier that night I stopped by J.W.'s farm and Cheech Mann told me they had gone carp fishing until after midnight. I drove to J.W.'s farm after driving by Carlton's house to make sure Carlton was home. A light was on and Carlton's truck was there. I got to J.W.'s at about four in the morning and J.W. came out. I didn't see anyone else. J.W. had just gotten in from carp fishing. J.W. wanted to drive his truck, so we rode in J.W.'s truck to Carlton's. J.W. had a pistol in his back pocket. When we

got to Carlton's we got out of the truck. J.W. reached into the bed of his truck. There was a lot of fishing gear in it. He grabbed a bag containing rolls of duct tape and a 2" x 4" board about three feet long. J.W. set the bag down and knocked on the door but there was no answer. After yelling and hitting on the door, Carlton cracked the door open and J.W. grabbed the knob. J.W. did the talking. We went into Carlton's den. Nobody else was there. J.W. told Carlton he wanted $1650. Carlton said he only had $400 but could have the rest by Monday. J.W. said he wanted the $400 now. Carlton gave the money to J.W., not me. Then J.W. said that wasn't good enough and told me to get the bag. I brought it in and J.W. told me to unwrap it. J.W. pulled out the pistol and pointed it at Carlton. He told Carlton not to move and told me to wrap Carlton up. I knew I was wrapping the tape so Carlton could be beat but was glad because it meant J.W. wasn't going to shoot him to death. After I done this J.W. hit Carlton all over with the 2" x 4" a lot. He was hitting him real hard and I was scared to say something. The tape was to keep his bones from breaking. He was just supposed to beat Carlton, not kill him. I never hit Carlton. When J.W. hit Carlton upside the head Carlton quit moving. He was knocked out. I thought he was dead at first but he was breathing. He was breathing when we left. We drove back to J.W.'s farm and got there at six a.m. J.W. kept his $150 and I got $250 that Carlton owed me. I didn't know J.W. was going to hit Carlton that hard. I went to McDonald's for a biscuit and then I went home. I didn't know Carlton was dead until I heard about it in the paper. This is the truth. So help me God. Harley Ames".

There was Detective Bunk Blanchard's report on his encounter with the Queen Bee and the subsequent discovery of the bodies in the well. Blanchard wrote that he had asked *"Miss Misty Street, a lawful resident of the premises, about the location of the suspect Fulcher on the night of the incident. She stated that Johnny Wayne Fulcher left the premises with Harley Ames at four a.m. and returned at six pm, stating to her that he had left to complete some business over a debt. Miss Street then indicated that she was fearful of retribution by the Defendant and that the Defendant had told her in the past that he had disposed of past murder victims by throwing them into a well located beyond the bounds of the curtilage."*

Interesting, thought Bob Lee. Blanchard had thrown in the word "curtilage". Bob Lee thought that there was no possibility the Queen Bee would have known, much less used, the word "curtilage."

"Curtilage" was a technical legal term meaning the area of land occupied by a dwelling and its yards and outbuildings. A person's "curtilage" included all of that space one would consider to be within one's residence and which one could reasonably believe to have an expectation of privacy. On a farm, the house, yard, and even garden would be considered to be within a curtilage, while the bottom fields would not. The Fourth Amendment to the U.S. Constitution protected the 'right of the people to be secure in their persons, house, papers and effects against unreasonable search and seizures..." and law enforcement officers such as Blanchard were required to obtain a search warrant before searching within a person's curtilage. The area outside the curtilage, often designated as "open fields" was subject to no Fourth Amendment protection and a search warrant was therefore not required.

Blanchard apparently had purposefully injected the word "curtilage" into the Bee's verbiage. He knew his job was on the line for not taking the safe path and waiting to get a search warrant before childish curiosity demanded that he and the other two detectives shine their flashlights down the wells. After all, the bodies had apparently been there for years. Blanchard's job security rested upon this being a legal and valid search of the well. No, he reasoned, he didn't need a search warrant. Whether or not the well was in fact within the curtilage, he was going to make a statement of law himself and decree that it was not. Not in the curtilage. Valid search. With no search warrant and no permission, up the creek. With no search warrant and Bee's permission, no problem. Therefore, Blanchard rationalized, he had a good search.

Blanchard's statement continued.

"After obtaining permission from Miss Street, who verified her address and lawful possession of the premises by displaying a duly issued driver's license, a well located beyond the bounds of curtilage was duly search by myself and Detectives Wade and Reece of the Rockingham Sheriff's Department. Detective Reece was lowered into the well and reported the presence of human remains so I, therefore, requested, and received within 45 minutes, the presence of Dr. Alonzo Carver, the Rockingham County Coroner. Over the next three hours four skulls, all of which appeared to be human, along with other bones, were

removed from the well and duly delivered to the aforesaid County Coroner. Further search of the premises, with permission to conduct said search being given by said Misty Street, revealed the presence of two sandwich bags containing green vegetable material and one sandwich bag containing a white powdery substance in a bedroom identified by Miss Street to be the bedroom of her and Mr. Johnny Wayne Fulcher. All three sandwich bags were duly delivered to the evidence room of the Rockingham County Sheriff's Department for delivery to the State lab for evaluation. Miss Street denied knowledge of the substances. The aforesaid detectives and coroner left the premises at approximately 10:30 p.m."

There were the Coroner's reports: One indicated the cause of death of Carlton Ray Purvis. Four separate other reports pertained to the remains of one middle-aged Caucasian male and three Caucasian females between the ages of 14 and 20 years, all yet to be identified. Bone breakage and cuts in the bones indicated that all four victims removed from the well of Johnny Wayne Fulcher's residence died of unnatural causes.

Also included was the statement of the Queen Bee, which dovetailed Detective Blanchard's report, and a statement from Cheech Mann, which corroborated Harley Ames' search for Johnny Wayne Fulcher on the night of Carlton Purvis's death.

There were also forensic reports substantiating the presence of Johnny Wayne Fulcher's fingerprints on the inner and outer doorknobs of the Purvis residence. Another forensic report matched tire marks in the Purvis yard with the tires on Fulcher's truck by the use of plaster casts.

Bob Lee could see Gerry Wiles' aim. Johnny Wayne was dead on in his sight.

Chapter 34

The old man was 90 years of age and as a young man had shaken the hand of a man who shook the hand of the great Abraham Lincoln. He was counseling his grandson. "Son", he said, "nobody wants to live forever. But nobody wants to die today, either."

Anonymous

Before Christmas, Bob Lee was sitting in his office when he got word that Ken Childrey was in the waiting room asking to see him.

A former member of the North Carolina Highway Patrol, Ken had resigned from the Patrol years earlier after running into a scrape over an affair with a young lady he had stopped while on patrol for no other reason than to get her telephone number. Complications arising from her complaining husband caused the Patrol to resort to its usual course of internal action by directing that the offending officer be transferred to another county a sufficient distance away. In Ken's case he simply decided to resign quietly from the Patrol and obtain his detective's license.

Bob Lee had retained Ken Childrey to investigate a number of domestic, civil, and criminal cases in the past, so Ken was the first person who came to mind when he had asked Judge Burgwyn to assign him funds to retain a private investigator.

Ken Childrey never should have been on the highway patrol in the first place. He liked to talk too much and had the countenance of just being too, well, nice.

Bob Lee rose from behind his desk and circled toward the door to greet his friend.

"Ken, come on in and have a seat. How've you been doing?"

The two shook hands and looked each other in the eye. They had been raised to do that. Bob Lee waved Ken in the direction of a seat and found his own behind his desk. Both slid their butts forward and made themselves comfortable.

"Just fine, Bob Lee. I'm just fine."

"And how's your Mama doing, Ken? How old is she now?"

"She's not doing too good, Bob Lee. I think she's losing her mind."

"Oh, I'm sorry to hear that..."

Ken went on.

"She's 91 now, and she's getting mean as a snake. Cusses a lot. Cusses a whole lot. I just don't know what to do with her, Bob Lee. A few weeks ago I took her to the Fisherman's Galley for supper, and I got up to get her some sweet iced tea over at the serving station because the young man who was going to wait on us was busy."

Ken adjusted himself in his seat. His feet came together.

"On my way back, I noticed the young waiter looking upset as he left our table. I asked Mama, I said, 'Mama, what did you say to him? Did you say anything bad?' And I swear Bob Lee, she looked me straight in the face and said 'All I said was I wanted some *damn* fish.' Can you believe that? My sweet Christian Mama, 91 years old, talking like that. Sayin' *damn*? Talkin' like a sailor!"

Ken was looking at his hands.

"I'm just about afraid to let her call her Daddy on his birthday 'cause there's no telling what she might say."

That caught Bob Lee's ear. He smiled.

"What's she doing, Ken? Talking to her Daddy in heaven?"

"Oh, no, Bob Lee. She talks to her Daddy. Calls him every birthday. And on Christmas."

"Are you telling me your 91-year-old Mama's father is still alive?"

"Well, yeah, Bob Lee, he is. He's 106 and lives by himself in a plantation house in northern Mississippi.

Owns a nice place in New Orleans he visits. He was 15 when she was born."

Bob Lee slid his body back up into his seat and sat up.

"You've gotta be kidding me, Ken."

Ken was matter-of-fact.

"No, and he don't need to be worrying about his little girl, not at that age he don't. Bad for his heart, I'd think".

Bob Lee was smiling.

"Well, doggone, Ken, I'd think he has a pretty good heart to be 106."

Ken smiled.

"Can't argue with you on that one, Bob Lee, but it might be starting to fail on him. I'll tell you something, Bob Lee... but you gotta promise not to tell Mama about this... but Granddaddy has always liked the young girls. I guess I got it honest, Bob Lee."

Bob Lee didn't interrupt Ken. Unknown to Ken, two things were happening at the same time: he was telling Bob Lee about his family circumstances and analyzing them as he spoke.

"He ain't as dangerous as he used to be, though, Bob Lee. I was with him in July down in Meridian and he drove me over to the Piggly Wiggly in his Buick. Well, a pretty young thing pushing a cart of rug rats caught his eye and he grinned like a teenager and said, 'Ken, ever hear the expression 'where there's a will there's a way?' I said, 'Sure, Granddaddy, 'course I have!' And he said, 'It ain't true, Boy! It just ain't true!' Kind of felt sorry for him. Know what I mean, Bob Lee?"

"No, not really, Ken. I mean, for God's sake, he's 106 and drivin' a Buick and..."

Bob Lee looked at his watch dial for two long seconds. He meant it as a hint.

"Well, Bob Lee, what's the guy got to live for if he can't..."

"Ken, let's get down to business, okay? You know we're here today about the Fulcher case and Judge Burgwyn has allowed me to retain a private investigator. I want you. Would you like to jump in on this one, Ken?"

"Sure thing, Bob Lee. What do you have in mind?"

"To begin, Ken, I need photos and measurements of the Fulcher home place. Specifically, I need to know how far it is from the house to the well where they found four bodies. You've probably read about that in the newspaper. I need measurements of how far the well is from every structure on the Fulcher farm."

Ken reached for his coat and pulled out his pen and a 3" X 5" note pad. He folded back 4 or 5 pages and wrote. After scrawling a few words, he looked up, and Bob Lee continued.

"An aerial photo would be nice. And a written drawing. I need that information first, Ken. Now Fulcher's girlfriend--Misty Street, who goes by the nickname of The Queen Bee--is living there and may not let you take pictures or measure at first, so that's why you're getting paid the big bucks, Ken. I don't care how you do it or what you've got to do to get it done, just get it done, Ken, okay?"

Ken looked up. He was curious.

"Why do you need these details, Bob Lee? What is it you want me to help you prove?"

"I've got to find out whether or not the well was within what was known as the 'curtilage,' Ken. Whether it was close enough to the house in relation to the whole farm to be considered within what the law calls an area where a person has an expectation of privacy. We both expect a little privacy if we pee in the bushes in our back yards, Ken. But we might not expect that privacy if we pee in the middle of an open field not far from the highway. Get it?"

"I think so, Bob Lee. What else?"

"Let's just start there. But there's something else, Ken."

"What's that?"

"You need to go get your mama some damn fish, okay, Ken?"

Chapter 35

"Lawyers I suppose were children once."

Charles Lamb

Edward Bryant Griggs, Esquire, a youthful 32 years of age, swung the knob behind him to close the door as he entered Bob Lee's office waiting room. He had just entered a couple of traffic pleas in District Court and the week had been unusually warm. He wore what was more or less his "Springtime uniform" for District Court: a solid blue sports coat, a department store white button-down shirt with a preppy yellow and blue tie, khaki pants with an alligator skin belt, and penny loafers.

Eddie Griggs was the only child of a local pharmacist and grade school teacher. His resume wasn't exceptional. In high school, he had earned above average grades despite meager efforts and played on the football and tennis teams as a well-liked, but not particularly athletic, participant. After high school, he continued to live with his parents and was hired as a part-time employee at the local Lowe's

Hardware by one of his father's customers. He also enrolled at Rockingham Community College and took college parallel courses so he could transfer to another school after two years. In his off time he either hunted or fished in the river with his buddies. After his two years at the community college, he was admitted and transferred to the University of North Carolina at Chapel Hill, and before graduation took and excelled in the Law School Aptitude Test, and then entered law school.

After his second year of law school in Chapel Hill, Eddie married his college sweetheart from Ellerbe, North Carolina, and immediately and directly participated in the conception of the first of his three children, a daughter, in student housing. After his graduation and passing of the North Carolina State Bar Examination, Eddie and his young family returned to his hometown of Mayodan, where he hung his law shingle, paid his father a nominal amount as rental in investment office space above his Dad's drugstore, and began his legal career dependent in large part upon goodwill earned by his father's pharmacy.

During eight years of law practice, he had, in addition to hundreds of District and Superior Court criminal pleas, tried hundreds of District Court Criminal cases, dozens of District Court Civil cases, two Superior Court civil jury trials, 19 Superior Court felony jury trials, and not a single death penalty case. He was at best a sufficient trial lawyer, neither wise nor great, and did not draw courtroom onlookers to appreciate his performances as more demonstrative attorneys did. That would come, if ever, only after having been tempered by additional years of experience in a consistent and almost daily courtroom trial practice.

Eddie was eager to cut his teeth on a capital trial with the Fulcher case. He had seen Fulcher in courtrooms on sporadic occasions and was well aware of his reputation and figured, in his estimation, that there really wasn't much to lose. He recognized that the case would be a learning experience that widened his exposure because of the local chatter about the lawyers involved. And just as important, he would be working under the tutelage of Bob Lee Pender, who had very politely and expertly waxed him as opposing counsel on previous occasions.

Bob Lee had just pulled the Fulcher file from his desk drawer when Ida buzzed to tell him she was sending Eddie in to see him.

Bob Lee fixed his eyes on Eddie's and welcomed him with his left hand on Eddie's elbow and his right hand in a firm handshake. He asked about Eddie's wife, children, and parents. Eddie thanked Bob Lee for asking and reciprocated with similar inquiries of Bob Lee's family. Bob Lee then suggested that the two of them grab a legal pad from his desk and retire into the conference room. After determining that Eddie was thirsty, he buzzed Ida and asked her to bring Eddie a Coca-Cola, always in a 6.5 oz. bottle that had become a signature of Bob Lee's office.

The pile of Discovery delivered on behalf of assistant district attorney Gerry Wiles was there. They sat and Bob Lee began.

"Eddie, there's what Gerry has sent me. Real quick, here's what it looks like from Gerry's view. Carlton Purvis owed Harley Ames money. Harley says it was over a truck, but, to me, it sounds like drug money owed to Harley. Harley lines up Johnny Wayne to collect the money, and says he'll pay him to help collect it. That's crucial, Eddie. Fulcher is getting paid money."

"Exactly what are you saying, Bob Lee?" Eddie was listening and doing his best to hone in on Bob Lee's pattern of thought.

"If Gerry can get his first degree conviction, they can't stick Johnny Wayne with the needle until they prove the statutory factors. It smells like they're going to try to prove armed robbery as an aggravating factor. Johnny Wayne just isn't allowed to walk in and threaten somebody with a weapon, whether it's a gun or a stick, just to get payment for helping Harley. If they prove armed robbery, they've proven a factor sufficient to give him the needle. I'm getting ahead of you, Eddie. There are four more factors Gerry announced in court and sent over that they're going to try to prove if they get a first-degree murder conviction. You need to read Harley's statement yourself."

Bob Lee waved his hand toward the discovery.

"Ida will make you copies of all of the notes and pleadings. In the meantime, would you mind, Eddie, doing some work on jury selection? I have some roadways from other cases I've tried that Ida can give you to serve as go-bys, but we need for both of us to be thinking about the jury."

"Sure thing, Bob Lee", Eddie answered.

Bob Lee picked back up.

"So Harley goes to find Johnny Wayne at Johnny Wayne's house. Johnny Wayne's fishing with his girlfriend. Do you know her, Eddie? Ever represent her? Misty Street. Also called Queen Bee. Big woman. White beehive piled on top of her head? Sometimes its pink. Has been around the courtrooms, either with Johnny Wayne or for herself."

"I represented her once, Bob Lee. Shoplifting about four years ago from the Rexall Pharmacy. Mean looking woman. Love that tattoo, though. Mesmerizing..."

"That's her. So Harley stops by Johnny Wayne's and Cheech Mann is at Johnny Wayne's and tells Harley that Johnny Wayne and the Bee are carp fishing up at Philpott Lake in Virginia. Now keep in mind, Eddie, that up to this point Johnny Wayne and Harley Ames agree 100 percent what happened."

Bob Lee went on.

"From here on out Johnny Wayne swears everyone else is lying. He'll look you straight in the eye and tell you that he and the Bee stopped by Carlton's house just to get some marijuana and cocaine to enjoy while they fished, that they were going to go fishing up at Philpott Lake but changed their minds and went up to Smith Mountain Lake instead, and that they got home just after six a.m. He swears up and down to this. "

Bob Lee understood Eddie was thinking that Johnny Wayne Fulcher was one of the ablest and most experienced liars in the county. But for both of them, if Johnny Wayne's version amounted to the best story presented to them, they'd just have to ride that pony all over town. And ride it with a straight face.

"Harley's statement, corroborated by Queen Bee's statement and by Cheech, is that Harley found Johnny Wayne at home later that night, that Johnny Wayne drove his truck and took a gun with him, and that between the two of them Carlton was wrapped up in silver duct tape and beaten to collect the debt. The coroner's report backs up that Carlton threw a blood clot from a dark bruise on his right leg to his lung that killed him. And certainly you've heard about the four bodies. Detective Blanchard is saying no search warrant was necessary because a person in lawful possession of the Fulcher House, the Bee, gave them permission to search the curtilage. I don't know exactly where the well house is in relation to the house, but we'll find out."

"So what would you like for me to head up, Bob Lee?" Eddie asked.

Bob Lee appreciated Eddie's deference.

"Well, Eddie, it's up to the two of us to decide, but my initial feeling is for you to head up jury selection. Opening statements to the jury: one for each of us, you first. I'll cross examine Harley and Detective Blanchard. You cross-examine the Bee and Cheech and the coroner. The coroner may or may not be laborious because we're talking either one or five bodies. We don't know yet."

Eddie nodded. He didn't interrupt Bob Lee. He was listening and, in his estimation, learning from a master at his trade.

"Closing statements? We'll each do one, with me second. And research. I'd ask you to research Blanchard's search of the Fulcher home place where the bodies were found to make sure the search of the premises and seizure of the evidence in the form of human bones was clean and proper. That's my first impression, Eddie."

An initial trial strategy had been set by the defense.

Chapter 36

"My father said there are two kinds of people in the world: givers and takers. The takers may eat better, but the givers sleep better."

Marlo Thomas

The Bee heard the crunch of gravel over Bob Barker's "The Price Is Right" bids as the truck made its way slowly down the driveway toward the farmhouse. Gravity had taken its toll on her braless breasts which, unfortunately to even the drunkest just-in-port sailor onlooker, exposed themselves beneath a sheer pink blouse. Coifed in her signature beehive hairdo and wearing Spandex stretched to its limits along with flip flops, a Walmart greeter would have questioned the suitability of her appearance.

The Bee walked from the den and palmed the screen door open. She watched from the unpainted front porch as a man exited a van. She noticed he was wearing a hard hat and blue jumpsuit and holding a clipboard. Before approaching closer, he spoke from beside the open truck door.

"Good afternoon, ma'am. My name is Marcus Larry Pegram, and I'm a contract worker here set out by Southern Telecommunications."

His blue coveralls lent the appearance of manly professionalism to The Bee. She was interested in checking out his ass. But she offered no greeting.

"Our corporate computers are telling us you might be having a loss of transmission because of a short or slight knick in your TV cable lines."

The Bee still didn't say anything. She just stared. The worker was a little uncomfortable.

"Have you noticed that your cable TV is not as sharp as you'd like it to be? Your TV should be sharp and clear as air. They want to make sure your line is fine, and your picture is clean and crisp. They've told me that if I find the problem, Southern will be glad to give you two-month's refund on your bill, and if I don't find it, they'll give you a month just for letting me check the problem out for them."

The Bee liked the sound of that. But she was skeptical.

"Who'd you say you were with? Who you with?"

"Southern Telecommunications, ma'am. Your cable people."

He reached to tilt his hard hat, and his voice became inquisitive.

"Is this the residence of a Mr. John or Johnny Wayne Fulcher? I've got to make sure I have permission from the right person, ma'am."

He was fumbling with his clipboard.

"Is this Mr. Fulcher's residence? I can't survey the problem and nobody can get a refund or free cable until I get permission from an owner or someone in charge."

"It is."

"Then you must be..."

"Mrs. Fulcher."

The man shut the door to the truck, took a few steps closer to the porch, and stopped, clutching the clipboard with both hands.

"Well, Mrs. Fulcher, would it be okay with you if I tried to find that leaking line? I won't dig up your yard, ma'am. Just a little hole if I find it. I've got a metal detector here, and I'll try to locate any lines around the yard that might be causing an interference, and I won't be digging much at all. I'm going to write down where I find it so it won't be so much trouble next time."

The man scanned toward his right and smiled in recognition of a bed of flowers.

"Your pansies are safe with me, ma'am. I love flowers, ma'am. I got that from my own mama. So they'll be safe. That is, of course, if you'll give me permission to do that."

The Bee had to give it a try.

"You reckon you can get me three months free service? I just don't know whether my husband would want you digging up the yard and all. He's going to get mad at me just for letting you do anything on this land without his permission. I think he'd want at least three months free cable whether you find a leak or not."

"Ma'am, it wouldn't be honest for me to promise you that. All I'm authorized to offer you is one month for letting me inspect and two months if I find it. But I'll tell you this. I promise I'll ask them when I turn in the report for three months free cable for you. Yes, ma'am, I'll do that. Would that be okay with you, ma'am, if I just honestly promised to ask them?"

He put pen to paper to memorialize his promise to try.

"If not, I'll just leave, and they can decide whether to just terminate service or let it keep leaking on you. I'm sure it's leaking on you, Mrs. Fulcher, and if I can find it, you'll get two months free service and a better picture, and you won't have to worry about them cutting it off on you. Or you can go back to one of those eight-foot satellite dishes that make your crabgrass look so good.

The cable worker took a moment to organize the papers on his clipboard.

"But I'll do whatever you say, ma'am."

The Bee decided. Better something for nothing than nothing at all.

"Go ahead, Mister. Just don't leave no holes."

A small grin appeared on the worker's face. "Don't you worry about that, ma'am. I'll go over this whole place for you, and you won't notice a single hole, I promise you that."

Marcus Larry Pegram, The Cable Guy, also known as Ken Childrey, Private Investigator, reached for the metal detector and a notepad in the van. He'd been slicker than pig snot on a radiator. He had free reign to measure the distances around the well in which the bodies had been found. He'd give those measurements to Bob Lee. Bob Lee would then have the information necessary for him to decide on how to proceed on the curtilage issue.

But it was what had been said about The Bee, and not what he was going to do, that was on Ken's mind as he watched The Bee waddle back into her hive.

Chapter 37

"Did you ever notice they never take any fat hostages? You never see a guy coming out of Lebanon going: 'I was held hostage for seven months and lost 175 pounds. I feel good and I look good and I learned self-discipline. That's the important thing.'"

Dennis Leary

Eddie Griggs had made his way up to the second floor of the jail and seated himself facing the door of the small conference room where he was to interview Johnny Wayne Fulcher. He opened his briefcase, lifted a note pad, slid on his glasses, and reached for an ink pen.

The deputy jailer led Johnny Wayne to the door, removed Johnny Wayne's handcuffs, and cracked the door open. "Here he is, Mr. Griggs."

Eddie Griggs stood and extended a handshake toward Johnny Wayne.

"Thank you, Deputy, for bringing Johnny Wayne down. Johnny Wayne, have a seat."

Johnny Wayne remained standing. Eddie continued as he began to sit down.

"I believe we've met before, when I represented Miss Street in that little shoplifting matter over at the One-Stop Shop. Have a seat if you will."

Johnny Wayne plopped into the plastic chair with his back toward the single door behind him. Eddie faced Johnny Wayne and the door and clicked his pen.

Johnny Wayne had grown pallid from sunlight deprivation after having been incarcerated for almost a month. He wore the same orange jump suit and flip flops he had worn at his bond appearance before Judge Burgwyn. A larger paunch had grown on his belly from his starchy diet and lack of exercise. His mullet was longer and unkempt. There was a recognizable odor easily identified by anyone who had ever been jailed. People have identified or often referred to what is known as the "stench of death." A less publicized, but just as memorable, aroma is known best by those who frequent local detention facilities as the "stench of jail."

Eddie attempted to raise the comfort level between himself and his client.

"Johnny Wayne, Judge Burgwyn has appointed me to work with Mr. Pender in providing your defense for the murder charge. Please call me 'Eddie.' We're in for a lot together, and we've got to work together, so you call me

Eddie, and I'll call you Johnny Wayne or J.W. whichever you prefer, if that's okay with you. Which would you prefer?"

"It don't make no difference what you call me, Eddie. Just get my ass outta here."

Eddie nodded and smiled.

"First, I want to ask you how you are doing. I know it's not home in here, Johnny Wayne, but how are you faring in here? Is there anything in particular I can do for you or anything you think the jailer would allow that I can bring you?"

Johnny Wayne was bitter.

"Yeah, I've already done told you what you can do for me. You can get my ass out of here."

Johnny Wayne's left fist was balled up.

"I ain't done nothing, Eddie. Nothing. You need to get them to try to find the real person who did this so I can get out. I don't give a damn what the Bee is saying right now, she and me were fishing up at Smith Mountain Lake in Little Bull Run Cove."

That brought the first question to Eddie's mind.

"I need to ask you about that, Johnny Wayne. According to Cheech Mann's statement he told Harley you had gone to Philpot Lake to go fishing, not Smith Mountain Lake. Now I realize that a person's got to pass the entrance of Philpot Lake to get up to Smith Mountain Lake. Smith

Mountain Lake is further away than Philpot. Did you tell Cheech Mann you were going to Philpot Lake or Smith Mountain Lake? Which did you tell him you were going to? As a matter of fact, was Cheech Mann even at your house, and what, if anything did you tell him?"

Johnny Wayne wasn't even looking at Eddie when he was peppered with these questions. He searched the ceiling, with his chair perched on two legs as he leaned back, and tapped a finger on the table. He didn't know why these questions were important.

"Look, Eddie, I don't know what any of that has a thing to do with anything. The Bee knows we were at Smith Mountain that night. Fishin' in Little Bull Run cove. She needs to tell the truth."

Fulcher brought the chair back down as he changed his line of thought.

"But, just to let you know, Cheech had been sleeping on the couch for about two days. He had a fight with his mama. I guess you could call it a lover's quarrel. He didn't have no place to go, and we felt sorry for him, okay? I told him to do some chores and cut some wood and that if he took anything he didn't own from around the house, he'd be real sorry. So Cheech was there. The Bee and I was just going fishing, okay? Wasn't no Act of Congress or anything. Just fishin'."

Eddie didn't interrupt with a question. He was taking notes.

"We told Cheech we'd be up at Philpot Lake so we went to Carlton's for just a couple of minutes, and I got some smoke and blow while the Bee waited in the truck. Nothing happened at Carlton's. It wasn't no big deal. I got my smoke and a little blow, and we left. I didn't have nothing against Carlton."

Fulcher noticed that Eddie was nodding as he wrote.

"Me and The Bee lit up a little smoke around the Carolina-Virginia line and when we got to the forks we decided to head up to Smith Mountain Lake instead. No big deal."

Eddie repeated what Fulcher had said.

"So you went to Smith Mountain Lake?"

Having to repeat what he had said irritated Fulcher. He scratched his leg.

"Yeah, Smith Mountain. Write that down. Little Bull Run Cove. Smith Mountain."

Fulcher leaned forward as Eddie wrote.

"Carp fishing is carp fishing. The fish don't know whether they're swimming in Philpot or Smith Mountain Lake, do they? They just bite when you know how to catch them. What difference does it make where we went as long as I wasn't at Carlton's house killing his sorry soul?"

Eddie was writing furiously to keep up with Johnny Wayne and explained his reason for asking.

"Harley's statement is saying he went to Philpot Lake looking for you. We thought we might have caught him in a lie about where he went. It sounds like from what you told him, Cheech thought you were going to Philpot and that's why he told Harley you were going to Philpot Lake instead of Smith Mountain Lake. It does seem to back up Harley's statement, though, that he did talk to Harley at your house that night. Not very good for you, Johnny Wayne."

Johnny Wayne's hand hit the table and his chair slammed back to its four legs. His voice became loud. He leaned forward, staring into Eddie's eyes.

"So are you telling me you believe those two fools? Do you believe what the hell they're saying? Whose lawyer are you, anyways?" Johnny Wayne's voice had risen to a yell.

"Who do you think you're representing here, Eddie? I've been here a month, and I don't need some jailhouse lawyer telling me he's believing the liars that put me here! Whose damn side are you on??"

Johnny Wayne had put the fear of God in Eddie. Eddie leaned back in retreat, and his voice got higher.

"Just calm down, Johnny Wayne. I believe you, Johnny Wayne. I believe you. But you need to understand that I've got to figure out what they're saying so we can catch them in a lie and get you out of here."

Eddie thought he had caught Johnny Wayne's attention.

"Do you understand that, Johnny Wayne? Me and Bob Lee are on your side. Now please, Johnny Wayne, let's stay calm here, okay? I've got my job to do, so don't think when I ask questions you may not like that I'm not on your side. I am, Johnny Wayne. I am. Work with me, okay?"

Johnny Wayne reared back so his chair perched on two legs and clasped his hands behind his neck. He looked across the table.

"Let's get it on, Eddie. What's next?"

Eddie wanted to get this over with as quickly as possible.

He noticed for the first time that Johnny Wayne was between him and the door, and not vice versa.

For the first time he grasped that he had taken the wrong seat.

The sense that something just wasn't right seized Eddie. Across the table sat an accused murderer with a hair-trigger temper who owned land with a well containing the corpses of four victims between him and his path of exit from the room.

Eddie Griggs had a nice wife and three beautiful, healthy kids. And Johnny Wayne was between him, the door, and his family. Oh, hell.

"I want to ask you about the location of the well, Johnny Wayne. I need to know how often you went to the well. Did you use it often, and how close is it to the house?

We've got our private investigator measuring distances from the well house to the barn and to the house and so on, but I'd like to know what you can tell me about your use of the well."

Johnny Wayne leaned toward Eddie. His chair came back to its four legs and both elbows rested on the table.

"You tell Bob Lee I don't know a damn thing about that well or even the well house. I don't use it. Haven't used it for years. It sits just on the inside of the fence that separates the barn area from the field and hasn't been used in years."

Fulcher was drawing slow circles on the table with his index finger.

"They can fingerprint it if they'd like, but they won't find anything of me there. It's just something down on the edge of the yard as far as I'm concerned."

Eddie noticed that Johnny Wayne's trunk was rocking back and forth and that the circles were being drawn faster. The cadence of his speech was quickening.

"If they found any bodies in there, then it's just some kind of coincidence, Eddie. Anybody could have thrown them in there. Anybody. But it wasn't me. Could have been anybody that comes down there, Eddie. We have a lot of parties, with people on Harleys or Indian Chiefs and friends drinking beer. A fight breaks out once in a while, and we don't think nothing of it. And I worked at the coast for a while. Anybody could have throwed somebody in there."

Fulcher paused and then tapped his index finger twice on the table.

"But it wasn't me because I don't have nothin' to do with that well, Eddie, not a damn thing. If I did, maybe I would have knowed somebody was down there. So since I didn't know nobody was down there that means I don't know nothing about the well, right, Eddie?"

Eddie was writing furiously. He didn't look up. He just murmured.

"Well, not necessarily, Johnny Wayne. They're probably going to say you knew they were down there in the first place, and..."

Johnny Wayne's hand hit the table again. He started to rise but quickly sat back down. He leaned forward.

"Listen to me, dammit. Just listen and hear what I got to say, Eddie." He pointed at his eyes. "Right here."

Eddie was intimidated. He returned the look.

"I ain't done nothin'. You can write that down. And if I hear you say one more time that I did do something I didn't do, it's really going to ruin your day. Do you hear me, Eddie? I didn't do nothing. Not a thing."

Johnny Wayne's voice rose again.

"As a matter of fact, Eddie, I don't think I want you messing with my case no more. You got that? You tell Bob Lee I just fired your skinny ass, you hear me, Boy? You're fired."

Eddie was almost stuttering.

"But Mr. Fulcher, I…"

Fulcher had taken total command.

"Go back to your traffic tickets, son. You're fired. I ain't going to take somebody else's murder just because you think I'm guilty, boy. We'll both go down before that happens, you hear me?"

Johnny Wayne was on a downward spiral. He was sneering. Eddie wished he had seated himself next to the door.

"I hear you, Johnny Wayne. I hear what you're saying. You've got it, and I understand perfectly. You don't want me to represent you, and if that's what you want, then that's what you get. I understand and I apologize if I have offended you in some way." Eddie's voice quivered and squeaked. A stage fright reaction took place. He was humiliated. Embarrassed. Petrified. "I'll be going now, Johnny Wayne. I'll be going. Let me get the jailer."

Johnny Wayne sensed Eddie's animal terror that permeated the room. Predatory instinct set off his motions to pounce. He noticed Eddie as he held his briefcase under his left arm and reached for the doorknob with his right.

In the same moment, and with a catlike movement, Johnny Wayne dipped into his jumpsuit and slid out an object stuffed within the confines of his underwear.

Fulcher stiff-armed Eddie backwards toward the far wall of the room. As Eddie spun to catch himself Fulcher rear-ended him and strung his left arm around Eddie's neck in a headlock. His right hand clutched half of a Mountain Dew can, jagged edges facing away from his hand, on Eddie's neck adjacent to the jugular vein.

Johnny Wayne was in sole control. His mouth was an inch from Eddie's right ear. His breath, warm to Eddie's neck, stank. Eddie completely surrendered.

"Listen, damn you. We might both go to hell today if you don't listen real good, you hear me, Eddie-boy? You hear me, Son?"

Eddie's voice was whispered, cracking.

"I hear you, Johnny Wayne...you don't have to..."

Johnny Wayne's grip tightened. His voice lowered and warm breath filled Eddie's ear.

"Shut up, Eddie. Just shut up. Do what I say. Do it, or you're going to bleed like a stuck pig. You got that, Sonny? Your neck's going to be squirting blood all over the walls. It's gonna look like one of those monkeys with the red butts slinging paint on a canvas in here; you got that? You hearing me? Just nod if you do, Little Man. Just nod."

Eddie nodded. Johnny Wayne picked back up.

"Now reach for that doorknob, and open it. You and I are going to stay like this, real close, so don't try nothing that's going to make me jab this can in your neck, got it? I will, Eddie, I swear I will. You tell everybody that they got to open the elevator door and get us downstairs, you hear me? You better do it right, Eddie, because the only way you're going to keep from getting stuck in the neck is for you to get both of us down there, you understand? Just nod, Eddie. Just nod."

Eddie nodded. Johnny Wayne tightened his grip again.

"Then let's do this. Now, real slow, reach for the door knob and open the door. Tell them what you have to say to get us downstairs. Do it good, Eddie. Your Mama and Daddy are countin' on you, Eddie."

Johnny Wayne gave Eddie a slight nudge. Eddie reached for the doorknob, slowly turned it, and pulled the door open. The two of them, with Eddie leading as Johnny Wayne held him from behind in a headlock with the jagged can to his neck, slowly exited the room. The elevator door was less than 15 feet away. For the first seconds they were unnoticed. Johnny Wayne whispered for Eddie to speak up.

Eddie's voice verged on the edge of weeping.

"Everybody listen up. Don't anybody move, please. Please don't pull out your guns. Please, stay calm!"

Jack and three deputies all turned from their clipboards toward Eddie and Johnny Wayne. Four hands rested on pistol handles.

"No, please, Jack, don't do anything. Please. Me and Johnny Wayne just want to go downstairs, Jack. Please let us go downstairs."

The deputies' elbows slowly flared out. Eddie thought they were going to draw their weapons.

"Please, Jack. Johnny Wayne's serious. I believe him. He's not going to hurt anybody just so long as we can go downstairs. Please get that elevator door open, Jack, so we can go downstairs. Please, Jack. I'm begging you, Jack. Please."

Jack knew Eddie's life depended on his answer. He spoke in an even voice.

"You're right, Eddie. Ain't no reason for anybody to get hurt. That door's coming open right away, Johnny Wayne. It's coming open. But don't anybody do anything stupid. Everybody stay calm."

Jack held out his arms in a display for Johnny Wayne that his weapon was off limits.

"Keep your guns where they are, boys, and Johnny Wayne, you stay calm, okay? We're going to get the two of your downstairs."

Jack motioned for the jailer to push the button, and the elevator doors opened. Johnny Wayne spoke.

"I'll be seeing you, Jack." Johnny Wayne had always liked Jack. "You take care, okay?"

The two stayed in the same position--Eddie in front, Johnny Wayne in back with the jagged can to Eddie's neck. They shuffled into the elevator and faced the deputies. Johnny Wayne told Jack to send the elevator down, so the doors closed and Johnny Wayne and Eddie found themselves alone within the confines of the elevator box.

Neither spoke. Both listened to the machinations of the elevator as it descended to the lower floor. Stress pervaded, with each man considering mortality in different terms. Eddie thought of his family. Johnny Wayne thought of the moment.

Johnny Wayne tightened his hold as the door opened, fully expecting to be faced with an array of guns aimed toward his face.

No one in the alcove. Johnny Wayne held on to Eddie, looking forward, left, and right as he nudged Eddie to the edge of the elevator door. He spoke in a low voice.

"Your car's in the parking lot outside the jail, right, Eddie?"

Eddie whispered a weak, "Yes, Johnny Wayne."

"Keys in your pocket?"

"Yes, Johnny Wayne."

Johnny Wayne then directed his attention to the outside world. His voice echoed as he shouted toward the steel exit door.

"Open the door! Don't do nothin'! Don't try nothin'! I'll put this man into a bloody sleep if anybody so much as burps, do you hear me??"

There was no response. But Johnny Wayne knew they waited.

"If I hear as much as a shuffle, I'm going to cut young Eddie's throat, do you understand? You willing to bet his life? You willing to take that gamble? If I so much as jerk a little his throat's cut, you get that? Just a twitch, and his wife's a widow. Don't be stupid. It ain't worth it. Open the damn door. Be easy. Be smart."

Johnny Wayne's yell rose to a rant.

"Open the door. And do it now! I'm giving you ten short seconds or Eddie's wife's a widow, you got that? One, two..."

The steel door leading to the outer jail hallway clanked as the brass key was inserted, turned, and used as a handle to swing the door open slowly. Johnny Wayne noticed the difference in the air from where he and Eddie stood at the elevator door. It smelled like freedom.

"Let's go, Eddie. Let's do this together. Ready? Let's go. Slow now."

Johnny Wayne and Eddie retained their positions. Eddie in front, Johnny Wayne with the headlock and jagged can on Eddie's neck from behind. They shuffled, with a wide-eyed Eddie looking forward and Johnny Wayne's head bobbing in all directions, anticipating an ambush.

When they reached the steel exit door leading to the public hallway outside the jail proper, Johnny Wayne called out.

"We're coming out. Don't try nothin'. You hear? Don't try nothin'!!"

The two shuffled out to an empty hallway. Working their way left, they hobbled past the bulletproof glass between the hallway and the front desk sergeant toward the exit door that opened to the parking lot. When they reached the door, Johnny Wayne issued instructions.

"Eddie, I ain't going to let go of you, but I want you to take your hand and reach into your pocket real slow and easy and get out your car keys, okay? Take your time, Eddie, but move real slow, you hear? Real slow."

Eddie's trembled so badly Fulcher feared he was going to collapse. Fulcher lowered his voice into one of reassurance.

"Now, Eddie, we're almost there. You go ahead and get your keys and reach up real slow and put them in my left hand, the one that's around your neck. You got that? And then we're almost done. Now, do it now."

Eddie gingerly reached into his pocket, found his key ring, and very carefully reached up and placed them within the reach of Johnny Wayne's left hand. Johnny Wayne had a question.

"Eddie," he whispered. "Where's your car? What color is it? Don't mess with me, Eddie, 'cause I don't want to cut your throat, but by all that's holy I will if you try anything smart. Where is it, Eddie?"

Eddie spoke low.

"Johnny Wayne, it's a tan Volvo station wagon just to the right of the door. It's the third or fourth car down on our right. I parked near the door, Johnny Wayne. Right outside this door and near it. On the right."

Eddie found his voice again.

"Now Johnny Wayne, let's be careful, okay? I'm working with you, Johnny Wayne. I've been going along with you. Now let's be careful and just get out of here without either of us getting hurt, okay, Johnny Wayne?"

Johnny Wayne was a realist.

"We'll just see what happens, Eddie. Now let's go. And slow, got that? Slow. Pull the door open and then head to the car, Eddie."

Eddie reached forward and gripped the doorknob. His reach was only a foot or so. When the door cracked, he and Johnny Wayne wound their way around the edge of the door to the door jamb, where they stopped. Johnny Wayne's grip had grown even tighter as they exited the building. No one in the parking lot, and they had a clear path to the Volvo.

The steel exit door had just shuttered shut and the two had travelled no more than 10 feet when the group appeared. No less than 20 deputies, half with high powered rifles, emerged from the side of the building, from behind patrol cars, from beside pickup trucks. All with their rifles pointed toward Eddie and Johnny Wayne. To one side stood the good Sheriff Efron Bailey, in a blue suit and holding a hat at his left side, and within 15 feet to the left of the Sheriff stood Judge Amos Burgwyn, wearing his judicial robe, craning his neck for a better view.

Everyone stopped dead in their tracks.

Johnny Wayne, mind racing as instincts calculated odds, measured options, and scanned the area, was the first to speak.

"Don't do it! Don't do it! We'll both die, I swear it! Sheriff, get 'em to back off, or I'll stick him in the neck!"

Eddie felt Johnny Wayne's grip tighten.

"You ain't giving me no choice, Sheriff. It'll be on your hands, Sheriff. Get 'em to back down, Efron. Do it or he dies!"

No one had particularly noticed that Fulcher had called the Sheriff by his first name. But everyone looked toward the Sheriff for a response. Silence ruled.

To the puzzlement of all, a voice from the Sheriff's left shouted.

"Blow his stinkin' head off! Shoot the son-of-a-bitch!! Blow his punkin' head off!"

It was Judge Amos Burgwyn, hands cupped around his mouth as if cursing a basketball referee.

"Quick! Shoot the son-of-a-bitch!!"

Johnny Wayne turned toward his right and the shouting voice. As he did, Eddie eyes rolled up and he slid down, dizzy and in his mind dying from a cut throat. His weight brought Johnny Wayne with him as he descended and melted into a dazed, sitting position. At least a dozen deputies, guns aimed, shouted, "Don't do it, Johnny Wayne! Freeze! Don't do it! Freeze!!! Freeze!!!!"

Johnny Wayne's sense of survival trumped. He dropped the jagged can and smiled into the crowd. His hands were up, and he slowly raised himself. Before he could fully stand, he was pig-piled on by no less than eight deputies, thrown to his belly onto the asphalt, and held still by sets of arms and hands. With his arms jerked behind him, handcuffs were slammed on and squeezed into the tightest positions. He was jerked back up by three sets of arms and pushed with hands on his back and head toward the jail door.

Other deputies rushed to help Eddie, who was amazed to be alive, to his feet. He looked down, rubbed his throat with his left hand, and held onto a supporting deputy with his right.

"Oh God, Oh God" were his only words. His wife and children were in his mind.

Judge Burgwyn never let up. "You shoulda' shot the son-of-a-bitch, Sheriff. You shoulda shot him."

Johnny Wayne's mind paralleled His Honor's. "I should've killed him," he was thinking. "We should both be in hell right now."

Chapter 38

"Lots of people want to ride with you in the limo, but what you want is someone who will take the bus with you when the limo breaks down."

Oprah Winfrey

Judge Burgwyn, so openly in favor of the public execution of Johnny Wayne Fulcher in the jailhouse parking lot, insisted that procedure be closely followed in the selection of an attorney to work as co-counsel with Bob Lee Pender in lieu of Eddie Griggs. Gerry Wiles let Bob Lee know he would oppose a mere oral motion given in open court by Eddie Griggs to withdraw as Fulcher's attorney. He insisted that a written Motion to Withdraw be filed by Eddie specifying a justifiable reason, in this case that a jagged can had been held to his neck by his client, to be relieved of responsibilities as attorney for Fulcher so an appellate court could not later rule that Fulcher had been denied effective counsel against his wishes.

The written record revealed Eddie's motion declared that "for unstated but specific reasons not herein enumerated the undersigned counsel and defendant are no longer able to work effectively together on the defendant's defense, and the defendant himself has requested that the undersigned withdraw as his counsel of record" as justification and cause for his withdrawal as counsel for the defendant.

Griggs' verified motion was properly filed, placed in Fulcher's court file and, after proper service and five-days' notice, Gerry Wiles, Eddie Griggs, Bob Lee Pender, and Fulcher stood in the Superior Court courtroom before Judge Burgwyn. Counselors Wiles, Griggs, and Pender appeared in their usual attire of coat and tie, while Fulcher was led into the courtroom in his usual orange jump suit and jailhouse flip flops. This time both of his wrists and feet were shackled.

After Wiles and Griggs recited the reasons for the hearing so the Court Reporter could enter them into the record, Judge Burgwyn asked Eddie Griggs if he had anything to add in addition to his verified motion. After Griggs responded "No, Your Honor," Judge Burgwyn asked Johnny Wayne Fulcher if he objected to Eddie Griggs's motion to withdraw as his attorney of record. Fulcher replied he had no objection to anything "but calling Eddie Griggs an attorney."

Judge Burgwyn then asked the Clerk for the name of the next attorney on the Capital list. The Clerk opened her notebook, looked down while lowering her glasses to her nose, and responded that Craig Emory Fitts, Esquire, appeared next.

Fitts, now 36 years of age, had graduated from Campbell School of Law at age 28. He was raised and schooled in eastern North Carolina and spent much of his four years as a United States Marine in the Middle East. He married shortly after his discharge from the Corps, enrolled and graduated from the University of North Carolina in Wilmington, and then spent three years earning his law degree at the Campbell University School of Law in Buies Creek, North Carolina. Craig and his wife had considered Craig's education a team effort that required both to work during Craig's college and law school days, but now an appreciative Craig was happy to be the sole breadwinner while his wife reveled in the care of their three sons.

Fitts had stayed in solid shape after leaving the Corps, looked everyone he conversed with straight in the eye, and kept his hair cropped short. He was a self-assured, no-nonsense, straight-in-your-face, tough bird with a quick mind. Johnny Wayne Fulcher would have had a rough, if not impossible, time convincing Craig to go down the elevator with a jagged drink can to his neck. Fitts would have taken his chances upstairs. He feared few men and would not have hesitated to fight Fulcher, even "in a phone booth." In a fair fight Fitts would have outlasted Fulcher easily and bested him. Fitts loved his wife and children, God, his country, his dog, guns, smokeless tobacco, and professional wrestling, in that order.

Fitts' legal experience was, at the very least, adequate. He began his career as an assistant district attorney working as an underling to his mentor Gerry Wiles. He prosecuted for the most part misdemeanor cases in District Court and assisted in guilty pleas in Superior Court. Fitts' aggressive personality made him a favorite of law enforcement officers wanting zealous prosecution of commonplace cases other assistant district attorneys would tend to dismiss or plea bargain. His courtroom assertiveness was offset by a smiling and engaging personality that allowed him and defense attorneys to agree to disagree and acknowledge that all were simply earnestly doing their jobs, however contentious the circumstances.

Fitts left the security of an adequate state salary with insurance and other benefits to open his own law office in the aging downtown of Madison, a mere three miles from Mayodan.

Although Fitts had worked in the District Attorney's Office, he was not yet well known in the local community. He joined the Rotary Club and volunteered to coach a youth team at the local Boys Club. He made it a part of his daily routine to have coffee before work in the local downtown diner and engage in conversations with the retired members of the Coffee Club who bantered over taxes and politics and offered advice on everything from politics to chicken feed.

And he became a hero of sorts. A local policeman on a three-wheel scooter persistently irritated the coffee-drinkers by issuing parking tickets in the form of brown envelopes that would be deposited with the $2 fine into the slot of red container affixed to the parking meter. Fitts became known as "the man who can get things done" by generously offering to take care of the parking tickets issued to complaining coffee-drinkers or other patrons ("Here, Bob, just give me that ticket, and it'll go away."). What the locals failed to realize was that Craig was simply surreptitiously placing $2 from his own pocket into the envelopes and sliding them into the red iron boxes when no one was looking. Those $2 tickets bought him more goodwill and word-of-mouth referrals than could have been earned by a dozen billboards.

Fitts signed up for court-appointed cases and represented many of the same people he had once prosecuted as an assistant district attorney. As time passed, these clients, and their relatives, hired him for divorces, traffic tickets, land issues, and wills. Within a few years he had tried felony jury trials and argued before the North Carolina Court of Appeals and Supreme Court.

With experience, his effectiveness and results improved. Fitts had served as co-counsel on one prior capital case "won" when his client received a life sentence instead of death. He would be ready for the Fulcher case.

Hearing no objection, Judge Burgwyn recorded in open court that Craig Emory Fitts would serve as co-counsel along with Bob Lee Pender in Fulcher's defense.

Both Gerry Wiles and Bob Lee Pender were pleased Craig would be on the case. Bob Lee knew he would have a stubborn fighter with a keen intellect in his corner. Bob Lee's pace was slower, more methodical, wizened, and predicated on past experience. In contrast, Craig would ably and deftly kick box his way through the trial. It was a good combination.

Even Gerry Wiles and Johnny Wayne Fulcher continued to share the common desire that Fulcher have competent, unassailable counsel. Johnny Wayne wanted lawyers with enough vinegar to ram his innocence down the system's screaming throat. Wiles wanted attorneys for Fulcher who would supply a written record that would later indicate tireless effort, skill, and proficiency during their defense of their convicted client that was unassailable if allegations of incompetent counsel were raised.

All in all, everyone was satisfied and content as they exited the courtroom that afternoon.

The happiest, though, was poor Eddie Griggs. He had no desire ever to set his eyes on Johnny Wayne Fulcher again.

Chapter 39

"Son, there are two kinds of people in this world. There are givers. And there are takers. Be a giver!"

Concetta Crescenzo, 1930

"Mr. Pender, Ken Childrey and Tommy Austin are out here to see you."

"Go ahead and send them on back, Ida."

Detective Ken Childrey followed Tommy Austin into Bob Lee's office. Bob Lee stood and greeted both of them, saying he was glad to see them again and motioning for them to have a seat as he circled around behind his desk. He had no idea why the two of them were together.

"I've got to ask both of you the same question. What are you two doing here in my office? Apparently something to do with the Fulcher case, Ken?"

Ken nodded.

"Yeah, Bob Lee, it does. Tommy has mentioned something to me, and it may or not be important."

"So what is it, Ken?," asked Bob Lee.

"Tommy and I bumped into each other at the John Deere dealership the other day. I knew Tommy used to ride his Harley with J.W. Fulcher and the Bee every once in a while, so I asked him if he might know anything about the case that might be of interest. I told him I was working for you, and Tommy had a lot of nice comments to make about you, and he said something that caught my ear."

Ken took a breath.

"Bob Lee, do you remember the report on the measurements of the Fulcher house I sent you? Better yet, do you remember the comment I made about the Bee calling herself 'Mrs. Fulcher'?

Bob Lee nodded.

"Keep that in mind, Bob Lee. Something did come up when I was talking to Tommy and, well, Bob Lee, I'll let you decide for yourself. You've known Tommy longer and better than I have, so let's get Tommy to tell you for himself."

Bob Lee had liked Tommy since the first time he met him. How they met is worth mentioning.

About seven years earlier Tommy had waddled into Bob Lee's office as bowlegged as if he'd ridden into town a Texas mule. He had been charged with the felonious assault of a female named Amanda Jane Reece. According to the warrant he had allegedly reduced the number of teeth in her head by five. Bob Lee asked Tommy what had happened.

"Well, Mr. Pender, it went this way. Me and Amanda Jane have been seeing each other for over two years. We've never had any cross words or an argument. We tried to court the proper way, Sir, so we never, uh, you know, uh, consummated our relationship, so to speak. We were going to wait until after we got married, Sir."

"That's really nice of you, Tommy." Bob Lee smiled, hoping Tommy would relax a little bit.

"So, Mr. Pender, last Friday night Amanda Jane came over to the house to eat a pizza and listen to music. We hung around for a while and opened a bottle of that wine from Portugal called Mateus. You know Mateus, don't you, Mr. Pender, that wine that comes in those funny-shaped bottles? The top don't screw on. It's got a cork."

Bob Lee nodded.

"So Amanda Jane and I started on a second bottle, and I put on some Johnny Mathis. I know Johnny Mathis sounds homosexual, Mr. Pender, but Amanda Jane and I like his music."

Tommy's mind had transported him back to the moment. He smiled.

"So where'd this warrant come from, Tommy?"

"I'm gettin' there, Mr. Pender. I'm gettin' there… One urge led to another, and, well, Mr. Pender, I had a real bad desire to go ahead and consummate our relationship. Nature is nature, you know."

Bob Lee smiled.

"But this was my Amanda Jane, so I asked her about it. She said it wouldn't be right, but that maybe we could compromise just a little bit and still be within the bounds of what's holy."

"Compromise? What do you mean?" Bob Lee asked as he adjusted his seating position.

Tommy looked down at his hands. He was embarrassed to say.

"You don't know what I mean, Sir?," he asked.

The thespian in Bob Lee rose to the moment.

"I *think* I may have heard of that before, Tommy. Yes, I'm sure. I *have* heard of that. Go ahead, Son."

"But she still just couldn't do it. So she asked me if I would mind dippin' it in a jar of ranch dressing just to make it, uh…"

"More… palatable?"

"That's just the word, Mr. Pender. *Palatable.*" Tommy was relieved. He smiled and nodded once. He knew his lawyer understood.

"Well, Tommy, ranch dressing just seemed like a good solution… we are from the South, after all."

There was a pause.

"So what does this story have to do with…?"

"As I said, everything was going just fine when all of a sudden, she chomped down on me. Chomped down like an alligator tryin' to chunk down a chicken!"

Tommy held both arms straight out with his right hand directly over his left hand. His hands came down in guillotine fashion and clapped.

"Let me tell you, Mr. Pender, in an emergency situation like that, there wasn't much time to think. In just a second, like a reflex, as quick as a whip, I balled up my fist and swung as hard as I could."

"And?"

"Well, Mr. Pender, when my fist was about two inches from the side of her head, I realized I was in the midst of a grievous mistake. A *grievous* mistake, Sir."

Bob Lee liked the way Tommy stretched out the words "A… Grievous… Mistake."

"When my fist hit her, it was right in the jaw. Her head shot off me like a golf ball, Mr. Pender. The bad thing, the most awful thing, was she still had a hold of me, Mr. Pender. Real hard. Like a barracuda or a shark or something."

Tommy looked down in the direction of his crotch, nodding his head left and right.

"I thought I had died and gone to hell. I looked down, and it was hanging by a string. Just a string. It was pitiful, Mr. Pender."

"What about Amanda Jane?"

"She was on the floor rolling around, spitting out teeth and checking on the rest. She lost five teeth by the time it was all over. We were both in a mess there on the floor. Blood and ranch dressing all over the couch, the table, the carpet. You'd have thought a 'coon got in the window and took ahold of us."

"So who called the Sheriff?"

"Not me, Mr. Pender," Tommy explained. "I didn't need no law. I needed a medical team. And a good one. Like from the Mayo Clinic or that hospital Marlo Thomas runs. So I called 911 and told them to send the fastest ambulance they could. They came and took us both to the hospital. I ended up in surgery in Winston-Salem."

Tommy's looked up at Bob Lee.

"The bottom line is, Mr. Pender, they put me under and sewed it back on. But I'll be honest, Mr. Pender, it's a mess. It points South when I walk West. Don't know if it will ever work like it used to."

"And the warrants?"

"Deputies were called to the hospital, and they took pictures of Amanda Jane, and the warrants were issued, Mr. Pender. I just couldn't help what I did, Sir. It was reflex."

Bob Lee eventually had the charges against Tommy dismissed after convincing the Judge at the probable cause hearing that it had been a matter of self-defense and that a little "jury nullification" was in order. Tommy had suffered enough.

It really hadn't been that difficult a case for Bob Lee to resolve. The Judge and assistant district attorney had been sympathetic. On the other hand, Tommy never forgot that he had been able to walk out of the courtroom that day because of Bob Lee, even if it had been with bowed legs.

And, as it turned out, Amanda Jane and Tommy got back together and married.

They hadn't had kids, though.

So that's how Bob Lee and Tommy first knew each other. And when Ken Childrey brought him into his office and told him that Tommy knew something, Bob Lee could bank on Tommy's story being true.

"So what do you want to tell me, Tommy?, " asked Bob Lee in the voice of an old friend.

"Well, Bob Lee, I really don't know what it means as far as your case is concerned, but Ken here seems to think it might mean something. Not last Spring, but the Spring before, about five of us got our wives and girlfriends and went to Bike Week down in Myrtle Beach. On the way down, we stopped at Little River for a fill-up and a stretch and, lo' and behold, there was the Bee working behind the counter in the Zippy Pik. I always did like that Bumblebee she has, Bob Lee. Ever notice it?"

Bob Lee smiled.

"Yeah, Tommy, I think I might have noticed it before. Not exactly my taste, though."

Tommy went on.

"Well, Bob Lee, it was like Old Home Week. Everybody knew the Bee and got a hug. She's gettin' big, you know that, Bob Lee? Used to be a hottie, but Lord, she's really been spending time at the trough. Anyway, I looked down and the Bee was wearing a wedding band and a name tag that said 'Misty Fulcher,' so I asked her if she and Johnny Wayne had finally tied the knot. She said 'I guess you could say that' and told me J.W. was helping out on a sick uncle's shrimp boat until he got better. Nobody had seen them for a while, so I asked her how long they had been there, and she told me they had lived there in Little River for four months and might be home in a month or two. I told the Bee we were staying at the Sun Surf Hotel on 38th North Boulevard and said she and Johnny Wayne ought to come join us for the Bike Weekend."

Tommy had the habit of using his hands to explain as he talked. That day was no exception.

"So, sure enough, she and Johnny Wayne showed up and partied with us and spent the next night at the hotel along with the rest of us. I made it my business not to drink too much around them because, you know, both of them can get mean. We left the next morning after eating at the Pancake House. I reckon they did come home before too long because the next time I saw them was at TapATop Bar a few months later along with a group of bikers from around here. But the Bee wasn't wearing a wedding band so I didn't ask her or Johnny Wayne nothing about it."

Tommy stopped.

"And, well, Bob Lee, that's about it. Ken wanted me to tell you that. I don't know why, but he wanted me to tell you that. Said it might be important."

Bob Lee nodded that it was indeed important. He had a question.

"Tommy, how many of you were there? How many people were in your group on bikes traveling together when you and the Bee were talking?"

"Well, Bob Lee, there would have been about eight of us there. I'd bet two would have been in the bathroom, so I'd guess eight. I don't know if everybody heard everything and circled their calendars and all because of what they heard, but I'd say eight."

Bob Lee slowly rose. His mind was rapidly reviewing what he had just heard.

"Tommy, could you wait outside in the waiting room for just a few minutes? I need to discuss some business with Ken. I'll have Ida bring you a Coca-Cola if you'd be so kind. And thank you, Tommy, for coming down here today and being so candid with me. I really appreciate you, Tommy. And before I forget it, tell Amanda Jane I send my kind regards, will you?"

"Sure, Bob Lee. It's always nice to see you, Mr. Pender. And God Bless," Tommy answered, rising and closing the door as he left the room.

When Tommy exited, Ken Childrey spoke up.

"Bob Lee, I don't know if it means anything, but out of the blue the Bee called herself 'Mrs. Fulcher' to me in her yard, and then Tommy tells me she called herself 'Mrs. Fulcher' down there in South Carolina. I don't know if it has a doggone thing to do with this case, Bob Lee, but it just sounded kind of odd to me, for some reason."

Ken reached up and scratched his head.

"I thought you should know. I've checked the Register of Deeds for five counties around us and the folks down in Raleigh, and Johnny Wayne and the Bee have never been issued a marriage license. The folks in Raleigh at the Bureau of Vital Statistics swear there's nothing to indicate they were ever married in North Carolina. After I talked to Tommy, I checked with the Bureau of Vital Statistics in South Carolina, and in Horry County, to see if they had been married in South Carolina. No dice. Never married there, either. I hope I'm not wasting time and money, Bob Lee, but I thought you should know. It just seems strange. And it might not matter at all as far as you're concerned."

Bob Lee spoke up.

"Good job, Ken. You're right, it may or may not mean anything. But here's what I want you to do, Ken. First, I want you to double-check with the South Carolina county and state offices to make sure one way or the other if Johnny Wayne and the Bee were ever issued a marriage license."

Ken was taking notes on a small pad he had taken from inside his coat pocket. Bob Lee continued, but spoke lower after he noticed Ken taking notes.

"I want you to run down those eight folks Tommy's talking about and get a statement from each of them detailing what they might remember about the Bee and Johnny Wayne being married. See if any of them remember the wedding band or name tag."

Ken was writing as fast as he could.

"Then I want you to go down to Little River and find out what you can from down there. See if you can get any employment records from the Zippy Pik Tommy referred to that indicate whether or not the Bee was married."

Bob Lee spun his Wake Forest College class ring on his finger as he thought of the next instruction.

"Check with the South Carolina Department of Motor Vehicles and see if any cars were registered or driver's licenses issued in the Bee's last name. Check on leases. Snoop around and see if you have any sources that might indicate whether or not either of them filed an income tax return in South Carolina that year. Do all that and more, okay, Ken? Just find out."

Ken was curious.

"So what are you shooting for, Bob Lee? Exactly where are you headed with this investigating?"

Bob Lee stood and dropped his legal pad on his desk. He squinted as he tapped his pen on the pad three times.

"I'm not positive, Ken. Just find out one way or the other if they were married by a preacher or justice of the peace or not. Once I know that, I'll be able to determine the ramifications, okay?"

Bob Lee moved toward his door, looking back at Ken.

"Let me step out here and thank my buddy Tommy again, Ken. He's been through more than you and I will ever know."

Chapter 40

"He who wants a rose

must respect the thorn."

Persian proverb

Craig Fitts had known of Bob Lee Pender before his first day at work as an assistant district attorney. Bob Lee's reputation had preceded their introduction to each other. Most of their encounters were within the courtroom proper, and as cases were tried and time passed Craig began mentally to distance himself from the surroundings of the courtroom and study the sources of Bob Lee's effectiveness. He learned that Bob Lee's strengths lay not in his particular knowledge of the law, which was extensive, but in the basic nature of his character.

Bob Lee had qualities not learned in classrooms or books. They spawned from life experiences and most importantly, from his descent of two honest and loving parents. He was sincere, well-read, respectful, and practical. Bob didn't demand. He appealed to people's better natures and brought them to the place where common values were shared. Judges and juries were comfortable with his countenance of simple goodness and understanding when Bob explained human failings so universal among God's children.

Years of human interaction in and out of the courtroom resulted in a sixth sense that more often than not detected deceit and half-truths from the witness stand. Attempted perjury resulted in sincere inflections in Bob Lee's voice conveying indignation such an offense could occur after a Bible-given oath in a hallowed courtroom. Judges and juries observing this good man's infuriated reaction to such disrespect could not help concluding that the witness must have been lying.

And, when he explained the law to Judges, they listened. They were aware that Bob Lee knew the law.

Fitts called Bob Lee's office the day after his appointment to the Fulcher case. He anticipated the Fulcher case, coupled with working with Bob Lee, was going to be a heck of a ride.

After stopping by Eddie Griggs's office to pick up Eddie's file on Johnny Wayne Fulcher, Fitts headed to Bob Lee's for their initial meeting of trial preparation. The two of them agreed Bob Lee would retain his previously assigned roles and that Craig would simply step into Eddie's shoes.

After all, Eddie had already prepared much of the jury selection material and researched a large portion of the search and seizure issues.

Jury selection was set for less than a month away. Bob Lee and Craig agreed to meet at 10:30 the next morning to pay Johnny Wayne a visit at the jail.

The two met at Bob Lee's office and rode to the jail in Bob Lee's Chrysler. They entered the jail vestibule, signed in as procedure required, waited until steel doors were unlocked and squeaked open, and rode the elevator to the second floor. When the elevator door opened neither Bob Lee nor Craig assumed that they would wait for Johnny Wayne in the lawyer's conference room. They would let Johnny Wayne go in first this time.

Jack brought Johnny Wayne to the conference room door. Johnny Wayne was dressed in his usual orange jumpsuit and wearing the same flip flops. He wore shackles on both his hands and feet. Jail had not been kind to him. He was, if it were possible, even more unattractive as a human being than when he had been arrested. He had grown paler as each day passed, and an atrophy caused by the lack of daily walking and unintended exercise seemed to have set in on his arms and facial muscles despite a starchy diet. His mullet was longer and his teeth even fuzzier and more yellow. He gave an initial impression to Craig of being withdrawn and possibly even beaten.

Jack spoke up and motioned toward the handcuffs and shackles.

"We're going to let Johnny Wayne wear all of that jewelry he's wearing on his hands and feet today, Gentlemen. Now Johnny Wayne, you go in first and have a seat. I'll send Bob Lee and Craig in when you're settled."

Johnny Wayne shuffled to the clink of his shackles into the conference room, sat in the orange plastic chair between the table and back wall, and rested his elbows on the table. Bob Lee entered, followed by Craig, and both stood above Johnny Wayne. Johnny Wayne eyes rose and he sized up Craig. He leaned forward in his chair, balled his fists, and his chest bucked up, just a little.

Sensing this, Craig Fitts spoke up.

"Now Johnny Wayne, or J.W., or Shithead, or Candypants, or whatever they call you, you don't know me, but I'm Craig Fitts and I was appointed to represent you in place of Eddie Griggs. I want you to know that I am *not* Eddie Griggs."

Fitts had emphasized the word "not." His voice rose.

"So get your elbows off that table right now. You hear me, Candypants? Get your filthy elbows off that table, sit up straight like a good boy, and look me straight in the face."

Johnny Wayne was silent. He removed his elbows, sat up in the chair, and looked into Craig's eyes.

Craig continued.

"Now J.W., I'm here to help Mr. Pender defend you. I'm helping him help you. We might not like you, J.W., but, speaking for myself, I like to win. I like to win my cases. Call it youthful exuberance or competitiveness. I don't give a rat's ass. But you're not going to mess me up on that, you hear me, Shit-for-Brains?"

Craig Fitts' and Johnny Wayne Fulcher's eyes were locked.

"I'm going to do everything I can within the law to win this case, not because I like you or because you're innocent, but because I like to win."

Fitts leaned and pointed his finger at Johnny Wayne's face.

"And you're going to do everything you can to help me do that, J.W. You got that? It's not about you right now, J.W., it's about me and Mr. Pender. We like to win."

Johnny Wayne liked what he was hearing. He started to lean forward, smiling.

"No, J.W., don't you lean forward. You lean back, and you listen to me on this one."

Fitts pointed and Johnny Wayne leaned back. Then Fitts placed his elbows on the table and spoke in a near whisper.

"Johnny Wayne, if you so much as twitch, if you so much as pass gas or burp, I'm going to beat the shit out of you. Right here in this little room. Now you may be thinking you can kick my ass, but I'm not thinking the same about you, Johnny Wayne."

A short moment passed.

"What I'm thinking is different. I'm thinking I can kill you, Johnny Wayne."

Fitts continued, his voice softening. The faces were less than a foot apart, with eyes of each riveted on the other.

"Let's see whose expectations we meet, if you want to, Johnny Wayne, yours or mine. I'll get Mr. Pender to stand back and near the door."

Bob Lee remained silent, transfixed by what he was observing.

"Nobody's going to call the deputies in here for help. That door's going to stay shut and I'm going to beat the hell out of you in those shackles and handcuffs you're wearing with my bare hands, Little Boy, until you're dead. I can do that, Johnny Wayne. I've beaten men who could make you their boy toy, J.W., and I'll do you in a heartbeat."

This talk was no threat. It was a promise.

"I'm no Eddie Griggs, J.W... Eddie's a nice man who didn't deserve what you did to him. I'm not nice when certain things happen, so don't you even think of it. You'll be blessed if they'll wheel you into that courtroom in a wheelchair, Johnny Wayne, I swear to God you will."

Fitts now spoke to Johnny Wayne like a child, telling him what to do.

"So just sit there and shut up unless we ask you something, and let us win your case, Johnny Wayne."

Fitts voice was low, calm, and deliberate, with each word measured and sincere and spoken with firmness.

"I don't want to beat the hell out of you and have to withdraw from this case. But you push the wrong button with me, Johnny Wayne, or move the wrong way too quick, or try to get slick with me, I swear on all that's holy that I'll do just that. I'll stomp you into the ground and not look back. The Governor'll give me a medal, and I'll be sent off like a hero to Disney World. Matter of fact, I might not get that medal 'cause the Sheriff out there'll just throw your sorry rotten corpse in the swamp, and your name will never be mentioned again, not anywhere in this county or this world."

Craig leaned back in his chair and spoke louder.

"Hell, Judge Burgwyn's mad 'cause they didn't kill you... you think anyone would say anything, Johnny Wayne? Your really think that? You'll just disappear like you were never even born. Poof!"

Fitts snapped his finger and waited for effect. Johnny Wayne sat still, unwilling to challenge him. Animal instinct was telling him to be cautious of the man across the table.

"So if you're feeling froggy, Johnny Wayne, you just jump right on up. Just hop right on up, and let's get it on."

Johnny Wayne didn't move an inch. Craig paused for a moment, and his voice dropped.

"Personally, as a man you don't amount to anything to me. You're nothing but a pile of shit I have to step around. But I'll do just that to get a not-guilty verdict in this case. I'm going to do everything in my power to get that not-guilty verdict whether you like it or not and even if I have to stomp you to get it. You can go to hell as far as I'm concerned. I'm selfish. I want to win this one."

Stone cold silence. Eye-to-eye.

Craig had not just earned Johnny Wayne's respect. At this point Johnny Wayne was ready to ask the man to marry him. Craig was going to fight. He sounded personal about it. He might not be fighting for him, but he was willing to fight.

Craig stood up straight and directed his attention to Bob Lee.

"Mr. Pender, I apologize for speaking this way in front of you. I did not mean to usurp your authority in this case. I will be quiet and ask that you take over from here, if you will."

Johnny Wayne raised the two fingers on his right shackled hand as if in class. He was looking at Bob Lee.

"Mr. Pender?"

Bob Lee looked up just as Johnny Wayne continued and pointed toward Fitts.

"Yes, Johnny Wayne?" Pender asked.

"I like this man. He's gonna be okay."

Bob Lee had purposely not interrupted Craig's lecture. Although it had been unplanned and unexpected, Craig's direct talk had solidified the trio's collective goal: a verdict of not guilty.

Game on.

Chapter 41

"We believe trial judges confronted with disruptive, contumacious, stubbornly defiant defendants must be given sufficient discretion to meet the circumstances of each case."

U.S. Supreme Court Justice Hugo Black

In North Carolina Superior Court judges presided over the disposition of all felony charges and only those misdemeanor charges which had been appealed by defendants from the lower District Court. They sat and held court, generally for terms of six months at a time, in those particular counties specifically assigned to them by the North Carolina Administrative Office of the Courts in Raleigh.

Superior Court judges traveled more than District Court judges. District Court judges, who rendered judgments only in lower-value civil cases and misdemeanor and infraction cases and made initial rulings on bonds and other pretrial matters in felonies, were generally relegated to preside in the judicial districts of their election and slept in their own beds every night. In contrast, Superior Court judges traveled more throughout the state and very often spent the work week miles away from home.

It was because of the traveling nature of a Superior Court judge's employment, coupled with the fact felony cases usually drew more publicity than mundane misdemeanors, that Superior Court judges often earned statewide reputations within the legal community. The civil cases they presided over involved greater demands for money than District Court cases, and the criminal cases involved the more sensational crimes that received newspaper and television attention. Attorneys swapped opinions and stories about the propensities and biases of incoming or sitting Superior Court judges as they shopped for those traits most favorable in a judge before filing a request to have a Clerk of Superior Court calendar a case for trial.

It was under this system that Gerry Wiles learned that the venerable and aged Honorable Cletus Marcellus from Edgecombe County had been assigned to preside over criminal cases during the Spring session of Superior Court for Judicial District 17A, which included Rockingham County. He could not have been more satisfied.

Judge Marcellus graduated from the Wake Forest School of Law as a student of Dean Carroll Weathers and Dr. Robert Earl Lee. He had been elected to the Superior Court Bench after serving as the district attorney in his coastal judicial district at a time preceding the bifurcated death penalty trial system in which juries decided whether or not a death sentence was imposed. The death penalty was mandatory in first-degree murder cases at that time, and Judge Marcellus had been assigned to preside over more capital murder cases than any other judge in the State of North Carolina.

And, for reasons best understood by those who attended these trials, defendants in capital murder cases presided over by Judge Marcellus had a particularly high conviction rate. It was during sentencing after these convictions that Judge Marcellus, with a dramatic flair and theatric authority that denied room for any other thought or attention, admonished many a defendant's weeping mother that "you have had your chance, Madam, and it is too late now." He would then point his index finger directly into the eyes of the convicted murderer and, with the audience in stunned awe, slowly, and painfully, enter the death penalty of the gas chamber or the electric chair and stretch out the words "until...you...are...DEAD!!".

No person, living or deceased, had sentenced more people to death in the history of the State of North Carolina than Superior Judge Cletus Marcellus of Edgecombe County, who became known as North Carolina's "Hanging Judge."

And, much to the delight of Gerry Wiles, no Superior Court judge had fewer reversals of death sentences by the North Carolina Supreme Court than Judge Marcellus. There were reasons for this remarkable consistency.

Only one Prima Donna was allowed in Judge Marcellus' courtroom. That would be Judge Marcellus. Judge Cletus

Marcellus, with those renowned bushy white eyebrows, a piercing stare, and a booming voice punctuated with an eastern North Carolina accent. He-ah. They-ah. "They're right here" was pronounced "They-ah rite he-ah!" by the Judge.

Flashy lawyers who ordinarily dominated courtrooms knew better than to cross the judge. He ruled with an iron hand and acted as his whim desired. Any attorney with the audacity to enter Judge Marcellus's courtroom in a sport jacket, and not a formal suit, was immediately jailed for direct contempt of court. Tardiness by an attorney or witness or whispering in court were also remedied by findings of contempt. Any mannerism, movement, or pattern of speech subjectively found to be irksome could give rise to His Honor's wrath. His controlling, arbitrary presence prompted panic attacks and stuttering in veteran lawyers.

Judge Marcellus genuinely loved to preside over trials. He was the peacock in the barnyard. In theory the district attorney controlled the pace and date and scheduling of trials, with the presiding judge merely acting as referee of the proceedings. In Judge Marcellus' courtroom, there was no lapse between trials. As soon as a jury left the room to deliberate, he would demand "Call your next tri-yal, Mr. District Attorney" and another trial would commence. His constant pushing for trial after trial resulted in assistant district attorneys, defense attorneys, detectives, patrol officers, and witnesses anxiously waiting in the halls outside the courtroom for their trials to begin, often for days at a time. Judge Marcellus did not want to waste one minute of the court's time. And he did not want to waste one minute of his being in control.

He took smirking pride in the fear he instilled. It was a common practice in North Carolina for district attorneys and defense attorneys to extend the courtesy of taking visiting Superior Court judges to lunch and to invite them to social events occurring during the work week. Judge Marcellus ate lunch alone. He spent nights alone in his hotel room.

Judge Marcellus was sincerely disappointed when mandatory death sentences were outlawed and determination of whether or not a defendant was sentenced to death was transferred by the bifurcated trial system to a jury. He initially resented it as another opportunity for a guilty defendant to escape justice and as another hoop for a wronged society to jump through to attain a just verdict allowing the State to kill the son-of-a-bitch as the Bible demanded.

This resentment evolved into a self-image of himself as a White Knight, a just avenger, cloaked with moral and statutory authority to overcome this hurdle. He began using his strengths as a trial judge in such a way so as to exert what he considered to be appropriate influences on juries to achieve righteous, and, therefore, death penalty, verdicts.

Judge Marcellus was able to bear this authority on jurors with such impunity because of two personal strengths.

The first was his thorough and encyclopedic knowledge of the North Carolina trial system and procedure acquired from books and decades of experience.

The second was more basic and, to many, insidiously simple and maddening. In North Carolina, there was no audio recording of what went on in a courtroom. Every word uttered by a witness, attorney, judge, or bailiff on the record was typed—transcribed—by a court reporter who generally sat within feet of the witness stand straddling a device that resembled a typewriter with fewer keys that typed in shorthand—a transcription machine. Since everything was typed and not heard on audio, voice *inflections* were non-existent in any record reviewed by the North Carolina Court of Appeals or the North Carolina Supreme Court.

Judge Marcellus developed an insidious talent for inflecting his voice into the written record in such a way that the most threatening, outrageous, and suggestive statements read as absolutely proper and in order in the written record of court proceedings. Any word or phrase, whether "Sir," "Ma'am," "Thank you," "Proceed," or "Answer the question," could be spoken with kindness or with opposite fierceness and the personal opinion of the speaker conveyed to the listener in such a manner as to influence opinions.

Judge Marcellus was well aware that inflection of voice was not reflected in written transcription. He became a master of expressing his opinion by nuances his voice carried while, at the same time, he remained acutely cognizant of the content of each word of his speech to protect the written record from attack in the event of appellate review.

For example, during jury instructions Marcellus would roll his eyes and quickly read the defendant's contentions in a boring monotone, but when he arrived at the contentions of the State, each word, with force and effect, would be stressed and enunciated with direct eye contact and such emotion that Judge Marcellus' unvarnished opinion of the defendant's guilt was clearly relayed to the jury. He could insidiously bait any witness and attorney who fell into his mercurial disfavor into whatever situation he preferred in what appeared to be the most gentlemanly way in the written record. And yet, when a death sentence was appealed to the North Carolina Supreme Court, the *written record* of comments and instructions, devoid of intonation of voice, indicated utter impartiality with absolutely no favoritism or opinion of Judge Cletus Marcellus.

Gerry Wiles was happy Judge Marcellus would be holding court during the term in which the Fulcher trial would take place. He knew that by simply being in the courtroom even he would be subjected to torment, aggravation, pressure, and threats from The Hanging Judge. There would be unnecessary stress and the need for silent, disciplined toleration.

And to think that he represented the State! Pity the poor defense, Wiles thought. He believed that by downing Tums and suffering through the anxiety, abuse, and diarrhea caused by Judge Marcellus it would all be worth it in the end. He would be on his home field, with the bases loaded against Johnny Wayne Fulcher, before a Judge who would typically umpire most calls--even if they weren't that close---the State's way.

He could not have asked for better odds.

Chapter 42

"Monkeys are superior to men in this: when a monkey looks into a mirror, he sees a monkey."

Malcolm De Chazal

Both Judge Cletus Marcellus and Johnny Wayne Fulcher felt provoked the first time they shared a mutual presence. Each sensed an uncomfortable familiarity with the other. This initial introduction occurred in the Superior Court courtroom of the Rockingham County Courthouse during the May session as set by the North Carolina Administrative Office of the Courts. Even by courtroom standards, it was riveting. Potential jury members had not yet been allowed into the courtroom on that sunny morning.

Two conspicuous onlookers were in the courtroom. Jamie Watson, U.S. Attorney Timothy Herndon's assistant, sat on the third row with yellow notepad and pen in hand. Also present and sitting in the fifth row was Sheriff Bailey's aide and confidante, Deputy Arnie Robertson.

Judge Marcellus had plopped into his seat on the bench, opened court, and directed the bailiff to bring the defendant into the courtroom. Assistant District Attorney Gerry Wiles rose from behind the prosecution's table while Bob Lee Pender and Craig Fitts stood behind the defense table when two deputies led the shackled and handcuffed Johnny Wayne through the side door toward his attorneys.

At the insistence of his counsel, Fulcher had been allowed a haircut before the trial was to begin. Fulcher was also permitted to wear a blue suit, shirt, tie, belt, and shoes Craig Fitts had purchased at Goodwill Industries. It was like putting lipstick on a pig. Johnny Wayne Fulcher would remain an unattractive, intimidating hulk with an obvious mean countenance no matter what the attire. His greasy hair spiked from his head, and his pale skin appeared almost cadaverous from a deprivation of sunlight during the incarceration since his arrest. His appearance was startling, even frightening.

Judge Marcellus had heard of Fulcher's escape attempt and was curious about the miscreant's demeanor. He immediately determined that a jury would sense Fulcher's clothing had been no more than a futile attempt to make him more presentable. Fulcher had heard jailhouse tales of The Hanging Judge's reputation and doubted he would get a fair trial.

When their eyes met, the courtroom was pervaded with the intensity of two fighting cocks, oblivious to their surroundings, being held nose to nose by handlers in a ring. They glared at each other as the deputies methodically unchained Fulcher beside his defense counsel.

The unspoken difficulties between the two lay in their similarities. Both were insecure bullies. Neither minded killing other people. Both were cold at heart.

Judge Marcellus spoke.

"Madam Clerk, please let the record reflect that court has opened outside the presence of the jury pool. Present is Assistant District Attorney Charles Wiles of the 15th District's District Attorney's Office. Also present are attorneys Robert Lee Pender and Craig Fitts of the North Carolina State Bar, along with the Defendant in the case of State of North Carolina versus Johnny Wayne Fulcher, a/k/a J.W. Fulcher. Counselors Pender and Fitts, I ask that you have your client take a seat and that he remain seated unless advised by this Court otherwise. It is my sole intent that Mr. Fulcher has a fair trial in which justice is served."

The Judge stressed the words "justice is served" and smirked toward Fulcher.

He couldn't help himself. He went on.

"Yessir, I will do everything in my power to assure that justice is *appropriately and properly served* in this trial and that Mr. Fulcher gets the fair trial he *deserves*."

Another smile appeared beneath those bushy eyebrows directed straight at Fulcher. Silence. The four eyes were locked.

Fulcher started to growl.

"Why you old son-of-a-bitch...I've heard about you. You ain't gonna do that to me, you bastard..."

Fulcher had been effectively baited. Marcellus had found it easy. Deputies descended toward Fulcher.

"Mr. Fulcher," the Judge thundered as he hefted himself forward from behind the bench, "you are hereby admonished and held in direct criminal contempt of court. I sentence you to thirty days in the county jail and direct that you be bound and gagged until further order of this court so proceedings may continue without further interruption."

Judge Marcellus's eyes left Fulcher long enough to turn to the Clerk.

"Madam Clerk, let the record show that all of the defendant's behavior and this court's ruling have taken place outside the presence of the jury venire. I hereby direct the deputies to remove Mr. Fulcher from this courtroom and to return him in ten minutes, *bound and gagged*. Court is adjourned for ten minutes."

Bob Lee dared not address the Judge. Craig Fitts took over. He leaned toward Fulcher and carefully whispered.

"Johnny Wayne, it's me, Johnny Wayne. It's Craig. Now listen, J.W." Fitts placed his left arm on Johnny Wayne's right shoulder and began patting it. He could hear Fulcher breathing. "You gotta keep cool. Just do as these nice deputies say, Johnny Wayne. We'll take care of it, Johnny Wayne. You gotta believe me. Just do what the deputies say."

Johnny Wayne glanced over toward Craig.

"That wall-eyed son-of-a-bitch."

Craig tried to soothe him.

"You're right, Johnny Wayne, but just go with these nice deputies." Craig placed his right hand on the defense table and rose with his left on Johnny Wayne's shoulder. "Here, I'll go with you. Let's go together, J.W."

Ten minutes later all counsel rose when Judge Marcellus re-entered the courtroom. All but Johnny Wayne Fulcher, who sat, shackled and gagged in the seat between Bob Lee and Craig.

Bob Lee stood.

"May I be heard, Your Honor?"

Judge Marcellus gave him permission to proceed.

"Your Honor, if it please the Court, I stand to apologize to this Court on behalf of my client. As you can see, and as the record has reflected, my client is bound and gagged because of inappropriate comments to this Court. I ask this Court to empathize with the emotions and stress of circumstance peculiar to all but a few. Mr. Fitts and I have spoken with Mr. Fulcher and received his permission for me to extend his full and sincere apologies to this Court."

Johnny Wayne's neck twitched. But he remained still.

"I say on behalf of Mr. Fulcher that he is sorry, that he regrets what was said, and that there will be no further inappropriate remarks."

Bob Lee had stroked the Judge. He had acknowledged that the Judge was in control. Bob Lee then appealed to his intellect.

"I might also remind the Court, if I may, that the jury pool will be entering this courtroom for jury selection, and their viewing Mr. Fulcher bound and gagged may cause an inappropriate influence in this case, Your Honor. The jury pool's first impression and view of Mr. Fulcher, who is by law presumed innocent, will be of a person bound and gagged in the courtroom. Such an appearance conveys a sense of guilt, Your Honor, when he should be, and is by law, presumed innocent. As Mr. Fulcher's attorney I simply ask that he be introduced to the jury in the frame of what our law provides, and that is as an innocent man. Our forefathers fought for the right to be presumed innocent at trial, Your Honor, and we all recognize that the presumption of innocence is the cornerstone of our judicial system. Mr. Fulcher maintains his innocence and does not want to be unfairly prejudiced by such a biased introduction."

Bob Lee then went for the jugular. Everything he had already argued had appealed to Marcellus' ego and logic. Now he appealed to the Judge's greatest trepidation, his fear of the humiliation of having a lengthy trial resulting in a death sentence overturned because of an error on his part.

"On the other hand, and I do not intend to speak for Assistant District Attorney Wiles, I do not think the State would want to have to defend this issue in an appellate court in the unfortunate event Mr. Fulcher is, in our opinion, wrongly convicted."

The only argument that resonated with Judge Marcellus was the last. He didn't want Johnny Wayne Fulcher's conviction and sentence of death to be overturned by the North Carolina Supreme Court because of prejudicial error. Having Fulcher's initial introduction to the jury in a bound and gagged condition would probably constitute such error, particularly in light of the fact there would be no explanation to the jury about why he had been bound and gagged. Marcellus might have been able to get by with the binding and gagging if Fulcher acted up in front of the jury. But probably not away from it.

It simply wasn't worth the risk to Marcellus. And, best of all, he had made his point with Fulcher. It was he who was looking down from the bench at Fulcher, and Fulcher who had to look up to see him. He could talk down to Fulcher, and Fulcher couldn't even speak with the gag stuffed in that filthy mouth of his.

Marcellus believed he had won. As always.

Judge Marcellus picked up where Bob Lee ended and spoke directly to him. He did not give Gerry Wiles the opportunity to respond. He spoke almost kindly.

"Mr. Pender, I accept Mr. Fulcher's heartfelt apology and acknowledge the stressful nature of these proceedings.

The sentence of 30 days for direct contempt of court will remain in effect. I cannot countenance such behavior, even in light of an apology. I represent our judicial system in this room and cannot by the mandates of my oath allow such disrespect."

The Judge paused to let his words take effect.

"I am going to order removal of the shackles and gagging as follows: Before the jury pool enters this courtroom, I am going to ask the deputies to remove the shackles and gagging from Mr. Fulcher. Not now, but before the jury pool enters the courtroom."

Judge Marcellus had taken care of Fulcher's past transgression. Then he addressed future decorum in the courtroom.

"I am also going to formally admonish Mr. Fulcher and remind him that no further outbursts of any nature whatsoever will be allowed. No noise, no sighs, no distracting gestures. Any such outbursts by anyone in this courtroom, particularly Mr. Fulcher, will result in this Court exercising its contempt powers as by law provided. And, if need be for purposes of completing this trial, I will consider appropriate remedies, including further binding and gagging to effectuate that goal. We are going to have a fair trial for Mr. Fulcher, and it cannot be interrupted because emotions cannot be controlled. Is there anything else, Mr. Pender?"

"No, Your Honor," Bob Lee responded. "We thank you. We thank the court for its understanding. For clarification, Your Honor, may Mr. Fulcher be unbound now so we can confer with him during the rest of this morning's proceedings?"

Judge Marcellus almost barked his response, but protected the record with a crafted response.

"Mr. Pender, you will remember what I just announced in clear and uncertain terms. I stated that before the jury pool enters this room, I will order the removal of the shackles and gagging from Mr. Fulcher. I have not ordered the jury pool to enter this room yet, have I, Mr. Pender?"

His voice began its inflection... an inflection of condescending sarcasm.

"Should I check with the Clerk to see if the record indicates whether or not I have ordered the removal of Mr. Fulcher's shackles and gagging, Mr. Pender, or can you and I agree that I have not done so yet? Could you please answer my question, Mr. Pender?"

Bob Lee agreed the record would not reflect that the Judge had ordered removal of the shackles and binding from Johnny Wayne Fulcher.

Judge Marcellus continued.

"I am happy to see we are all in agreement as to the contents of the record," Judge Marcellus continued. "That being the case, I understand that the assistant district attorney has brought to this Court's attention that there are a number of motions pertaining to the parameters of the questions the assistant district attorney and defense counsel may ask potential jury members pertaining to their qualifications to serve on the jury." He looked down at the assistant district attorney. "Is that correct, Mr. Wiles? Do you and defense counsel wish for this court to rule on the parameters of the voir dire, particularly including religious and other leanings of opinion of jurors as they pertain to the death penalty?"

"Yes, Your Honor, "Gerry Wiles said as he rose, "there are such motions."

For the next two and one-half hours Johnny Wayne Fulcher sat in the courtroom, shackled with gagging in his mouth, gazing intently at Judge Cletus Marcellus. During his own comments Marcellus often looked directly back down at Fulcher and then smiled into his next sentence. And, when counsel argued positions, Marcellus took periodic breaks from the drone of argument to enjoy a stare down at the defendant trash sitting behind the table beneath him.

Each could have killed the other. Both hated what they saw in the other.

What each saw was himself.

Chapter 43

"Individuals play the game, but teams beat the odds."

US NAVY SEALS Team aphorism

As they left for the day's lunch break and entered the hallway outside the courtroom, Bob Lee Pender and Craig Fitts were greeted by a hurried introduction from Jamie Watson of the U.S. Attorney's office in Roanoke. She already had caught the eye of Fitts, a married man who remained physically and psychologically incapable of resisting mentally undressing an attractive woman, no matter where or what the circumstances.

"Mr. Pender and Mr. Fitts. My name is Jamie Watson and I work for the U.S. Attorney's Office in Roanoke for U.S. Attorney Timothy Herndon. May I have just a moment?"

Craig Fitts stepped forward.

"Why sure, Miss Watson," Craig Fitts said as he stepped forward. "It is 'Miss' Watson, is it not?" Fitts was staring directly into her eyes.

Jamie ignored him. She looked at Bob Lee.

"Mr. Pender, I'm sure you know Tim Herndon has been investigating Ricky Dean for racketeering and a number of other offenses for several years now. He's sent me down here to monitor this trial. Mr. Herndon believes Ricky Dean is being assisted in a huge drug, prostitution, and non-tax paid liquor operation with the cooperation of local law enforcement officers from Virginia into North Carolina and on to Tennessee. That includes law enforcement officers here in Rockingham County, Mr. Pender and Mr. Fitts."

"Of course, Miss Watson," Bob Lee spoke up. "We've heard those same accusations. We live in this county and don't need to have our ears close to the ground to have heard those rumors. So what does any of that have to do with us? Why are you bringing up this old information?"

Jamie got to the point.

"Carlton Purvis was killed within days of a subpoena requiring him to appear before the federal grand jury in Roanoke."

She paused, waiting for a reaction.

"I'm sure you must know that. We suspect, but cannot prove, that Purvis was killed to prevent his testifying before the grand jury. I'm sure you know that, too. Anyone involved directly or even indirectly in the murder of

Carlton Purvis for that reason would not only be guilty of murder, but also of obstruction of justice and depriving Carlton Purvis of his constitutional right to life. Federal offenses."

Bob Lee was ready to leave.

"Miss Watson, we're trying Mr. Fulcher's murder case here in the state courts of North Carolina. That is the location where are our efforts are directed, and nowhere else. Are you offering us some kind of assistance in the defense of Mr. Fulcher?"

Jamie's attention was directed solely toward Bob Lee. Fitts had pissed her off and creeped her out.

"We suspect local law enforcement here in Rockingham County might be connected to the killing of Carlton Purvis. This suspicion is based primarily on coincidence, Mr. Pender and Mr. Fitts. We don't have anything definite or hard to prove that. Suspicion, but more than we believe to be mere conjecture."

Craig Fitts interrupted her.

"Miss Watson, Mr. Pender has told you we're here to try the Johnny Wayne Fulcher case. Our sole intention is to have Mr. Fulcher's innocence affirmed. We're really not worried about Mr. Herndon or Ricky Dean or any other people in the world but Mr. Fulcher right now. What does any of this have to do with our client's innocence?"

Her eyes didn't waver. She accepted his stare-down challenge.

"It looks like they may have a good case against your client, Mr. Fitts. You know the State's case. Your client has told you what he knows, if anything, about Carlton Purvis's murder. He may not have killed him. Or he may have acted alone. Or for Ricky Dean. Or for someone in the sheriff's department, maybe even the sheriff himself. After all, one of the skeletons found in the well was of a man who had been acquitted of child molestation."

Jamie moved on to her next point.

"Fulcher could very well be an enforcer of some sort for the Sheriff or Ricky Dean. We don't know. Or Mr. Fulcher could have been set up by someone in the sheriff's department. The point is, gentlemen, we in the U.S. Attorney's office don't know. What we do know, though, is that Johnny Wayne Fulcher might know."

Bob Lee was interested in Jamie Watson's view, but once again his lunch was being interrupted, and he wanted to leave the courthouse. Hunger eluded Fitts as he concentrated on the daylight between the open top button on Jamie's blouse and her breasts.

"Well, we do in fact know the answer to a lot of the questions you have, Miss Watson," said Bob Lee, unperturbed by the young lady's insistence. "And the answer is very simple. Mr. Fulcher had nothing to with Carlton Purvis's murder. Nothing at all. He was miles away and doesn't really care who was involved except to the extent that he is exonerated. He is not guilty. That being said, what exactly are you getting at, Miss Watson?"

Jamie looked at both of them. Fitts never looked up.

"Tim Herndon wants to get to the bottom of what Sheriff Bailey and Ricky Dean are doing down here in Rockingham County. We respect your attorney-client privilege. But if Johnny Wayne Fulcher is truly innocent, and if he has worked for Sheriff Bailey in any form whatsoever in the past, we ask that he inform us of that fact and the extent of his efforts on the Sheriff's behalf."

She then made promises.

"We will in turn put the full force of our investigative sources to work to prove Mr. Fulcher's innocence. We will follow up on any leads he can give us. The State has the sheriff's department and SBI working against your client, gentlemen."

The plusses were adding up.

"You have a single detective. You would have the FBI working for you. An arrangement can be made to grant Mr. Fulcher immunity from federal and possibly state prosecution for anything he reveals to us."

Fitts couldn't help himself. He had little respect for the Feds. And Jamie Watson had spurned his leers and dared him to challenge.

"Isn't it a little late for that, Miss Watson. The charges have been pending for months, and you suddenly show up on the first day of the trial? Where has all this help you and the FBI are offering been all that time? And isn't that the same FBI that has already had Ricky Dean and our Sheriff arrested and convicted? Oops, I was mistaken. It must be the same investigative bunch that leaked Carlton Purvis's name to the press and got him killed. Oops, I must be right. Let's go, Bob Lee."

Bob Lee and Craig turned as if they were starting to walk away. Jamie wanted to make herself clear before they left.

"I just want you to know that the U.S. Attorney's office is very interested in this trial. It will take any help it can get from any source, particularly Mr. Fulcher, if necessary. If there is anything Mr. Fulcher knows of substance, you can use me as a conduit to Mr. Herndon to seek help or discuss some kind of deal."

Jamie glanced toward the empty courtroom.

"You want your client set free. We want Ricky Dean and his associates in jail. There may, or may not be, a commonality of interest. If there is, just let me know. That's all I wanted to say."

Bob Lee Pender found it difficult to be rude to a lady, even to a rude lady. But he was ready to leave.

"Miss Watson, I thank you for your thoughts. We will take them to heart. I cannot divulge whether or not your approaching us as you have will be discussed with our client. But I can tell you, we will keep what you have told us in mind. I hope you have a nice lunch, Miss Watson. Now, if you will excuse us..."

Chapter 44

"When you go into court, you are putting our fate into the hands of twelve people who weren't smart enough to get out of jury duty."

Norm Crosby

Bob Lee had turned the task of jury selection--voir dire-- primarily over to Craig Fitts. The court had allowed the employment of professional jury consultants, both female, and over the next two days Gerry Wiles, Craig, and Bob Lee questioned potential jurors on everything from their religion to their employment to their beliefs on the death penalty. The jury consultant for the State sat to the right of Gerry Wiles and the jury consultant for Johnny Wayne Fulcher sat between Bob Lee and Craig. Neither consultant spoke. Both passed notes of advice or opinions or simply engaged in whispered conversations during the process.

Judge Marcellus informed the jury of the nature of the charges against the defendant. He reminded the jury in his cursory way that Fulcher was presumed innocent and that they would be bound by a solemn oath to follow his instructions as a judge over their own leanings.

Each juror could look at the judge, but not into a mirror, and vow that the benefit of this reasonable doubt and the presumption of innocence was being granted Fulcher. But there were no honest denials that Johnny Wayne Fulcher, sitting in his ill-fitting suit to the right of his two defense counsel, faced the burden of proving his innocence. Whether he liked it or not, most of the jurors would never admit even to themselves that they felt in the core of their souls he was probably guilty. After all, the State wouldn't have gone to the trouble and expense to prosecute an obviously innocent man. "Let's just wait and see what the Defendant has to say about whatever evidence they produce," they would be unwilling to admit thinking, "and it'd better be good."

Assessing the leanings and biases of potential jurors was important to the litigating attorneys. Just as important was the opportunity for each potential juror to be introduced to, and determine his or her own independent impressions of, the prosecution and defense lawyers trying the case. This pivotal time was when the measure of influence over a jury of prosecuting and defense attorneys often took place.

And this intuitive sense was where Bob Lee excelled over the other attorneys. As hard as they tried to be earnest and personable, Gerry Wiles, Gerry's assistant, and Craig Fitts were unable to suppress their competitive countenances. Their airs were ingratiating, their smiles a bit slanted, their questions stilted and unnatural sounding after being read from notes.

Bob Lee, on the other hand, with his off-the-rack suit and disheveled shirt and tie, gave the impression of being a down-to-earth good man who didn't particularly want his life interrupted by his participation in a jury trial. Nonetheless, he was compelled to do so out of an innate sense of right and wrong and appeared to be making a heartfelt attempt to help each juror get to the bottom of an important matter and do right. He could have been the kindly uncle or brother of any of the jurors.

Bob Lee didn't come across as concerned about convincing jurors of anything. He conveyed a sense of interest in joining them, in assisting them, as an equal partner on a journey to the truth. The road to truth in this case would end, as Bob Lee saw it, with validation of Johnny Wayne Fulcher's innocence.

His questions were straightforward, with direct eye contact, and asked with a genuine interest in both the person and the response. His comforting approach relaxed the jurors to the point that each had the sense they were on a simple visit obligated to determine an important truth. It wasn't an act, and the jurors knew it. Bob Lee was exactly what he was and no more, exactly where he wanted to be and nowhere else, and doing what he was born to do and nothing else.

After the second day of voir dire, the jury pool of over 200 potential jurors had been culled to the magic twelve, with two alternates selected in the event one or two of the twelve became ill or unable to continue serving.

The jury in the case of State of North Carolina v. Johnny Wayne Fulcher, a/k/a J.W. Fulcher consisted of six white women, one black woman, three white males, and two black males. The alternates consisted of a black woman and a young white man. The ages ranged from 22 years to 64 years. Eleven of the fourteen were employed, and four had college degrees. Seven of the twelve attended Protestant church services on a regular basis. None would refuse to follow their oath as jurors, and all swore to follow the judge's instructions and impose the death sentence if the State proved each necessary element beyond a reasonable doubt.

The jury was impaneled after the prosecution and defense agreed upon its makeup. The jury consultants quietly left the courthouse during recess, and the twelve plus two returned to the courtroom. They were seated in two rows of seven to the immediate left of the prosecution and defense tables. The witness stand was within eight feet of the jury box and faced the counsel tables and courtroom audience.

One juror, a white, 52-year-old man with a college degree, was married and a deacon at his Presbyterian Church. He worked as an assistant plant manager at the local packaging plant. Bob Lee and Craig pegged him early on to be the jury foreman. Bob Lee and Craig agreed this juror would most likely lead the other eleven in the direction of his impressions, most probably because of his education, his appearance, and his social status. They dubbed him "The Leader" and agreed as a matter of strategy this particular juror would be the one to convince of their arguments. The Leader sat on the second row, second from the right.

A juror of less noticeable stature sat on the front row, fourth from the right. The juror was also a white man, 60 years of age, and wore suspenders and black-laced shoes with thick soles. His work-worn hands served as evidence he worked as a brick mason building chimneys. He was referred to as "The Mason" by Pender and Fitts.

The Mason spoke little, but the words he used were those of meaning. He relied upon his own integrity and an understanding of the limited honesty of others. He considered himself a charter member of his own Church of Expediency—follow the Golden Rule, but make sure you stay a step ahead of the next guy who presumably doesn't. It made his life simpler and more orderly. This understanding of human weakness extended to his seemingly contrarian business practice of asking for only a small deposit before he began construction of a chimney. The remaining balance would be due after the chimney was completed. In nearly all cases, the balance was promptly paid. Occasionally a debtor would place more immediate desires ahead of the just debt owed The Mason, but The Mason never availed himself of the services of an attorney to collect the money owed. He simply waited. Inevitably, time would pass, the weather would turn cold, and anticipation of a glowing fire to warm the debtor's home would arise. This expectation was met with disappointment when the first fire lit in the new chimney filled the house not with warmth but with bellowed smoke and soot. The indignant debtor would predictably appear at The Mason's house to complain about the faulty workmanship. The Mason's response was simple and direct. "Your chimney will never work as long as you owe me the money. It simply will not work. You can blame it on the stars or the Lord or on the fact you haven't paid a just debt. But it simply will not work until you pay what is owed." And here's where The Mason's honesty again served his purposes. They believed what he said. His reputation was one of truth. Within a day or so the debtor would scrounge up the money, and once the debt was paid and a receipt properly given, The Mason would ask the homeowner to leave his home and chimney while The Mason went to the premises to wave his magic wand to correct the situation. Arriving at the defective chimney with ladder in hand, The Mason would ascend to the top of the chimney, chuck one or two rocks or bricks down the chimney, and listen as the large pane of "insurance glass" he had secretly inserted six feet below the chimney cap during construction shattered. The fireplace magically drew as it should. The Mason had his money. All was good.

Johnny Wayne overheard his counsels' opinions and began to pay specific attention to The Leader. The Mason and other jurors were simply wall-paper in the background. As the trial was set to begin, Johnny Wayne could be seen looking down at his hands, over toward his counsel, and then toward The Leader. The Leader noticed.

The Bailiff called "Oyez, Oyez!" and the Judge appeared through the door behind his bench. All stood, were told they could sit, and the rumble of movement descended into quiet.

The Mason sat in his seat, facing forward, quiet, already seeming ready to doze.

Johnny Wayne Fulcher was set to be tried for his life.

Chapter 45

"There is no client as scary as an innocent man."

J. Michael Haller, Criminal Defense Attorney,

Los Angeles, 1962

Judge Marcellus allowed both the State and the defense to make two opening statements each to the jury. Bob Lee informed the Court only he would be making a single opening statement, and hearing this announcement Assistant District Gerry Wiles offered to do the same.

Judge Marcellus informed the jury that nothing Mr. Wiles or Mr. Pender said was evidence and each intended nothing more than to lay out their versions of what the evidence might show.

With that understanding, the first words during the prosecution of The State of North Carolina vs. Johnny Wayne Fulcher, a/k/a J.W. Fulcher were spoken by Assistant District Attorney Gerry Wiles to the impaneled jury. To the right of the State's counsel table stood the table for the defense, littered with yellow notepads, pens, and documents. Bob Lee sat to the left facing the judge's bench, with Johnny Wayne in his ill-fitting suit and Craig Fitts to the right of Bob Lee.

Gerry Wiles rose from his seat and circled around to the front of his table and faced the jury. The Leader's eyes locked with those of Wiles. The Mason watched the tip of his own left shoe tap the side of his right.

"Ladies and gentlemen of the jury..."

Wiles directed his efforts toward explaining in clarity to each juror how the evidence would show beyond a reasonable doubt that Johnny Wayne Fulcher was indeed guilty of murder of the first degree of Carlton Purvis. The horror of the murder itself, he believed, would be self-evident as the testimony and exhibits unfolded so no effort was made to inflame the jury's emotions for the time being. He instead appealed to their minds and intelligence. His statement was clear and full of explanation of how the facts proven through the State's witnesses and tangible evidence would match up with every element of the crime of first-degree murder. And, he reminded each juror, once the State had presented such clear evidence of each element of the crime, it was then each juror's solemn duty to follow the oath each had taken upon a Holy Bible and return a verdict of guilty of first degree murder against Johnny Wayne Fulcher.

It was Bob Lee Pender's turn.

Bob Lee stood before the jury without notes. Some jurors noticed his dress wasn't particularly sharp, his shoes were scuffed, and he wore an inexpensive watch. Bob Lee began simply by reminding the jury Johnny Wayne Fulcher was indeed presumed to be innocent. As his statement progressed, Bob Lee often smiled, gave a kindly stare into the eyes of each juror, and nodded his head in a positive way as he made points about the heavy burden of proof the State was obligated to meet to prove Johnny Wayne Fulcher guilty beyond a reasonable doubt of each element of first degree murder.

Pender spoke of God, their oath, and the heavy duty to follow their oath given to our Holy Maker. He reminded each juror that it would be their obligation to return a verdict of "not guilty" if he or she had not been convinced beyond a reasonable doubt from the evidence presented. A "sense" or gut feeling was insufficient. Evidence was key, he argued. Cold, hard, evidence presented to them. Not supposition. Evidence.

He was, perhaps, the only person in the courtroom who noticed almost imperceptible nodding in agreement from jurors in return. No juror had looked at his or her watch. Each juror seemed to have a connection with Bob Lee, except for The Mason, who gave no inclination of interest in anything but staying awake as he looked toward the floor. Bob Lee dared not promise the jury anything at this point. But he was not hesitant in reminding the jurors that Gerry Wiles had indeed made very strong promises of what the State would prove and pointed out that with the stakes so high that it was only fair, and only right, to hold Gerry Wiles to each promise he had made.

Bob Lee then asked the jury to follow along with him as he searched to discover where the mistake had been made that led to Johnny Wayne Fulcher, an innocent man, being charged with the murder of Carlton Purvis.

When the opening statements were completed Judge Marcellus directed his attention toward the assistant district attorney.

"Call your first witness, Mr. Wiles."

"Yes, Your Honor."

And with that exchange Gerry Wiles called his first witness, Dr. Alonzo Carver, the Rockingham County Coroner. Dr. Carver had testified in no less than seven previous murder trials. He was comfortable taking the stand and adept in the bounds and limitations evidentiary rules placed on him as he explained what the State wanted the jury to hear.

Wiles asked the doctor his name, address, and occupation. He reviewed the doctor's education, degrees, and credentials and then asked the Court to allow the doctor to testify as an expert in the field of medicine.

After these preliminaries were concluded, Wiles got to the gist of the doctor's testimony. Dr. Carver explained he had performed the autopsy on Carlton Purvis who was, he testified for the written record, in fact deceased. He had been called to the Purvis residence by the Rockingham

County Sheriff's Department and viewed the body before it was removed to the county hospital.

Jurors cocked their heads when the coroner described how the body had been wrapped in silver duct tape. Particular interest was exhibited by The Leader, who wrote furiously on a notepad allowed by Judge Marcellus and bobbed his head between himself and the witness, attorneys, and Fulcher. The Mason never even looked at the doctor and seemed detached.

The jurors heard for the first time of the duct tape. Dr. Carver described how Purvis's face, eyes, neck, trunk, and limbs had been covered, leaving only his hands, feet, and mouth visible. Purvis had died in the dark. Then, to assist the coroner in his testimony, Wiles introduced photographs of Purvis's body lying on the floor of his home which the coroner said fairly and accurately depicted the scene as he viewed it at the time of his arrival. Carver gave his opinion that, based upon the accumulation of body fluids at the time he first viewed the body, the decedent Purvis had been dead for no less than 24 or more than 36 hours.

Wiles then let Carver take the jury through his testimony to the autopsy. Photographs of the Purvis body before and after removal of the tape were allowed into evidence despite objection by the defense as being inflammatory and overly prejudicial. Carver gave an extended explanation of the process of the autopsy and his findings.

Carver explained Carlton Purvis had been the victim of a severe beating with some type of heavy blunt object. There were no cut marks. Interestingly enough, there was only one contusion above Mr. Purvis's neckline, on his left forehead, but none on his untaped hands or feet. The rest of Mr. Purvis, Carver described, was a mass of purplish/black contusions covering almost the entire portion of the taped flesh. Photographs were once again used to explain and show the results of the beating.

Wiles then asked Carver an interesting question. With Purvis having suffered such an intense and severe beating, could Carver please tell the jury how many bones he found broken in Carlton Purvis's body?

Dr. Carver looked straight at the jury.

"None, Mr. Wiles. Absolutely none."

Wiles feigned disbelief. "But how could this improbable circumstance be, Dr. Carver?"

"Wrapping the body in duct tape insulated and protected Mr. Purvis's bones from being broken by the blows. That may or may not have been the intention of the perpetrator or perpetrators, but that is the net effect. The tape protected Mr. Purvis's bones from breaking when being struck by a heavy blunt object." Carver used a chopping motion with one arm onto his other. "But the tape did not protect Mr. Purvis from suffering numerous painful, severe contusions, or bruises. The blows would have been torturous in their nature, intended to inflict intense, immediate pain rather than cause permanent physical damage."

Bob Lee boomed an objection. Bob Lee believed Carver knew better than to render an opinion as to intent or to describe the blows as "torturous." Carver had to be forced to play by the rules.

"Objection! His opinion as to intent is without a factual basis!"

Judge Marcellus ruled.

"Sustained. The jury will disregard the witness's last statement."

Marcellus's instruction would have had the same import had he instructed them not to think of an elephant.

Wiles asked Carver if he was able to render an opinion on the cause of death of Carlton Purvis. "I most certainly can," Carver answered.

"Each of the bruises you see in the photographs is a source for the body to throw a clot, Mr. Wiles. Any one of these contusions could release a clot--gelled blood--to another part of the body. The more bruises a person has, the more the odds increase that a clot can be thrown. In this case, a blood clot was released from a bruise caused by a contusion or contusions resulting from a blow or blows by a blunt object by a third party or parties and rested near the lung of Mr. Purvis, where it cut off circulation of life-sustaining blood and the oxygen in the blood and resulted in Mr. Purvis's death. That organ of the body then, in layman's terms, suffocates." Carver held his hand to his throat in a choke. "In short, Mr. Wiles, the beating caused Mr. Purvis to throw a blood clot that killed him. We often see this result in automobile accidents or leg injuries and take measures to prevent such events, such as having a patient wear knee socks or take blood thinners. In this case, no such preventative measures were given Mr. Purvis, and as a result of the factors I have previously mentioned, Mr. Purvis died. The clot was formed, released, and shut down air and life-sustaining oxygen to a necessary organ, in this case, the lung."

Wiles asked Carver if he had a proximate cause of death of Carlton Purvis.

Carver said he certainly did.

"The proximate cause of death of Mr. Carlton Purvis was a severe beating about his body with a blunt object or objects causing severe multiple contusions that resulted in a blood clot being released to his lung. His death was unnatural and caused by severe trauma instigated by a third party or parties."

In short, Carlton Purvis had been murdered.

Despite objection by Bob Lee, Judge Marcellus allowed the opinion of Dr. Carver to be considered by the jury.

Bob Lee and Craig decided to conduct only a cursory cross-examination of Dr. Carver. It was apparent Purvis had been murdered. Neither wanted to insult the jury's intelligence by arguing otherwise in the face of such gruesome photos.

Besides, the issue wasn't whether or not Carlton had been murdered.

The question was who had done it.

Chapter 46

"Until my ghastly tale is told,

this heart within me burns."

Samuel Taylor Coleridge

The Rime of the Ancient Mariner

Harley Ames, capitalist, overseer, and manager of The Train Stop, strode to the witness stand wearing his blue funeral suit. He gave an earnest "I do" when his oath was administered. Facing the assistant district attorney, he had been coached to turn to the jury and to try to make eye contact when answering his questions.

Ames gave his name, address, and stated he was the manager of the bar, restaurant, and motel known as The Train Stop. When he first mentioned "The Train Stop," he nodded his head and looked at the jurors to find them nodding that most of them, too, knew of the establishment. And, no doubt, its reputation.

When the assistant district attorney asked if he had known the now-deceased Carlton Purvis, Ames testified that yes, he had known Carlton Purvis as a patron of the bar and restaurant for more than ten years before his death. Purvis had come to The Train Stop on a regular basis and the two of them had become well acquainted.

Checking off his list of questions, Assistant District Attorney Wiles led Harley Ames down the chronological path of Ames' story. Yes, Purvis had told him he wanted to borrow $1500 to buy a Chevrolet pickup truck, and he had loaned Purvis the $1500 in cash. Purvis had promised to repay him by the 15th of the month but had not done so. Carlton Purvis had instead "made himself scarce" and quit coming to The Train Stop. Ames had called Purvis, but Purvis avoided him.

Ames was performing nicely. He seemed genuinely distressed even to be involved in the court case and was relating well with the jurors.

"I really didn't know what to do. Carlton had a reputation for associating with people of low character, such as thieves and drug dealers, so I thought if I could find someone who he might be afraid of he might just go ahead and pay the money," he explained to the assistant district attorney and jurors. J.W.—that's what we call Johnny Wayne for short--came into The Train Stop. It was on a Tuesday, and I asked him if he would like to make a little money. Fulcher said 'Sure,' so I told him what it was all about. I told him I'd give him $150 if he would get me the $1500 from Carlton, but that I'd appreciate it if he could get the whole $1650 out of Carlton."

Ames faced the jury.

"I believed Carlton could get the money and pay me back if he wanted to. He knew folks with a lot of money, or so he said at The Train Stop. It was just a matter of getting him to do it."

Harley Ames gave this testimony with an earnest, straight face. A master thespian.

"So," Gerry Wiles asked, "how did Ames propose getting Carlton to pay up?"

"It wasn't that hard, Mr. Wiles. Johnny Wayne and I would show up at Carlton Purvis's house and tell Carlton he was overdue and needed to pay up. If he didn't pay up, J.W. was going to kick his..., give him a licking, and tell him we'd be back in a week or so. Not a bad licking, just a licking. Not kill him or anything, or even hurt him real bad. Just a smacking around so he'd get the message. Whoop up on him so he understood he'd have to pay."

Ames paused. Contrition was in order.

"I know how bad what we did sounds, Mr. Wiles, but that's the only way folks like Carlton Purvis understand. I don't mean to be talking poorly about the dead, Mr. Wiles, but court don't mean anything to people like Carlton, Sir, and even he would've understood what it was all about and why he was getting shoved around. But that's all that was supposed to happen. If Carlton didn't pay up, J.W. was supposed to thump and smack on him some, not hard enough to make his ancestors dizzy, but just so he'd get the message and pay up when we came back."

"So, then," Wiles asked, "What happened?"

"Well, Mr. Wiles, J.W. and I agreed we'd go on an early Tuesday morning. We figured Carlton might have been gone on a weekend, so we decided on a Tuesday morning. Early, like 5 a.m. or so. Right after the sun came up, and the grass was dewy."

Ames took a breath.

"So on the night before we were set to go see Carlton, I went to J.W.'s house to see J.W. to make sure we were still 'on' to go early the next morning. J.W. wasn't home. A fellow by the name of Cheech Mann came out. He's here in the courtroom, Mr. Wiles, sitting right over there."

Cheech Mann held his hand head high and smiled toward the jury as Ames pointed a boney finger in his direction. No juror smiled back or nodded.

"Cheech told me J.W. and his girlfriend Misty had gone carp fishing and wouldn't be home until late. So I rode over to Carlton Purvis' house, and, yes, sure enough, his truck was there and his lights were on. So I left there and waited at my place until about four in the morning and then went back to J.W.'s farm."

Johnny Wayne sat up. He hadn't seen Harley Ames that night. He tried to lock eyes with Ames, but Ames wouldn't look at him. Ames was busy on stage, occupied with remembering his script.

"J.W.'s lights were on, and he came out when I drove up." Ames leaned toward the jury as his right index finger swept in the direction of Johnny Wayne. He dared not look in Johnny Wayne's direction.

Fulcher's hand hit the table. Hard. He let out an audible "Oh, Hell."

The Leader's head swung abruptly toward Fulcher, while several other jurors covered their mouths. The Mason, from all appearances dozing, didn't bother to look up.

"Mr. Lee," Judge Marcellus boomed toward Bob Lee. "This court will not, under any circumstances, allow any outbursts or interruptions by the defendant. Does your client understand that?"

Bob Lee stood up. Craig furiously whispered aloud to Fulcher, who with clinched fists had his entire being honed in on Ames, to think, to be smart.

Bob Lee quickly addressed the Court.

"Yes, Your Honor, he understands that," Bob Lee popped up as he addressed the court. "We apologize."

"Then," Marcellus directed Wiles, "You will continue."

Wiles asked Ames what happened once Fulcher left the inside of his house.

"J.W. wanted to drive his truck. He told me he and his girlfriend Misty had been carp fishing and hadn't had much luck. I noticed J.W. had a pistol in his back pocket and I said 'J.W., we really don't need that thing, do we?' and he said 'No, not unless Carlton decides he needs his.' So we drove on over to Carlton's house. His porch light was still on and his truck was there."

"And what happened then, if anything?" Wiles asked.

"We got out of the truck and went up to the porch. J.W. got a two-by-four out of the back of his truck and a blue gym bag that had duct tape in it. The board was about as long as a baseball bat."

"And then?"

"Carlton wouldn't answer the door, but J.W. kept hitting on it, and finally Carlton opened the door, just a little bit. Carlton was standing there in his shorts with a T-shirt on. When the door was cracked open J.W. grabbed the knob and said we needed to talk to him, and talk to him now."

"And what were you saying or doing?" Gerry Wiles asked Ames.

"I was just following J.W. I didn't say nothing. I followed him into the den. J.W. told him we wanted the money. $1650. Carlton said it was mighty early in the morning and that he didn't have that kind of money laying around, that he had only $400. Said he would have the rest by Monday. His wallet was on the kitchen table so he emptied it and counted it—there wasn't any left—and handed over $400 in tens and twenties to J.W. He asked to hold onto a $5 bill so he could get a biscuit and coffee for breakfast. J.W. took that $400, but then he told Carlton the $400 wasn't good enough."

Ames' didn't dare look in the direction of Johnny Wayne. The sense of Johnny Wayne's seething stare was enough to bring him to the edge of breaking.

"J.W. pointed to the bag of duct tape and told me to unwrap a roll. He pulled his pistol, it was a .38, and pointed it right between Carlton's eyes from about three feet. I spoke up and said, 'Easy, J.W., easy,' and he told me to shut up. You don't tell J.W. what to do."

Ames' hands visibly trembled. He gave the appearance of being on the verge of weeping. He *had* to perform. His life depended upon it. There was no question Johnny Wayne would slice him to pieces if he ever got out of jail.

"I didn't want old Carlton dead. I knew Carlton. He was my friend. I just wanted my money. That's all. My money. Nothing more."

Wiles reassured Ames. "Take your time, Mr. Ames. Take your time. I know your testimony is difficult, but I must ask you the next question. What happened next?"

Ames nodded his head in appreciation. He returned to the script. He had almost convinced himself the story he was passing to the jury had actually happened.

"So I got the tape out quick because I figured J.W. wanted him taped up and beat and not shot dead. I was really relieved at the thought J.W. wouldn't be shooting old Carlton. So I got the tape out as quick as I could."

Wiles asked Ames to explain the duct tape to the jury.

"It's pretty common knowledge around some parts that if a man's taped up, he can be beaten with a bat or a stick and the tape keeps his bones from getting all broke up. It ain't supposed to kill no one."

Wiles nodded back.

"It'll hurt like crazy, Mr. Wiles, but the bones won't get broke. Just bruises a person really bad. It's a way to send a message without having to kill a person. And that's all I wanted to do. I just wanted Carlton to get the message."

Harley Ames reminded himself to create a distance between him and Johnny Wayne Fulcher. "I didn't want him killed. Honest to God I didn't. I really didn't."

Fulcher was staring at Ames in sincere disbelief. He was thinking of what he was going to do if he ever got his hands on Harley Ames. What he would do before he threw him down his well.

"So J.W. told me to tape him up," Ames continued. "J.W. was really mad and acting crazy. Waving the gun around. Pointing it at me and Carlton, playing with the hammer of the gun. I wasn't sure if he was acting this way just to scare Carlton or because he really was crazy."

He looked again at the jury.

"I ain't afraid to admit it. I ain't afraid at all. It scared me. He had that pistol. He could've shot both of us. You don't argue with a crazy man with a gun. A man points a gun at you, and it's like looking down the barrel of a cannon—that's how big it gets. Makes you feel like your eyes are going to pop out of your head. So I got the tape on old Carlton as quick as I could. Carlton and me knew J.W. was going to shoot him if he put up a fuss, so Carlton stayed still and did a little whimpering. But he didn't fight me, not with that pistol in J.W.'s hand. I didn't put none of the tape on over his mouth or nose, but I pretty much wrapped him up."

Harley Ames looked down at both of his hands. He paused for effect.

"All those pictures Dr. Carver showed. I was the one who put that tape on," Ames barely whispered.

He got quiet. He put both hands together and laid them in his lap. Then he looked down and closed his eyes as if he were praying.

Quite a presentation.

"And then J.W. started hitting him with that two-by-four. Hitting him hard. Kicking him upside the head. Tomato-faced him. It scared me to death. He was like a crazy man. I mean, Mr. Wiles, I was scared to death and who could blame me? I thought he might just knock the taste out of Carlton's mouth and then quit, but he didn't. I couldn't do nothing to stop him. The Good Samaritan himself would have kept on walking… I was thinking J.W. was going to beat him to death, right in front of my eyes. I just stood there, almost frozen and scared. I kept sayin', 'J.W., that's enough…don't hurt him too bad, J.W.….that's good, J.W., he's got the message now.' But J.W. kept on smacking him with the board and kicking him, kicking him like a dog. He was out of control, calling Carlton names and such."

Ames stopped again to collect his thoughts. He had to make sure his tale was being repeated correctly and with effect. Wiles helped him along.

"So tell us, Mr. Ames. What happened next?"

Ames looked at Wiles instead of the jury.

"There wasn't anything I could do, so help me. He hauled off and hit Carlton one time on the side of the head, and Carlton quit moving. I thought J.W. had done gone off and killed him, but Carlton was just knocked out. I asked J.W., I said 'J.W., you didn't kill him, did you?' and J.W. just looked down at old Carlton and didn't say nothing. Carlton was breathing, though. I told J.W. that Carlton had gotten the message, and we needed to go. I did everything I could do to get him away from Carlton and out of there."

He spoke with an earnest voice.

"So we left. Carlton was alive when we left. He was breathing and he rolled over to his side and I heard him give off a moan. I thanked God he was alive."

Harley Ames had actually said that he had "thanked God."

"We went back to J.W.'s farm. It was just around sunup, around 6:00 o'clock or so. J.W. kept his $150 and I got the rest of the $400, which was $250. I told J.W. we'd see if Carlton was going to pay me the rest. I told J.W. he wouldn't hear from me unless Carlton didn't pay the rest. He said OK just to let him know and he'd go back, I shook his hand, and I went my own way. I got some breakfast at Lefty's and went home to bed."

The jury had listened intently. Ames sounded so factual, so sincere.

Wiles then asked when he learned Carlton Purvis was dead.

"I read about it in the paper. I thought Carlton had just been whopped upside the head and knocked out. That's all, just knocked out. Not dead. And then the paper said he was dead."

Ames reached for his face.

"It scared me, scared me real bad. I didn't want no part of no murder, Mr. Wiles, no part at all. I just wanted to get my money. I know a lot of the folks in this room don't like the method I used, Mr. Wiles, and I appreciate that. But you gotta understand that there are some people that don't know nothing else but duct tape and a bat, and Carlton was one of them. That's the only reason I called J.W., Mr. Wiles, to get my money. Not to kill old Carlton. Truth be told, Mr. Wiles, I really liked Carlton. I knowed the man for years, for God's sakes. I just can't believe it's happened."

The assistant district attorney asked Ames how he had come to talk to law enforcement about what had happened at Carlton Purvis's house.

"Once again, Mr. Wiles, you've got to realize who we're dealing with here. On one hand, all I wanted was my money. Carlton ended up dead. The paper said he had been murdered. I knew what had taken place was wrong. I could be charged myself with taking part in the murder. J.W. himself could have turned on me and said I did it. All of these charges could have fallen on my shoulders, and my shoulders alone, when I didn't even want Carlton dead."

He knew the jurors might doubt his morality. But no one in the courtroom could look at Johnny Wayne Fulcher without a sense that he was capable of doing anything to protect himself. He just had that look. So Ames made his stronger argument.

"But most of all I knew I was the only witness, other than Johnny Wayne, who saw what had happened. I went to Mr. Blanchard because I had heard a lot about Johnny Wayne Fulcher, and Johnny Wayne Fulcher is the last person on this earth I want after me, Sir. I respect your office and the power you have as a district attorney, Mr. Wiles, but I had rather have 100 of you after me than one Johnny Wayne. There ain't no way I'd sell an insurance policy to anyone Johnny Wayne Fulcher was after, Mr. Wiles, so I went and called Arnie Robertson at the sheriff's department to help me get what had happened sorted out. I didn't want no part in no murder, Mr. Wiles. No part at all. I ain't no killer."

Ames waited a moment.

"And I sure didn't want to get killed by J.W. like J.W. had done to Carlton. What he did was crazy and mean.

Crazy and mean. Wasn't no doubt in my mind he'd want to keep me from tellin' anyone what I saw he done. Wasn't no doubt at all. Not one iota."

Wiles had one more question.

"So, Mr. Ames, have you been promised anything whatsoever by our district attorney's office, knowing that you could be charged with a number of offenses at any time by our office?"

"Mr. Wiles," Ames answered sincerely, "You and your office haven't promised me a thing. Not a thing at all. I'm just trying to be honest, get this case behind me, and deal with the Lord for having been there in the first place. That's all I'm trying to do. To do what's right."

Gerry waited a moment for the effect.

"Thank you for doing that, Mr. Ames. Thank you. No more questions at this point, Your Honor."

Fulcher had become fixated on The Leader. The Leader continued to write on his notepad. Fulcher sensed that The Leader was accumulating proof to verify to the other jurors during deliberations that Ames had been telling the truth. Fulcher then turned to gaze at Ames. Ames was a dead man once he got out, he swore to himself. Dead.

Marcellus looked at the defense table.

"He's your witness, counselors!"

Chapter 47

"Never, never, never on cross-examination ask a witness a question you don't already know the answer to... Do it, and you'll often get an answer you don't want, an answer that might wreck your case."

Harper Lee

Bob Lee was at bat. Fulcher sat between Bob Lee and Craig Fitts, hands gripping at the armrests of his wooden chair.

"Mr. Ames, you have testified you are the manager of The Train Stop, is that correct?"

Harley Ames smiled and nodded.

"Mr. Ames, for the record, I would ask that you answer audibly rather than by nodding so the court reporter can take down every word of your testimony. So, are you are the manager of The Train Stop?"

"Yes, Mr. Pender, I am."

"And you have been the manager for several years, have you not?"

"Yes, Sir."

"And you receive a weekly paycheck from the owner, do you not, with taxes and social security taken out?"

Ames looked toward Assistant District Attorney Wiles, wondering why Bob Lee was asking these questions. Wiles returned no hint.

"I do."

"And this paycheck you receive, Mr. Ames, this paycheck you receive comes from a bank account in the Commonwealth of Virginia, does it not?"

Wiles rose from his seat and spoke up. "Objection as irrelevant, Your Honor."

Before Bob Lee could respond, Judge Marcellus spoke up. He overruled the objection, commenting that he was going to give Mr. Pender some leeway and that he hoped Mr. Pender would quickly bring the relevance of the question to light.

"Answer the question, Mr. Ames. Is your paycheck written on a Virginia bank account?"

Ames smiled.

"Why, yes, Mr. Pender, it is. I don't see what that…"

Bob Lee interrupted him.

"And you are well aware, Mr. Ames, that Carlton Purvis, the deceased, had been subpoenaed to testify before a grand jury in the Commonwealth of Virginia, Roanoke to be exact, in relation to a federal investigation concerning alleged illegal activities related to the operation of The Train Stop by its owner and yourself less than a week before his death, correct?"

Wiles shot up and yelled, "Objection!"

Ames was oblivious and didn't hear. He looked at Bob Lee, determined to blurt out his answer.

"No, Sir, I didn't know that when he was killed, Mr. Pender. I'm sure I didn't know that before he was killed."

Judge Marcellus spoke up.

"Objection sustained as to the form of the question."

Marcellus held the palm of his left hand toward the attorneys and drew a bead on Harley Ames.

"Mr. Ames, I instruct you to remain silent if an objection is made by any of the attorneys in this room. Once I rule on the objection, I will tell you whether or not you may answer the question. Do you clearly understand these instructions, Mr. Ames?"

Harley blinked.

"Uh, yes, Sir, I understand you, Your Honor."

Judge Marcellus directed Bob Lee Pender to continue and allowed him to rephrase his question.

"Mr. Ames, I want to ask you a question about your state of mind. Have you ever come to believe, whether or not your belief was correct, that Carlton Purvis, the deceased, had been subpoenaed before he died to testify before a grand jury in Roanoke, Virginia about a federal investigation concerning alleged illegal activities related to the operation of The Train Stop by its owner and yourself?"

Harley Ames shifted in his seat.

"Well, yes, Sir, I did think that. I'd heard something about that."

Bob Lee acted inquisitive. "You had heard something about that? When did you hear that, and from whom?"

Ames felt as if he was playing with fire. The only way out was for him to go 50/50, to lie about part of it and tell the truth about the other half.

"I'm not sure how I heard it, Mr. Pender. I can't swear under oath who I heard it from. I just don't know."

A better response finally came to Ames mind.

"But I do remember I heard it just before he died, Mr. Pender. I remember thinking I'd better get paid before he got arrested or got put in jail or something."

Bob Lee needed to pin Harley Ames down on what he was saying. The Devil was often in the details. Experience had taught Bob Lee that a lying witness was likely to get confused trying to conjure up small details in the midst of untruthful testimony.

"So it was your understanding that he had been subpoenaed, but that he had not yet testified?"

Ames was unsure of what Bob Lee was doing. He shifted in his seat.

"Well, uh, yes, Mr. Pender. I guess you could say so. Yes, he hadn't testified yet. But that didn't have anything to do with him owin' me the money!"

Bob Lee inflected his voice so it sounded as if he, and the jury, were having their levels of intelligence being insulted by Harley Ames.

"Of course, it didn't, Mr. Ames. Of course, it didn't."

Bob Lee gave a slight smile and asked his question condescendingly.

"So I ask you, Mr. Ames, are you telling these twelve good people on the jury that the stars just happened to line up correctly, that Mr. Purvis just happened to owe you money, that you happened to show up at the subpoenaed Mr. Purvis's house with Mr. Fulcher, that Mr. Purvis just happened to be killed against your wishes while he was under subpoena, and that it just so happened that this occurred the same week he had been subpoenaed to go to Roanoke and tell the Grand Jury there anything and everything he might know about you and The Train Stop?"

After a pause, Bob Lee pushed the issue and asked incredulously with a raised voice, "Am I correct that your testimony to the jury is that this amazing coincidence occurred?"

Ames floundered in Bob Lee's sudden attack.

"Mr. Pender, it's not exactly like that."

Bob Lee pressed the issue. Ames was trapped. He directed his attention to Judge Marcellus.

"Would the Court please direct Mr. Ames to answer my question, Your Honor?"

Marcellus turned to Harley Ames. "You will answer the question 'Yes' or 'No,' and then you may explain your answer, Mr. Ames. Now answer counsel's question."

"The answer, I guess, is yes, Mr. Pender. But I didn't know whether or not he had testified. I swear to God I didn't."

Bob Lee shot back with sarcasm.

"Of course, you didn't, Mr. Ames. Of course, you didn't. But you will acknowledge, at the very least, that you do know the answer to that now, do you not? He didn't testify because he was killed between the time he was subpoenaed and the time he was to testify, was he not?"

Ames paused before he answered.

"Apparently so, Mr. Pender."

"'Apparently'? 'Apparently'? Have you seen the photos of Mr. Carlton Purvis wrapped in duct tape, Mr. Ames?"

Ames surrendered. Yes, Carlton was definitely dead, he said, and he did know Purvis had been subpoenaed to testify before the federal grand jury. He insisted, once again, that he did not know whether or not Carlton Purvis had testified before the Grand Jury in Roanoke before he died.

"And you are telling this jury that it just so happened, that it is mere coincidence and happenstance, that Carlton Purvis, a man you knew only as a customer, a person you knew only as someone to whom you loaned money in a truck purchase, was murdered days after he was chosen by the U.S. Attorney in Roanoke out of four billion people on this entire earth to testify before a grand jury about the goings-on of the very business you managed? That is what you are telling this jury, is it not, Mr. Ames?"

Ames was squirming.

"All I know…"

Bob Lee took control and cut in.

"Yes or no, Mr. Ames, then you may explain your answer as His Honor has instructed you. Would you like for me to repeat my question?"

"No, Mr. Pender. No need. The answer is yes. What happened is what I've already told these folks. That's what happened."

"I'm sure it is, Mr. Ames." Bob Lee's intonation was one of condescension, of disbelief. The jury sensed Bob Lee's sincerity, his righteous indignation that the courtroom was being tainted by less than the truth, the whole truth, and nothing but the truth.

He continued.

"And was it your understanding, Mr. Ames, that this federal investigation involves alleged, and I emphasize 'alleged', prostitution, gambling, drug trade, and moonshining activities occurring in the very business you manage here in Rockingham County?"

The courtroom was silent while Bob Lee waited for a response.

"Was this your understanding on the day Mr. Purvis died, Mr. Ames?"

"I've heard all kind of stories, Mr. Pender." Ames was tired, aggravated. "So yes, I thought that."

"And this 'owner' of The Train Stop, Mr. Ames... have you told him that you, a trusted employee, associated with Johnny Wayne Fulcher, whom you have sworn has deadly propensities, and with Carlton Purvis, who for some reason unstated today was of enough interest to the U.S. Attorney that he was in fact subpoenaed to testify before the federal grand jury about the operation of the business you operate for the 'owner'? Have you told the owner any of that, Mr. Ames?"

By now Ames had almost surrendered to Pender's intense questioning. "No, Mr. Pender. I have not," he answered quietly.

Bob Lee had him trapped. "Not told who, Mr. Ames? Not told the 'owner'? Please tell the jury just who the 'owner' of The Train Stop is, Mr. Ames."

Ames was quiet. Answering "Ricky Dean" was a death sentence. The Sheriff would know how he had answered. He was desperate for protection. He looked at Wiles, his eyes begging.

Wiles looked at his ink pen.

"I think..."

Bob Lee interrupted.

"You think? You think??"

The question turned into a demand. Wiles offered no objection, no protection to Ames.

"Tell us a fact, Mr. Ames. Who is your employer at The Train Stop?"

Harley Ames re-checked with Wiles. Their eyes met. The jury watched the two of them silently communicating.

"His name is Mr. Ricky Dean, Mr. Pender. Mr. Ricky Dean." Ames was internally gasping for air, trying to distance himself from appearing to have double-crossed Ricky Dean. "We hardly know each other, though, Mr. Pender. I think he just owns the building, but I don't know for sure. We don't really know each other."

Bob Lee nodded and spoke as if he were a disbelieving parent, invoking gentle sarcasm.

"Of course, you don't, Mr. Ames. Of course, you don't know your employer whom you worked for daily and report to on a regular basis as manager of his business. That is what you would have us believe, would you not?"

Bob Lee didn't push for an answer. He allowed a pause in the questioning to let the jury stew in Harley Ames' lies.

"Mr. Ames, could you tell us... The Train Stop has never, ever been investigated by the Rockingham County Sheriff's Department for prostitution, drugs, gambling, or moon shining, of your own knowledge, has it?"

Bob Lee knew the jury was familiar with The Train Stop's reputation for "all of the above."

Ames was relieved the subject had veered from Ricky Dean. "Why, of course not, Mr. Pender, not that I know of."

Bob Lee asked, "So your answer is 'no', Mr. Ames?"

"Yes, Sir, the answer is 'no'."

"And I presume you know Detective Bunk Blanchard of the Rockingham County Sheriff's Department, do you not, Mr. Ames? Detective Blanchard is sitting right over there, Mr. Ames, just behind Assistant District Attorney Wiles. You know Detective Blanchard, do you not?"

Harley Ames looked over at Detective Blanchard and nodded.

"Why sure, Mr. Pender, I know Bunk. I've known him for years. He gave me my first speeding ticket when he worked for the Reidsville Police Department. He comes in to eat at The Train Stop on a regular basis. Likes our food, I think. Yes, I know Detective Blanchard."

Bob Lee softened.

"Let me ask you a question, Mr. Ames. Knowing Detective Blanchard as you do, with him coming into the restaurant regularly, having known him for years and all, you would consider him an honest man, would you not?"

"Why sure I would, Mr. Pender. None more stout, Mr. Pender. None."

"As a matter of fact, you've spoken with him about your testimony today, have you not? You gave him a statement that was written down and signed by you, did you not?"

Ames nodded. "Why yes, I did that, Mr. Pender."

"And you have told the grand jury that the first person in the Rockingham County Sheriff's Department you spoke with was Mr. Arnie Robertson, correct?"

"Yes, Sir. He was."

"Not Detective Bunk Blanchard, but Arnie Robertson of the sheriff's department, correct?"

"Yes."

"And Mr. Robertson is Sheriff Efron Bailey's chief assistant, is he not?"

"That's my understanding, Mr. Pender."

"And Mr. Arnie Robertson is not in the detective division, but instead works as the chief aide to the Sheriff, correct?"

"Yes, Sir. I believe so."

"And you've testified that you read in the newspaper where the detective division of the sheriff's department had reported on the Carlton Purvis murder, did you not?"

"I did, Mr. Pender."

"And instead of contacting your friend Detective Bunk Blanchard, the same Detective Bunk Blanchard whom you view as an honest man that you've known for years and who eats at your table on a regular basis, the same Detective Bunk Blanchard of Rockingham County's Detective Division that was investigating Carlton Purvis's murder, the first person you decided to contact was the right hand man of the Sheriff of this Rockingham County, the same sheriff who has never caused an investigation of The Train Stop for prostitution, gambling, drugs, and moon shining to be instituted despite an apparent interest on behalf of the federal authorities, correct? Your testimony is that you contacted the chief aide to the Sheriff instead of your good and admired friend, Detective Bunk Blanchard of the detective division, correct?"

Ames almost shouted.

"I contacted Arnie Robertson because I know him."

"I'm sure you do, Mr. Ames. I'm sure you do."

Pender shook his head in feigned disgust and looked down while his point sunk in with the jury. He then spoke lowly, and deliberately.

"You have testified, after all, that you are the manager of The Train Stop. And you must have known Arnie Robertson, the right hand man of our high sheriff, very, very well, did you not? At least much, much better than you did Detective Blanchard, who regularly ate at your establishment, did you not?"

The insinuations were not denied. The innuendo was clear.

Bob Lee Pender was going after the iconic Sheriff Efron Bailey in an effort to save Johnny Wayne's life.

The courtroom audience was spellbound. Jurors were staring wide-eyed at Bob Lee Pender. Attacking Sheriff Bailey simply had never been done. Rockingham County had considered it blasphemy. Dangerous.

But even Gerry Wiles failed to object to this line of questioning. No one, at any time, in any manner, had ever insinuated corruption by Sheriff Efron Bailey in open court.

Until that moment.

During the rest of the afternoon, and the entire next morning, Bob Lee pelted Harley Ames with question after question, knowing the answer before each was asked. Inconsistencies, Harley's previous criminal convictions, wild coincidences, self-serving statements, all brought forth and clearly laid in each juror's lap.

By the end of the ordeal Harley Ames was in tatters. Confidence in Harley Ames' word had been shattered, and yet a few confusing facts remained. This testimony was still early in the trial, but already each juror subconsciously acted as "detective" trying to piece together the puzzle, particularly The Leader. Carlton Purvis had been murdered. Harley Ames was somehow involved, and his involvement had led, for reasons still questioned by the jury, to Johnny Wayne Fulcher being indicted. And there was the unspoken fact that lowlifes congregate with lowlifes. If Harley Ames was seedy, he'd seek out the worst to do the dirty work. Johnny Wayne fit that bill. But Harley Ames' word was, at this point, far from sufficient to convict Johnny Wayne of first-degree murder.

Harley Ames did not repeat his bouncing step as he retreated from the witness stand. Judge Marcellus instructed that he remained under subpoena and was not to leave the proceedings until properly excused by the court. Ames passed between the counsel tables, took a seat alone on a courtroom pew far removed from any officers of the sheriff's department, and quietly left the courthouse during its next recess. Word later spread that he moved to a trailer near the North Carolina Outer Banks town of Corolla, but no one ever knew for sure.

Chapter 48

"You shall not bear false witness against your neighbor."

Exodus 20:16

"No one has ever been betrayed by a friend."

Anonymous

Gerry Wiles stood. "Your Honor, the State will call Mr. Raeford Mann to the stand."

Cheech Mann rose from the front bench behind the railing that separated Gerry Wiles' prosecution table from general seating and approached the witness stand. His stringy wrist and hands and neck stuck out from his black cowboy shirt with pearl snaps instead of buttons. His hair had been Brylcreamed over the top of his forehead. A huge silver buckle hung from the front of his blue jeans. He gave the impression of a washed up wanna-be set to troll in a line-dancing club, except the lighting in the courtroom was better. His fingers, brown from tobacco tar, stuck out, as did the yellow crud-laden fuzz on his teeth. There was simply nothing redeeming about the man.

Mann took his oath with his wrist bent instead of pointing up, which was an assumed waste of words, and took the witness stand. He faced the assistant district attorney and quickly answered the introductory questions about his name, address, and employment, which he described as "disabled." Then Wiles got down to business.

"Mr. Mann, could you tell the jury whether or not you know the Defendant, Mr. Johnny Wayne Fulcher?"

Mann explained that yes, indeed, he did know Johnny Wayne Fulcher—who he called "J.W."-- and had been a friend of his and Misty for a number of years. As a matter of fact, Mann explained, when J.W. and Misty had get-togethers, and also on other occasions, he had spent the night at Fulcher's residence.

Wiles got to the root of his questioning.

"Could you tell the jury whether or not you saw Mr. Harley Ames on the night of August 15th of last year?"

"Why, Yes Sir. Yes Sir, I could."

"So, did you see him?"

Cheech was basking in the limelight. He smiled, canvassed the courtroom, and nodded at the jury. He was dressed up. The center of all attention in the courtroom. The only person he wouldn't look at was Johnny Wayne, seated behind the defense table. He feared Johnny Wayne. Wiles was having to pull every answer out of him.

"Yes, Sir, I did."

"And at what time did you see him, Mr. Mann?"

"Time?"

"What time did you see Mr. Ames on the night of August 15th of last year, Mr. Mann?"

"Oh, I reckon it was between 11:00 and midnight. Before midnight. Harley Ames came driving up."

Wiles had to make it clearer to the jury.

"And where were you when he came driving up on the evening of August 15th, Mr. Mann? Where were you?"

"I was at J.W.'s house. He was lettin' me stay there for a couple of nights. I was out of work and all, and I didn't have no money or nothing to eat, so he and the Bee let me stay on the couch for a couple of days."

The jury was not impressed. A few looked around the courtroom. Cheech scrambled for something to say.

"That Bee can cook. Let me tell you, she can cook when she wants to."

Wiles didn't care about the Bee's cooking.

"So tell us, Mr. Mann, tell us what happened when you saw Mr. Ames. Did you speak to him?"

"Well, he came driving up looking for Johnny Wayne. Told me Carlton Purvis owed him some money and he and Johnny Wayne was going to go collect it."

Mann didn't dare look at Johnny Wayne. He continued on.

"Yep. He told me he and Johnny Wayne was going to get that money and that he needed to find Johnny Wayne so he'd make sure he got it. He and Johnny Wayne was in that money thing together, that's what he said. He wanted to see Johnny Wayne, but I told him Johnny Wayne and the Bee had gone carp fishing. That's what I told him."

Wiles wanted to make it clearer.

"Had Mr. Fulcher told you he and his girlfriend were going carp fishing earlier in the day, Mr. Mann?"

Bob Lee did not voice an objection to the Judge despite Gerry Wiles' "leading the witness" by asking questions that included a suggested response. The questions were inconsequential to Bob Lee.

"Yes Sir, Mr. Wiles. He told me he and The Bee—that's what we call his girlfriend, Misty Street--was going carp fishing up at Philpot Lake or Smith Mountain Lake, I wasn't real sure."

Mann sounded proud and extended his finger toward Wiles.

"Left me in charge of his place. Told me to feed his dogs and that they'd be back in the morning. So that's what I told Harley. I told him where they went."

"So tell us, Mr. Mann, did Mr. Harley Ames tell you anything else before he left?"

Mann looked at the jury, just as he'd been told to do.

"Yes Sir. He told me to have Johnny Wayne call him just as soon as he came in. Told me he and Johnny Wayne was going to go get that money no matter what they had to do to get it. He wanted his money."

Wiles cupped his hand to his ear in a feigned inability to hear so he could re-ask the question for double effect. It was an old trick, and Bob Lee shook his head, rubbed his forehead, and almost laughed.

"I'm sorry, Mr. Mann... I'm not sure I heard you correctly. Did you say Harley Ames told you he and Johnny Wayne Fulcher were going to get money from Carlton Purvis, no matter what they had to do to get it? Is that what you said?"

Bob Lee still didn't object. He couldn't help but look toward the ceiling and roll his eyes, though. He was simply letting Assistant District Attorney Gerry Wiles sow distrust among the jurors by tying himself into faith in Cheech Mann's word. He knew that if the jury lost faith in the Assistant District Attorney he was halfway home to an acquittal.

"Why yes, Mr. Wiles. That's what I said. That's exactly what Harley Ames told me. And that he wanted his money."

Fulcher's eyes lasered in on Mann. Mann had just put himself on his list to be dropped into Johnny Wayne's well.

Wiles announced to the Court.

"No more questions at this point, Your Honor."

Marcellus gave the go ahead to Bob Lee Pender. Craig Fitts remained silent and slid a yellow piece of paper past Johnny Wayne over to Bob Lee. Bob Lee paused, took a look at the note, set it down, and then smiled in the direction of Cheech Mann.

"I have just a few questions of you, Mr. Mann. First of all, Mr. Mann, you are more commonly known in the community as 'Cheech Mann,' are you not?"

"Why you know I am, Mr. Pender. I am."

"So let me ask you a little bit about your past, Sir. Could you please tell the jury whether or not you have been convicted of any criminal offenses within the past 10 years that carry active sentences of 60 days or more?"

Mann gave a sideways grin.

"Oh, Mr. Pender, you know I have. I can't remember exactly what."

Bob Lee offered to help. He had a stack of papers over four inches thick which obviously appeared to be Cheech

Mann's criminal record in his hands, leafing through it and squinting for detail. The stack was not referred to verbally, but from his handling of it the jury had a good idea what was in Bob Lee Pender's hands.

"In the interest of time, Mr. Mann, is it fair to say that you have been convicted of no less than 14 criminal violations of drug laws that carry sentences greater than 60 days incarceration in the past 10 years?"

"If you say so, Mr. Pender. You've got it in front of you."

Bob Lee smiled.

"Oh, I can't say so, Mr. Mann. You will have to be the one to say so or not. Have you?"

Cheech did his "Aw, shucks," nod and answered.

"Yeah, Mr. Pender, I have. At least that many. I don't know how many exactly, but it's been a lot. I've had this problem with drugs and alcohol, Mr. Pender. With the help of the Lord, I fight them every day."

"And how many breaking and entering and larcenies, if any, have you been convicted of in the past 10 years, Mr. Mann... would you say no less than eight?"

"I guess so, Mr. Pender." Cheech caught himself and gave a slight chuckle. "Ok. Yes. Eight."

"And let me ask you about contributing to the delinquency of a minor. Would you admit or deny that you have been convicted of no less than two violations of that law in the last ten years, Mr. Mann?"

Mann became indignant.

"Mr. Pender, one of them told me she was 15. One of those wasn't fair!"

"So if she was 15, it would have been fair, Mr. Mann?"

Wiles tried to end the misery. "Objection!"

Bob Lee turned toward Gerry Wiles and, knowing the jury was watching him, shook his head and gave a smile of disbelief that the State of North Carolina would attempt to put a citizen to death based upon the word of a witness such as Cheech Mann.

"Question withdrawn, Your Honor."

It came time for Bob Lee to twist the knife.

"Mr. Mann, you mentioned you were out of work. You haven't held down full time employment in years, have you, Mr. Mann?"

Mann adjusted his seating. He could barely look at Bob Lee because Johnny Wayne sat so close.

"No Sir. I'm disabled. I've been disabled for years, Mr. Pender. Matter of fact, I have a claim for Social Security disability I've filed again pending. I'm hoping to hear on it soon."

Two of the male jurors' heads jerked. One of the females twisted her neck down and around toward Mann and frowned.

Bob Lee and the courtroom bailiffs were well aware of Cheech Mann's "bad back." He had used his so-called back pain as an excuse for years as an inability to pay fines before Judges in the open courtroom.

"It wouldn't be your back, would it, Mr. Mann?"

Mann smiled. "Why, yes, Mr. Pender, it is my back. You're exactly right. I've had back problems for years. Comes and goes, and sometimes I can hardly move."

"And you live with your mother, too, is that correct, Mr. Mann?

"Why, yes, Mr. Pender, I do."

"And I believe she also receives Social Security Disability, does she not?"

"Yes, Mr. Pender. Poor thing has all kinds of problems, too."

Pender changed his line of questioning.

"Mr. Mann, you stepped forward and told authorities about what had happened on the night of August 15th, did you not?"

"Yes, Mr. Pender, I did. It was the right thing to do."

"And when you stepped forward, Mr. Mann, it wasn't that far you stepped was it? You were in the Rockingham County Jail when you stepped forward, were you not?"

Mann readjusted his seating position, almost raising himself by his elbows as he sat.

"Why yes, Mr. Pender, I was. For nothing. They said I stole some cigarettes, but when the police came, they didn't read me my rights or nothing and violated the Do-Right Rule. My rights were violated, Mr. Pender, and I didn't do nothing. They didn't have nothing on me because they violated the Do-Right Rule."

Pender dared not ask about the Do-Right Rule...

"And the first person you spoke to about Mr. Purvis, it wasn't Detective Bunk Blanchard, who was investigating the Purvis death, was it? You didn't tell Mr. Blanchard first, did you?"

"No, Sir, I didn't."

"Okay, Mr. Mann. Could you please direct your attention directly to the jury and tell each and every one of them the very first law enforcement officer you discussed this story to that day in the Rockingham County jail when you were in custody in violation of your civil rights. Tell them who you told."

"I told Mr. Arnie Robertson."

"Did you say Arnie Robertson, and not Mr. Bunk Blanchard?"

"Yes, Sir. What difference does that make?"

Judge Marcellus spoke up.

"Just answer the questions, Mr. Mann."

"Well, yes, it was Arnie Robertson."

"And in between jobs, Mr. Mann, you've been known to do a little work for Harley Ames, have you not?"

Mann's eyes darted around. He was looking straight at Pender, uncomfortable.

"No, Sir, not that I can remember."

Bob Lee pounced.

"Are you telling this jury you can't remember if you've ever sold a little marijuana now and then for Harley Ames, just a little, to pick up a little pocket change? Is this your testimony to the jury, Mr. Mann?"

Mann thought he was fighting back. The bit dog yelped.

"I'm going to plead the 5th Amendment on that, Mr. Pender. You're trying to trick me. I plead the 5th!"

Judge Marcellus rolled his eyes. Bob Lee was smiling. He had Mann where he wanted him. The jury was disgusted with Cheech Mann, undergoing the mental linkage of the Sheriff, Arnie Robertson, The Train Stop, Harley Ames, and Johnny Wayne Fulcher.

Bob Lee seemed to ease up on Mann.

"Mr. Mann, I've noticed your clothes. I must admit, Mr. Mann, that you give a handsome appearance today, Sir."

Mann eased up on his grip of the witness chair. He sat up straighter, pulled on one of his sleeves, and brushed the front of his shirt with his left hand. He smiled, relieved that the questioning had changed, and welcomed the compliment.

"Thank you, Mr. Pender."

Bob Lee had seen Cheech in court on several occasions for either getting into fights at Moon's Danceland on Highway 220 near Madison or for driving drunk after leaving the bar.

"Those boots you have on, Mr. Mann, they look like boots you might wear if you go dancing. You don't dance, do you, Mr. Mann? You don't wear that nice outfit and go woo the young ladies dancing, do you, Mr. Mann?"

Wiles objected and, as he did, both he and Bob Lee started to rise. Judge Marcellus waved them down and barked, "Overruled." Even he was finding Cheech Mann repulsive.

Bob Lee kept feeding Cheech's ego.

"You can answer the question, Mr. Mann. Do you kick up your heels with the young ladies in that outfit?"

Mann was grinning. He was a stud muffin, at least in his own mind.

"Why, yes, Mr. Pender, I have been known to step out every now and then. I like to go out at least every other week or so."

"And while you're out dancing in those nice boots, and drinking a cold one between dances, do you ever wonder why you haven't gotten those Social Security disability checks you've been waiting on for that bad back, Mr. Mann?"

Wiles objected. Bob Lee raised his left hand and gave a pained smile as he shook his head toward the disgusted jury.

"No need for him to answer that, Your Honor. No need at all. No more questions."

The Leader laid his pen on the notepad to rest his writing hand.

The Mason continued to stare downward. Various words bounced in his head. "Damned Democrats. Welfare. Social Security Disability. Crooked Sheriff. Liars."

Chapter 49

"The details are not the details. They make the design."

Charles Eames

Gerry Wiles stood.

"Your Honor, the State would call Detective Bunk Blanchard to the stand."

Detective Bunk Blanchard, dressed in a dark suit with a blue tie and an American flag pin inserted in his lapel rose slowly from the front pew of the courtroom. With a steady stride, he made his way to the witness stand, faced the clerk, and when asked if he swore to God to tell the truth, the whole truth, and nothing but the truth, answered with clear eyes.

"I most certainly do. Yes, I do."

He then seated himself and calmly faced District Attorney Wiles.

The assistant district attorney began by asking Detective Blanchard to recite his name, occupation, years of employment in law enforcement, and the fact that he was the lead investigator in the Carlton Purvis murder. Blanchard's credentials, along with certificates of achievement and the various investigative schools he had attended during his career, were disclosed to the jury.

Over the next hour and a half, the detective explained his initial involvement in the murder investigation beginning with his arrival at the residence of Carlton Purvis and the cadaver's condition as described by Dr. Carver. He explained his relationship with Harley Ames and how Harley had come to him in fear and regret and spilled his guts to implicate Johnny Wayne. This testimony was nothing new. It was intended to reemphasize, and bolster, the testimony of previous witnesses called by Wiles.

The detective explained how he had been dispatched to the residence of Carlton Purvis on August 18th. The sheriff's department had received a report from a third party caller that a person might be deceased at Mr. Purvis's residence. Two deputies had responded to what was then labeled a Wellness Call and verified Purvis's death. They had reported their findings to the sheriff's dispatch office and these circumstances had been conveyed to the secretary in the office of the Detective Division of the sheriff's office. Being on duty, Detective Blanchard took the call from the secretary and went to the scene to begin his investigation.

"And what was the situation so far as Mr. Purvis's body when you arrived, Detective Blanchard?" Wiles inquired.

"Mr. Purvis was lying on the floor within the den of his residence. There was a strong, unbearable odor resulting from decaying flesh in a hot, enclosed environment that necessitated our opening the doors and windows of the premises. Furniture had very apparently been displaced. Mr. Purvis was obviously, in my opinion, deceased. His corpse was wrapped up in silver duct tapes, mummy-like, just as Dr. Carver and Harley Ames earlier described, Mr. Wiles."

Wiles then laid the foundation necessary to introduce photos of the scene taken shortly after Detective Blanchard's arrival on the scene. Once these preliminary steps were done, each photograph was laboriously identified, described in minute detail, and introduced into evidence before being passed, one by one, to the jury. No death is pretty, but this one, exacerbated by the tape, the bloating, and the pool of body fluid around the corpse, was particularly affective. Jurors studied, imagined the odor, shook their heads, and passed each photo to their neighbor until all had been studied and committed to memory. Blanchard then related that Coroner Carver had been summoned to the scene and undertook his examination of the body ending with the results related through Carver's earlier testimony.

To corroborate Harley Ames' testimony, Blanchard testified that yes, fingerprints of both Ames and Johnny Wayne Fulcher had been discovered on the outer doorknob of the Purvis residence and at numerous other locations within the abode. Once again, foundations were laid so large photographs of the fingerprints could be used to illustrate Purvis' testimony, introduced into evidence, and passed among the jurors.

Wiles then moved on to the plastic casts of tire impressions left on the Purvis lawn, impressions that were an exact match to Johnny Wayne Fulcher's truck. These molds, laid on a table in front of the twelve jurors, served as additional tangible evidence that Johnny Wayne Fulcher had been at Carlton Purvis's residence on the night of the murder. Some jurors might have doubted the existence of God, but all believed in science.

With this portion of Blanchard's investigation completed, it was time for Wiles to move on to Blanchard's discovery of the bodies in the well at Fulcher's residence, along with Fulcher's admissions to his girlfriend Misty. However, Judge Marcellus had other ideas. The day was late, and he wanted to get in nine holes of golf before dark.

"Bailiff, you can close Court until 9:00 tomorrow morning. Sharp."

Chapter 50

*"When you get to that level, it's
not a matter of talent anymore because
all of the players are so talented. It's about preparation,
about
playing smart and making good decisions."*
National Basketball Association All-Star
Hakeen Olajuwon

The next morning Judge Cletus Marcellus entered the courtroom. All present, including the jury, stood as the bailiff began his "Oyez! Oyez!" to open court.

Judge Marcellus directed that everyone be seated and instructed Detective Bunk Blanchard to take his place on the witness stand so the questioning ended by yesterday's recess could resume.

The day before the detective had explained his initial involvement in the event and his arrival at the residence of Carlton Purvis and the cadaver's condition as described by

Dr. Carver. Simple repetition re-enforced the district attorney's case. Corroboration boosted the memories of each juror and clarified the picture.

But Gerry Wiles intent in calling Blanchard wasn't simply to bolster his previous witnesses' testimonies.

The jury needed to learn that Johnny Wayne Fulcher was a mass murderer. A woman killer. With not just one casualty. Three young women. And another victim, this one a middle-aged man. Any one of Fulcher's prey could have been a juror's son or brother or daughter or sister or niece. And not murdered in the heat of passion with bodies left for families to provide a good and decent burial. But killed by brutal, painful beatings that resulted in broken and cut bones. And then, with an indecency that revolted even the hardest heart, the broken bodies of the man and three young girls had been thrown down a dark, dank well-shaft to rot in sitting water while loved ones searched, waited, and prayed for their safe return.

"Detective Blanchard, were you present when Johnny Wayne Fulcher was arrested?"

"I was, Sir. Yes, I was."

"And where did this take place, Sir?"

"Mr. Fulcher was arrested at his residence, at his farm, where he resided with Misty Street. Ms. Street was present at the time of the arrest."

"And did Mr. Fulcher resist arrest?"

"No, Sir, he did not. He was taken into custody and delivered to the sheriff's department by a deputy."

"And did you follow the deputy with Mr. Fulcher to the jail after Mr. Fulcher was taken into custody?"

"No Sir, I did not. I stayed at the residence and spoke with Ms. Street."

"And what, Sir, did you..."

At this time Bob Lee rose from his seat to interrupt.

"Your Honor, may Mr. Wiles and I kindly approach the bench?"

Wiles looked at Bob Lee with a look of consternation. He had been interrupted on the cusp of his bombshell.

"For what reason...?"

"Mr. Wiles, with his Honor's permission, could we approach the bench? May we, your Honor?"

Judge Marcellus waved his hand toward himself. "Approach."

Both attorneys laid their elbows on the bench and faced the Judge. Bob Lee whispered up.

"Your Honor, we would like for you to excuse the jury to the jury room while a voir dire is conducted as to the compellability of a witness."

"Compellability?" Wiles chirped up, agitated. "He's a detective for God's sake, Bob Lee."

Bob Lee didn't respond to Wiles. "Your Honor, this is a murder case and I would ask that you give me some latitude here. Please excuse the jury so a voir dire can be conducted. Otherwise I will have no choice but to ask the questions that you are refusing to be asked in the absence of the jury in the very presence of the jury. Doing that could prejudice this case and result in a reversal by an appellate court in the event of a conviction."

Bob Lee dropped his whisper and spoke in a low voice. He tapped his finger on the bench with insistence and addressed his thoughts to Judge Marcellus.

"I want to make sure that there is no error in this case that could result in a reversal in the event of a conviction. Having the voir dire in the absence of the jury would assure that Mr. Fulcher has been given a fair trial and that any verdict could not be overturned on that basis."

Bob Lee might not have had the best legal argument, but when he spoke once again to Judge Marcellus about avoiding a reversal, the judge listened.

"Take your seats, Counselors."

The Judge addressed the jury. "Ladies and gentlemen, I'm going to ask you to excuse yourselves while we conduct some important legal business in your absence. I assure you that your being excused has nothing to do with anything any of you may have said or done. We simply need a short while to figure out some important matters."

Detective Firth remained on the witness stand while the bailiff escorted the jury to the jury room. The Leader grabbed up his papers. The Mason simply looked in the direction of his travel. He had not looked at any of the witnesses, the attorneys, or Fulcher.

Judge Marcellus looked at Bob Lee.

"Mr. Pender, I understand you have some questions of this witness. You may proceed."

Bob Lee turned his attention to Detective Blanchard.

"Detective Blanchard, I understand that you spoke with Ms. Misty Street after Mr. Fulcher had left the premises of his farm to be processed at the Rockingham County jail, is that correct?"

"Why, yes, Mr. Pender, I did."

"And you repeated a large portion of this conversation in your written report pertaining to this case, did you not?"

"Why, yes, Sir, I did. I did in fact."

Bob Lee knew from the detective's written report exactly what point he intended the detective to prove. He asked each question with firmness, knowing the answers before Blanchard's responses. Blanchard, on the other hand, had no idea of the ultimate object of the questioning and could do little more than weakly agree with each question.

"Well, Detective Blanchard, I draw your attention to a particular aspect of that report, particularly that portion when you first discussed Ms. Street's residence. Ms. Street told you she lived with Mr. Fulcher, did she not?"

"Yes, Sir."

"And you verified Ms. Street's residence by examining her driver's license, did you not?"

"I did."

"And, after some conversation, Ms. Street told you she was afraid of Mr. Fulcher, did she not?"

"She did, Mr. Pender. Yes, she did."

"And then Ms. Street told you that Mr. Fulcher had told her that he had thrown bodies in a well that is located within a well house on the edge of the yard, next to a field, did she not?"

This was the first time Judge Marcellus heard about the bodies. He had already developed a keen and sincere disgust for the very existence of the Defendant Johnny Wayne Fulcher. But mention of the bodies caused his back to flex and for him to lean toward Blanchard.

And Blanchard found it difficult to believe his ears. Bob Lee was bringing up the subject of the four bodies himself!

"Why, yes, she did, Mr. Pender. She told me Johnny Wayne Fulcher had told her he had killed people and thrown them in a well located in the well-house."

"And she told you the door to the well house was locked, did she not?"

"Yes, Sir, she did. As a matter of fact, it was locked. Just like she said it would be."

Bob Lee wanted to retain control. "Thank you, Detective Blanchard, but if we could please stick to answering the questions asked, I'd appreciate it..."

Blanchard surrendered to the courtesy in Bob Lee's voice. "I'm sorry to have added something, Mr. Pender."

Bob Lee picked back up. "So, with the well house being locked, you needed a key to get in, didn't you? Or did you knock the door down?"

"Oh, no, Mr. Pender. Ms. Street gave the key to me."

"That's just what your report says, Detective Blanchard. She didn't physically give you the key, did she? Wasn't the key hidden, and didn't she tell you where the key was?"

Blanchard's smile disappeared, and he answered somewhat defensively. "Well, Ms. Street told us it was hidden."

"That's correct, Detective Blanchard. Let's clarify that, shall we?"

"Okay."

"The key was not actually given to you by her handing the physical key over to you, was it? It was hidden, and hidden not just from you, but from Ms. Street also, was it not?"

Blanchard had no idea where Bob Lee was headed. Wiles was powerless. Nothing to object to.

"She gave me the key by telling me where it was." Blanchard was being elusive.

"Ms. Street told you the key was hidden from her, but she knew where it was, and that Johnny Wayne Fulcher didn't know she knew where it was, didn't she?"

Blanchard took the offensive.

"Yes, Sir, that's exactly what she said. And she said that she lived there as a lawful resident and had proof of the residence and that Johnny Wayne didn't know that she knew where he had hidden it. And from what she told me, the key was found at her own lawful residence, Mr. Pender."

Bob Lee remained unflustered.

"And Ms. Street told you the key was hidden under a rock at the right corner of the well house, and that's exactly where you found it. Correct?"

"Yes, Mr. Pender. It is."

"And you found the key exactly where it was hidden by Mr. Fulcher, used the key to unlock the well house, looked in the well house and eventually discovered four bodies at the bottom of the well, did you not?"

Blanchard reverted to his confusion about why Bob Lee could possibly want all of this brought into evidence.

"Yes, Sir, we did. Me and my deputies found the bodies. There were the broken bones of three young girls and one middle-aged man. That's all that was left."

"And you wouldn't have found those remains at that moment had you not used that key that Ms. Street told you about, would you? The key led to the bodies, didn't it?"

Blanchard simply returned a confused look to Pender. Pender didn't wait for an answer to the question.

"And--and I don't mean to be repetitious, Officer--but, when you get down to brass tacks, if Ms. Street hadn't told you where the key was, you wouldn't have found the bodies when you did, would you?"

"Well, not right then, but we would have found them sooner or later."

"Officer Blanchard, you hadn't found them up until that day, and on that day you found them because Ms. Street told you where the key was, correct?"

"I guess so, Mr. Pender."

"Guess?"

Pender waited for an answer. Blanchard realized Pender was attacking the validity of his search of the well house and was, somehow, boxing him in to keep the bodies from being discussed before the jury. He turned to seek refuge from Judge Marcellus only to be instructed, "Answer the question, Detective Fitts."

"I'm sorry, Mr. Lee. No, Sir, we would not have found them, not at that particular moment. But we would have eventually found them."

Bob Lee inserted the knife...

"And the search warrant... Which magistrate gave you a search warrant to go into the well house?"

Blanchard smiled. "We didn't have a search warrant, Mr. Pender. We didn't need one."

Bob Lee twisted the knife and asked the next questions in an incredulous, soprano voice.

"You didn't? You didn't need a search warrant?"

There was no need to await a response. Bob Lee lowered his voice, slowed his cadence, and asked inquisitively, "And I'm sure you called a magistrate or the district attorney to get their legal opinion on that, did you not?"

"No, Sir."

"And the well house is within the fence of the yard separating it from the field, correct?"

"It is," Fitts replied.

"I think you referred to the well house as being 'beyond the curtilage' in your report, did you not, Detective?"

"I did," Fitts answered.

"But on second thought, considering the well house was within the fence and a stone's throw from the house, isn't it apparent that you made an honest mistake in typing the word "beyond" and actually meant "within the bounds of the curtilage"?

Fitts was squirming.

"Well, Mr. Lee, I guess the Judge could decide whether it was or not. That's for him to decide."

Bob Lee finished up. "I thank you for that, Sir. No more questions."

Assistant District Attorney posed a few questions for meaningless clarification. Judge Marcellus then asked Bob Lee, "Are there any other witnesses you'd like to call, Mr. Pender?"

Bob Lee stood.

"Yes, your Honor. I would call Ms. Misty Street to the stand, Your Honor."

Chapter 51

"Many of life's circumstances are created by three basic choices: The disciplines you choose to keep, the people you choose to be with, and the laws you choose to obey."

Charles Milhuff

Misty Street shot up from the second row pew where she sat. True to form, she had worn a red miniskirt stretching to just below her waterline and coifed her white hair into a beehive that made her height total over six feet. The bumblebee tattoo, broadened to six inches in width by reason of simple gravity, weight, and time, brought to mind a colored Rorschach inkblot as jurors' eyes were magnetically drawn to the edge of her see-through blouse. Her aging silicone torpedoes, suspended by a NASA-inspired designed bra made of Kevlar aramid fiber sold only in Greensboro's Target stores, threatened to break their carriage and dive-bomb to the floor like a pair of overfed bulldog puppies.   Pink, pink frosted lipstick highlighted her lips.

She was in the spotlight! Her moment had arrived!

Misty carefully laid the purse containing little more than her cosmetics on the pew, and strutted her 175 pounds of flaccid flesh on pressured three-inch heels down the alley between the counsel tables. She paused between the tables, resplendent in the aura she cast among the recesses of her mind and looked, not at Johnny Wayne, but to the Judge.

Judge Marcellus was not impressed. "Ms. Street, approach the witness stand and take a seat." He had seen a thousand like her. Or at least he thought he had.

Misty took her oath and faced Bob Lee. She glanced at Johnny Wayne, fought back a smile, and surveyed the courtroom. Judge Marcellus directed Bob Lee to proceed.

"Could you tell us your name, please?"

"Why, Mr. Pender, you know who I am." She drew her knees together, folded her hands in her lap, and batted her eyes. "I'm Misty Street."

"Do you prefer I address you as 'Miss Street' or 'Mrs. Street' or 'Mrs. Fulcher'?"

Misty was caught off guard.

"Excuse me?"

"We'll come back to that, ma'am. Let me ask you a couple of questions about Mr. Blanchard, if I may, and then we'll circle back, okay?"

Misty nodded with a frown. She was curious about why he had questioned her name.

"For the time being I'm going to call you 'Miss Street,' okay?"

Misty was nonplussed. There was a bob in her head. "Whatever..."

The "Whatever" struck Judge Cletus Marcellus's ear like a brick. His hand hit the bench with a slap, and he raised his voice. "Miss Street. Answer the question with a reply. Any more smart answers from that mouth of yours or any insolent or disrespectful attitude displayed by you will land you in jail. Remember where you are. You are in a courtroom. Better yet, you are in my courtroom. You are hearing your one and only admonition, a warning. Are you clear on what I'm saying?"

The right hand of Misty Street reached weakly toward the microphone that sat to the right of the witness stand. She quivered a "Yes, Your Honor." Misty was shaken. She had been in a jail cell before and didn't like it.

Bob Lee asked His Honor for permission to proceed. It was granted.

"Now. ma'am, please listen. You were in the courtroom and heard Detective Blanchard testify that you told him where the key to the well house was hidden, were you not?"

"I was, Mr. Pender, Sir," she answered in a contrite voice.

"Mr. Fulcher had hidden the key from you, had he not?"

"He did, Mr. Pender. He wouldn't let me go in it. Told me not to go in it. Didn't think I knew where the key was, but he dug it out in front of me when I was looking through the window about two months before."

"How far were you from him when he 'dug it out'?" Bob Lee asked.

"I was inside the house looking out the window, and he was at the well house."

Bob Lee was trying to be more specific for the record.

"So could you please estimate, just for the written record, please, how many feet away Mr. Fulcher was from you when you were inside the house, and he was at the well house 'digging out' the key? Just an estimate, please."

"I'd guess about 200 feet, Mr. Pender. Maybe 175. No more than 175 feet."

Pender was appreciative.

"Thank you, Miss Street. 175 feet. So, you never told him you knew where it was, did you?"

"No, Sir. He might have killed me."

"You were very, very afraid that Mr. Fulcher might find out that you knew where he kept his secret key and harm you because you knew, were you not?"

The Queen Bee thought she had Johnny Wayne where she wanted him.

"You know better than that, Mr. Pender. You know J.W. from court and from the street. You know I'd end up in the bottom of that well with the rest of them if he knew that I knew where that key was. You know I would."

"So you told Detective Blanchard where the key was, and you gave Detective Blanchard permission to go into the well house?"

"I did."

"But even you didn't have permission to go into the well house from Mr. Fulcher himself, did you?"

Misty spoke up.

"No, he wouldn't let me go in there. He didn't want me to go in there! There was a reason..."

Bob Lee interrupted and changed course.

"And your name isn't on the deed to the farm where you were staying, is it, ma'am?"

"No, I just live there. He inherited it. But it's my house, too."

"Do you still live there?"

"Yes, Sir, I do."

"But it's not titled in your name, is it?"

"No, Sir, it is not."

Bob Lee switched subjects again. He intended to keep the witness unsettled.

"I'd like to clarify your name, if I may, ma'am. Could you help me do that?"

Misty turned on her "sweet" voice.

"I'm not sure what you're asking, Mr. Pender."

"I'm going to ask Mr. Ken Childrey to stand up from the third row, ma'am. Mr. Childrey came to your house about three months ago and took measurements of the yard. Do you remember him?"

Ken Childrey stood and was surveyed by the witness. "Is that the cable guy?" She squinted. "Yeah, I remember him. He measured my yard for free cable. I never got it!"

Bob Lee decided to circle back around. "And you remember Mr. Childrey being out in the yard measuring things, do you not, ma'am?"

"Yes, Sir, Mr. Pender. I remember. He was trying to find out why our cable was leaking."

"And if I were to call Mr. Childrey, the cable guy, to the stand and he were to testify that he had measured and the distance from your back door, the one leading to your back porch, and the door to the well house was 193 and one-half feet, would you disagree with him?"

Misty nodded her head.

"Why, Mr. Pender, I couldn't call him a liar. He had his tape and all."

"Do you remember identifying yourself as 'Mrs. Fulcher' to him? Do you remember doing that, telling him your last name was Fulcher?"

Misty paused to think.

"Well, yeah, I suppose I did tell him that. He had an offer for free cable so I told him I was Mrs. Fulcher. I had to do that to get free cable, which I never got. So what of it?"

Misty hesitated and snapped her head toward Judge Marcellus. She had caught herself crossing a line with His Honor. She quickly corrected herself.

"I mean, Yes, Sir. I did."

Bob Lee pursued the issue.

"I'd like to back up a few years, ma'am. You and Mr. Fulcher lived together in South Carolina for over a year about two or three years ago, didn't you? It was down in Little River, South Carolina, I believe..."

"Why, yes, Mr. Pender, we did. J.W. worked on a shrimp boat, and I got a job, too. We both worked." She looked over at Johnny Wayne, who was leaning forward with both elbows on the defense table. Their eyes met. Johnny Wayne gave one of his slight country grins and nodded his head.

Bob Lee smiled. He became conversant with her, trying to get her to loosen up.

"You're exactly right, ma'am. You worked. I believe you worked at the Zippy Pik right there in Little River. Worked a lot of hours, I bet."

Misty chirped right in. "Yes, Mr. Pender I did. I worked there and brought home the bacon. J.W. spent his money on beer and such."

"I'm sure he did, ma'am. I'm sure he did. But what I wanted to ask you about might sound kind of strange, but it has me a bit confused. A mutual friend of ours named Tommy Austin tells me he was in Little River for Bike Week a couple of years ago and saw you at work. He tells me your name tag read 'Misty Fulcher' and that he's willing to come testify, and bring some of his friends to testify, to that as a fact if you disagree with him. If Tommy Austin had said that, would he be a liar, ma'am?"

Misty adjusted a bra strap with her shoulder and looked toward one of the ceiling lights. "Well, I just wore that tag. We never went to no preacher, Mr. Pender."

"Oh, I understand that, ma'am. You didn't ever go to a preacher, but weren't you wearing a wedding band about that time, ma'am?"

"Yeah, I guess I was. J.W. wanted me to wear it to keep men from hittin' on me at work."

"And your paychecks and the forms you sent in to South Carolina for tax purposes had your name down as 'Misty Street Fulcher', did they not?"

"I guess they did, Mr. Pender. Yes, they did."

Bob Lee pushed the issue.

"Ma'am, didn't you file joint federal and State of South Carolina income tax returns with Mr. Fulcher that year?"

"Income tax returns?"

"Yes, a joint federal and a state income tax return. One where you sign your name on the bottom of both. Where you sign your name, saying everything in those returns is true. Under penalty of law. You wouldn't commit a state or federal offense and lie about something like that, would you, ma'am?"

"Oh, no, Mr. Pender. No, Sir, not on purpose." She was trapped.

"You filed a joint return with Mr. Fulcher as husband and wife that year, didn't you?"

Misty hesitated.

"If you say so, Mr. Pender."

"Ma'am, it's not what I say, it's what you say. Did you or did you not?"

Misty clenched her teeth. Her voice rose.

"Yes, Sir, we did."

She went on the attack.

"And there warn't nothin' wrong with that, Mr. Pender, 'cause we felt like we were married. We were married in the eyes of God and everyone else, even if we didn't get no license. We told everybody we were married because it was between us. We was married between us. And between everyone who knew us. That's what mattered!"

Bob Lee seemed to give in. He lowered his voice, and asked his next question almost apologetically.

"I suppose those were better times, were they not, Mrs. Fulcher? You and Mr. Fulcher have had good times, and you have had bad times, but you always ended up together at the end of the day, did you not?"

She was looking at Johnny Wayne. They hadn't been in each other's presence since the night of the arrest. She had been lonely.

"We loved each other."

Misty removed a tissue from her bra.

"We had something special. Ain't nothing wrong with that. Ain't nothing wrong with soul mates doing like we did. Ain't no man going to judge us on what we did, so I won't say I'm sorry. It's between us and God."

Bob Lee was quiet.

Then he softly agreed. "Yes, Mrs. Fulcher, it is."

Misty testified in a murmur, twisting the tissue in her hands and looking down.

"Sometimes people work problems out and sometimes they don't. That's why I took off the ring. Ain't nothing illegal about that. Ain't nothin' wrong with that, either. That's between me and God. That's what it is."

Bob Lee reassured her. "No, Mrs. Fulcher, there's nothing wrong with that," he said quietly.

Bob Lee put his hand on Johnny Wayne's shoulder. He looked at Johnny Wayne, and then he looked at Misty.

His voice was kind.

"Mrs. Fulcher, let me ask you one last question. Do you want to testify against your husband?"

Misty Fulcher broke down.

"No, God help me! I do not! May God strike me dead if I do. I won't do it."

Bob Lee thanked the witness. Voice inflection or not, Misty Street's testimony was in the written record. He looked in the direction of the assistant district attorney.

"Your witness, Mr. Wiles."

Wiles had no questions. She was a flake.

Chapter 52

"Truth hurts. Maybe not as much as jumping on a bicycle with the seat missing, but it hurts."

Leslie Neilson

Misty stepped from the witness stand, sobbing.

Judge Marcellus asked Bob Lee if he had any further witnesses. Bob Lee said no, but that he would like to be heard by the Court regarding the admissibility of evidence. Marcellus seemed interested.

Bob Lee rose from behind the defense counsel table.

"Your Honor, I ask this Court to suppress anything and all evidence whatsoever that pertains to any discoveries by the sheriff's department within the well house located on Mr. Fulcher's property for numerous reasons. Let me spell them out to you."

"The first reason is that the sheriff's department was required to obtain a search warrant before it searched the well house. The following facts are undisputed:"

Bob Lee laid one finger of his hand in the palm of the other.

"First, that Mr. Fulcher was the sole owner of the land."

Then the second finger.

"Second, that Misty Street, or Mrs. Johnny Wayne Fulcher, cohabitated with Mr. Fulcher on Mr. Fulcher's land."

"Third, that in the absence of Mr. Fulcher, Detective Bunk Blanchard obtained a key to the locked well house based on information given to him by Misty Street, or Fulcher."

"Fourth, that the location of the key was Mr. Fulcher's secret from Misty Street, or Misty Fulcher."

"Fifth, that the well house is located within the curtilage of the Fulcher home place. Despite the opinion of the Detective—and it is no more than an erroneous opinion—this Court should rule as a matter of law that the well house, being 193 feet from the house and within the fence and mowed area of the yard, is within the curtilage."

Bob Lee Pender was laying it out.

Step by step.

"Everything I have pointed out is undisputed, Your Honor. All of it," he said with conviction.

"Let's look at the next step down this path: What is also undisputed, and unsaid until this moment, is that Mr. Johnny Wayne Fulcher had, as the Supreme Court of this nation and this state described, an 'expectation of privacy' in whatever lay behind that locked door. We do not dispute that Misty Street, or Mrs. Misty Fulcher, could give permission for the deputy sheriff to search what I will call 'the open estate' of Mr. Fulcher, that is, those areas within the curtilage in which *both* Mr. Fulcher and Misty had access. There is *no* individual expectation of privacy within those areas."

Pender held both hands before him, palms in as if he were cradling a ball.

"But when we're talking private places within the curtilage, such as locked diaries, a car where the other party or spouse isn't allowed to have a key, the Supreme Court has repeatedly held that the expectation of privacy *requires* the State to obtain a search warrant."

He pointed at Detective Blanchard.

"There were no exigent circumstances requiring an immediate search, Your Honor. None. No emergencies or evidence being destroyed. A search warrant *could* have been obtained. It was not. Mr. Fulcher was in custody, and Detective Blanchard had until the end of eternity to make a simple phone call and obtain a simple search warrant as required by the very Constitution our forefathers fought and died for. He failed to do that."

Bob Lee paused and looked down. After a telling moment his head rose, and he stated what he contended to be a fact.

"The evidence should be suppressed and ruled inadmissible by this Court."

Judge Marcellus was almost nodding his head. All three attorneys--the Judge, the district attorney, and Bob Lee-- knew this law.

Bob Lee continued.

"And let me give you the second reason this evidence should be suppressed, your Honor. I earlier told the Court that we questioned the compellability of a witness in this case to give evidence against Mr. Fulcher."

Bob Lee lingered for effect. He turned, looked at Misty, and pointed as he made his pronouncement.

"Your Honor, Misty Street Fulcher is the lawful wife of Mr. Johnny Wayne Fulcher."

Misty sat expressionless. She had no idea of the ramifications of her living in South Carolina with Johnny Wayne Fulcher. Bob Lee was about to explain them to her.

"Your Honor, North Carolina General Statute 51-1 defines the elements of a valid marriage. There must be a marriage ceremony, whether you're getting married in a church or before a civil servant. And there must be two witnesses. If you don't have a marriage ceremony and two witnesses in North Carolina, you aren't married."

"Mr. and Mrs. Fulcher moved from the State of North Carolina and took up residence in the State of South Carolina. They became South Carolina residents. They signed a joint income tax return designating the Great State of South Carolina as their residence. They held themselves out to the public and to their friends as husband and wife."

"As the court may know, the laws in South Carolina and North Carolina differ in regard to the requisites of marriage."

Bob Lee looked down at his notes. He continued with his argument.

"South Carolina recognizes *common law* marriages. For a common law marriage to be recognized, the parties must live together and hold themselves out to everyone as being husband and wife even if there is no marriage license or certificate."

He placed his right hand on Johnny Wayne's left shoulder and glanced toward Misty again.

"In this case, there is no disagreement about the facts. The facts are undisputed. Mr. and Mrs. Fulcher lived together in South Carolina. They held themselves out to the entire world as being husband and wife. Mrs. Fulcher wore a name tag at work holding herself out as 'Mrs. Fulcher.' Her paychecks were made out to 'Misty Fulcher.' She filed joint federal and state income taxes as a person married to Johnny Wayne Fulcher. She even wore a wedding band. Since that time, no divorce proceedings have been filed or adjudicated."

Bob Lee got to the bottom line.

"Johnny Wayne Fulcher and Misty Street remain in the status as husband and wife. Plain and simple. As husband and wife, Mrs. Misty Fulcher is, by virtue of North Carolina General Statute 8-51, not compellable to testify against Mr. Fulcher. She has testified under oath that she does not wish to do so. The written record reflects that and that fact is undisputed by the State."

Wiles remained seated and scribbled notes as Pender continued.

"There's one more link in this chain, Your Honor. The only way for the hearsay evidence of Detective Blanchard, that being the testimony by Mrs. Fulcher that she told him where the secret key was hidden, to be admissible is if that evidence is corroborated, or backed up, by the witness who made the statement. In this case it is Mrs. Fulcher. Mrs. Fulcher is refusing to testify and therefore will not, and cannot, corroborate it."

Bob Lee reached his logical conclusion.

"Detective Blanchard's testimony of everything pertaining to what was on the other side of that locked well house door is, therefore, inadmissible."

There was one last plea.

"We ask this Court to concur with these contentions."

Bob Lee slowly lowered himself into his seat and pushed the notes lying on the defense table to the side. He had worked hard. It was time to rest a bit as he listened to the assistant district attorney's contentions.

Chapter 53

"Drunk logic: She's only ugly in the face."

Unknown

Judge Cletus Marcellus was visibly upset in his consideration of Bob Lee Pender's presentation. He was watching a filthy murderer of at least five people sit on the verge of being set free because an idiot detective had been too eager to take a peek and too lazy to even inquire about the necessity of obtaining a search warrant from the district attorney's office.

"What do you have to say about what Mr. Pender has just argued, Mr. Wiles?" the Judge asked.

"Your Honor, I would ask for a brief recess to conduct some quick research into the validity of Mr. Pender's arguments and the weight this Court should grant them."

Judge Marcellus was not buying that. He blasted into Gerry Wiles.

"Mr. Wiles, you and I have both heard the evidence and the arguments. We have fourteen good fellow citizens, twelve jurors and two alternates, sitting in that jury room, and I'm not going to make them wait one second for you or anyone else to go look up the law. The burden is on you to have been ready to defend all evidence you intended to present, and now you have the opportunity to do just that."

The courtroom became quiet. Marcellus waited and then spoke up.

"Let me hear what you have to say, Mr. Wiles."

"Your Honor, I..."

Judge Marcellus interrupted him.

"I have two questions to ask you, Mr. Wiles. I ask these questions of you solely in your capacity as a district attorney for The People. The first is very simple: Did Mr. Fulcher have a reasonable expectation of privacy against all persons in the world in what was behind that door after he locked the door and hid the key? Mr. Pender has not disputed the facts as you have presented them and has accepted them, at least for the purposes of his argument, as being true. Did the Defendant Fulcher, or did he not, have a reasonable expectation of privacy?"

Wiles was almost visibly shaking. Fulcher had been within his grasp. He had finally had him. Before day's end he might be on the street.

"Your Honor, Mr. Fulcher did not have a reasonable expectation of privacy. He simply placed the key under a rock where it was visible to the whole world that he was either taking it out or putting it back. Anyone could see him do that. As a matter of fact, that's what Misty Street saw him doing."

Judge Marcellus challenged him.

"Mr. Wiles, it is not in dispute from the very evidence that you yourself presented that Misty Street or Misty Fulcher, whichever you prefer, told both Detective Blanchard and this Court that Mr. Fulcher hid the key from her. She discovered where it was. How could he not be seeking privacy, even if for the wrong reasons, which this Court is absolutely not allowed to presume, if he was hiding the key?"

Wiles knew he was grasping for straws and simply irritating Judge Marcellus with the paucity of logic in his contentions.

"Your Honor, if I tried to hide an elephant in an open field, I would not be entitled to claim privacy if someone saw me trying to do so. Mr. Fulcher was in an open space, visible to the whole world, when he tried to hide the key. If we want to presume facts, let us presume this: the key was never hidden because Mr. Fulcher was so poor at hiding it! Any expectation of privacy under such circumstances should not be found to be 'reasonable.'"

Judge Marcellus nodded, but inwardly he was not convinced.

"Mr. Wiles, let me ask you a second question, which contains two parts: Is Misty Street in fact the wife of the defendant and therefore Mrs. Johnny Wayne Fulcher, and may you, as the State, compel her to testify against Mr. Fulcher?"

Wiles knew that to argue that Misty Fulcher was not in fact the common law wife of Johnny Wayne Fulcher and that he could compel her to testify was a losing proposition. He changed the subject.

"Your Honor, I respectfully argue to this Court that the marital status of Misty Street is irrelevant to this matter and merely a red herring that only confuses the issues."

Marcellus looked interested.

"And?"

Wiles had gotten the judge to nibble.

"Your Honor, the defendant is attempting to exclude the statements of Misty Street as hearsay. I argue to this Court that the statement may have been hearsay, but that it falls within one of the exceptions to the hearsay rule. One of the exceptions in which such a statement is admissible is as a 'spontaneous utterance'. It is clear from the evidence that Miss Street's statements were made under trying circumstances and in the heat of the police coming to her house and making an arrest."

Marcellus looked as if he had been let down.

"That's it?" he thought.

Wiles waited for a question from the Court.

Marcellus leaned back and asked, "Is there anything else, Mr. Wiles?"

"No, Your Honor."

"Mr. Pender, anything you would like to say to rebut any of Mr. Wiles' arguments?"

Bob Lee rose. "No, Your Honor."

Marcellus was visibly disgusted. He rose from his seat, pointed to both counsel.

"Court is recessed for five minutes, Bailiff. Have the jury in the box in those five minutes. Counsel, get yourselves into my chambers. And do it *now*."

Chapter 54

"What is the origin of my own anger? Is it the ego defending its territory, or is it something that has its source in the desire for the well-being of all?"

Jean-Yves Leloup

Bob Lee and Wiles sat in the exact seats pointed to them by Judge Marcellus. Marcellus did not remove his robe or take a seat. He chose to stand behind his desk, arms waving from beneath his robe like the Angel Gabriel, and staring from beneath his uncombed, white, wiry eyebrows down at the two counsel.

"Mr. Wiles, am I correct in assuming that Detective Blanchard is your last witness and that once he has testified you will rest the State's case?"

Wiles was almost sheepish.

"Yes, Your Honor, that is our case. Detective Blanchard's testimony will complete our case."

Marcellus raised his chin, looked through the window onto the courthouse lawn, and spoke.

"Gentlemen," he began, "you both know that I'm only a referee here. I'm supposed to call them as I see them and let the jury decide which way it's going to go. That's what I do, and that's what I'm going to keep doing."

The judge turned to face the lawyers.

"I sit there, rule on the law, and keep my mouth shut while you two guys duke it out and try to sell your goods to a jury. Nobody on that jury is supposed to look up at me and get an idea what I'm thinking when deciding if a defendant is guilty or innocent."

Bob Lee suppressed a chuckle at His Honor's disingenous suggestion that he didn't try to sway juries.

His voice began rising.

"But the door is shut, and I'm going to tell both of you what I'm thinking. No, not what I'm thinking. What I'm wondering..."

Neither counsel dared to interrupt. His Honor commanded the stage.

Judge Cletus Marcellus was not known for admitting he didn't know everything. He started his question with an inquisitive tone.

"Wiles, in what corner of the back side of a filthy, stinking, manure-filled horse barn did you dig up that idiot Detective Blanchard or Deputy Fife or whatever his name is? Who in the hell caught your good sheriff having sex with a stud monkey and blackmailed him into hiring, or what kind of political favor could he possibly owe to cause him to hire an apparently cross-bred, half-witted imbecile without the patience of a three-year-old wanting to pee in his pants? A sniper wouldn't take that guy out! So stupid he couldn't wait to get a simple rubber-stamped, pre-printed form search warrant from one of his friendly magistrates?"

The Judge apparently suffered from an inability to control his blood pressure. His face had turned beet red and droplets of spittle shot from his mouth as his voice boomed.

"He could have gotten a search warrant in ten minutes, for God's sake! What the hell was he thinking, Wiles? Where did Efron Bailey dig up this guy?? Bailey had to be drunker than Cooter Brown when he hired that guy. Is he Bailey's kid by a girlfriend? Why is he on the payroll? You need to impanel a grand jury and do a world-class investigation on what kind of dirt that idiot detective must have on Sheriff Efron Bailey to cause Bailey to turn a murder investigation over to him."

Wiles sat quietly, frozen, providing the Judge with his attention. Marcellus' hand slapped his desk.

"Or, better yet, maybe you should call '60 Minutes' and have them do a piece on what kind of gene pool in this county would elect such an idiot as sheriff to hire Blanchard as a detective."

Gerry Wiles didn't dare interrupt His Honor. Marcellus was outraged at Detective Blanchard and had directed his venom toward Sheriff Bailey and Blanchard instead of Wiles. Wiles desperately preferred to keep it pointed in that direction. He was intimidated, his voice unsure.

"Judge Marcellus, I don't…"

"You're most certainly right you don't, Mr. Wiles. You're damned right, you don't. You don't have a snowball's chance in hell to put away a filthy murderer who has killed at least five people because of that idiot, three of them just young girls. Kids, for God's sakes. Kids! It doesn't sound like this Carlton Purvis character was such a loss. Fulcher probably did us a favor. But four others, thrown into a well. Good Lord, Wiles, what in the name of Mary is that guy doing as a detective?"

Gerry Wiles had nothing that was safe to say to Judge Marcellus at this moment. He simply looked down at his hands, almost contrite in his attitude.

"Let me tell you what I see at this point, Mr. Wiles. Mr. Pender sitting over here has done his job. Your evidence about the well house is not going to be admitted. It's my decision, and I'm not going to allow it to be introduced into evidence. There's no way I won't get overruled by the Court of Appeals if I let it in. No way. And I'm not going to look like some fool idiot and stand up in that courtroom and put on the record that I think that Deputy Fife out there didn't have to get a simple search warrant. Hell no, I won't do that. He could have gotten a search warrant, and he should have gotten a search warrant, if for no other reason than to cover his own ass. He had time to get one, and he didn't. He should have. All three of us know that."

Wiles was looking at the Judge. Bob Lee examined the scuffs on his shoes to avoid eye contact, poker-faced. He was smiling inside.

The Judge went on.

"So that leaves you with the coroner's report about the cause of death and the testimony of Harley Ames, an obvious drug dealer. He's an obvious drug dealer who was there when the killing took place trying to collect a debt and could have done it himself. He has every reason to lie to cover his own tracks."

Marcellus turned from angry to sarcastic.

"Oh, and let's not forget the right reverend and highly credible Mr. Cheech Mann. I've seen Mann time and time again in this courtroom, Mr. Wiles. Is that as good as the State can do in this case? Is Cheech Mann's word what the State is relying on to put a man to death? He may not be the Father of This Country, but he could arguably be the Father of Rockingham County."

Marcellus placed his right hand on his desk and leaned over Gerry Wiles. Wiles barely dared to peek up.

"Wiles, you've got enough to get to the jury. I can't rule on the credibility of your sorry-assed witnesses. The law doesn't allow that. The jury's got to do that. That's what the law requires. And theoretically they could believe your witnesses and find Fulcher guilty. So even though you don't have a snowball's chance in hell of having them believe your witnesses and winning this case, it's going to go to make it to the jury because that's what the law requires. And they're going to be laughing about your witnesses and send Fulcher home after taking up all of these days in this fine courtroom."

Neither attorney responded to the Judge. Marcellus had the floor.

"The only chance you'd have, Mr. Wiles, is if Fulcher were insane enough to take the stand and let you cross-examine him about those four bodies, which he's not going to do because of his constitutional right to not take the stand. It's going to the jury, and the jury's going to deliberate for less than an hour before it comes back and lets a man who has killed five people back on the street."

Marcellus looked out the window.

"And maybe that's how it should be, gentlemen. The State has not proved its case beyond a reasonable doubt. Too often we forget that the issue in these cases isn't whether or not the defendant did or did not commit a crime. *The only issue for the jury to decide is whether or not the State proved every element of the crime beyond a reasonable doubt.* I just heard Bob Lee remind the jury of that fact the other day, but still we attorneys often forget it. It's that simple: Did the State prove it? Did it prove it beyond a reasonable doubt? In this case, Mr. Wiles and

Mr. Pender, the State has not proved it, and the jury will correctly decide that it did not. And that's how it is."

The judge began rubbing his own neck with his left hand.

"Right now I don't like it, and I weep for the families of those poor people in the well, but that's how it is."

There was a moment of quiet. Neither attorney had the courage to make a comment on the judge's remarks. Marcellus retained command of the room.

"Gentlemen, we're going to go back into that courtroom, and I'm going to rule in favor of Mr. Pender's motion to suppress any testimony or evidence that would allow the bodies in the well house to be admitted. Then Mr. Wiles is going to rest the State's case."

Marcellus looked over at Bob Lee. He then went through his projection of the coming events in the trial—one, two, three…

"I presume Mr. Fulcher is going to rest on his constitutional right to remain silent and not testify. Mr. Wiles will then make his pitch to the jury and try to convince them that, in essence, they should convict Mr. Fulcher on the word of the Honorable Mr. Harley Ames. Mr. Pender will then give his arguments to the contrary. I will then instruct the jury, and I predict the jury will return a verdict of not guilty before the end of the day, allowing me a long weekend with my wife at the coast in Kitty Hawk."

Marcellus then issued a directive.

"Mr. Wiles, before I rule, I want you to get Sheriff Efron Bailey's skinny ass up in this courtroom. Front row. And tell him I said for him to take off his damn hat when he walks into my courtroom and that he's better not smile or wave hello at me."

The judge began walking back around behind his desk, his back to the attorneys, with his right index finger wagging toward the ceiling.

"You tell that incompetent, Bible-thumping son-of-a-bitch sheriff of yours that if he's not on the front row of that courtroom when I walk in that, so help me God, I'll contrive some reason to incarcerate him for contempt of court in the jail of an adjacent county and that I'll personally stop by the jail to make sure he's there at midnight. I mean that, Wiles! I mean that! *Get him here.*"

Wiles was prompt. "Yes, Sir, Your Honor. I'll see to it."

Bob Lee Pender hadn't muttered a sound since entering Judge Marcellus' chambers. After all, when a judge is in the process of announcing a ruling that's falling in the lawyer's favor—right or wrong—a good lawyer never, ever interrupts him. A good lawyer keeps his mouth shut and lets it fall. And a better lawyer flees the courtroom before the judge can change his mind.

Bob Lee rose from his chair and quickly followed Gerry Wiles from the judge's chambers. He didn't linger to thank Judge Marcellus.

Chapter 55

"In a closed society where everybody's guilty, the only crime is in getting caught."
Hunter S. Thompson

"Well, I think we tried very hard not to be overconfident, because when you get overconfident, that's when something snaps up and bites you."
U.S. Astronaut Neil Armstrong

Within ten minutes Judge Marcellus seated himself on the bench and looked directly at the High Sheriff seated on the front row. Deputy Arnie Robertson sat in full uniformed regalia to his right, with Detective Blanchard to his left. The jury remained in the jury room. Marcellus knew local newspaper reporters and even a reporter from a local television station were in the courtroom. Abby Trimyer, who had leaked the federal grand jury subpoena of Purvis in her newspaper, had driven from Roanoke for the trial and sat among the reporters, small legal pad and Scripto pen in her hands. Jamie Watson, U.S. Attorney Tim Herndon's agent, had also arrived from Roanoke but refused to acknowledge, much less speak to, Abby Trimyer and intentionally sat two rows ahead to both avoid having to see Abby and also be within Abby's line of vision.

On the second row from the rear sat an unnoticed and indistinguishable courtroom observer. Even Jamie Watson didn't know or recognize Paul Gil Reed, her boss's informant who had machinated all that was taking place within the walls of this courtroom. Reed had succumbed to a human weakness---curiosity. He had kept up with the trial in the newspaper and had driven from Leasburg simply to watch the proceedings as an interested bystander. The more he watched Johnny Wayne Fulcher, the more comfortable he grew with the idea that he had taken part in an innocent man having been charged with the murder of his daughter's drug pusher. Innocent of at least that killing. But four bodies in the well. The man was an apparent animal. At least he had contributed in part, however unnoticed, in keeping Johnny Wayne Fulcher off the streets for the time he awaited trial.

Marcellus began his ruling, looking not at counsel or the clerk, but directly into the eyes of the sheriff. He strove for media reportable drama.

"Madam Clerk, let the record reflect that court has been re-adjourned and that this Court has before it the admissibility of evidence pertaining the discovery of not one, not two, not three, but four additional unsolved murders that have taken place during the administration of the current sheriff of this county."

The judge noticed the reporters' pens scratching their legal pads. He slowed his speech and lowered his voice.

"These four murders were particularly heinous, particularly cruel. Hack marks on the bones of the corpses. Three young women, just beginning their lives and full of promise. A man. All most assuredly with loved ones. All precious. Thrown into a dark, dank well to decompose, lost to those who loved them, deprived of even a simple ceremony of burial. Thrown away like trash. These four could be the family members of any person in this county, loved and cherished, and disrespectfully disposed of as if these children of God were simple filth."

Marcellus's gaze did not leave Bailey. The reporters scrambled to write every word.

"Unfortunately, no one will probably ever be convicted of these four murders. Unfortunately, oversight, or the lack of oversight, of the detective division in this county's sheriff's department has allowed an investigation so incompetent that the law will not permit any reference of the fate of these four unfortunates to be admitted into evidence in this trial. There is no question in this Court's mind that Detective Blanchard should have, as the law clearly requires, obtained a search warrant in this case. No question whatsoever."

Sheriff Efron Bailey did not shake his head in disapproval. It wasn't worth the risk of what a challenged Judge Marcellus could do to him.

"Detective Blanchard had the time; he had the means; he had the basis in law to obtain one had he made an effort to do so. But he did not. His immature, amateurish, childlike eagerness to open that door overshadowed what the law required him to do before he opened it, and that is that he obtain a search warrant as by law provided."

Blanchard, seated next the sheriff, clicked his ballpoint pen twice.

"There is no need for me to rule on the admissibility of the evidence based on objections raised pertaining to husband/wife privilege. I do not rule on that issue here. I do not do so because the evidence is clear that the defendant in this case had a reasonable expectation of privacy of all that was behind that door locked by his hidden key. "

Marcellus's voice raised. He continued to speak directly to Sheriff Bailey.

"That is not to say that Detective Blanchard is solely responsible for his failure to obtain the required search warrant. This failure to obtain a search warrant and the inability of the State of North Carolina to prosecute a suspected murderer of these four blessed, innocent victims, citizens who could be a member of any loving family in this county, rests not solely in the hands of Detective Blanchard. It lies in the hands of the person who hired Detective Blanchard, the person who is responsible to train and oversee Detective Blanchard, the person who entrusted this investigation with Detective Blanchard."

The Judge leaned forward. He spoke louder--not just to the High Sheriff--but also to the reporters.

"Let this word go forth. Responsibility for the murders of four innocent victims in Rockingham County going unpunished lies in the hands of Sheriff Efron Bailey."

The courtroom was still, noiseless except for the scratch of reporters' pencils and pens on paper. Twenty seconds elapsed as the Judge continued to stare at the High Sheriff.

Judge Marcellus then looked down at Johnny Wayne Fulcher. "A cowardly murdering bully--whoever it might be--has apparently gotten away with four murders, but he can't hide behind his mother's skirt forever. Justice is this world, or the next, always prevails."

Johnny Wayne hands rhythmically opened and stretched and then turned to fists. Marcellus was taunting him. "Coward." "Bully." "Mother's skirt." Marcellus was now on the same list for a visit as Harley Ames and Cheech Mann when he got out of jail.

For the first time since court had resumed, Judge Marcellus addressed Assistant District Attorney Gerry Wiles, this time in a lower voice.

"Mr. Wiles, is there any further evidence to be produced by the State?"

Wiles stood.

"No, Your Honor, the State rests."

Bailey had not been spoken to with such disrespect in more than 20 years--not even by his wife. He feigned indifference. Instinctively his mind turned to physical revenge against Judge Marcellus. He stood, hat in hand, tapped Blanchard on the arm, and whispered as he turned toward the rear of the courtroom. "Let's go."

Judge Marcellus heard him. "Yes, Sheriff, you leave. You do that. You go do that. But Detective Blanchard is under subpoena, and he will remain seated."

Marcellus then directed his attention to Bob Lee Pender and Johnny Wayne Fulcher.

"Mr. Pender, could you and Mr. Fulcher please stand?"

Pender and Fulcher stood. Although he hadn't been asked, Craig Fitts stood along with them. Marcellus continued and addressed both of Fulcher's attorneys instead of speaking to Fulcher directly.

"As you know, Counselors, under our Constitution a defendant has the absolute right to refuse to take the witness stand to testify."

Marcellus looked at Fulcher. Fulcher stared back. The mutual hatred was thick. Marcellus was still angry, disgusted, with the Sheriff and watched his words, knowing that the Clerk was transcribing with exactness every word uttered, but was insidious in his tone.

"This constitutional right applies to even the *guiltiest, the most evil*, the *most untruthful*, the *worst* elements of humanity that could walk into a courtroom. I'm *sure* you have explained this right to Mr. Fulcher. I'm sure you've explained to Mr. Fulcher that, *if he wishes to do so*, he can exercise his Constitutional right and refuse to take the stand *in his defense*."

Each inflection was intended to insult Fulcher. To challenge, dare, and game him.

Bob Lee began to address the court. "Yes, Your Hon…"

Marcellus interrupted him. He had noticed Fulcher licking and biting his own lips during his baiting.

"I'm not through, Mr. Pender. I want to make sure that everyone understands that in America a guilty person can hide in the bushes and cannot be forced to testify. Your client, who is *presumed* innocent, can do just that." The Judge was smiling through his insulting tone directly at Fulcher.

Fulcher took the bait. Bob Lee could hear a low guttural sound coming from Fulcher. Fitts reached around and patted Fulcher on the shoulder, "Cool, Johnny Wayne. Be cool, Man. Cool."

"So tell me, Mr. Pender, does your client choose to exercise his right to testify, or does he wish to remain where he is and not testify that he did not kill Carlton Purvis in his..."

Marcellus paused briefly, and then shot an arrogant, provoking smile in Johnny Wayne's direction.

"*defense?*"

Before Bob Lee could answer, he detected a growl from Fulcher directed toward Marcellus. In a flash, Fulcher shot up from his seat and pointed a shaking finger at Marcellus. Bob Lee and Craig followed, with Craig turning to Fulcher and attempting to reach around his back for a pat in an effort to calm the situation.

It was too late. Fulcher's eyes were locked on Marcellus. His legs bumped into the table as he stepped forward, shaking the finger of one hand and positioning his other hand on the table as if he were going to pounce.

"Are you sayin' I killed Purvis? Are you sayin' I'm too chicken shit to deny it? You can kiss my ass, Marcellus. You can kiss my lily-white ass! I ain't killed Carlton, and I ain't gonna sit here and take this shit. I wanna testify! You can't keep me from doin' that. It's my right!"

Bob Lee was thunderstruck. "Wait, Johnny Wayne, wait. Give me a second, Your Honor. I need just a moment to speak with my client."

Craig turned toward Fulcher, attempting to whisper in a hushed tone loud enough to be heard. "Johnny Wayne, Johnny Wayne. C'mon, Man. We talked about this. Don't do this, Johnny Wayne!"

Fulcher stared straight at Marcellus. He had lost control. Craig's words had fallen on deaf ears. Marcellus didn't dare interrupt.

"Hell, no, Bob Lee! I don't want a moment or a second. I'm going to testify! It ain't your ass on the line, Bob Lee. This son-of-a-bitch is tryin' to keep me from tellin' the truth. If I don't deny it they're going to think I admit it. I didn't kill ol' Carlton. I'm gonna tell all twelve of those bastards."

Bob Lee tried again. "Your Honor."

Johnny Wayne got louder. His right hand pushed Craig Fitts away.

"Judge, I want to testify. If I have to fire Mr. Pender and Fitts right here and now, I'll do that. But you just told me I've got that right, whether you like it or not. I want to tell them I didn't do it."

Marcellus stayed quiet. He raised his hand to cover his faint smile.

Bob Lee faced the bench. "Your Honor, if I may be heard. I would ask that I be given five minutes to consult with my client."

Marcellus turned on his insulting voice. He smiled at Fulcher and was patronizing. "Oh, I'm sure Mr. Fulcher would like to speak with him, wouldn't you, Mr. Fulcher?"

Fulcher took the bait again. "Hell no, you son-of-a-bitch. I ain't going nowhere. I want to testify!"

Marcellus protected the record. He looked at the clerk, and then at Fulcher.

"Mr. Fulcher, do I correctly understand that you do not wish to consult further with your counsel, that you waive your right not to testify, and that it is your affirmative and your positive desire to testify in your own defense?"

Fulcher stood tall and bored into Judge Marcellus's eyes. Both of his hands were on the defense table.

"You're damn right it is, Judge."

"Mr. Fulcher, before you testify, I'm going to hold you in direct contempt of court for your disrespectful and profane language used by you in open court as is evidenced by the written record in this cause. I sentence you to 30 days in jail for direct criminal contempt of court and advise you that if your profane language persists, this court will consider having you gagged. Do you understand me, Mr. Fulcher?"

Fulcher looked up. "You're just trying to keep my innocent ass in jail, you son-of-a-bitch. I want to testify. Now. And you can kiss my..."

Bob Lee interrupted, loudly. "Yes, Your Honor. He understands perfectly. Now, Your Honor, if I could have five minutes..."

Marcellus addressed the bailiff. "Bring the jury back in, Mr. Bailiff."

Chapter 56

"But Mousie, thou art no thy lane (you aren't alone)

In proving foresight may be vain;

The best laid schemes o' mice an' men

Gang aft a-gley (often go awry)

And lea'e us naught but grief an' pain

For promised joy."

Robert Burns *"To a Mouse"* 1786

Craig Fitts had been assigned the direct examination of Johnny Wayne. He and Bob Lee were required, naturally, to prepare and presume Johnny Wayne could and would testify. The odds that their far-fetched hope that Bob Lee's long-shot motions to suppress evidence exposing the jury to the bodies in the well and the testimony of Misty Fulcher would be granted had been slim.

Judge Marcellus had assessed the situation accurately. If Bob Lee won either of the motions, it would be too risky, even foolish, to put a wildcard Johnny Wayne Fulcher on the stand. The defense could simply argue that the State of North Carolina had not proved its case beyond a reasonable doubt.

Yet in this case, a miracle of sorts had occurred. Each piece of the defense strategy had, if only by the hands of the Gods, fallen into place. The evidence had fallen into each needed slot, and the Judge had refused to allow the damning evidence to be presented to the jury.

And, just as quickly, every effort to accomplish that task had been laid to waste by the temper of a fool and the guise of a fox.

Craig stood and limply announced, "Your Honor, we would call Mr. Johnny Wayne Fulcher to the stand."

Johnny Wayne rose from behind the counsel table and began to approach the witness stand. Every juror measured his gait, his dress, his hands, his eyes. Had they been dogs, they would have sniffed his privates.

Fulcher's eyes glazed as the clerk read the oath, and after a brief silence following the question, Johnny Wayne agreed that yes, he would tell the truth, so help him God. His very countenance laid the question before several jurors whether he had in fact believed in not just The God, but A God.

Fitts had written each question he intended to ask Fulcher on yellow-lined paper. He had spent hours in the jailhouse reading the questions, re-writing the questions, and rehearsing the questions and answers with Fulcher.

Fulcher's life existence was on the line. He had difficulty remembering some of the answers and using the proper voice intonations in his answers. Time and time again he was reminded not to swear and instructed to look at the jurors as he gave his answers.

Despite all, Fitts had one major asset in his presentation.

Details. The essence of truth.

Fitts had asked Johnny Wayne about his presence and whereabouts during each second of the night Carlton Purvis died. Johnny Wayne's memory of the time he had left to go fishing, what he ate for dinner, how many fish he had caught, and other small, minute details gave his story a sense of credibility. No matter how many times Fitts tried to corner him, Johnny Wayne had an answer for where he had been that particular night. Fitts became convinced of Johnny Wayne's truthfulness which, in his presentation, enabled him to convey a sense of earnestness and hopefully a contagious belief in Johnny Wayne's alibi to the jury.

After all, "alibi" does not mean a person is lying about his or her whereabouts. It is simply a translation of Latin meaning "in or at another place." And Johnny Wayne Fulcher had in fact been somewhere else during the Purvis killing. Practicality demanded that Fitts convince the jury of this fact, although technically the burden was on the State to prove—beyond a reasonable doubt—that the alibi was a fabrication. The law did not demand that Fitts prove this. Reality did.

Fitts believed the defense retained a credible chance as long as Fulcher stuck to this script and the correct answers. Fulcher had convinced him that, despite all, despite the unequivocal fact he was a sorry sack of humanity, he had been carp fishing on the night of August 15th and had been nowhere in the vicinity of Carlton Purvis.

It was Craig Fitts' simple and heavy job to convey that fact, and gut feeling, to the jury through Johnny Wayne's testimony.

Craig's biggest fear revolved around the four bodies in the well. Judge Marcellus had ruled the State could not introduce the evidence of the bodies in the wells as the State presented *its case in chief.* After all, no further evidence could have been presented by the State of North Carolina after Assistant District Attorney Gerry Wiles rested his case unless and until the defense presented evidence of its own. Once the defense presented evidence of any sort, the prosecution was allowed to present additional evidence to discredit, or refute, the evidence presented by the defense.

So a *distinction* had to be acknowledged. Judge Marcellus had *not* ruled that Johnny Wayne could not be subjected to questions regarding the four bodies *during cross-examination* of his testimony by Assistant District Attorney Wiles. *Once Johnny Wayne decided to waive his Constitutional right to remain silent* and present evidence in his defense by taking the stand to testify, he had opened himself up to the possibility of having his testimony discredited by cross-examination by Assistant District Attorney Gerry Wiles.

In short, once Craig had finished asking Johnny Wayne his prepared questions, Johnny Wayne Fulcher was fair game for Gerry Wiles. And if the jury learned about the bodies, the prejudicial effect of their existence could be devastating even though they were not directly associated with the death of Carlton Purvis.

So in the seconds between the time the trial was in his and Bob Lee's back pocket and the minute Fulcher insisted he be allowed to testify against their advice, Fitts had to anticipate mentally and prepare to argue to Judge Marcellus a fine point: Even though the evidence of the four bodies might be relevant to impeach Johnny Wayne Fulcher's testimony and theoretically show to the jury that anything said by Fulcher was untrustworthy, the *prejudicial effect* of allowing such testimony into evidence *outweighed the probative effect* of allowing Fulcher to be impeached.

Fitts would argue that the jurors might find Johnny Wayne Fulcher guilty of the Purvis murder simply because of the existence of the four bodies in Fulcher's well and not because of the true issue in the trial. Had the State proven beyond a reasonable doubt that Fulcher had killed with malice aforethought not the four people in the well, but the single individual named Carlton Purvis? A witch hunt could and should not be allowed, he would argue. The State had to stick to its hunt of a specific and particular game. And this hunt could pertain only to the murder of Carlton Purvis.

And so the kickoff took place. The oath had been given, and Fulcher was on the stand.

Fitts stood to address the Court.

"May I proceed, Your Honor?"

"Proceed, Mr. Fitts."

Eleven of the jurors looked not at Fitts, but at Fulcher. He was still being measured. The Leader had his notepad perched on a knee, held by one hand with grasped ink pen in the other. Only The Mason seemed indifferent. Johnny Wayne had noticed he had the attention of everyone except The Mason, but then again, The Mason seemed old and disinterested. Sleepy. Old furniture. Of no effect. He did not realize or appreciate that The Mason had heard every word, every inflection, every nuance, and, at this point, The Mason was his greatest ally on the jury.

Fitts had notes or, better yet, the script before him. He looked up at Johnny Wayne and, in a conversational tone, asked Johnny Wayne a simple question.

"Could you please tell the jury your name, your address, and your occupation?"

"My name is Johnny Wayne Fulcher, and I live at 1130 Chinquapin Road, Stoneville, North Carolina. I work in construction and sometimes the fishing industry."

Fitts then went on to humanize Fulcher before the jury. He asked him about his childhood, where he went to school, his job, his farm, and his relationship with Misty. He asked Fulcher if he would be permitted to call him "Johnny Wayne," further personalizing him to the jury members. He allowed Johnny Wayne to brag about his proficiency as a fisherman.

Fifteen minutes of relaxed, mundane, introductory exchanges and even banter were interrupted by a direct question to a more relaxed, humanized Johnny Wayne.

As part of the direct examination Fitts had prepared questions--and answers--pertaining to Johnny Wayne's character defects. Had he ever collected money violently for Harley Ames or anyone else?

"Yessir, I have." Johnny Wayne sounded contrite. "But not on that night. That's not why we're here today, is it? Isn't this about Carlton Purvis?"

Had he been convicted of assaults and beatings?

"Yes, Sir, I have. But that was in the past and not on the night Carlton Purvis died." Fulcher looked at Craig Fitts and then to the jury. He asked, "We're not here about that, are we?"

"Johnny Wayne, I want to ask you the most serious question of your life. I want to ask you a question and I want you to look me and these twelve good people sitting over there." He pointed to the jury. "Right in the eyes and tell us the truth, Johnny Wayne. Can you do that, Johnny Wayne?"

"Why sure, Mr. Fitts, I can do that."

"Johnny Wayne, did you kill Carlton Purvis?"

"Mr. Fitts, I swear to God on all that's holy that I didn't kill Carlton Purvis! I wasn't nowhere near him that night, Sir."

Fitts was soft in his presentation. Inquisitive.

"You weren't? Then tell us, Johnny Wayne. Tell us. Exactly where were you on the night of August 15th?"

"I was carp fishing up at Smith Mountain Lake with Misty, Mr. Fitts. Carp fished all night. That's where I was."

Fitts decided to start early on the morning of August 15th.

"Johnny Wayne, if you would, I want to start from the time you woke up on August 15th until the night of August 16th. Now that's about 36 hours, do you understand that? I want you to tell the jury where you were each second of those 36 hours. What time did you wake up on the morning of August 15th, Johnny Wayne?"

Johnny Wayne proceeded to explain the exact time he woke up, who cooked his breakfast, even what he had for breakfast. He discussed what television shows he watched that morning, what chores he performed, what he had for lunch, and where he ate it. Minute detail of every moment of the day was presented, leading up to the bait he had purchased to go fishing and how much he had spent. The music and songs he and Misty listened to on the radio as he fished on the banks of Smith Mountain Lake were given, along with how many beers he had drunk and the marijuana he had smoked and the fish, along with the size, he had caught.

All this detail had the most desired of effects in a courtroom. The ring of truth. Arguments can be made, testimony presented, articles of evidence introduced, but the most powerful of all evidentiary traits is the guttural, base instinct that what is being heard is true. It can be difficult to remember and keep the details of a lie straight. But even someone as simple as Johnny Wayne could speak with a voice of genuine reality when what is being said is truthful. It was in the intonation, the earnestness, and the exactness that the unmistakable candor was revealed. And on that day, at that moment, in that courtroom, Johnny Wayne Fulcher conveyed a sense of veracity that, coupled with the feints and slips of Harley Ames and Cheech Mann, injected an unmistakable reasonable doubt into the State's case against him.

Fitts continued his soothing tone and questions throughout the morning and into the afternoon. Question after question about a humdrum day in the life of Johnny Wayne Fulcher punctuated by a killing far away and removed from his actual presence.

It came time for Fitts to wrap up his direct examination and present his innocent client as a victim.

"Mr. Fulcher, you have been in the custody of our sheriff's department for how long now?"

"Since August 18th, Mr. Fitts. Over nine months since I was able to go fishing or walk on my farm."

Fitts closed it up.

"Do you know anything, or did you have anything to do with, the killing of Mr. Carlton Purvis?"

Johnny Wayne looked straight at the jurors.

"No Sir, Mr. Fitts. I knew Carlton and liked him. I got no idea who did that to him."

Fitts waited a moment for the denial to have effect.

"No further questions at this point, Your Honor."

Judge Marcellus addressed Assistant District Attorney Wiles.

"Your witness, Mr. Wiles."

Chapter 57

"Even a blind pig

finds an acorn now and then."

American Southern Expression

Gerry Wiles was desperate and, at this point, hoped for, at best, an honorable loss. An honorable loss would be, within the measurements of his mind's eye, jury deliberations that lasted at least two hours before the "not guilty" verdict was returned.

He was down by six, it was fourth and 20, four seconds were left, and no timeouts remained. Time for a "Hail Mary" pass.

Wiles had noticed The Leader and his copious note-taking. Throughout the trial all the jurors, except The Mason, had swung their heads between witnesses and attorneys as the evidence unfolded, but none had seemed so engrossed or taken notes like The Leader.

The first words out of Wiles mouth were, "Mr. Fulcher."

Fulcher had been distracted by The Leader. The Leader was vigorously shaking his pen, up and down. He was out of ink.

'Mr. Fulcher," Wiles continued, "I want to ask you a few questions."

The pen shaking continued. Johnny Wayne found himself looking at The Leader. The Leader stared intently at the pen, shaking harder and harder. It wouldn't write. He shook it again. Suddenly the pen shot from his hand, striking the rear of the seat to his right and falling beneath the seat of a female juror three seats over. The Leader leaned forward, looking, searching, totally preoccupied with his once airborne pen.

Judge Marcellus was oblivious to The Leader's plight. He had leaned back in his chair, hands crossed over his copious abdomen, looked upward, and waited for the next question and answer. The only ones seemingly aware of the situation were The Leader, Gerry Wiles, and Johnny Wayne.

For Wiles, it was a distraction he could not afford. For The Leader, the loss and recovery of the pen became, for reasons best understood by the preoccupied Leader, a matter of major concern. A Life Mission.

For Johnny Wayne, The Leader's lack of attention became an irritant. Throughout the trial, The Leader had listened to every word and paid attention as each bit of evidence had been presented by the State. He had paid more attention to Cheech Mann's testimony than his, for God's sakes!

It became a matter of respect and regard. Johnny Wayne felt he was being dismissed by The Leader. A simple pen had become more important than The Leader hearing his side of the story.

He had become a matter of disregard by The Leader. Treated like common dirt, just as he had been his entire life.

Belittled.

Trashed as a man in front of the entire courtroom.

Fulcher lasered his gray eyes toward The Leader. The stare of a wolf upon its prey. The Leader never sensed the look, but other jurors did.

Wiles had seen Fulcher's temperament. Fulcher had a tendency to forget his immediate environment, where and who he was with, and zone in on any target of his anger. He had never developed even a modicum of discipline when slightly offended for real or imagined reasons.

In open court while on trial for his very existence, he had cursed the most feared judge in the State of North Carolina. Fulcher had no redeeming qualities, was bad to the bone, and lacked self-control.

The jury had not yet met the real Johnny Wayne Fulcher.

"Mr. Fulcher, tell the jury how many times you have gone to collect money using force and violence for Mr. Harley Ames, Sir."

Johnny Wayne was irritated by the question, but more so by the fact that The Leader kept peering, not at him, but toward the seat under where the pen lay. Fulcher's chin turned left and right, facing Wiles and then The Leader. The Leader scanned the area of the lost pen. Fulcher's answer to the question was of little consequence. Locating the pen was. The Leader looked not at Fulcher, but at the floor. Fulcher was being dismissed as less significant than the pen.

"Not never, Mr. Wiles. That's a lie."

The tone of Fulcher's voice had hardened to the extent that even The Mason became interested. For the first time, The Mason looked up, turned his head, and looked directly toward the face of Johnny Wayne.

Straight into the eyes of evil. Undeniable depravity.

Fulcher caught sight of The Mason's head rising. He stared back. Their eyes locked. For seconds.

Neither blinked. They recognized what they saw in the other.

"Are you telling this jury that you've never been paid to collect money for somebody, Mr. Fulcher?"

Fulcher's voice was low. He was engaged in a stare down with The Mason.

"That ain't got nothin' to do with this kangaroo court, Mr. Wiles. Nothin' at all."

Judge Marcellus shot up in his seat. With both hands reaching forward and planted on the bench, he stretched his neck toward Fulcher.

"The witness will answer the question. Mr. Fulcher, I decide what does and does not have to do with this case. Answer the question."

Fulcher never looked toward Marcellus. His gaze left The Mason and twitched in the direction of The Leader. The Leader was still rummaging beneath the seat of his juror neighbor. His look returned to the eyes of The Mason. Nothing else was seen or contemplated by Fulcher but the Mason's returned stare and the fumbling Leader.

"I've picked up a buck or so doin' that, Mr. Wiles."

Wiles pressed. Fulcher continued to look toward the jury, boxed between Wiles' questions, the Leader's distractions, and The Mason's gaze.

"So, do you ever hide money you might collect around your farm, Mr. Fulcher? Around the farm, like, let's say, in the well house just behind your house?"

Fulcher's gaze returned to The Mason. They were eye to eye. He looked at Wiles and then over at The Leader. The Leader had leaned forward, groping toward the pen, oblivious to the testimony being rendered.

"What the hell does the well house have to do with anything, Mr. Wiles? I don't know a damn thing about no four bodies in the well. Nothin'! And you've been told by the Judge here that the dead man and those damn dead girls ain't got nothing to do with this case, so I ain't answering your question. You hear me??"

Fulcher gripped the armrest of the witness chair and started to rise from the witness chair as if he were going to charge the assistant district attorney. He lowered his body when he noticed two of the bailiffs moving in his direction but raised his voice to a shout.

"Screw that dead pervert and those dead girls, Mr. D.A.! And screw you and the horse you rode in on. You hear me, Mr. Wiles?"

The courtroom went electric. Jurors' eyes widened, except for The Mason. He simply turned forward and looked toward an untied shoelace. The Leader looked up, trying to determine the cause of the excitement.

Fitts shot up in his seat.

"Objection! Objection!" he roared.

Marcellus didn't hear a sound Fitts made.

"Mr. Fulcher! You will answer the questions and not argue with the district attorney!"

Fulcher hadn't heard a word. His mind was swirling. He swung his attention from the assistant district attorney toward the jury box and stared at The Leader.

"What are you doing, you son-of-a-bitch? Huh? Looking for your pen? Just what the hell are you doing? Answer me before I reach over and squeeze an answer outta that chicken neck of yours," Fulcher yelled.

The Leader gazed up. His chin grew limp. Fulcher was talking to *him*!

Evil. Vile, revolting degeneracy.

And then to The Mason. "And what the hell are you looking at, old man? What the hell are you looking at?"

By now two voices were being raised. To the point of screaming.

Marcellus had lost control of his courtroom, something that simply could not be. He was habitually calm to protect his record from a successful appeal. But he had lost control of himself, with a tinge of unexpected joy, shouting for Fulcher to be quiet and directing the bailiff to take him into custody.

Fitts and Bob Lee were on their feet, leaning over with their palms on the counsel table, powerless.

And Fulcher. Fulcher went for broke. He stood up, facing the jury box. A towering figure, leaning forward, stabbing his boney finger at the jury. He screamed at its terrified members.

"Let me tell you son-of-a-bitches something! Every one of you! You ain't gonna find me guilty! I ain't done nothin'! No, you ain't gonna find me guilty. I'll come to your houses and cut every one of your throats if you do!"

The jurors leaned away, with mouths agape. The female jurors pulled their clutched handbags up to their chests.

"I swear to God I'll cut babies out of bellies and break into your houses when you're asleep and cut the heads off your children! I'll hang your dogs in trees! I'll burn you out! Do you understand me? Do you think I won't do it? You just try me, you sons-of-a-bitches!"

Marcellus stood from behind his bench. "Handcuff and gag the defendant, bailiffs. Do it! Do it *now*!"

Fulcher wasn't through. He wanted to make sure the jury understood what he had to say.

"I ain't done nothin', you hear me? You find me guilty, and I'll send you and your family straight to hell! I'll hunt you down when I get out, so help me God I will. You just try me!"

For one of the few times in the trial the three attorneys were silent onlookers. All three stood. Wiles didn't say a word. He didn't need to. He had made no mention whatsoever about the four bodies in the well. Fulcher had. Fulcher brought it up, loud and clear. Time and again.

And the jury had listened. They had heard about the dead man and three girls thrown into Fulcher's well from their mass murderer, a serial killer. A dangerous, raving maniac in every sense of the word.

Five bailiffs descended upon Johnny Wayne. Jurors fled their seats without consideration of permission from the judge. Fulcher fought to pull away from the bailiffs, screaming, writhing to get away and reaching toward the jurors. The jurors scrambled into the open courtroom and toward the hallway, seeking safety and refuge at any place other than the jury box.

"I swear I will! You hear me! You'll be dead meat! I'll cook and eat your children! I swear it!"

Fulcher was dragged from the courtroom as the last juror, an elderly man, backed out of the jury box.

The Leader had picked up his pen from beneath Juror No. 4's seat as he fled.

When order had been restored, Judge Marcellus directed that each juror return to the jury box. He instructed the jury to consider only the testimony and exhibits properly introduced into evidence and that Mr. Fulcher's behavior was not to be considered as evidence against him.

Judge Marcellus's instruction was meaningless at this point but required for the written record.

He then recessed court for the day and instructed the jurors to return at 9:00 a.m., sharp, the following day.

Chapter 58

"When the solution is simple

God is answering."

Albert Einstein

Court properly resumed at 9:00 a.m. the next morning as instructed by Judge Marcellus.

Marcellus asked the bailiff kindly to return the twelve jurors and two alternates to the jury room while the Court conducted some brief business.

Fulcher remained in a holding cell watching the proceedings on a television monitor mounted on a ply board stand beyond reaching distance of his bars. Another television screen sat on a stand beside the court reporter making Fulcher visible to all within the courtroom. He was quiet and could hear the proceedings taking place in the courtroom.

Fitts was also in the room with Fulcher and observable, along with a microphone that allowed him to communicate to an earpiece worn by Pender, on the screen. Fulcher's handcuffs and shackles were not detectible.

Gerry Wiles declined Judge Marcellus' offer for Mr. Fulcher to re-take the witness stand so he could resume the cross-examination that had been interrupted the previous day. When asked if the defense wished to conduct a re-direct examination of Mr. Fulcher or had additional defense witnesses it chose to call, Craig Fitts rose and stated the defense rested its case.

That meant it became time for the State and the defense to present closing arguments. Bob Lee Pender first made perfunctory Motions to Dismiss and asked for a mistrial based upon yesterday's outburst. Both motions were denied. Marcellus refused to allow the defendant's outburst to be cause for him to avoid a jury's determination of the facts in the case.

The jury was brought back into the jury box. Judge Marcellus thanked the two alternate jurors for their service and informed them additional service on their parts was unnecessary because none of the original twelve jurors had, thankfully, been excused because of illness or other just cause.

It now came time for the case to be presented to the jury for an initial determination of one single issue: had the State presented sufficient evidence proving beyond a reasonable doubt that the defendant Johnny Wayne Fulcher was guilty of the first-degree murder of Carlton Purvis?

But first, oral arguments for both the State of North Carolina and the defense would be made.

The defense went first. Criminal procedure dictated that since the defense had presented evidence in the form of Johnny Wayne's testimony the State would be allowed to make the final, and not first, closing argument.

Bob Lee Pender rose, glasses in hand, and approached the front of the jury box to make his final argument to the jury on behalf of the Defendant Johnny Wayne Fulcher.

Pender began by thanking the jury for its service and patience under such difficult circumstances. He apologized for his client's behavior and did his best to attribute it to the stresses of an innocent man standing trial for his life.

For an hour and a half, he concentrated in meticulous detail solely on the evidence, or lack of it, linking Johnny Wayne Fulcher to the murder of Carlton Purvis. He repeated time and time again the heavy burden of proof beyond a reasonable doubt the State which was required to prove before the jury would be entitled to return a guilty verdict, even if they *felt*, or *thought*, or *sensed* Fulcher was guilty. That wasn't enough—they must *believe*, not *to* a reasonable doubt, but *beyond* a reasonable doubt, that the State had proved every element of murder in the first degree before they could return a verdict of guilty.

Bob Lee raised his voice, stressed, and stretched out the word "be-yond." The oaths taken when each juror had placed his or her right hand on the Holy Bible, the very word of God our Maker, he reminded them, demanded complete acceptance of the Judge's instructions regarding the burden of proof. Each and every word of the phrase "*beyond* a reasonable doubt" must be strictly adhered to in their deliberations. They had no choice, he insisted. No choice at all in following the Judge's instructions. Their oaths and our Almighty God himself demanded that they do so.

By this point, Bob Lee did not consider a unanimous verdict of not guilty as a real possibility. He didn't need the votes of twelve jurors to survive. He needed simply one. One lone wolf juror could cause a mistrial. A deadlocked verdict. With a mistrial would come a re-trial, with Johnny Wayne having a second chance to keep his mouth shut.

Bob Lee needed just one juror, so he eyed each of them, one at a time, trying to read faces and the depth of individual involvement in his arguments. He sensed at least four were ever so slightly nodding their heads when he spoke of reasonable doubt and their holy oaths. The jury's sincerity and collective goodness contrasted with all that had been seen and heard during the trial and brought to mind the sweetness and innocence of the hearts of his own beloved mother and father. Bob Lee felt unsettled and manipulative as he tapped into these traits for the sake of Johnny Wayne Fulcher, but his reluctant acceptance of the rules of the game which placed the heaviest burden of proof, "proof beyond a reasonable doubt," on the State trumped the values inculcated in him by his good and loving parents.

Bob Lee spoke for nearly two hours before thanking the jury for its communal vow to abide by its holy oath to follow the law regarding "proof beyond a reasonable doubt." He slowly circled back toward the defense table, head bowed, and took his seat.

Assistant District Attorney Gerry Wiles then rose to face the jury. His remarks were short. He agreed with the able counsel for the defendant that the case did, in fact, rest on whether or not the State had proven its case beyond a reasonable doubt.

Wiles then made a very simple, direct argument.

"I am not going to review each and every element of the State's case as Mr. Pender has done. You are all wise and intelligent people who have exhibited extraordinary patience. I'm not going to bore you with that repetition."

"You have been asked by the judicial system to leave your jobs, your families, and your homes to sit here in judgment of Mr. Johnny Wayne Fulcher. But you have not been asked to leave at home your good old common sense at home. Simple common sense. You brought that here with you into this room of justice and did not leave it at home."

Juror heads gave slight nods of agreement. Wiles paused, waiting for it to sink in further.

He pointed at Fulcher's empty seat between Bob Lee and Craig Fitts, mindful that every word, but not mannerism, was being typed by the court reporter.

"You have *heard* what you *heard*." The court reporter's typed record would reflect that this reference could be attributed to what the jury had heard pertained to the State's evidence. Wiles intended for his insinuation to be heard by each juror as a reference to Fulcher's personal threats against each one of them.

After a long pause, Wiles looked back at Fulcher's empty seat.

"You have *seen* what you have *seen*." Again, Wiles knew the typed record would suggest that this reminder was a reference to the exhibits introduced into the trial. But each juror took Wiles' statement as a reminder of the Fulcher who had turned into an animal before their very eyes. None doubted Fulcher would have cut each of their throats had he been able to reach them.

"Now, ladies and gentlemen, I ask that you go into the jury room and do your duty."

Wiles turned and slowly approached his counsel table. All juror's eyes were on him with the assumption his closing argument had finished.

Midstep, Wiles slowly turned, faced the jury, and approached the rail at the front of the jury box. He bent at the waist, firmly placed both hands on the rail, and surveyed the eyes of each juror as each gazed intently back. Ten seconds passed.

And then he implored them.

"One of the purposes of trial for murder is to protect us all from murderers. *You must protect society. Do what is right!*"

That was it.

A mad dog was on the loose. The dog may have been blameless and come into this world as a cute and precious puppy, but now it was mad and dangerous. The jury had to put the dog down not necessarily because of what the dog might have done, but out of self-defense.

Wiles had spoken less than five minutes when he sat down.

Judge Cletus Marcellus then brought out his large orange binder containing North Carolina's Pattern Jury Instructions. He read various instructions the jury was to follow during its deliberations, with the most important related to the elements of the crime of first-degree murder and the burden of proof.

And during the instructions, Judge Cletus Marcellus justified his statewide reputation as the feared Judge Cletus Marcellus. He used his inflection of voice. His instructions regarding Proof Beyond a Reasonable Doubt made the heaviest burden of proof in law seem light and perfunctory. He gave instructions that Fulcher's outburst was to be disregarded, but these directions sounded disingenuous and could not possibly have erased any juror's memory of the terror inflicted by Fulcher. By the completion of Marcellus's instructions each juror was convinced beyond a reasonable doubt not just of Fulcher's guilt, but also of the Judge's belief in Fulcher's guilt.

The jury retired to weigh the evidence. Over the next hour and a half jurors rationalized and justified in his or her mind a verdict of guilty. Leading the deliberations was The Mason, as Jury Foreman. The Leader barely spoke a word, thumbing back and forth through his notes hunting for some written utterance he was unable to locate.

The Mason had no qualms arguing for a guilty verdict against Johnny Wayne. He didn't particularly care if Fulcher had in fact killed Carlton Purvis or not. All the platitudes about oaths and burdens of proof were touchy-feely, sounded nice, and made the heart feel warm, but Fulcher was a particularly dangerous person. The Mason did not share other jurors' personal and unspoken fears of personal harm by Fulcher. He feared no man and trusted in God in regard to his personal safety. But he was wily enough to use the undeclared stigma of fright shared by fellow jurors to subtly convince them against all reason that the State had indeed met its burden of proof beyond a reasonable doubt.

The shared trait of all jurors was that each was a creature of survival. They convinced themselves to do right, even if it was wrong. Each persuaded himself to find Johnny Wayne Fulcher guilty of the first degree murder of Carlton Purvis.

The Mason tapped on the door of the jury room and informed the bailiff that a unanimous verdict had been reached. Within minutes, the jury, the attorneys, Fulcher, and the courtroom spectators stood as Judge Marcellus entered the courtroom. Marcellus asked if a verdict had been reached. The Mason, who had been elected jury foreman by his peers, stood and announced in open court that the jury had unanimously agreed upon a verdict of guilty of murder in the first degree while The Leader sat silently and double-checked his watch for the time.

The Carlton Purvis murder had been solved. Johnny Wayne Fulcher had murdered him, and murdered him in the first degree. The same Johnny Wayne Fulcher, who, in fact, had been carp fishing at Smith Mountain Lake on the night and at the time of Carlton Purvis's death.

Justice had been served.

The trial then proceeded to the issue of whether Fulcher should be sentenced to death for the murder of Carlton Purvis. After half a day's presentation of evidence, Assistant District Attorney Wiles argued the death penalty should be imposed because the circumstances included factors justifying imposition of the ultimate penalty: The murder was particularly heinous and cruel; it had been committed in the commission of a felony, that is, armed robbery; and it was committed for pecuniary gain. In Fulcher's defense, Pender addressed the sanctity of life and appealed to what he knew in his heart was residual doubt among the jury of Fulcher's guilt. After further instructions the jury returned to deliberate and, after two hours of consideration, returned a verdict.

The defendant Johnny Wayne Fulcher was to be sentenced to death.

This dog had to be put down.

Even Paul Gil Reed, sitting in the back of the courtroom, understood that. It was natural law.

No one was happier than Judge Cletus Marcellus.

No one.

Chapter 59

"Nowadays there is no honor, only drama.

Your friend today can be your enemy tomorrow."

Unknown

Fulcher stood behind the counsel table between Bob Lee Pender and Craig Fitts. Handcuffed with feet shackled, he looked up at Judge Cletus Marcellus.

Sheriff Bailey and Arnie Robertson had shown up for the sentencing and sat in the third row. The two non-communicating ladies from Roanoke, Abby Trimyer from the Roanoke <u>Times</u> and Jamie Watson from U.S. Attorney Tim Herndon's office, sat on opposite sides of the courtroom, each refusing to glimpse at or acknowledge the other.

Marcellus couldn't have been in a better place. He was doing what he enjoyed most.

"Mr. Fulcher, do you have anything to say before I impose sentence?"

"Yes, I do, Judge. I sure do."

"Then go ahead."

"Judge, I done a lot of bad things in my life, and I know life ain't fair. But I swear on all that's holy that I didn't do no harm to Carlton Purvis and that I wasn't nowhere to be found around him on the night he was killed. I swear I wasn't. I was fishin', for God's sakes."

Fulcher gazed up at the ceiling. Then he turned his head and scanned the courtroom.

He faced the Judge again.

"Judge, I don't know what this farce is all about. I really don't. I've been sittin' in a stinking cell keepin' my mouth shut for months now, waitin' for some kind of help. Waitin' to be told it was over and I could go home now. Waitin'. That's what they was supposed to do, but they ain't. And I ain't done nothing wrong, Judge. Nothing."

His voice raised a level.

"Now I know what happens when I'm sent to Raleigh and put on death row. I know I won't be in the general population, and I won't be allowed to wander around. And I'm tired of sittin' in a godforsaken cell by myself. I've been patient, waitin' for them to come and tell me this is all over and thank you and that I can go home now. But it don't appear like they're going to come and look after me like they're supposed to."

Fulcher's paused, glanced down at the table, and then up at Marcellus. His voice rose.

"And they're sittin' here in this courtroom, Judge, listenin' to what I'm saying as these words leave my mouth, and they don't stand up, they don't raise their hands, they don't do nothing. They know I didn't hurt ol' Carlton. They know that. But I know where I'll be in Central Prison, Judge, and it ain't pretty. I'll be in a cell 23 hours a day and let out an hour a day to stretch."

He turned his head around again and looked at Sheriff Bailey and Arnie.

"I've been waiting and waiting for some help, Your Honor, but it seems like those that I've helped in the past don't want to help me today. Everybody's keeping their mouths shut. I ain't got no reason to keep mine shut about what I've done for other people, like the Good Sheriff sitting there, when I was told to do it. No reason at all."

Sheriff Bailey fumbled with his hat. He shook his head. Jamie Watson noticed the movement and leaned forward to hear each and every one of Johnny Wayne Fulcher's words.

"Judge Marcellus, I want to cut a deal. We got everybody right here in this courtroom for us to cut a deal. The Sheriff and Arnie are here, and we can cut a deal."

"I ain't about to go to that chicken pen and sit in there by myself. I want to tell what I know and what I done when Arnie sittin' back there told me to do it for the Sheriff or his buddy Ricky Dean.

"I'm sure you heard of Ricky Dean, Judge. I don't mind serving time, but I ain't goin' to do 23 hours a day in a six by eight cell for something I ain't even done in the first place. Arnie and the Sheriff sittin' back there were supposed to take care of me. So to hell with them! Judge, I want to cut a deal. I'll talk."

Marcellus asked Fulcher a question.

"Is there anything else, Mr. Fulcher?"

"No, Your Honor, I just want to cut a deal."

"Well, Mr. Fulcher, it's just too late to do that. Now, are you finished talking?

"Yes, Judge.

"Then I'd like to sentence you to death."

And that he did.

Chapter 60

"What is the use in rushing

if you are on the wrong road?"

Proverb

Jamie Watson squeezed the phone and didn't wait for the receptionist to announce that she was answering the U.S. Attorney's Office in Roanoke.

"Give me Mr. Herndon, Juanita. Now! It's me, Jamie. Give me Mr. Herndon, now!"

U.S. District Attorney Herndon picked up his receiver. Jamie's tongue almost ran out of her mouth. She was breathless. She started forgotting to call her boss "Mr. Herndon".

"Tim, Johnny Wayne wants to talk about Ricky Dean and Sheriff Bailey. He was sentenced to death not five minutes ago and started demanding in open court that he be allowed to cut a deal and tell what he knows about Ricky Dean and Sheriff Bailey."

Herndon leaned forward.

"Slow down, Jamie. What are you talking about?"

"Johnny Wayne Fulcher is flipping, Tim. He wants to talk. You know and I know we could never rely on his word to convict anyone, but he does know things. Important things."

Herndon listened.

Jamie continued. "Mr. Herndon, I'm asking—no, I'm begging—you to do whatever it is you do to wave that magic wand of yours and get Johnny Wayne Fulcher out of the cell he's going to be sitting in tonight in Rockingham County and into federal protective custody."

Her voice became instructive. Demanding.

"Call whoever you have to and do whatever you need to, and do it now. Call the Attorney General if you can. If you don't, the best source you've ever had in the Ricky Dean investigation may be dead by dawn."

Tim Herndon thought out loud.

"For God's sake, Jamie! The man's just been given the death sentence! And I'm supposed to bust him out tonight? Are you kidding?"

Jamie dropped her voice to sound less demanding. She turned to reason.

"Tim, just remember I'm on your side. You've busted your butt for years on the Ricky Dean case. You really have. You've worked hard."

She had stroked Herndon to get what she wanted. It was time for another angle.

"There's finally been a breakthrough, Mr. Herndon. No, it may be better than that. It may be exactly what you need after all these years. He talked about Sheriff Bailey's right hand man Arnie Robertson. He did everything but spit in their faces in open court."

Herndon hadn't said a word.

"There's a bad rift, Tim, and we need to jump into the middle of it. Arnie Robertson might even flip if pressure is put on him. All I know is that you've got to trust me and act fast. If you don't, Fulcher's a dead man and dead quick."

Herndon started to ask, "But what the hell can I..."

"I don't know, Mr. Herndon. I'm just telling you how it is. If you don't do something now, right this second, the best chance you ever had of nailing Ricky Dean is out the window."

"God help you if you haven't told me everything, Jamie," Herndon threatened.

"I'm on your side, Tim. I'm telling you everything."

Within five hours, six federal agents, accompanied by four agents from the North Carolina State Bureau of

Investigation, arrived in Wentworth at the Rockingham County jail. State and Federal agencies in Virginia and North Carolina had collaborated. In hand were writs signed by a federal judge and the Governor of the State of North Carolina demanding the physical custody of Johnny Wayne Fulcher for protective custody as a material witness in a major ongoing investigation being conducted by the Federal Bureau of Investigation. Newspapers and the local television station had been notified by an anonymous caller of their arrival. Crowded outside the jail door were the ten agents, newspaper people including Abby Trimyer, and a rolling television camera.

Sheriff Efron Bailey entered the throng with a group of his deputies, hat in hand, and politely asked, "May I be of service to you gentlemen?"

Presented with the writs, the Sheriff, eyes blurred by the camera lights, was asked by the lead federal agent, "Sir, do you intend to comply with the federal judge's writ and the Governor's command and deliver the person of Johnny Wayne Fulcher to our custody?"

The Sheriff hesitated, taking it all in.

"Why, of course, I do, Sir. Of course, I do."

He turned to a subordinate.

"Jailer, would you please have Mr. Fulcher arrange his personal effects and bring him to these kind gentlemen?"

The Sheriff asked the agent. "May I ask where Mr. Fulcher is being taken? He was, after all, just convicted of murder on this date in our county?"

The agent was abrupt.

"No, Sheriff, you may not. No, you may not."

With that, the Sheriff turned, smiled and nodded at the camera, and left the room.

Within 90 minutes, convicted murderer Johnny Wayne Fulcher was cramped with four federal agents in the bowels of a small jet aircraft, handcuffed and shackled, traveling 462 knots per hour and 32,000 feet above the State of South Carolina, secretly bound for protective custody among the 1940 inmates in the Federal Penitentiary in Atlanta, Georgia. The older agent leaned over and whispered.

"When we get where you're going, your name is Stan Bailey. The papers showing that are waiting for you in Atlanta. You're being brought down there for supposedly robbing a bank in Greensboro. Do you understand that? No more 'Johnny Wayne Fulcher' while we work your deal out, okay? It's 'Stan Dailey.' Just remember it. The guy who robbed the bank in Greensboro. To everyone, including me. The guards, the cooks, the other personnel. Stan Dailey. No middle name. Bank robber. Greensboro. You got those three things? And don't make any friends. No whining or complaining. Keep to yourself and keep your mouth shut while the deal is cut. You're going to be given a good lawyer to help you. Listen to him, and he'll tell you what to do and get you out of this mess. You got that? Stan Dailey. Bank robber. Greensboro."

Johnny Wayne nodded his head. 'Stan Dailey.'

He still had no idea of his destination.

But Ricky Dean did. As a matter of fact, Dean had already notified his guard and inmate contacts within the Federal Prison in Atlanta of the arrival of Mr. Stan Dailey, the bank robber with no middle name. They were waiting.

Waiting to greet him.

Epilogue

"Money is not the most important thing in the world.

Love is.

Fortunately, I love money."

Jackie Mason

It was 7:30 a.m. on Tuesday, and Bob Lee Pender sat in the fourth booth from the front door of Lefty's Grill studying the <u>News and Record</u>. No matter what the restaurant, five stars or a local dive, he always ate facing the entrance instead of with his back toward the door. This practice began as a young lawyer after he had received threats during a contentious trial and instinctively became more alert of his surroundings. It had become a lifelong habit. Although people would often recognize him and interrupt his meal, taking this position was worth it. He could always see who—or what—might be coming. It felt safer.

This summer morning Bob Lee was enjoying a breakfast of brains and eggs, a biscuit with honey butter, grits, fried apples, orange juice, and coffee. He had entered to the usual "Mornin', Slick!" from the black beehive-hairdo adorned Maxine. Any of the ladies who waited on him knew to pour his coffee, chirp "Good mornin', Mr. Pender!", and ask whether he wanted the brains and eggs or just fried eggs that morning. Bob Lee scarcely looked up from his paper and announced his choice before reaching in the direction where his morning cup of coffee was usually placed.

Bob Lee failed to pay specific attention to the man dressed in a suede jacket who caused the bell over the entrance door to jingle. The person wore sunglasses in the cafe, something of an oddity in the Mayodan community, and was definitely not a local.

But Bob Lee continued to read on, searching the op/Ed page not for insight into a topical issue, but for a columnist who agreed with his opinion of a particular manner. He would scan the articles of the columnists who irritated him and then devour each word of those who lined up with his vein of thought. After all, everyone loves affirmation.

The man in the suede jacket approached Bob Lee's booth.

"Excuse me, Sir. Are you Mr. Bob Lee Pender? The attorney? Attorney Bob Lee Pender?"

Pender's head swung up. He had been interrupted.

"Why yes, Sir, I am. And you are…?"

"Let me introduce myself, if I may. My name is Enos Thigpen, Mr. Pender. I'm from Sudley, a small town in upper Virginia."

Thigpen extended his hand to shake Pender's. Pender held the paper in his left hand as he released his coffee cup and reached up with his right hand, obviously annoyed at being interrupted. He retreated to his newspaper. "Nice to meet you, Mr. Thigpen."

Thigpen was oblivious to the brush-off. He looked toward the seat on the other side of the booth. "May I, Mr. Pender…?"

"Mr. Thigpen, I don't want to sound rude, but I'm reading my paper and having my morning breakfast."

Bob Lee returned to the newspaper.

"If you need to talk to me about a case, I'd appreciate it if you'd call my office and my nice secretary will set you up with an appointment so we can discuss whatever's on your mind in a more professional atmosphere. But right now I'm just having my coffee and reading this paper before I start a very busy day, so if you'll excuse me…"

Ignoring Bob Lee's comments, Thigpen sat in the booth opposite Bob Lee.

"Oh, Mr. Lee, this isn't about a specific case. Nothing like that at all. It's more of a general question, Mr. Pender, and I think you might be interested in the nature of the question."

Bob Lee nodded in disagreement and tossed his napkin forward. He was being distracted during his damn breakfast! The reason for this disruption had better be good...

"I must ask you, Mr. Pender. Those are brains and eggs you're enjoying this morning? Is that what they are? I do believe I'd rather eat a mouthful of bees before I ate those, I do."

Bob Lee held a spoon in his right hand.

"So, is this what you do for a living, Mr. Thigpen? Do you wake up every morning, seek out anonymous diners in cafés in small towns across America, and interrupt folks having their morning coffee to become their food critic? Is that what you do?"

Thigpen showed a slight grin. Pender continued.

"Is that what you do? Who trained you? Eddie Haskel?"

Thigpen finally smiled. "I apologize, Mr. Pender. I really do."

Pender wanted him gone. "Well, the answer to your question is 'yes,' they are brains and eggs. You can put that in your notes. So if you'd excuse yourself, I'd like to get back to my paper."

"No, Mr. Pender, the real question I have of you is whether you might be interested in being placed on retainer for a client who is willing to pay you a substantial monthly retainer? A retainer simply to be on call in the event your services are deemed to be needed."

Pender bit.

"Two questions, Mr. Thigpen. The first is: Who's the client? And the second is: What do you mean by 'substantial'?"

Thigpen had come to the table prepared.

"Mr. Pender, the word 'substantial' is, as you know, relative. A lot of money to one man is a pittance to another. So my client has asked that you simply tell him how much it would cost him for you to be ready to represent him 24 hours a day, seven days a week, every day of the month, and he, in return, will simply pay what you ask. Whatever you ask, and don't be afraid any amount you ask will be considered insulting. Your services are well worth paying for. It's that simple. You tell him what you think is reasonable and 'substantial.'"

"As far as 'who' would be your client, Mr. Pender, let me simply say that your potential client was very, very impressed with your recent representation of Mr. Johnny Wayne Fulcher."

Bob Lee smiled.

"I lost that case, Mr. Thigpen. Fulcher's going to be on death row whenever he shows back up. Everyone knows from the papers that the Feds have him and I have no idea where he is or whether he's alive or dead. I haven't heard a word from him. Even his appellate attorney can't find him."

Bob Lee twirled the cup in his hand.

"Is that what you're about, Mr. Thigpen? You think I can tell you where Fulcher is? Well, I can't Mr. Thigpen. I can't tell you anything. You can write that down, too."

Pender looked back at his paper. Thigpen smiled.

"No, Mr. Pender. I'm not here about Fulcher. That matter will take care of itself. I'm here about you."

Pender cocked his head.

"And you, Mr. Thigpen. Who the hell are you? You're from northern Virginia. How the hell do you know about the Fulcher trial?"

Thigpen deflected the question. He was working toward the purpose of his visit.

"Mr. Pender, the client who has asked me to come speak to you was, as a simple onlooker, very, very interested in the Johnny Wayne Fulcher trial. *Very* interested."

Bob Lee watched his spoon as he stirred his coffee. Thigpen went on.

"The client has varied business interests in Virginia, the Carolinas, and Tennessee. He has asked me to convey to you that he was very impressed with your command of the courtroom."

There was a short pause.

"He may be in need of similar capable and vigorous representation in the future in Rockingham County and has asked me to delve into any interest you may have in representing him should the need arise. He believes that it is possible proceedings could be instituted against him and in state and even federal courts, and that these proceedings could be instituted immediately or in the near future."

Bob Lee wanted to square the deal up so there were no loose ends.

"And the name?"

"Mr. Pender, why do you think I'm here on behalf of this other person? Why wouldn't he be here himself?"

Pender didn't push the issue.

"So you're telling me I can name my price and simply have to be available? That I will receive a monthly retainer regardless whether or not services are actually performed simply to be available?"

Thigpen came with obvious authority.

"Yes, Mr. Pender, you have a correct understanding of what I was directed to convey. Except for one small aspect that should be mentioned. The monthly retainer can be remitted either by check or, should you prefer, in cash with no written receipt being expected to be returned by you. Or, for that matter, part by check and part in cash. It's a simple income tax issue. You decide."

Bob Lee reached back for his paper. He became rude, sounding insulted.

"Mr. Thigpen, if you don't mind, I'd like to get back to my paper. I don't mean to be impolite, but you have thoughtlessly interrupted what is, for me, a morning ritual. I do not conduct business in my home, at my farm, in my church, or in this café. I do my business in my office and in the courthouse. And not, once again, here in the Lefty's Grill."

There was a pause. He became abrupt.

"So, if you will excuse me, Mr. Thigpen..."

Thigpen started to rise.

"I apologize for interrupting your breakfast, Mr. Pender. I really do. I'll be leaving now, Mr. Pender, but I may stop by sometime after you've had a reasonable time to consider what we've spoken about. I hope you have a good day, Sir."

Pender returned to his paper and reached for his cup. He refused to recognize Thigpen further.

"I will, Mr. Thigpen. Have a good one yourself. There's the door. It's for people who are leaving. *Now please use it.* And let me get back to my newspaper."

Bob Lee had dismissed Thigpen. Thigpen rose, smiled, and noticed that Pender refused the small courtesy of even looking up from his paper.

Thigpen walked through the café and reached for the handle on the exit door.

Bob Lee's head rose, and he called across the room in a neighborly tone. "Thigpen!"

Thigpen stopped as he pulled the door open and looked towards Pender's table.

"Tell Mr. Dean I'll think about it, and please get back to me on Friday, okay?"

Thigpen nodded, smiled, and pulled the door shut as he left the café.

About the Author

The author is a lifelong resident of Rockingham County, North Carolina, where he practices law as a small-town trial attorney and engages himself part-time as an unpaid and un-mentored apprentice handyman ("If it ain't broke, I can fix that!"). Married to the beautiful and genteel "Miss Julie" and the proud father of twin sons Michael and Victor, the author quietly but noticeably suffers from McDonald's paunch, denial of male pattern baldness and the effects of decades of exposure to gravity on his physique, and wanderlust.

The author graduated from the University of North Carolina at Chapel Hill and the Wake Forest University School of Law. He has practiced law in Rockingham County for, according to his courtroom adversaries, too long.

He is a firm believer in the undeserved grace of an Almighty and Omnipotent God. Nothing else could explain all this.